Just to Hear 'I Love You'

An Alternate Tale of Jane Austen's *Pride & Prejudice*

Sarah Johnson

This is a work of fiction based on the characters in Jane Austen's *Pride and Prejudice'* and is otherwise completely the product of the author's imagination. Any resemblance to real persons, whether living or dead, is purely coincidental and not intended by the author.

Cover Design by: Peculiar World Designs
Section Dividers and Headers by: Media Militia
Title Font: Jellyka Delicious Cake
Title Font Courtesy of: Jellyka Nerevan from CuttyFruty
Floral References and meanings: The Language of Flowers, by Kate Greenaway

ISBN—10: 1500734012
ISBN—13: 978-1500734015

Dedication

To my husband of sixteen years, Paul. You are truly my own Mr Darcy.
Without your love and support I would have never found the courage to
complete this journey. *Thank you!*

Acknowledgments

The inspiration for a deaf character came from reading a letter Jane Austen wrote in 1808 in which she mentioned talking with her fingers. Her second eldest brother, George, was deaf and mute. Though little is known of what caused his impairment, it is known that he knew how to sign. So it is Jane Austen herself that has inspired this tale.

I have a wonderful editing team and I would be remiss if I did not take this opportunity to personally thank them for their hard work and wonderful ideas. So thank you to Anita, Linnea, Linda, and Rose for all the time and energy you have put into this story with me. Also thank you to my brother, Joshua, who has done the tedious task of formatting my eBooks. I could not do this without the support of each of these wonderful people, so from my heart to yours—*Thank You!*

Prologue

January 1799

COLD! *So cold!* She could not open her eyes because of the shooting pain it caused. She had to fight! Move, she told herself. Tiny pin pricks all over her body! She could not continue like this—she had to stop—she needed to be warm. Suddenly she felt her body go limp—floating in a weightless suspension somewhere. *Where am I?*

Suddenly everything changed. Even without opening her eyes she could tell the difference. Warmth encompassed her whole being and she no longer felt the sharp pain of needles poking her.

Opening her eyes, she saw that she was standing in a field of flowers. The sun shining overhead was just enough to be bright and warm, but not overpowering. She looked all around. As far as her eye could see were rolling hills—fields covered with flowers of every kind. It was like looking at a rainbow poured out over the lands.

Off in the distance she noticed a tree on top of one hill. She wondered about its lone existence and suddenly she was there, beneath its shade. She turned all around, spinning so her dress came up, then she saw someone. She stumbled to a stop and looked to the lady who appeared before her.

"Mama? Is that really you?" The little girl standing by her side looked just as she imaged her baby sister would have looked at that age. "Lydia?"

The lady reached down and grasped the hand of the child beside her, then they turned to walk away. Suddenly she turned back, reaching her hand out to Mary, the words coming from her lips echoing in Mary's mind— *'Come with me, my child. I love you'*.

She stretched her arm, trying with all her might to reach them, but the harder she reached the further away they became. Everything around began to fade. The sunlight grew dim and the flowers on the distant hills disappeared. Mary looked all around and when she looked back to where the tree should have been, there was nothing. Complete darkness encompassed her world.

She felt her way a few steps, but was so unsure of her footing that she stopped. "I cannot see! No! I must be able to see!" She collapsed on the cold ground below her, the darkness engulfing her to the deepest part of her soul. She did what any young girl of eight years would do—she began to cry for her Papa until she was so tired she could no longer remain awake. Finally she gave in to the drowsiness and sleep overtook her.

Heaviness surrounded her. Her arms were weary and something was weighing down her entire body. Slowly she opened her eyes and the familiar surroundings of her room came into view. The once bright floral wallpaper was faded and peeling, just as she remembered. The bed curtains were pulled back and tied at the corner posts of the bed. A chill in the room was driven away with the roaring fire in the fireplace, but something was wrong.

She looked around and saw her father sitting in the chair across the room. His head was resting in the wing and one leg was crossed over the other, an open book laid across his knee—*just as she remembered him*. She smiled and tried to sit up.

Suddenly she saw someone come running into the room, making it to the side of the bed before Mr Bennet could. *Elizabeth!* Oh she looked so tired! She was saying something, her lips were moving, but nothing was coming out.

Mary's brow furrowed and she looked around at the faces now surrounding her bed—*Elizabeth… Papa… Aunt Philips…* the next face that came into view was that of Doctor Jones. He was saying something to the others, then he reached out his hand and felt her forehead. His fingers were ice cold and she cringed at the sudden feel of them on her skin.

Aunt Philips was nodding at what he said, then she handed him a cup of tea. He turned back and lifted her head, helping Mary drink the awful tasting liquid, then he helped her lie down again, pulled the blankets high to her neck, and tucked them in all around, all the while talking to the others.

Nothing—she heard nothing. Not a sound, not a twinge, not even what one would expect to hear when you plug your ears up and hear your own heart beating. *Silence.* Deep, dark silence, then everything went black once again as sleep overtook her body.

When she awoke again she saw Elizabeth sitting in the chair that had now been moved to right beside the bed. Elizabeth was holding Mary's favorite book in her hands—one their mother read to them often. It contained a list of flowers and what meaning they held, as well as pretty drawing throughout—some from the author and others drawn by their mother.

Mary looked back to Elizabeth's face and realized she was reading aloud, but once again nothing was heard. She reached up to her ears, pulling at them frantically as tears began to well in her eyes. She felt her father's strong arms wrap around her, pulling her into a tight embrace. She looked up into his eyes and saw him moving his mouth, but she did not know what he was saying. She could do nothing but cry in his arms. Even her crying was in silence.

The words she heard her mother say rang out in her mind—*'Come with me, my child. I love you'… 'I love you'… 'I love you'.* Would she ever again hear those words?

Summer 1807

The crowded coach ambled down the road. She was certain the letter that preceded their unexpected journey would arrive only hours before they did and she hoped her uncle would think to have a footman waiting at the appointed stop. That was something they did not think about until after the missive was on its way. Oh well, there was nothing they could do about it now.

The heat of the summer day was making the conditions inside the carriage almost unbearable. Mary decided at the next stop she and Elizabeth would try to sit next to a window instead. Until then, she would remain in the tiny space

3

available to them in the middle of the carriage, glad to at least not have to listen to the babe that was in obvious distress across from them. *Poor thing— even he cannot handle this heat.*

The four hour coach ride would leave the two sisters a mile from their relations home on Gracechurch Street and they would have to walk from there. Luckily their uncle did send someone to escort them. Neither of them knew exactly where they were going, but they followed closely as the footman led the way down the crowded streets of London.

Before they knew it the two stood before the door of an unfamiliar home in an equally as unfamiliar city. The bustle of the busy street faded around them and they stood shoulder-to-shoulder, each grasping the other's hand as the footman knocked and then stepped back to enter through the servant's door.

Almost immediately the door swung open and the familiar face of their aunt appeared. She embraced and greeted the two, and then ushered them into the small home and into the sitting room.

Mary sat where their aunt indicated, taking a cup of tea when it was offered, and watched as Elizabeth spoke with their aunt of the tragic events the two had left behind in Hertfordshire. Mary looked down, refusing to know what was said—it was too much to bear in detailing the loss they had suffered all over again.

Finally she felt someone touch her arm and she looked up into the teary eyes of her aunt. The words that formed on the lady's lips would forever be forged on her heart—*you are welcome to live here with us, both of you.*

Her life was not one filled with much acceptance, even from the small neighborhood in which she had spent the entirety of her fifteen years, but she knew somehow they would make a life here.

Elizabeth reached over and squeezed her sister's fingers, then she signed, "Uncle has gone to Hertfordshire and will return when everything has been settled."

Having never been as proficient at signing as her nieces were, Madeline let Elizabeth do the service for her as she told them both of the black crepe, muslin, and bombazine materials already being pulled from the shelves at their uncle's warehouse. They were to be fashioned into the mourning clothing the two would be required to wear for the next year. Some material had already been draped around the home on the doorways and in the proper places, and Madeline's maid was currently dying a dress for her to wear until more could be fashioned in the coming weeks. Black ribbon had been delivered already and was to be placed appropriately by the household staff as the day wore on.

Madeline reached for Mary's hand and when the younger girl looked up at her face, she said slowly, "My maid is awaiting you above stairs and bath water is being prepared already so you can wash the smoke from your hair." She smiled, "Your Uncle has even brought back some scented oil from his warehouse that may help."

Tears filled her eyes. She thought no one noticed—thought she was unseen in the dramatic hours since their family had suffered so great a loss—but her aunt saw what the girls needed and was prepared to do everything in her power to provide for their well-being. The tears began to run down her cheeks and in the next moment her aunt's arms were around her in a strong embrace, her hand running soothingly through Mary's long knotted hair. When Mary was finally calmed again, Madeline led the two up the stairs and to the room they would share. Then she went to the nursery to check on her own children. They were all asleep for their nap. She nodded to the maid who sat in the corner.

When her husband returned from burying Mr Bennet and their nieces, Jane and Kitty, who did not make it out of the fire at Longbourn, they would need to discuss the possibility of moving to a larger home. With their three children and their nieces now living with them permanently, this one would become too small very quickly.

She returned downstairs and sat at her desk, pulling out paper to begin the necessary letters to others who would need to be told of the family's loss.

An hour later, Mary came back down the stairs. Finding her aunt at the desk, she retrieved a chair and sat, watching as she completed the task before her.

Madeline looked to her niece and smiled, "You have always had lovely hair. Did the oil work in removing the smell?"

Mary lifted a section of her hair and smelled it, smiling slightly as she nodded her head.

"Would you like to help me dip the edges of these pages in ink?"

Mary nodded again, and her aunt helped her set up an area where the tedious task could be completed with minimal mess. When the two were done, Madeline retrieved the traditional black melting wax and they sealed the letters, then stacked them on the desk to be posted the next day.

Madeline stood and held her hand out to her fifteen year old niece, "Come, you can join me in the garden."

She took the offered hand timidly and went with her aunt outside into the small space they had made into a garden. It was only large enough for one bench that seated two comfortably, but it was nicely designed and a peaceful retreat in the middle of the bustling town all around them. The high wall covered in ivy at the back was meant to keep the noise to a minimum, but Mary would not notice such things. What she did notice was the Spruce Pine tree that grew in the back corner. She smiled as she recognized it from her mother's book of flowers—'*hope in adversity*'.

With a determined stride she went to the tree and ran her hand over the needles, smiling when they made her palm itch. She had to believe what it meant was true. She had to hold onto the hope that all this would be a distant memory for them one day. She had to trust that the physical limitations that had held her back since she lost her hearing at the age of eight would not become a deterrent to what the future held.

She felt her sister come up beside her.

"Are you well?" Elizabeth signed.

Mary turned and signed back, "Yes, I am well. And you?"

Elizabeth gave a small smile and reached for her sister's hands, holding them tightly in her own. "*We* are well."

Chapter 1

April 2, 1811

He raced furiously through the familiar lanes, dodging the carriages littering the streets in the late afternoon; an ominous feeling settling deep within him. He tried to push it aside, but could not outpace it. *What did she do? Will I arrive there in time to save her from whatever has occurred?*

Finally arriving at the very house where he delivered his sister just four weeks prior, he jumped down from the horse, tossed the reins to the stable hand, and nearly knocked over the butler as he threw open the door to rush inside.

"Mr Darcy... sir... we did not expect you..."

"Where is she? *Where is my sister?*" He hastened from one room to the next, flinging open doors as the staff followed behind him.

"Sir?" The housekeeper was trying to determine what had taken place to bring her employer here so unexpectedly. "We know not what you mean?"

It was then he saw the sheets over the furniture and the minimal staff present. "Where is everyone? WHAT is going on here Mrs Lewis?"

"Sir, your sister left three days ago."

"*WHAT?* She was to remain here until next week when I was to collect her for our Easter holiday at Rosings."

"Yes, that is what you said when you delivered her, but when you sent orders to have the house closed up immediately upon her taking her leave I assumed your plans had changed."

"NO! *I did not write to you!*" His stomach lurched as he closed his eyes and asked, "Where is the letter?"

"Right this way, sir," she quickly went downstairs to her work—room, the master of the house following closely behind. With shaky hands she rifled through the crate on her desk until she came across the correspondence. "Here it is, sir."

He was taken aback. The imprint in the wax was indeed the Darcy seal, and the writing was eerily similar to his own. If he did not know better, he would say he wrote it. He wadded it and threw it onto the desk, cursing loudly in frustration. Seeing the shocked look on the housekeeper's face he quickly apologized, "I am sorry, that was uncalled for. I heartily apologize for assaulting your ears, Mrs Lewis."

"Do not concern yourself, Mr Darcy." She picked up the wrinkled letter, smoothing and folding it before she placed it back in the crate, "Are you saying you did *not* write this?"

His hand ran agitatedly through his long dark curls, his brow furrowing further as he answered, "No, I did not, but I think I know who did." He slumped into the chair as he asked, "What has occurred over the last four weeks? Who has visited my sister?"

"Mrs Younge had a visitor a few times; a man. He seemed nice enough, but he only came two or three times and stayed only a short while," she answered. "At first I thought I recognized him, but I could never determine what was so familiar about his features. I just assumed his appearance was similar to someone I have seen before."

"Do you remember his name?"

"No sir, but he may have left his card. Would you like me to ask Mr Porter?"

"Yes... please do. Was this man the only visitor?"

8

"No sir, there was another—a young lady named Miss Bennet walked along the beach with your sister nearly every morning. She returned with Miss Darcy several times when their walk was completed."

"Miss Bennet? Hmm... I do not recognize the name. Do you know where she is now?" he asked.

"She was staying with her aunt and uncle. I do not recall their name, but I do remember her saying something about Addington Street."

"Is that not but a few streets away?"

"Yes sir, very close indeed."

"Are there any footmen still employed, or have they all been let go?"

"All but one have gone, and he is on an errand at present. If it would be any help to you, my son worked in the stables but has stayed on until I could close up the house," the housekeeper offered.

He pulled out a coin and handed it to her, "Send him to find out everything he can about Miss Bennet and her relations. Tell him I will pay double if he comes back before nightfall."

"Yes sir," she replied. The housekeeper started to leave the room, and then turned back. "Sir, we did find two letters in Mrs Younge's room after they left. They were under her mattress. Would you like to see them?"

"Yes, please," he answered wearily.

She searched through the crate once more, unearthing the two missives. Handing them to the master, she quietly replied, "I will be back directly, sir." She left to find her son.

He opened the first letter, reading it quickly. It did not contain any useful information, so he folded it and went on to the second. He recognized the handwriting immediately and scanned to the bottom. When he saw the name *'George Wickham'* scrawled across the paper he knew he was going to be sick. He barely reached the chamber pot before his stomach lurched, expelling everything he had eaten last, and then some. After a few minutes he heard the housekeeper's calming voice again, her motherly hands smoothing back his hair and mopping his face with a cool cloth as he sat against the wall.

"Sir, you are as white as a sheet! Are you well? Would you like some tea?"

"Yes, thank you, Mrs Lewis."

"You just sit here and I will get Mr Porter to help you to a chamber where you can rest."

"No, no, I must find my sister," he started to stand but realized he did not have much strength.

"Sir, I do not know what has happened, but if it is as I fear, you will have a long journey ahead of you tomorrow. When my son returns with the information about Miss Bennet I will let you know, but until then, it would be best if you rest."

Darcy looked at the familiar face looking down at him; the stance she took with her hands on her hips made him smile a little. "You are as obstinate as your sister Mrs Reynolds."

She put the cloth into the cool water, wringing it and replacing it on his forehead. "I will take that as a compliment, sir. Now sit here and I will return in just a few minutes." At his nod of acceptance, she left the room, quickly finding the maid to have a room prepared and then on to have Mr Porter help their master upstairs. She felt as if she, too, would be sick. Mrs Lewis dearly hoped what she feared for Miss Darcy was not true.

Two hours passed slowly and he was just descending the stairs when the housekeeper stepped into the hallway, walking in his direction.

"Oh, Mr Darcy, I was just coming to tell you what James learned."

He quickly ushered her into an empty room, closing the door for privacy as she lit a candle on the mantle. "What did he say, Mrs Lewis?"

"The house is indeed located on Addington Street, and the relations' name is *Gardiner*. He spoke to their stable boy and the couple is at the theater this evening, but Miss Bennet stayed home."

He quickly reached for the door handle. "Have my horse readied immediately, and tell your son I will pay him extra if he will guide me to the house. I wish to be on the road as soon as I speak with her."

"Sir! You mean to speak with Miss Bennet even though her relations are away for the evening?"

"I have no choice, Mrs Lewis. My sister must be found. I will return soon. See to it the carriage is ready when I return."

"It is a very dark night. Would it not be better to wait until first light to travel?"

"No... I cannot leave my sister in the clutches of... that is... *no—I must leave as soon as I speak with Miss Bennet.*"

Within minutes he was following James, his horse's reins held tight in his grip as they walked rapidly down the streets. The boy indicated a certain house and Darcy paid him the promised fee and tied his horse to the post before knocking on the door and presenting his card to the butler.

"I am sorry Mr Darcy, but the Gardiners are not at home."

"I am here to see Miss Bennet."

"Sir, as I have already said, the Gardiners are not home. You will have to come back tomorrow," the servant stated as he tried to close the door to the unexpected visitor.

Darcy pushed it open and entered the hall, a fiery look in his eye. He discerned which door must lead to the sitting room. His hand was poised on the handle to enter when the old butler caught him. "Sir, I *insist* you leave… immediately!"

"Do you know who I am?" he turned around to face him. "I can have you thrown into the street never to be gainfully employed again if I so choose. Now, as I said, I am here to see..."

"Thank you Henderson, I will speak with our visitor."

Darcy spun around to see a young lady a few years older than his sister, though not quite as tall. "Are you Miss Bennet?"

The butler addressed her. "This is highly irregular and your uncle would not like it, Miss Bennet."

"I understand, and thank you for your concern, but all will be well," she said to the alarmed butler. She addressed Darcy, indicating with a gesture of her hand the sitting room from which she had just come. "Please step this way, sir."

As soon as the door closed he faced her, nearly growling in his question, "Where is my sister?"

"Sir, if you will sit, we can discuss this in a reasonable manner."

"*WHERE* is she?"

The frantic look in his eye would have frightened anyone else, but Elizabeth's courage rose as she lifted her chin higher and squared her shoulders, answering firmly, "Unlike my uncle's servants, I cannot be intimidated by your threats. Now, if you will *sit down* we might discuss this calmly."

"You must tell me where she is! It is of the utmost importance."

In a flourish of impertinence, she replied hotly, "As we have yet to be introduced, I do not know who you are, much less who your sister is, so I cannot very well answer you, sir."

"I am Fitzwilliam Darcy, and my sister is Georgiana Darcy," he answered harshly. "Now where is she?"

Elizabeth took a deep breath, "Sir, we need to sit."

He was about to object yet again when he noticed something odd about the way the young lady was walking. She tried to hide a wince of pain, but he could tell it was taking all her effort to stay composed. He was just about to apologize and offer his help when she accidentally kicked the leg of a chair. Her face went pale and he caught her as she started to fall. Realizing she had fainted, he lifted her in his arms and carried her to the sofa, placing her there before stepping into the hallway to call for help. By the time he returned with the housekeeper, she was awakening.

"Oh, Miss Bennet, are you ill?" The housekeeper nearly pushed him out of the way in her haste. "What has happened?" She turned her menacing looks on the unexpected visitor. "What did you do?"

"No, no… he did nothing," the young lady assured the housekeeper between heavy gasps due to the tremendous pain. "Please help me sit upright."

The housekeeper assisted her to a more comfortable situation and propped an obviously swollen ankle on some cushions. When the young lady dismissed her, the housekeeper looked at Darcy. "It might be best if I sit in the corner, Miss Bennet."

"Thank you for the offer, but I assure you, your presence will not be required," she said in dismissal.

"Very well." The housekeeper eyed Darcy warily. "I will be right outside if you need me."

As soon as the door closed Darcy turned to the young lady. "I am very sorry... I did not know of your injury."

"No offence is taken, Mr Darcy. Please have a seat and we can discuss your sister."

Darcy sat on the edge of the chair, looking as if he was ready to bolt from the room at any minute. "I am listening."

"She is no longer in Ramsgate."

His looks became darker. "Yes, I gathered as much from my servants, but where is she?"

"I would guess she is a fair distance to Gretna Green as we speak," Elizabeth looked at the man across from her.

"Where would she get such a notion, and how do *you* know about such plans?"

"Before you start issuing accusations of which you know naught, I must advise you of my ignorance of the scheme."

"Am I supposed to believe you? If you knew, why did you not try to stop her?"

Elizabeth sat with shoulders straighter in defense, the movement making her hiss in pain. "I *did* try to stop her, but her companion, *whom I assume your family hired after much careful consideration*," she said as she rolled her eyes sarcastically, "convinced her otherwise, *sir.*"

The battle of wills between Miss Bennet and her inquisitor was interrupted when a couple, a little older than Darcy, entered the room. The lady went to Miss Bennet's side and the gentleman immediately focusing on Darcy. "Sir, I must ask you to leave my house at once."

"I will not go until I obtain the information for which I came!"

"NOT from my niece, you will not!" The master of the house pointed to the doorway where two burly footmen stood.

Darcy knew he needed to ascertain what Miss Bennet knew, but he doubted her uncle would be inclined to let her speak with him further. When they were in the hallway, he again tried to have his say. "It is imperative that I speak with Miss Bennet."

Edward Gardiner looked at the tall man standing before him, assessing his demeanor carefully before he replied, "*She and I* will be at our leisure tomorrow morning at ten o'clock to speak with you."

"I must leave town tonight, sir." Darcy was insistent.

"I *will not* put the health of my niece at risk. If what you must discuss with her is of such dire importance, then you will stay in Ramsgate tonight. I will not be gainsaid *or intimidated*, sir."

Knowing he would only make things worse if he tried to force the issue, Darcy bowed curtly. "You may expect me at ten, sir."

Edward watched as the man walked out the door, untied his horse, mounted and rode away. Returning to the sitting room, he saw his wife trying to arrange the cushions for Elizabeth's comfort. "Perhaps she could use some tea, my dear?"

Madeline Gardiner looked to her husband and nodded, "I will speak with Mrs Walters."

When they were alone and the door was closed, Edward drew a chair close to his niece. "Now tell me, what is happening Lizzy?" Elizabeth tried to look away, but he placed his finger under her chin, drawing her eyes to his. "I have allowed you to be vague until now about the events which have transpired, but after your persistent visitor tonight, I feel I must insist upon knowing all."

Elizabeth knew it was time to tell him everything. Taking a deep breath, she tried to keep the tears from her eyes as she explained.

Edward listened intently, asking a few questions where they were warranted. When she finished, he reached for her hand in his fatherly fashion. "You must tell him."

"Yes, I know. I was trying to get him to calm himself so I could."

"Well, let us hope tomorrow morning when Mr Darcy returns, he will be more apt to listen. I assured him of our being available to see him at ten o'clock."

"You will be with me when I tell him?"

"Yes; you will not have to do this alone." He saw a look of relief come over her features, "For now, I think it best you retire. I will fetch John and we will help you upstairs."

"Thank you, Uncle." Elizabeth squeezed his hand, smiling when he lovingly squeezed hers in return.

When she was finally settled in her room, her swollen ankle propped upon several pillows, she began to review the events of the evening. She knew the terror she saw in Mr Darcy's eyes had driven him to be brash, and she was grateful for Uncle Edward's assurances he would stay with her tomorrow when the man returned. She could not help but smile at the protective manners of her uncle. He was more a father to her and her sister than their own father had been. She was grateful to have such a loving family.

Darcy went back to the house, surprising the housekeeper with his sudden arrival.

Worried, she followed after him as he slowly climbed the stairs. "I thought you were leaving town immediately, sir? Was your carriage not ready when you arrived?"

He looked sheepishly back at her, feeling every bit the boy who needed to be scolded for how he had treated Miss Bennet this evening. "I cannot speak with Miss Bennet until tomorrow morning. Please have my horse ready by half past nine."

"Would you like something to eat or drink, sir?"

She had served his family at various Darcy homes since he was very young, and she was happy to come here to Ramsgate when he mentioned sending his sister. He knew she meant well, even if her tone was that of a mother. "No, I require nothing else. Thank you, Mrs Lewis."

He continued to his chamber, feeling the great weight on his shoulders of everything he had learned today compounded with the events of the last few months. He sat on the bed to remove his boots, catching sight of his disheveled appearance in the nearby mirror. *I cannot believe I arrived to speak with her looking like this,* he thought. *I would not be shocked to find she takes me for a lunatic.* He ran his hand through his grimy hair. The dirt on his hand displayed how long and hard he had ridden. Removing his jacket, cravat, and waistcoat, he washed the dust from his face and neck before sitting before the fire. He was tired, but he doubted sleep would come easily tonight.

Pinching the bridge of his nose and hoping to ward off the coming headache, he leaned back, stretching his toes to the heat emanating from the coals, and sighed. *She is right,* he told himself. *This is entirely my fault. I was the one who failed to check Mrs Younge's references and insisted we hire her immediately. I was the one who did not warn Georgiana of that scoundrel's threats against our family. I very well could have spared the time to come here with her, and yet I did not. Her downfall is entirely my fault.*

For the first time since his mother's death, Darcy felt tears he could not control well up in his eyes. Before he knew it they were spilling down his cheeks, soaking his shirt. He sat before the fire all night, the uncomfortable chair not giving his tall frame much respite as sleep eventually claimed him. The dreams plaguing him did not offer much rest for his weary heart.

He awoke early, his swollen eyes from hours of crying obvious in the mirror above the washstand. With a deep sigh he turned away from his visage, hoping he would not look this terrible when he went to speak with Miss Bennet in a few hours. *Miss Bennet.* The memory of her standing there, arms folded like armor over her chest, firmly informing him she would not be intimidated, ran through his mind. As he pulled the cord to have the servants heat water for a bath, a small smile formed on the corners of his mouth. *I doubt anything could intimidate you, Miss Bennet,* he thought to himself.

Fitzwilliam Darcy was not wrong in his assessment of the young lady he hardly knew. Elizabeth Bennet's life was one of hardship and pain, especially these last four years, but in every circumstance she and her sister seemed to have exactly enough strength to face whatever fate threw at them with a determination many ladies, or even gentlemen for that matter, did not possess.

Chapter 2

he Bennet sisters had lived with their uncle and aunt for four years now, and both were of the age to marry. While Elizabeth was excited at the prospect before her, Mary was not certain marriage was ever attainable for her. As their guardians though, it was up the Gardiners to introduce their nieces to the wonders of the *Season*. The family would first go on an extended holiday. After much discussion, Ramsgate was their chosen destination. Plans were made, a house let, and both girls looked forward to a month by the sea.

When the departure day finally arrived, Madeline Gardiner peeked her head into Elizabeth's room. Seeing her sitting in front of the mirror, Aunt Gardiner entered and walked over to stand behind her. "Are you ready to travel?"

Elizabeth smiled. "Yes, I am ready." She reached up to affectionately grasp the hand resting on her shoulder. Closing her eyes as she said, "Aunt Maddie, I have a feeling our lives are about to change." She opened her eyes, meeting her aunt's through the mirror. "How, I cannot tell you, but I know this holiday will be a time to remember for the rest of our lives."

"I hope so, my dear. I have loved having you both here with us, but you are of an age now to have your own homes. I know you are apprehensive about being out, but I believe you will find someone as special as you are with whom to share your life."

"I hope so, too. Perhaps I will meet him while we are in Ramsgate?"

"That is a good possibility, but if not, I am certain your uncle will have your calendar full when we return. He has been looking forward to the day he can show off the prettiest girls in Town, and you *know* how much he loves company," she teased.

"Oh, Aunt Maddie, I dearly love you both and will miss you when I do finally move away."

She squeezed her niece's hand, "Well, you are not leaving yet, so let us not think meanly of the future. Come, we must be on the road. I have a feeling your little cousins will prove to be quite the challenge these next few days."

Elizabeth stood and reached for her spencer, threading her arms through the sleeves. "It is a good thing the new carriage is large enough–I would not relish a trip of this length in the old one."

"Your uncle used this as an excuse to find something larger, but truly, it was needed. Our family has grown significantly in the last four years, and with the children growing up—well, it was just time."

They left the room, Elizabeth telling her aunt of the games she and Mary had devised to play with the children on the long ride.

Madeline chuckled as she followed Elizabeth down the stairs, "I do appreciate your efforts, though somehow I doubt my boys will be entertained by your efforts. It is only the promise of playing along the beach which has made Henry agree to be on his best behavior while we travel."

The Gardiners had four children. Eight year old Juliana reminded Elizabeth and Mary of their eldest sister Jane. She was always prim and proper, happy to sit with her elder cousins as they embroidered or read. Juliana lovingly guided her younger siblings in everything they did, and six year old Emma was now beginning to act much like Juliana, though it was more of a challenge for her. Emma dearly wished to be just like her sister, but she did not yet possess the ability which often comes with age to sit still quite as long as was required for some of their activities. What she lacked in calmness though she more than made up for in fortitude. Whenever she sat beside her older sister, she imitated precisely how Juliana sat, how she held her cup, even how she tilted her head. Emma was determined to one day be just as graceful.

The two had their mother's light brown curls and their father's blue eyes. Mary always said she loved those eyes because they were the one feature she remembered of her own mother. Edward Gardiner and his two late sisters, Frances Bennet and Martha Philips, all shared that common feature.

As much as the Gardiner girls embodied what society felt proper young ladies should be, their boys could not be more opposite. Five year old Henry was precocious, always getting into situations which confounded his parents. His bright red hair made attention turn to him when he came into a room, and his green eyes seemed to always hold a secret he did not wish to reveal. The youngest of the family was baby Joseph. He would soon turn two years old, and though he was definitely the most rambunctious of the Gardiner children, he did not get into as much trouble as his older brother Henry. The brothers were a force to be reckoned with when they combined forces, as their nursemaid learned all too often.

Mary and Elizabeth spent hours preparing for their holiday. They perused every book Elizabeth could find at the circulating library on the entertainments Ramsgate held, and soon a list of places they wished to go and things they wished to see emerged. Everything from visiting certain tea shops and seashell hunting, to watching the parade of soldiers on the promenade and viewing the ships in the harbor, was on their list.

The journey was long, and at times did prove to be difficult with the little ones, but they were all soon enjoying the city and all it held. Mary found the sea air invigorating and enjoyed joining Elizabeth daily as they took in the culture around them.

Eager to collect all the shells they could during their five week holiday, Elizabeth and Mary went to the seashore every morning to scour the sand for interesting sea life. It was on one of these early excursions that they met Miss Darcy and her companion, Mrs Younge. The girls began to meet nearly every morning. Usually Mrs Younge would leave her young charge in Elizabeth's care. Elizabeth did not think this odd until Miss Darcy began to speak of a man who was paying her court, unbeknownst to the Darcy family, and that her suitor was urged on by the encouragement of Mrs Younge. Knowing Miss Darcy was too young to be involved in such a scheme, Elizabeth tried to talk with her about what it might do to her reputation, but Miss Darcy was not willing to hear what Elizabeth had to say on the matter. Miss Darcy instead assured the Bennet sisters of the gentleman's affection. While Miss Darcy insisted he was of good character, there was something in the gentleman's eyes, the one time they met, that Elizabeth could not trust.

Elizabeth determined to talk some sense into the girl one last time, and if nothing came of it, she would write to the Darcy family, letting them know it was imperative they come to Ramsgate for the good of their youngest relation. It was this letter, delivered to his house in Town and signed only *'from a concerned friend'*, which made Fitzwilliam Darcy travel to Ramsgate. The note did not give particular details, saying only that it would be in the family's best interest if someone came to Ramsgate to check on Miss Darcy.

Elizabeth did not expect the girl's brother to arrive at her doorstep, nor for him to be so hostile. She hoped he would be more willing to listen this morning when he returned to speak with her. Feeling more courageous after a good night's sleep, she expressed to her uncle a desire to speak with Mr Darcy alone. Edward felt his presence in the room was essential, especially after his intrusion the previous evening, and assured his niece he would sit in the corner, giving them sufficient privacy while they talked.

A knock at the chamber door pulled her from her revelry. She bid the person enter and Aunt Maddie opened the door.

"I came to see if you need assistance this morning, but I see you have completed your toilette already. I love how you arranged your hair."

Elizabeth's fingers went to the dark curls piled on the back on her head, fingering the braid wound around them, "Mary saw this on someone at the beach last week and thought it would enhance my curls."

"It is very becoming, my dear," Madeline replied. "Are you ready to go downstairs?"

"Yes. I believe I may be able to put some weight on my ankle today."

"Elizabeth Bennet, I love you as if you were my own child," she placed both hands on her niece's shoulders as they both looked into the mirror in front of Elizabeth, "but you are mistaken if you think I will allow you to cause permanent damage to your ankle by walking on it too soon. It needs time to heal, especially after you kicked a chair leg last night. John will carry you to the sitting room to await your visitor."

Elizabeth sighed, "I fear I shall not be able to walk along the beach again before we leave."

Madeline kissed her niece's cheek, "If you will promise to stay off your ankle, I will promise to find a way for you to visit the shore at least once more before we return to Town."

Elizabeth smiled, "Thank you, Aunt Maddie."

"You are more than welcome, my dear. Now, you stay here and I will return directly with John," she said, turning to leave the room.

Elizabeth was comfortably settled when the clock struck ten. Their punctual visitor knocked on the front door at the stroke of the hour.

"Thank you Henderson, I will get the door," Edward dismissed the butler and opened it himself. "Welcome, sir."

"Thank you. I am sorry I did not have the opportunity to be officially introduced to you last night," Darcy bowed. "Fitzwilliam Darcy."

"I am Edward Gardiner, and as I am sure you surmised, I am Miss Bennet's uncle and guardian. "Before I allow you to speak with my niece, I would like a few words with you in private, if you will please follow me this way, sir." He led the way to the deserted dining room, closing the door behind them. "I know why you are here, but I would caution you to not lose your temper as you did last night. I will not have my niece's recovery thwarted because of you upsetting her in any way."

"I offer my sincerest apologies for my actions last night, sir," Darcy assured the older man.

"After speaking with my niece of the particulars of the situation, I cannot say I would not do the same. However, today is a new day, and nothing good will come of a repeat of last night," Edward warned.

"Yes sir, I understand."

With a nod, Edward led him to the sitting room, nodding to Elizabeth and choosing a chair in the corner, as promised.

Darcy bowed, "Please accept my apologies for my rude behavior last evening, Miss Bennet." When he rose up from his low bow his eyes caught some bluish marks on the side of her face.

Elizabeth felt him staring, her fingers reaching up to touch her eye and cheek tenderly as she turned away from him. "Please excuse my appearance, Mr Darcy."

"No, no, it is clear you have been injured. I did not see the bruises last night."

"There was not much light then," she observed. "Please be seated, sir."

Darcy sat in the chair opposite the sofa on which she lay, her foot propped up by some cushions, "Were you in an accident of some kind?"

Elizabeth looked nervously at her hands as she answered, "I tried to catch a carriage as it sped away."

"Why would you do such a thing?" he asked, full of curiosity.

"I was trying to convince them to stop, sir." She looked back up, catching his eye as she said quietly, "Your sister was in the carriage."

Darcy paled. "I am very sorry, Miss Bennet. I misjudged you and I must offer my most sincere apologies once again. I should not have barged in here as I did."

"I too feel I owe you an apology for my temper last evening. It was impolite of me to speak as I did, accusing you of causing all this with your sister."

Darcy sat forward in the chair, "What did you say that I did not deserve? I forced my way into this house when I knew your uncle was away, and I was rude to you and the staff." He stopped and took a deep breath, quietly saying, "I *truly am* at fault for my sister's situation, and I appreciate your pointing it out to me."

"Yes, well, it was not my place, sir. I am sorry." At his nod of acceptance, she continued, "I take it your family received the note I sent?"

22

"You are the *'concerned friend'*? I have to say, after I had time to think last night I thought you might be. My cousin and I share guardianship of my sister–my parents are no longer alive."

"Oh, I did not know. Miss Darcy did not speak much about her family."

"No, we usually do not speak of our parents." He closed his eyes and swallowed hard, "Please Miss Bennet, tell me all you know of the situation with my sister."

Elizabeth told him how she and her younger sister Mary met Miss Darcy, and all she knew of the girl's companion and the gentleman of whom Miss Darcy often spoke.

"Did you ever see him?"

"Yes, twice, and both times there was something about his eyes that unsettled me."

"Do you know his name?"

"No, he was never properly introduced to us, and your sister was careful not to say his name when we spoke of the situation," Elizabeth explained, immediately thinking of something that might help. "Although, my sister may know from... *well*, she just may know." She turned to get her uncle's attention, "Uncle Edward, can you please have Mary join us?"

He eyed her, "Are you certain?"

Elizabeth thought for a few seconds before she answered with a nod, "Yes, I am certain."

Edward left the room with a warning glance at their visitor, and Elizabeth used the time to speak with him about Mary. "Mr Darcy, there is something I must tell you about my sister. When she was eight years old, Mary suffered an injury that led to her losing her hearing. She is deaf."

"Oh," Darcy was taken aback.

"I think she may know his name because Mary *hears* others by watching how they form their lips when they speak." Noticing his hesitancy, she added quietly, "Please do not stare at her when she comes in the room; it makes her very uncomfortable."

"Oh, yes... of course." He heard Mr Gardiner in the hall and stood to be introduced to Miss Bennet's sister.

Edward looked at Mary as he said steadily, "Mary, this is Mr Fitzwilliam Darcy, Miss Darcy's brother." He then turned to the visitor, "Mr Darcy, my niece, Miss Mary Bennet."

With their greetings exchanged, Mary went to Elizabeth's side, sitting on the edge of the sofa so her sister could talk with her using their language of hand symbols. Darcy tried not to stare, but it was a rather odd display. Miss Bennet moved her mouth as if she was speaking, but nothing came out, and both were moving their hands in strange ways. He assumed it was a way for them to communicate. When Miss Bennet looked back at him he realized he was staring and looked away.

"Mr Darcy, my sister is certain the man's name was George, though the last name is a bit harder to determine. She thinks it may start with a W—I—C sound."

"Wickham!" The color in his face drained immediately and Darcy sat back down heavily in the chair. He finally looked back at the sisters, "It is as I feared. I must leave for Gretna Green immediately."

Mary shook her head no and turned to Elizabeth, moving her hands again.

"Mr Darcy, my sister says they are not going to Gretna Green. They said something about going to another town, but being unfamiliar with the names, she could not make out what it was."

He turned to Mary and quickly asked, "Miss Mary, would you be able to choose this place out of a list of names?"

"Mr Darcy, you must speak more slowly to my sister. When one speaks quickly the lips do not form words the same way and she cannot understand you," Elizabeth explained.

"Oh... I... am... sorry," he replied, this time drawing out every word very slowly.

Elizabeth chuckled, "Sir, it is not necessary to go quite *that* slowly. Just speak at a normal, moderate tempo."

"I do apologize, Miss Mary."

Mary moved her hands in response and Elizabeth replied, "She understands, Mr Darcy."

"Do you think you would be able to select the name of the town if you saw it written?" he asked again, this time at the appropriate speed.

Mary nodded and turned back to Elizabeth, moving her hands again.

"She says they were also speaking of going to London first, so it is possible they are there instead."

"Thank you," Darcy stood and looked at both young ladies, "for everything."

"We wish you luck in finding her, sir," Elizabeth said while Mary stood and curtsied.

Edward walked out to the hall with their visitor when Darcy was ready to take his leave, "I hope you find her in time."

"I hope so as well. My cousin is in Town still with his regiment, so if they are there, we will find them. Thank you, Mr Gardiner." He started to walk out the door, and then turned around, "I wish to pay for your niece's medical care."

Edward put up his hand, "That is not necessary. She has been far worse off of her own accord before this."

"Nevertheless, my sister is the reason she was injured, and I feel it is my duty. Please. I insist."

"We had her examined, but there has been no reason for a doctor to be called again, Mr Darcy. As soon as she is healed enough to endure the journey we will be returning to Town," Edward replied.

Darcy extended his calling card, "If you will not allow me to pay for a doctor, at least let me offer my carriage to return you and your family to Town. It is well sprung and will help with Miss Bennet's comfort."

Edward accepted the card, offering his own in return, "Thank you. I will let you know."

Darcy gave a short bow, "Again, I am sorry for the trouble my family has caused yours. I will have a list sent over for Miss Mary to look over and see if the locations look familiar. My staff will be at your disposal in any way you need."

He tapped the card on his palm, "I will let you know what comes of the list. I pray you find your sister, Mr Darcy."

With a quick bow, Darcy exited, returning to his residence to assemble a list for Mary and to inform his staff of his offer to Mr Gardiner.

As Darcy rode to Town to meet with his cousin and start their search for Georgiana, he could not get the Bennet sisters out of his mind. He wondered what they had been through to engender such obvious mutual love and devotion. He began to wonder if the lack of such feelings between he and Georgiana could be the cause of her recent rebellious actions.

Chapter 3

Three weeks later:

"ir, there is a Mr Fitzwilliam Darcy to see you," the butler told his master when he was bid enter at the knock.

"Oh? Please show him to me." Edward Gardiner replied, shuffling the mail in front of him into a neat pile as he awaited the unexpected visitor.

Greetings were exchanged and soon the two men were seated. "So what brings you to my home, Mr Darcy?"

"I was in the neighborhood and wished to enquire of Miss Bennet's recovery. Is she well?"

"Yes, she is much improved. In fact, she and her sister have gone for a walk in the park across the street," Edward replied.

Darcy sat up a little straighter, "Sir, would it be acceptable if I speak with your nieces today? I wish to thank them for their help in recovering my sister."

"I appreciated the note you sent and was glad to hear she was returned without consequence."

"Yes, my cousin, Colonel Fitzwilliam, with whom I share guardianship, employed some of his contacts in the Army, and with Miss Mary's information we located my sister quickly. That is why I wish to offer my gratitude in person."

"I am glad Mary could be of service to you. She has had a difficult life and most people do not give her much credit. To be honest, I did not think you would either."

"Had I not been in such a dire situation, I wonder if I would have as well," Darcy said honestly. "One thing I have learned from this entire circumstance is that I desire a bond such as your two nieces possess, though I doubt I will have the opportunity with my dear sister."

"What my nieces have was born of life's harshly dealt blows which have united them. Both grew into strong ladies and taught me much in the time they have been with us," Edward replied.

"If you do not mind my asking," Darcy broached the sensitive subject, "how long have you been their guardian?"

Edward chuckled, "Four years, and that is all I will say. If you want to know more, you have my permission to speak with my nieces. I would not feel right telling their story."

Darcy stood, "I may do just that. Thank you." He started to go, then turned back to ask, "Where in the park, sir?"

"They can usually be found feeding the ducks."

With another bow of thanks, he left, waving his footman away and walking towards the park. Darcy could see them sitting on the bench throwing scraps of bread to the ducks in the small pond. As he walked towards them he noticed how similar they looked from the angle of his approach. It was clear to anyone observing them that they were sisters. He and Georgiana were nothing alike; he looked more like their father and Georgiana was almost identical to their mother in stature, not that she remembered their mother much. Anne Darcy died when Georgiana was just a babe, and their father also five years ago, leaving the siblings alone. Darcy kept his sister in the right schools and did everything his family suggested, yet this was the second showing of her defiant nature since Twelfth Night, the first being when the school she attended contacted him saying she was caught sneaking out of her room several times.

He was starting to think perhaps what she needed most was to be in a true family. His aunts and uncle assured him this was how things were done for girls her age, and he usually followed their suggestions, but in this case, *he* was at fault for what took place.

Darcy stopped beneath a tree. Not wanting to interrupt, he leaned his shoulder against the rough bark as he watched the playful manner in which Miss Bennet interacted with her younger sister. She drew Miss Mary out with a vivacity he had never seen before. He was lost in thought until the two ladies and their maid stood to return home. Miss Bennet saw him and waved, winding her arm through her sister's as they walked towards him.

"Mr Darcy, it is good to see you again. What brings you to this tree? Do you not have such fine specimens where you reside?"

He could not help but chuckle at her teasing manner, "I must say, it is the prospect of speaking with you that brought me to its boughs. Good morning to you both," he bowed to each. "I called on your uncle, and he said I could find you here."

"What can we do for you, sir?" Elizabeth asked.

"May I walk with you for a minute?"

"Yes, of course, although we are just returning home." Mary began to cough.

"Are you well Miss Mary?" Darcy asked, concern evident in his voice.

"She will be well, Mr Darcy, it is merely a cold my cousin passed along to her. She is feeling much better though and wished to feed the ducks."

"I am glad to hear she is improving then."

They arrived at the house and the maid accompanied Mary inside. Darcy saw Mary lean down and move her hands, saying something to her young cousin who immediately nodded his head and closed the door. The next thing he knew the curtains of a nearby window moved and the red-haired boy peered out, watching the two intently.

"It seems we have an audience."

Elizabeth turned to where he indicated, then smiled and waved, receiving a frown in return. "He wanted to go with us, but he is still feeling a little too ill for such a trek." She turned back to the caller. "Was there something I can help you with Mr Darcy?

"Oh, yes, please excuse me. I just wished to thank you and Miss Mary for all your help."

"My uncle told us of your finding Miss Darcy. Is she recovered from the ordeal?"

"Yes... yes she is doing much better." He was about to say his goodbyes and walk away when he stammered, "Miss Bennet, I would like to extend an invitation to your family to join me for dinner one evening next week."

Elizabeth turned to look at him fully. Standing two steps up from him gave her the advantage of looking the tall man straight in the eye. "Sir, I can tell by your clothes and demeanor you are obviously very wealthy. However, my uncle is in trade. Did you know?"

He looked down, a bit stunned, "No... no, I was not aware of that."

"Yes, well, it is only his success in business which allows us to live in such a neighborhood as this. When Mary and I came to London they lived on Gracechurch Street within sight of my uncle's warehouses, but the house was too small for their own growing family plus me and my sister, so my uncle moved us all here to Brunswick Square."

Darcy stood a little taller and looked her in the eye with great determination, "Miss Bennet, it matters not to me whether you are from this side of London or not. Your family helped me, and I wish to continue the acquaintance. Please tell your uncle of my invitation and I will have the particulars written and sent here as soon as possible. I must first speak with my uncle to know which evening next week they are available, as I wish my family to meet all of your family. Good day, Miss Bennet." He gave her a respectful bow and turned to go, looking back again and tipping his hat to her when he reached his carriage.

Elizabeth stood watching the fine equipage roll away, rendered speechless by what she had just heard. In the years she had lived in London, this was the first instance a person of such standing acknowledged her or her family. When she returned inside and told her uncle, he gave her a hug. "Well, I do not see why this is such a shock to you, Elizabeth. You are, after all, a gentleman's daughter."

"Yes, that is true, but for the last four years I have been nothing more than an orphan taken in by my uncle and aunt who are in trade." Tears welled up in her eyes.

Edward pulled out his handkerchief and dabbed her cheeks. Kissing her forehead, he replied, "When the invitation comes I will be sure your aunt accepts in a timely manner. Mr Darcy seems like the kind of gentleman who could make our lives a bit more interesting, does he not?"

Elizabeth dried the last of her tears and chuckled at her uncle, "Indeed he does."

Darcy returned home in such a jovial mood that even the tedious task of answering all his piled up social engagements was done with a small smile on his lips and an extra flourish when he signed his name.

Richard Fitzwilliam stood watching his cousin from the open doorway. He was smiling—*actually smiling!* The shock of seeing such a rare sight was made even more momentous an occasion when he also thought he heard him humming. Shaking his head, he strode into the room and sat down across from Darcy, "All right, who are you and what have you done with my staid and serious cousin?"

Darcy looked up from the letter he was just finishing, "Good day to you Fitz. What brings you back so early? Did you not have drills all day?"

"It was decided the turn of this weather did not lend itself to such so easily, so we begged off until tomorrow."

"Oh? Did the weather turn? It was such a lovely day earlier."

Fitz looked over to the window where rain poured down like buckets being dumped from the heavens. A crack of thunder was heard in the distance. "Seriously, who are you and what have you done with my cousin?"

"Am I not allowed to be of a pleasant attitude?"

"While that is permitted, it is such a rare sight that you have me wondering if something has addled your mind. What exactly has engendered such from you today?"

Darcy pressed his ring into the cooling wax of the last letter sat before him, then he stacked it on top of the others on the tray. "I paid a call this morning, and it was pleasant. That is all."

"Ahhh, the truth is revealed. Just who has made you smile on such a dreary day as today? No—wait—let me guess. Was it Miss Lindstrom? *No, no, she usually can only induce half a smile from you, and only if she does not open her mouth. Hmmm...* Lady Rowley is not in Town yet, so it could not possibly be Lady Julia who has inspired your joviality."

Darcy rolled his eyes as he stood, walking over to the window to look out at the rain. "She could never inspire such from me. Have you seen her eyes? One never knows if she is looking at you or the person beside you, and unlike others, I am in no great need to pad my purse with her sizable dowry."

"I have a feeling even her eyes will not be a deterrent this Season. It seems I have reached the end of my list, so it would be best if you just tell me who you paid a call on earlier."

"Miss Bennet."

He thought, saying allowed, "*Miss Bennet... Miss Bennet...,*" then looked over at his cousin, "I do not recall where I have heard that name before."

"I met her in Ramsgate—she and her sister, Miss Mary, provided me with the information that led us to Georgiana."

"Oh, right; I do not believe you mentioned her name but once. Just what precipitated such a call?"

Darcy turned around, smiled at his cousin, then strode purposely from the room as he said clearly, "I am to have a dinner party."

"A dinner party!" Fitz was so shocked it took him a few seconds to realize his cousin had left the room. He followed after him, catching up at the stairs. "Just when is this dinner to be, and what is the occasion?"

"Must one need an occasion to have guests over?"

"Anyone else, I would say no. You—well, you have never been known to be so gregarious."

"Well Maybe I ought to be." He patted his cousin on the shoulder, "I have written to your father asking when they are available next week, and as soon as I hear from him I will make my plans accordingly. I believe I will enjoy having the Gardiners here—it is time we liven the place up, would you not say?"

"Gardiners? Just who are they?"

"Miss Bennet's relations—her uncle and aunt. I will invite them, Miss Bennet, and Miss Mary, as well as your parents, and we shall have a lovely evening."

He snorted, "Good luck with your plans—you lost me when you included my parents in the same sentence as *lovely evening*."

"They may not be the best choice, but I will not allow Georgiana to think she is to be hostess for me, and my Aunt Edith is not yet in Town for the Season." Darcy turned to continue up the stairs. "I expect you to be here as well, so have your man prepare your nice uniform."

Fitz shook his head and watched Darcy walk away up the stairs. *Just who is this Miss Bennet that she could inspire such odd behavior from my cousin?* He determined to find out all he could from his cousin over the next few days about the Gardiners, and especially about Miss Bennet and her sister.

Sarah Johnson

Chapter 4

arcy was sitting at his desk when his cousin came in the door.

"Well," Fitz replied as he sat down opposite his cousin, moving his sword with the practiced ease of a well—seasoned soldier, "my father has found out the inevitable."

"And what is that?"

"That your guests this evening are in trade," he sighed.

Darcy sat up a little straighter, "Will they be cancelling then?"

"No, amazingly enough, my father wishes to come and meet this paragon of a family you have talked up to them, and he has convinced my mother as well. However, my brother will have nothing to do with this *scheme*, as he calls it."

"There is no loss there; Milton can do as he pleases," Darcy mumbled. "How did they find out about Mr Gardiner being in trade?" Darcy asked.

"It was not too difficult. It seems my father's new doctor lives in Brunswick Square and the gentleman was all too eager to speak of his neighbors," Fitz said.

Darcy looked at his cousin, "Did he tell them of Miss Mary's condition?"

"I knew you would ask me that," Fitz stood and began to look at the many books on the shelf, running his finger down the spines of some. "As far as I could surmise from the conversation, they know nothing of her condition, but I did not want to come right out and ask. If she does not speak this evening they may just perceive her to be shy."

"Oh, excuse me," they heard Georgiana say from the doorway. "I did not know you were busy, brother. Hello Fitz," she gave a small curtsey to her cousin.

Darcy stood, "What is it, Georgiana?"

She looked from one to the other, then sighed heavily and sat down primly on the edge of the chair. "I do not feel well, and I was just wondering if I could stay in my room this evening?"

"I cannot believe you would ask such when you have treated Miss Bennet and Miss Mary as you have. If it were not for them, you would be married to that conniving scoundrel as we speak." Darcy leaned down to look directly at his sister, "You will attend the dinner, and you will offer your apologies to Miss Bennet for the injuries you caused her."

She looked back at him with an icy glare, "And what if I choose to not do as you say?"

Fitz snorted, "You know Darcy, when we were at Aunt Catherine's for Easter she was very eager to invite Georgiana to stay with her and Anne until the summer. She talked constantly about how wonderful it would be to have someone to read Fordyce's sermons aloud to her and someone our dear cousin could accompany on the pianoforte."

"But Anne cannot play the pianoforte..." she stammered.

"Yes, well, try telling *that* to Aunt Catherine," Fitz said flatly.

The girl looked down at her hands, the room silent as she considered the threat. Finally she stood, "I will be ready to apologize. With your permission, I wish to do so when the ladies separate from the gentlemen after our meal?"

"Yes, that will be fine." Darcy walked around the desk to his sister's side, "Georgiana, we are not trying to make your life miserable, but it is up to us to help you see what does *and does not* constitute a good decision."

She looked up at him, the harshness back in her eyes as she replied, "Then why have you waited until now to do so?" She turned and marched from the room, leaving both gentlemen reeling at her vehemence.

"I should have all along, my dear sister," Darcy whispered, *"I should have all along."*

Elizabeth knew Mary was nervous and did not wish to attend the dinner. She always was before they went anywhere, but she knew she could talk her into going. "I promise you will be well, Mary," she told her. "You will not have to say anything, just as all the other dinners we have attended with Uncle's associates. I do not know why, but I trust Mr Darcy. He is a good gentleman. Uncle Edward and Aunt Maddie will be right there too, so what could go wrong?"

After much cajoling and promises of the numerous books Elizabeth would give her sister if she attended this dinner, Mary finally decided to go and at least try to enjoy the evening. The two dressed in their finest gowns and joined their aunt and uncle for the carriage ride from Brunswick Square to a lavish home in the Mayfair district. Elizabeth was astonished when she saw the tall, ornate façade of the house on Hill Street in which they were to dine that evening. She knew Mr Darcy was affluent by the quality of his clothing, but his London home was beyond what she ever imagined. She stepped down from the carriage and looked up at the red brick that towered six stories above her, the white window casements setting off the uniqueness of this building from the others along Hill Street. She smiled when her uncle offered his arm, allowing him to lead her past the columns and up the steps to the entrance already standing open for the visitors.

A maid took her wrap then stepped away as Elizabeth's eye was drawn around the large entrance hall, her gaze taking in the stairs as they wound their way to the upper floors. She stopped when her eyes caught a large landscape that hung in a prominent place on the wall.

"This way, Miss," the butler interrupted her thoughts.

She turned from the beautiful painting to follow her relatives into the sitting room, where Mr Darcy stood with another gentleman, shorter than himself, though still taller than her uncle. The features of the two were as different as they could be, with Mr Darcy's dark hair and nearly black eyes and the other gentleman's light blonde hair and blue eyes. In a way, Elizabeth thought the gentleman resembled Miss Darcy more than her own brother did. He stood out from the blues and light wood tones of the surrounding room because of his bright red uniform.

Darcy stepped up, "Welcome, Mr Gardiner, Mrs Gardiner. Miss Bennet..." his eyes stopped on Elizabeth for just a second longer than the others as he bowed to her, then he continued on, "Miss Mary. I am pleased you all could join us tonight. This is my cousin, the Honourable Richard Fitzwilliam, Colonel in His Majesty's Army. His parents will be along shortly, and my sister will be joining us directly." He glanced with a nod at the housekeeper who stood by the door. Knowing what he needed immediately, she went to find Miss Darcy. Darcy was glad to have devoted staff who knew his needs so well that words were not always necessary. His attention was drawn back to the group before him as his cousin's easy nature was clearly on display for his guests.

"It is a pleasure to meet you all," Fitz said as he bowed.

Edward stepped forward, "I believe Mr Darcy has spoken of you, Colonel. Would you be the cousin with whom he shares custody of Miss Darcy?"

Fitz looked to his cousin, "Yes I would be, Mr Gardiner." With a sly expression aimed at Darcy, he continued, "It is not every day I have the opportunity to hear how my cousin behaves when not in my company, so if you will indulge me, I believe we may pass the time pleasantly as we await the others."

Elizabeth could not help smiling as her uncle and the colonel walked by the fire to take two chairs, their instant camaraderie evident to all. She scanned the room and stopped when she realized Mr Darcy was watching her. She felt her cheeks grow pink and was grateful for her aunt's insistence they all sit to await the others.

Mr Darcy chose a seat near the ladies and they talked of trivial things until Miss Darcy came into the room. He stood to greet her and was just about to sit again when the Earl and Countess Danver were announced, completing the guest list for the evening.

Introductions were made and the group could instantly feel the change in the atmosphere when the new arrivals joined their small gathering. The tension continued to rise until dinner was finally announced. The gentlemen took their positions beside the ladies. Fitz offered his arm to Mary, the earl took Georgiana's arm, and Mr Gardiner had the privilege of escorting his wife, leaving the countess and Elizabeth to their host, Mr Darcy.

Darcy followed behind the ladies, noting the reactions of his aunt as Elizabeth walked through the hall. Elizabeth could not help but notice again the painting that caught her eye when they first arrived.

Seeing where the eye of the young lady was drawn, the countess asked, "Do you like it?"

"Yes, it is breathtaking."

"That is *Pemberley*," she replied, "my nephew's estate in Derbyshire."

Darcy listened to them, curious about what Miss Bennet would say when she found out just *how* wealthy he was, especially after their conversation on the steps of her uncle's home the previous week.

"Is it not the most marvelous house you have ever seen? So grand and exceptional in its stature; it truly is a beauty to behold both inside and out." The countess added with obvious jealousy in her voice, "The works of art in the gallery and the sculptures around the grounds can be equaled only by a handful of estates in all of England."

"Oh my, yes, it is gorgeous, but the house is not what drew my eye immediately. The land surrounding it is well maintained and the gardens are lovely, but to see such a place where nature seems to be brightened by its presence, and yet it is not overwhelming to the beauty of the wood and hills all around. Why, even the sheep grazing off in the distant field do not seem out of place. *That* is what is so breathtaking."

Darcy felt the corners of his lips raise a little with her description. He stepped up to the two ladies, looking at the picture with them. "I feel the same way, Miss Bennet, though few are drawn to what I love most about Pemberley. They usually see only the grandeur of the estate and gardens, not the surrounding countryside and hills, the wood and rivers."

"Oh, but they miss so much, sir. The land itself seems to direct your eye to the manor as if born from the nature surrounding it, giving it a picturesque quality," she replied quietly.

The countess saw her nephew's small smile and knew this could not be good. She cleared her throat. "Well, as the others have already left the hall, we must hasten to join them."

Darcy put his arm out to Elizabeth and she accepted it without hesitation. As if it was a second thought, he extended his other arm to his aunt, escorting them to the dining room where everyone was waiting.

When they were all seated, Darcy noticed a distressed look on Mary's face. Looking to her sister seated across from her, he watched Miss Bennet move her lips without making a sound. Mary closed her eyes for a second and took a deep breath, her features showing a much calmer demeanor when she opened them again. He was intrigued at this exchange and looked to his own sister, noticing her haughty demeanor mirroring that of his aunt and uncle. He sighed silently, wondering if he too carried that same look at times. He would have to ask Fitz later.

As the meal progressed, Darcy noticed his sister's countenance growing more jaded and he wondered at his acquiescence to her plea to offer her apologies to Miss Bennet when the ladies separated after the meal. *Maybe everything will be well,* he told himself, though he could not shake the uneasy feeling of something going terribly wrong this evening.

When the time came, Lady Danver rose and the ladies departed the dining room, leaving the gentlemen to their brandy and cigars. Edward pulled a package from his jacket pocket, holding it out to his host, "I thought we might enjoy these this evening."

Darcy unwrapped the brown paper, impressed with the cigars encased within. He lifted one to his nose to better investigate. "That is an interesting and pleasant combination of spices, Mr Gardiner. I thank you for the offer and would be pleased to smoke these this evening." He held out the offering to his guests and all three took a cigar and followed Darcy to the library. The men were soon ensconced in the comfortable chairs, each with a glass of brandy and a lit cigar, puffs of the sweet smelling smoke rising into the air.

"Hmmm, I would have to say these are among the best cigars I have ever had the privilege of smoking, Mr Gardiner," Fitz replied.

"Thank you, colonel. They were wrapped especially for this evening," Gardiner said with a smile.

"From your own stock I presume?" the earl asked.

He turned to the older gentleman, "Yes, my lord. I have several businesses, but one of my newest ventures is a cigar shop. This particular blend of spices was suggested to me by my business partner, Mr Stone, who recently returned from India with some new spices and recipes."

The earl nodded, complimenting the blend again as he puffed on the cigar. If my nephew must invite people from trade into his home, he thought, at least it is someone with connections to a good cigar. I wonder if he can acquire French brandy. The earl's thoughts were interrupted by the laughter of the other gentlemen. Obviously he had missed something, so he shifted in his chair, took another puff of the sweet cigar, and began to listen to the younger gentlemen as they talked of London's current events.

When a half hour had passed, they returned to the drawing room where the ladies awaited them. All were dismayed at the spectacle before them as they entered. The countess and Miss Darcy were standing toe to toe against Miss Bennet and Mrs Gardiner, with Miss Mary cowering behind her two defensive relations.

"Explain this," Darcy demanded.

The countess turned to her nephew, vehemently crying out, "I cannot think you knew of this... this... *falsehood* which has been perpetrated upon your household this evening. These people have brought a person who belongs in *an asylum* into your home, and I have found out my niece was also exposed to her presence while in Ramsgate!"

"What? Whatever do you mean?" the earl asked his wife as he stepped to her side.

She pointed her finger angrily at Mary, "She belongs in an asylum I tell you!"

"*THAT IS ENOUGH!*" Darcy's voice was heard over the cries of his aunt. He walked to Mary, slowly and quietly asking her, "Are you well Miss Mary?" She nodded her head and looked down at the floor as Darcy turned back to his guests. "Where she belongs is in the bosom of a loving family, not an asylum, and as far as I have been able to see in every interaction I have had with the Gardiners and the Misses Bennet, that is exactly where she is."

"I will not have my niece exposed to such people," the countess angrily replied.

The earl saw the look in Darcy's eye and wisely urged his wife, "Perhaps it is time we leave."

"Yes, perhaps it is," Darcy bowed shortly, trying to keep his rising temper in check.

"Come by Berkeley Square on the morrow, Darcy," the earl said, receiving a curt nod from his nephew before he pushed past his son in the doorway, refusing to even look at him, and escorted his wife from the house.

As soon as the front door closed Darcy turned to his sister, firmly stating, "It is time you retire." He watched her walk up the stairs with her head down before turning to his guests, "Mrs Gardiner, I do humbly apologize for whatever my relations have said this evening against your niece." He turned to look at the other guests as well, "I sincerely wish to further our acquaintance, whether my family chooses to accept my decision or not."

"Sir," Gardiner replied, "perhaps it would be best if you have some time to think about the implications of such actions."

"No, I know my own heart in this matter," he said fervently. "I am my own man and not bound to the strictures they wish to place on me."

"Are you certain?"

"Yes sir, I am. I wish to continue our acquaintance and hope to have you and your family here again soon." He turned back to Mrs Gardiner and Miss Bennet, "Would you please tell me what led to the display we walked in on this evening?"

Elizabeth took a breath and squared her shoulders, "Miss Darcy felt it necessary to inform your aunt of my sister's apparent madness, saying she once saw Mary waving her arms around in a wild fashion with a crazed look in her eye, and that she feared for her life when around my sister."

"I take it what she truly saw was Miss Mary using her hands to speak with you?"

"Yes, my sister rarely signs in front of others, but in Ramsgate she did so a few times in front of Miss Darcy," Elizabeth explained.

Fitz stepped into the conversation, "I think it is time we have a serious talk with our charge. Thank you Miss Bennet." He then looked at Mary, walking over to garner her attention. When she finally looked at him, he said, "I am sorry my cousin was so mean spirited towards you this evening. Please know she does not speak for everyone in our family. My father and mother do not have as much control as they wish over our family. I apologize on their behalf, even if they would refuse to do so themselves."

Mary gave a nod, a small smile at the corners of her lips until she once again looked to the ground.

"I think it is time we take our leave as well, Mr Darcy," Gardiner replied. "Come girls," he held out his arm to Mary and his wife, Elizabeth following after them to the hall.

Darcy placed the cape around Miss Bennet's shoulders and watched as she followed her family out the door, happy to see her turn back to look at him when her uncle helped her into the carriage. He stepped back inside and closed the door, his mind racing with all that had happened this evening.

"I think I will retire," Fitz said. "We both need to speak with Georgiana tomorrow morning, and if tonight is any indication of what my father will have to say tomorrow, you will need your rest as well."

"Thank you Fitz. You are the closest thing I have to a brother, and I am grateful to have your support in this matter."

"Well, you *were* always nicer to me than Milton ever was," he joked, then nodded and went up the stairs to the room he had called his own ever since he came to live with his aunt and uncle at only thirteen years of age.

Darcy stood in the hall staring at the painting of Pemberley, his mind remembering the words Miss Bennet said about the picturesque qualities of the landscape. A smile tugged at his lip as he thought of all she said.

Sarah Johnson

Chapter 5

arcy walked into the dining room, the dark circles under his eyes telling of his lack of sleep. He nodded a greeting to his cousin, retrieved a cup of tea and a plate from the sideboard, then sat down in his usual seat, dismissing the servants from the room before he asked, "What are we to do with her?"

Fitz sighed, "I do not know, Darcy. I was up half the night myself trying to find a solution. Her attitude is being perpetuated by my parents, so I think she must be separated from them. Beyond that, I really do not know."

"First, she will apologize to Miss Mary and the rest of her family, for her behavior last evening," Darcy replied. "Only this time I will be in the room for the entirety of it."

"I may go with you just to help keep an eye on her," he offered.

"Your presence would be greatly appreciated."

"When do you want to leave?"

"If you are free this morning, I think it would be best to go as soon as an appropriate hour arrives."

Fitz stood up from the table, "I happen to be free until later, so I will go immediately and make sure Georgiana is dressed in time." He looked at his watch and snickered, "I think three hours should give her plenty of time to dress for the occasion, do not you?"

"You know she is not an early riser," he chuckled.

"Yes, well, as my new soldiers learn very quickly, I can be quite the motivator to get them out of bed." He smiled, "Who knows, this may be just what she needs to see how wrong she has been lately."

"Well," Darcy said as he stood, "it cannot hurt to try."

Elizabeth and Mary had just returned from their walk in the park, Mary going upstairs to lie down for a few minutes to hopefully rid herself of a sudden headache, when the three visitors were announced to the two remaining ladies in the sitting room. Mrs Gardiner greeted their guests affably, "Mr Darcy, Miss Darcy, Colonel Fitzwilliam, it is good of you to call today. Unfortunately, my husband is not home at this time."

"We do not wish to disturb your household madam, but I brought my sister to speak with Miss Mary."

Elizabeth spoke up, "She is resting right now. Can I be of service instead, sir?

"Oh," the colonel said, "is she not feeling well?"

"It is only a slight headache."

"I am glad to hear it."

"I would like to speak with Miss Darcy, if that is acceptable you?" Elizabeth said, looking pointedly at Mr Darcy.

"Yes, of course."

Georgiana looked up at Darcy, hoping he would not force her, but his firmly set jaw told her he would not change his mind. She slowly followed Miss Bennet outside into the garden to a bench amongst the flowers.

"Please have a seat, Miss Darcy," Elizabeth said as she, too, sat. "I do not know what happened to the sweet girl my sister and I met when we first arrived in Ramsgate, but your recent actions have made me think you were not forthcoming with your true opinions in the beginning of our friendship."

"If anyone has not been forthcoming, it has been you, Miss Bennet," she said with disgust clear in her quiet voice.

"Why do you say that? When have I ever been dishonest with you?"

"You never told me you are from trade," she looked icily at Elizabeth.

"You are correct; I did not, because my sister and I are gently born. My uncle however is a very astute and fortunate man of business, but I do not see how that would be of any importance to us meeting daily to collect seashells."

Georgiana looked affronted by Elizabeth's answer, but did not say anything in response.

"Everything you did in Ramsgate aside, what you said of my sister last evening was wrong. It is incomprehensible to me why you would say such things, but if it is from lack of information I will assure you of the facts today. My sister Mary was a normal child, born without any impairment in speech or hearing. However, when she was eight years old, we were skating and a thin part of the ice gave way. My older sister ran for help while my friend and I pulled Mary from the freezing water. She lost her hearing completely because of the fever that resulted from the accident. When you saw her moving her hands around in Ramsgate she was not mad and her mind was not addled, she was signing. It is her way of communicating."

"Oh," Georgiana said quietly, looking down at her hands. "So she cannot speak?"

"She can speak, but what comes out is oft times not very clear because she cannot hear her own voice, so she prefers to use signs when talking to others, especially those outside of our family," Elizabeth explained.

"I am sorry—I truly thought she was mad," Georgiana said flatly.

Something about the girl's demeanor made Elizabeth believe she was just acting concerned for the sake of her audience. "Miss Darcy, if you believed so, I wonder why you waited this long in our acquaintance to voice your concerns."

Georgiana glared at the lady seated beside her. "I am only here because my brother insisted I apologize."

"Well it will not be possible today as my sister is above stairs resting. I will let her know you came." Elizabeth stood, watching the girl as she walked back inside, her head bowed in what appeared to be a humbled posture, but Elizabeth was not fooled. She was about to follow when Mr Darcy stepped outside to talk with her.

"Thank you for speaking with my sister, Miss Bennet. She seems a little more repentant than before," he replied, looking back through the open door at Georgiana as she stood beside Fitz.

Elizabeth sighed, "Unfortunately, I do not think so, Mr Darcy. I think she knows how to look the part very well, but I doubt her heart is touched."

Darcy looked back to her, "My cousin and I have been trying to decide what to do with her, but neither of us have the answer. We pulled her from school a few months ago, and it is obvious by her subsequent behavior that what happened in Ramsgate was a continuation of the same problems." He paused, looking at her for a minute before he tentatively asked, "What would you do, Miss Bennet?"

She chuckled, "Besides turn her over my knee? I would probably look into hiring another companion; one well investigated and older, whom Miss Darcy cannot manipulate to do her bidding."

"Yes, that may be our only option. Thank you; I will speak with my cousin about your suggestion."

"My uncle may be able to help you find someone," she offered.

"I will speak with him as well then." He bowed, thanking her once again and saying he would have his sister draft a letter of apology to Miss Mary so as not to upset her any further, then the visitors took their leave.

Elizabeth sat outside in the garden thinking of how she could help the situation, but until Miss Darcy was ready to change, there was really nothing more she could do other than protect Mary from the girl's vitriol.

Saturday, May 4, 1811

Fitz looked across at Darcy, "Your turn."

He took a shot and missed, the cue ball bouncing in a random pattern across the table.

"Thanks for the set—up." Fitz lined up his shot and ended the game. "What has you distracted?"

"Nothing... I am not distracted."

"Oh, right! This is the first time in five years I have won a game of billiards against you when you broke, and you say you are not distracted? I do not believe you." Fitz went to the sideboard and poured them drinks, handing one to his cousin as they both sat down beside the fire. "Come on, you know you will end up telling me anyway."

Darcy stared into the small flames, his glass untouched on the table as he twisted his ring back and forth. "Do you think I am haughty like your parents and my sister?"

"No," Fitz said quickly.

"I just wonder... if Georgiana had not run away and if Miss Bennet and Miss Mary had not helped us find her, would I have invited the Gardiner's to dine at my house?"

"Well of course not–you would not have met them," he joked.

"You know what I mean Fitz."

He chuckled, "Just teasing Darce. In my *honest* opinion, yes you would. After all, your friend Bingley's money comes from trade, and that has never stopped you from inviting him to dinner or being seen with him around Town."

Darcy sat thinking silently for a few minutes before he finally asked, "Would my father?"

"No, I do not think he would. Uncle George was, in many ways, just like my father. They were raised with the beliefs the generation before them thought were most important–that of perpetuating the culture of our great England

and keeping the classes divided," Fitz said. "Our parents' generation does not see the changes on the horizon. New manufacturing methods and smarter inventions are ushering in a new time, and it is people like you who will change the future. You have enough stature and wealth to not be held back, and I know you support these new ideals." He looked intently at his cousin for a minute before he continued. "One day you will give in to Aunt Catherine and marry Anne, or perhaps you will stand up to her and marry some other lady, and then it will be up to you to teach your children what is important to our future."

Darcy's voice was barely above a whisper, "What if the wishes of your parents and Aunt Catherine are not what I desire for my life?"

Fitz drank the last of the liquid in his glass. Hoping to get his usually quiet cousin to open up a little more, he asked, "What *do* you want?"

Darcy sat thinking for a minute before he replied, "I want a companion who will challenge me to be a better person. Someone who sees me for me, not for Pemberley or whatever amount of money the gossips think I possess this year. I want to enjoy the things in life that money cannot buy, and a person by my side that will enjoy those things with me. I want affection to be my guide, not the strictures of our society." Even as close as the two cousins were, having nearly grown up as brothers, Darcy had never voiced these desires to Fitz in the past. He finally picked up his drink and took a sip, "So what is it you want?"

"What do I want?" He snorted, "Unfortunately I do not have the same opportunity to be so choosy."

"If you did not have to think of the financial aspect, say some wealthy relation gifted you with a piece of land large enough to allow you to sell your commission and join the landed gentry, what would you want?"

He looked at Darcy, warningly voicing, "Do not even think about it, Darce. We have already discussed Rose Bluff, and my opinion has not changed. A man does not want to feel obliged to someone else for the rest of his life because of such a gift."

"Who said I was talking of me? This is a hypothetical situation."

"Well, just know I would never accept such a gift, as I have told you numerous times before."

"I will make note of that. Now, what would you want?"

"If I did not have to consider my finances... hmmmm... I have never really thought about it before. I guess I would want what you said–someone who understands me and for whom I have affection." He stretched his arms high above his head and stood, "But, it is not likely to happen, so one day I will settle down and marry someone rich enough to let me sell my commission. Until then, I will avoid any and all dalliances that could have me walking down the aisle with any lady on my arm. My mother might not like it, but I intend to hold out on marriage until I am old and grey."

Darcy stood too. "I think I may be ready to find a wife."

The two started walking slowly up the stairs to their chambers. "And do you have any ideas on who it should be?"

"No, but I know who it should not be; Aunt Catherine will not like my decision."

"Well, well, well, Darce, it seems you are growing up on me. Here you are putting your foot down to Georgiana, willing to stand up to Aunt Catherine, and wishing you would find love all in just a few weeks' time." He jokingly puffed out his chest, "I am so proud."

"Perhaps if I settle down it will cause you to want to settle down as well."

"Oh no, I told you, not until I am old and grey, and I hear blonde hair does not turn too early. You, on the other hand, had better find your lady love soon, or this on the side near your ear might start to detract from your charmingly dark looks," Fitz joked.

"Whether I have grey hair or not, I am determined to find a lady who will appreciate every single one of them, no matter their color."

Fitz laughed, "Good night, Darcy. I will see you in the morning for our interviews. What time did you say they will begin?"

"Nine o'clock," he replied. "I hope we are able to find the right person for the job."

"Yes, Georgiana needs a firm hand this time," Fitz agreed.

The next week

"Well, I think we have a list of potential companions," Darcy stretched his hands over his head and yawned. "Now comes your part–investigating these ladies again. Please be thorough, as we must be assured we do not have a problem like we did with Mrs Younge. I could not bear losing Georgiana because of my own oversight."

"Darcy, you must stop blaming yourself for Georgiana's mistakes."

"I am the one who failed to find Mrs Younge's prior connection to Wickham."

"You did the best you could with the short time you had, what with Georgiana being pulled from school so suddenly. No school would put up with a girl sneaking from her room, and we did not know at the time it was to meet with Wickham. That is behind us, now, as I told you yesterday, I have already investigated these applicants, and any one of them would do nicely. We will sleep on it, and tomorrow we may know which one of these three ladies stands out as the best choice."

"Hmmmm... perhaps Miss Bennet could assist in choosing?"

Fitz eyed his cousin, "Just what could she help with beyond having suggested it?"

"She is very perceptive, Fitz. I think I may see if she will meet with these ladies and give me her opinion."

He chuckled as he walked away to retire, "I had a feeling before when you invited... then you introduced their uncle at your club, but with this, now I am certain..."

"Certain about what?" Darcy looked at him inquisitively.

Fitz tilted his head, his face completely serious when he said, "Yes, I believe so. I will have to see them together, but I do believe it will be quite the match."

Darcy rushed to catch up to his cousin, "Just what are you mumbling about?"

Fitz stopped and turned to Darcy, "I would like to go with you when you speak with Miss Bennet about these ladies."

"Yes of course; we can go tomorrow." Darcy watched as Fitz once again walked away, still mumbling to himself.

Darcy retired to his chambers and readied himself for bed. As he lay unable to sleep, he thought about marriage, making a list in his mind of what qualities the next Mrs Darcy would need to possess. He would find her this Season and be married by autumn. Unfortunately, that would mean accepting invitations to events he usually tried to avoid, and it would mean dancing when he really did not enjoy being a spectacle, but he would find the lady over these next few months—*he was determined.*

Sarah Johnson

Chapter 6

Saturday, May 11, 1811

"ood afternoon, gentlemen," Edward said to the visitors as he entered the sitting room. "We did not expect to see you today. I am sorry to say, my wife and nieces are unavailable to greet you. We have been invited to a small gathering, which of course means they need new gowns. Have a seat," he indicated the chairs. "Can I offer you some refreshments?"

"Yes, thank you."

Edward nodded to the housekeeper who left to prepare the tea. "Is there something I can help you with, or is this purely a social call?"

"It is not purely a social call," Darcy replied, "but it is Miss Bennet with which I wished to speak."

Gardiner pulled out his watch, checking the time before he said, "I expect their return soon. Can I tempt either of you with a cigar while we await the ladies?"

"Now *that* is something I will never pass up," Fitz replied.

They enjoyed the friendly discourse in Mr Gardiner's study until they heard the ladies return from their excursion, then they joined them in the sitting room. Greetings were exchanged, and Darcy, eager to speak with Miss Bennet, suggested they walk out in the garden. The four younger people went out to enjoy the bright flora surrounding them. The Gardiners watched from the sitting room, both noticing that there was a great connection forming between Mr Darcy and their eldest niece.

Fitz was sitting on a bench next to Miss Mary and watching his cousin's interactions with Miss Bennet as Darcy led her slowly through the garden when he realized how rude he was being. Turning to his companion, he said slowly, "I am sorry, Miss Mary; please accept my apologies for not speaking with you."

Mary nodded, the corner of her lips rising just a little.

He looked around at the flowers. Picking one from the garden beside him, he ran his finger over the soft petals, "I have always heard tell that when one sense is lost the others are heightened to help compensate. Is that true Miss Mary?"

She nodded, watching his lips carefully as he continued.

"You know, I have met many a soldier who has been injured in battle, some who have even lost their hearing from being too close to a blast from a cannon as it was fired. Until now I never thought of the difficulties they must face in adjusting to life after coming home." He looked at her for a moment before he quietly said, "Meeting you is starting to change the way I see everything around me." He held the flower out to her, "And I must thank you."

Mary reached for the vibrant petals, their fragrant smell filling her nose as she lifted it and took a deep breath. Looking back to the colonel, she nodded her head in thanks, smiling fully when her eyes met his again. She then pulled a notebook out of her pocket and began to write, handing it to her companion when she was through.

Fitz read the note aloud, "*Do you know what these flowers around us mean?*" Then he looked up to answer her. "No, I cannot say flowers have ever been of much interest to me. Will you enlighten me?"

She again wrote her answer, watching his reaction as he read aloud, "The Royal Oak tree, whose leaves we sit beneath, stands for '*bravery*'. The flowers we sit amongst have various meanings, but my favorite is the Chinese Chrysanthemum. It will not bloom until the leaves begin to fall from the trees, but its meaning is *'cheerfulness under adversity'*. Also the Spruce Pine over there means *'hope in adversity'*. It is the adversity in life that has taught me to appreciate the small things that bring me cheer."

Fitz saw in her answer the strength of character which carried her through the darkest times in her life. "You planted it here for this reason?" At her nod he looked around them, "Did you plant all of these?"

She once again took the pencil in her left hand and wrote her answer, then gave it back for him to read. "My aunt and sister helped with the planting, but I am the one who chose these particular plants surrounding this bench. It was my favorite place to sit when we first moved here, so my aunt suggested I have the choice of which blooms would surround it. My sister chooses for color and visual appeal while I choose purely for meanings—just as my Mama did her garden."

Fitz looked up once again after he read her explanation. "You fascinate me, Miss Mary. I would not have guessed such things meant so much to you. So what other hidden accomplishments do you possess, madam? Do you play the pianoforte?"

She shook her head no and chuckled at such a question.

"Embroider?"

She wrinkled up her nose and shrugged her shoulders.

He chuckled, "Not very well, I take it. What about painting?"

She shook her head no again, and wrote, "I draw; but mostly just flowers and other simple objects, but I am working on doing people. My mother was an accomplished artist, but she never got to teach me."

When he saw the words written with a shaky hand, he felt compassion for her. To lose one parent when one was so young—and then to lose the other just a few years later. It was a great deal to bear. "I shall have to talk you into showing me your drawings sometime. With your love of flora, you will adore Pemberley." He immediately realized what he said and stammered as he looked down, "That is, if you ever have the chance to visit my cousin's estate." Mary's hand touched his arm and he looked up at her face, "I am sorry; I forgot I must look at you, otherwise you cannot tell what I am saying. I do apologize."

She nodded, and wrote in her notebook, handing it back to him. "It is clear to some of us just what the future holds for my sister and your cousin. I am happy for her–she deserves to marry the best of men."

"I happen to agree with you. So what of you, Miss Mary? What is it you are looking for in a marriage partner?"

"Me?" she wrote. "I will never marry."

"Why not?"

"Who would want me, sir?" she wrote, turning her head away when he verbalized what she wrote.

Mary felt his finger on her chin as the gentle pressure tried to turn her back to face him. She turned, closing her eyes and swallowing hard. When she opened them again and met his eyes she felt her pulse start to race at his words.

"Do not discount your own charms." Fitz reached over and plucked one of the blooms at his feet, handing it to her.

Mary took it in her fingers and tried not to laugh, but it was too much to not at least smile with mirth. She wrote, "Do you know what this one means?"

"No, I cannot say I do."

"This is one my sister insisted on having here beside my bench. It is a Ranuculus, or a Persian Turban, and it means *'You are radiant with charms',*" she wrote.

Fitz could not help but smile, "Well then, it seems I have chosen the perfect bloom for this moment." He could not bring himself to admit, whether aloud or even to himself, that he was indeed dazzled by her radiant charms.

They continued to talk of the other flowers surrounding them until it was time to leave. He determined to search through his cousin's library to see if it contained a book with the meanings of foliage, as he found it now fascinated him.

In the carriage as they rode back to Darcy House Fitz began to think of what he had told his cousin just a few days before. Yes, he did wish for affection, especially after meeting Miss Mary, but without his parents' support, he did not

58

see how they could ever marry. For the first time in his life Fitz was fearful of what he was starting to feel for this young lady. Not wanting his cousin to see the battle warring within him, he began to tease Darcy about his attention to Miss Bennet.

When Darcy retired that evening he thought about his conversation with Fitz and what he wanted in a wife. *Could Miss Bennet be the one?* He already knew she possessed so many attributes which were important to him, and he could honestly say she was very handsome. *Maybe it is time to invite them back over for dinner, or better yet, on an outing*, he thought, *only this time without the rest of my family around. The Gardens—we should go to the Pleasure Gardens! Hmmmm, maybe Bingley will be available to join our party? I wonder if Aunt Edith has arrived in Town yet.*

Edward walked out into the hall from his office, a headache starting to pound right behind his ears. Almost as if she knew she was needed, Maddie exited the sitting room at that same moment.

"Oh, Edward, you must rest, my dear. This much work is not good for your health," she admonished him.

"I know I have been quite busy these last few weeks, but I believe we have finally completed the majority of the paperwork." He closed his eyes and ran his hand wearily over them. "We have a lot of procedures to go over before Mr Stone returns to India. You would not think the acquisition of one business could cause so much trouble for my books."

"I am just grateful for Mr Stone's acquiescence in going by himself as I am quite reliant on your being here in England with me," she said as she lovingly wound her arm through his and walked beside him up the stairs.

They were nearly ready for bed when Maddie remembered the missive that was delivered earlier. Pulling it from her pocket, she handed it to her husband. "I received this note today. It is an invitation to join Mr Darcy's party at Vauxhall Gardens."

"I cannot say I am surprised. Mr Darcy does seem to be taken with Elizabeth."

"Yes, that is clear for anyone to see, though I doubt either of them realize it themselves yet."

"This is for Friday," he said as he laid it down on the table.

"Yes it is."

Edward looked at his wife, "No, I will not give up the tickets I purchased months ago for your birthday just so Elizabeth can visit the Pleasure Gardens. A man must have some time with his wife," he lifted her hand to his lips.

"I knew you would say that, so I answered Mr Darcy immediately, declining the invitation and explaining the situation. He wrote back with this," she said as she pulled out another note from her pocket and opened it to read aloud to her husband.

"Mrs Gardiner,

I thank you for your quick response, and as fate would have it, my aunt, Mrs Edith Darcy, was visiting when your note was delivered. She wishes to meet your family as well, and when I told her of your previous plans she offered to act as a chaperone for your two nieces. I know you do not know her, but I would trust her even with my own sister. She is nothing like my other relations and will not judge you as harshly as they have.

If you do not feel comfortable with such an arrangement, perhaps we can make the trip next week instead?

Thank you,

Fitzwilliam Darcy"

Edward pulled his wife closer as he took the note from her hands. "If Mr Darcy trusts this aunt, and she has offered to chaperone so we can still go to the theater, then who am I to intrude upon such plans?"

Maddie smiled, "I will write to him first thing tomorrow. Do you want to tell the girls, or should I?"

Edward stood, drawing her closer, "I will leave that to you. For now, I just wish to go to bed."

Maddie kissed his cheek, "Thank you Edward; I could not ask for a more loving husband."

The next morning Maddie was sitting at the table with her nieces and children. "Elizabeth, I received an invitation yesterday that may interest you."

"Yes Aunt? What is it?"

"You and Mary," she added as she signed to her, "have been invited to join a party that will visit Vauxhall's Pleasure Gardens this Friday. Your uncle and I cannot go of course, as we have other plans, but we feel confident in the chaperone that will be provided."

"Vauxhall? Oh my! Who has sent the invitation?"

"Mr Darcy," she answered, smiling when she saw Elizabeth's cheeks become pink. "Mrs Darcy, his aunt, will be joining him, as well as a few friends, and he has assured us of his regard for their discretion." Maddie looked over to Mary who was helping Henry cut up a roll. She reached over and gently placed her hand on Mary's arm, drawing her attention. "Mary, he has assured us they are nothing like his other relations. I wish you to go as I know you will enjoy the flowers."

Elizabeth looked at Mary pleadingly. She had always wanted to go to Vauxhall Gardens, but before now the opportunity never presented itself.

Mary looked between her aunt and her sister a few times before she finally gave a small smile and asked, "What time are we to leave?"

"Mr Darcy says he will send a carriage to pick you up at ten."

"Does Mr Darcy indicate how large this party is to be?" Elizabeth asked.

"He says it will be only a few close friends, seven total, with you two included. His other guests will include Mr Charles Bingley and his sister, Miss Caroline Bingley, and possibly another couple, Mr and Mrs Gilbert Hurst, along with his aunt, Mrs Darcy."

Maddie took Mary's hand in hers, "You will be well, my dear. It is time you get out more. Who knows, maybe you will meet some new friends among Mr Darcy's group. Have faith Mary–Mr Darcy knows of your difficulties, and he would not set out to humiliate you."

Mary signed, "Yes, he has been solicitous of my needs."

Elizabeth excitedly grabbed her sister's hand. "We will have such fun."

"I know you have wanted to go for ages," Mary said to Elizabeth. "Is Mr Darcy's cousin to be there as well?"

"The note did not say anything of the colonel or Miss Darcy joining the group."

"Everything will be well, I know it will," Elizabeth encouraged.

They will have fireworks once the sun has set, and I know you would enjoy the display."

Mary nodded, "Yes, I have always wanted to see them."

The two sisters soon left on their usual morning walk in the park, Elizabeth's excitement over the invitation evident in her constant chattering to Mary. *Maybe it will be as fun a day as Aunt Maddie says,* Mary thought as she sat on the bench beside the pond. *Fireworks—! Oh I cannot wait!*

Chapter 7

Friday arrived and the sisters were excited to join their host and his friends as they explored the many walks and exhibits.

Elizabeth looked over at Mary as they stopped to take in the exhibition in front of them. Catching Mary's eye, Elizabeth gave a hand gesture asking if she was feeling well. The small nod she received was enough to calm her fears and she turned back to the others.

Mrs Darcy was an amiable lady, though her eyes were always carefully watching everything that took place. She did not have the disapproving glares of the Danvers, and for that Elizabeth was grateful. Mary seemed much more at ease in her presence. Mrs Darcy did not fawn over Mary either, which was another good mark of her character.

Mr Charles Bingley was a good-natured gentleman with a ready smile for everyone, so very different than their host, Mr Fitzwilliam Darcy. *Fitzwilliam... hmmmm*, Elizabeth thought, *that name seems to fit him*. Her cheeks became a bright pink with embarrassment as the thought crossed her mind, especially when Mr Darcy chose that moment to turn and ask her a question. She stumbled with what must have been a decent enough answer, though she could not remember, even seconds afterward, what was said by either of them.

Her attention turned to the other three in their group–Mr Bingley's two sisters and his brother—in—law. Mr and Mrs Hurst were a quiet couple, hardly saying ten words the whole of the day to anyone except Miss Bingley. Now *there* was an interesting lady indeed. Caroline Bingley was the younger of the two sisters, though she was older than their brother, by several years Elizabeth would guess. Miss Bingley latched onto Mr Darcy's arm as often as she could, even pretending to sprain her ankle once just to have a reason to grasp his arm. Her brother quickly stepped up, offering to escort her back home, but she decided it was not necessary and a short walk with his escort seemed to work out the slight bit of pain she felt.

"Are you ready Miss Bennet?"

Elizabeth was torn from her reverie with the melodic sounds of Mr Darcy's voice. She looked over and saw his hand held out to help her up a step. She reached out, stepped up, and then looked where he was leading her. Her heart stopped nearly as fast as her feet.

"Is something wrong, Miss Bennet?"

"Oh... no... I am sorry Mr Darcy... but I cannot... that it..."

He stepped into her line of sight, breaking her view of the large balloon behind him. "Are you well?"

Her voice was barely above a whisper, "I cannot..."

His answer in return was nearly as quiet as her own, with such tenderness that Elizabeth had to look into his eyes when he said, "Please have no fear; I will be right beside you." The look in his dark gaze seemed to say to her, *please trust me*.

She closed her eyes and took a deep breath before she answered with a nod, "You promise?"

The corner of his mouth rose just slightly, barely perceptible to anyone, even her, as he replied, "Yes, I give you my word."

With a slight squeeze to her hand, he led her over to the basket where the others in their party awaited them. Mr Darcy placed Elizabeth's hand on his arm and stepped just a bit closer to her side as the guide lines were unlatched and the basket lurched up, causing her stomach to object. She closed her eyes to keep from becoming sick.

It was Mr Darcy's voice that drew her back to the moment when he said,

"Open your eyes and see the world around you, Miss Bennet."

She did as he suggested and was surprised at the beauty that lay in front of them. She started to look down until he said, "No, just look out, not down. Focus on something far in the distance." She followed his long, slender finger as he pointed out to the miles that stretched in front of them, "Do you see the ships near the bridge? That one with the big white sail is just coming into port while the others are preparing to unload their cargo." He turned her gaze to the left, "Over there we can see the church spires as they raise high above the townhouses. If you look this direction," he leaned down to her level and pointed way off into the distance, "that tiny dot there is the square where you live."

Elizabeth slowly felt the wild palpitations of her heart calm as London unfolded around them. She was not yet brave enough to move, but she needed to check on her sister. Closing her eyes once more, she quietly said, "Mr Darcy, I fear my turning around would cause an unpleasant experience for both of us. Would you please tell me how my sister is doing?"

Darcy turned and reported, "My aunt and Mr Bingley are standing beside her and she has a smile on her face as she gazes out over the landscape below." He turned back to her, "I take it Miss Mary does not fear heights as you do?"

"No, she is much braver than I when it comes to activities such as this."

"Did you never jump from the loft in the barn or climb trees when you were younger? I have to say, Miss Bennet, you struck me as someone who loved to live life on the edge of danger, especially after hearing of your heroic efforts to stop a particular carriage."

"That was a very different situation," she looked up into his eyes, a small smile just touching the corner of his mouth. "As for your other assumptions, a tree is much lower to the ground than this balloon, sir, and my mother would have been scandalized forever, even in her grave, if she found we were jumping from the hay loft," she said with an arch of her brow and a lilt to her voice.

Caroline stood behind the couple and could not believe it when she heard Mr Darcy give out a low chuckle at the hoyden standing next to him. What did *she* do to garner such attention from the solemn bachelor? Caroline knew something must be done to separate Mr Darcy from this woman. Her eyes focused on the backs of the two as her mind began to form a plan. *Surely*

65

his family would not approve of such attention being fostered upon someone whose closest relations are in trade? I must find a way to speak with Lady Danver soon and apprise her of this unfortunate situation. The couple continued to talk as if they had not a care in the world.

"In truth, Mr Darcy, I have always been a bit of a cautious individual and that has saved me from many a broken bone or scraped knee. My sister Mary on the other hand was always found in trees before her accident. It made her change her ways, but she still retains her love for adventure."

The basket jolted a bit and Elizabeth clutched his arm a little tighter. It was all Darcy could do not to wrap his arms around her shoulders to help ease her fears. "I believe you are braver than you think, Miss Bennet," he said quietly in admiration.

Mary stood with her face in the wind, her neck extended up and her chin stuck out as the balloon floated through the air. She could not believe the sights below and would turn this way and that looking at everything. A few times Mr Bingley pointed to something in particular and she would turn to see what he said. With a small nod of acknowledgement she would turn back to the breathtaking views all around. At one point she must have frightened him as she looked down at the ground directly below them, because he grabbed her arm to steady her. She thanked him with a nod, then slowly leaned over again, enjoying the rush through her body as the wind whipped around the ribbons of her bonnet. Their balloon ride ended all too soon for Mary, but her spirits soared the rest of the day with the memories and feelings she would never forget.

Darcy wearily sat in front of the fire; his head leaned back against the wings of his favorite chair, a book opened on his lap, and his nightly cup of tea cooling on the table beside him. He looked up when he heard the door open. "I did not expect to see you this evening," he said as his cousin entered the library and sat in the chair opposite his.

"I did not expect to be here either, but I found myself in need of quiet and my parents were not as indulgent to my needs as I knew you would be."

Noticing the strain in his features, Darcy asked, "Is there something troubling you?"

Fitz sighed, "Nothing you can help with, Darce."

"You know you are like a brother to me. I would do just about anything for you."

"I know you would, but it is not your place." He stood to pour himself a drink before heavily sitting back down again. "No, what is troubling me is not in your control."

Darcy asked barely above a whisper, "Are you being sent to the continent again?"

"No, not yet, but papers did come across my desk which would indicate my regiment is likely to go early next year."

Darcy stiffened as he sat up. Putting the book on the table, he picked up his tea and stirred the tepid drink, his face contorting when the liquid touched his tongue.

Fitz chuckled, "If you hate the taste so much, why do you drink that horrid mixture every night?"

"Mrs Reynolds insists upon its health benefits."

"I think I will stick to my scotch," he held up his glass in salute before he drank the burning liquid down in one gulp. "So tell me about your day–how was your Vauxhall Gardens excursion?"

A smile crept over Darcy's face as he set down his tea again and stared into the fire, telling Fitz about how Miss Bennet reacted to everything they saw. At Fitz's prodding he also told about the others in the group, though Darcy did notice a certain interest when he mentioned Miss Mary. Soon, the highlights of the day's events having been told, the cousins sat in silence, both taking comfort in the pleasant stillness surrounding them.

After several minutes, Darcy's voice cut into the stillness, "Fitz, I know you have refused in the past, but I would like to give you..."

"No, as I have said every time you bring this up, I will not accept your charity, Darcy."

"It is not charity! You are as close to a brother as I have ever had, and I only wish to give you what would rightly go to a brother if my parents had been so blessed. Rose Bluff is a nice piece of property and would provide you the means to leave the military."

"I do not mind my service to the Crown. It is what is expected of an earl's second son and what I have been raised all my life to do."

"What of marriage though? Are you forever resigned to stay a bachelor because of the expectations placed on your shoulders?"

"You know nothing of expectations," Fitz replied forcefully.

It took everything in him to not explode at such a statement, "*I* know nothing of expectations? Who do you think you are talking to here? I am not your brother *Milton*."

Fitz sat forward, "I am sorry Darce; I should never have said such to you." Standing, he began to pace. "If anyone understands expectations, it would be you. The idea of marrying a lady only for her wealth is distasteful to me and would most likely lead to an unhappy union, so what is the rush? I will earn my keep in the King's Army until I am too old to do so."

"I wish to help you Fitz. Not because I do not think you can handle the military life, but because I wish to see you happily married one day, with little ones running around here along with my own children."

Fitz reached for the door handle, "Sorry Darcy. I know you mean well, but I cannot accept such a gift from you. Please do not bring it up again." With that he retired for the night, hoping his cousin would respect his wishes. Until now he had resisted with much more ease. Since meeting Miss Mary Bennet he found he secretly longed for the life Darcy described tonight, but he knew it was not for him. He was raised to be in the military and would need to prepare himself mentally for the battlefield he was soon to face once again. Daydreaming of a life he could not have would not help.

With his resolve set, Fitz gladly accompanied his cousin to the Gardiner residence the following morning. Not long after their arrival he found himself walking through the nearby park with Miss Mary on his arm, Darcy and Miss Bennet having walked a little faster, separating themselves from the group. Turning to face Miss Mary, he asked, "Did you have a pleasant trip to the Gardens yesterday?"

Mary nodded.

Fitz looked around and saw his cousin circling the duck pond. He indicated the bench where they could wait, sitting in such a way as to easily converse with Miss Mary. "So tell me, was my cousin as exclusionary yesterday as he is today?"

Mary looked at the couple walking slowly around the water and a small smile played on her lips. When she looked back to Fitz she noticed he was watching her mouth intently. With a blush she looked down at her lap. His movement brought her eyes back up to his lips as he continued to talk.

"What was your favorite part of the Gardens, Miss Mary?"

She immediately withdrew a map from the previous day out of her reticule, and with a big smile she pointed to the brightly colored balloon display.

"Ahhh, a woman of great brevity, indeed. I would have thought the flowers would be your favorite part. Was this your first time going up in a balloon?"

She nodded yes as she drew out her ever present notebook and a pencil from her reticule, writing down something before she handed it to him. "The view from up there was breathtaking!"

He chuckled, "I would have to agree with you there. I only wish I would have been available to escort you myself as I dearly wished to see your face as you took in the stunning sights. I hope your escort was solicitous of your needs?"

Mary blushed as she nodded. *A little too solicitous at times*, she thought to herself.

Fitz felt his stomach tighten at her reaction. *Was she affected by Bingley?* It would be rude of him to ask, but that is exactly what he wanted to know—*needed* to know. Noticing his cousin and Miss Bennet as they completed their trek around the pond, he stood and held out his arm to Miss Mary. As they silently walked back to the Gardiners' house his heart began to ache for what he knew he could never have.

The cousins stayed for tea and Fitz enjoyed talking with Mr and Mrs Gardiner while Darcy spoke exclusively with Miss Bennet, Miss Mary only making small gestures with her fingers when she was asked a direct question. Fitz was intrigued by the smooth and effortless way in which she spoke. When Mr Gardiner indicated he must return to his paperwork, Fitz asked if he could have a moment of his time. The two excused themselves and Fitz followed their host to his study at the back of the house.

"What is it you need Colonel?"

"Sir, I was just curious about your niece."

"Ahhh, you too have noticed the particular attention your cousin is paying to her lately," he sat, indicating the chair opposite for his guest.

"Well, yes sir, I have. It was not *that* niece of which I was speaking though. Actually, I wished to ask you something of Miss Mary."

"Oh? Please go on Colonel," the slightly older man tried to look intimidating, but he doubted it affected the war—hardened soldier in front of him.

"I am curious about the hand gestures she uses to speak. Is it something she was taught, or something she came up with herself?"

Edward looked at the gentleman across from him. After assessing him, he stood and took a book from his shelf, holding it out, "This is the book from which she learned her signs. Perhaps you wish to borrow it?"

Fitz stood and took it, looking down at the well—worn leather binding. "Thank you, sir. I will leave you to your business."

"Colonel, I have only one request."

He turned back, "Yes sir?"

"Do not raise her expectations."

"Sir, while I understand your caution, I know my own situation all too well. It is obvious to me where my cousin's attentions are paid, and I only wish to make Miss Mary as comfortable around my family as she is around yours."

"You believe Mr Darcy's attentions are honourable?"

Fitz squared his shoulders and looked directly into the man's eyes. "Sir, my cousin has never given his affections lightly nor bandied about Town as others of his set often do. I know him better than anyone else, and I know he is losing his heart to your niece. I doubt he is even aware of the depth of his feelings yet, but I would not be surprised if he is soon asking for an audience with you."

"Thank you Colonel. I appreciate your candor and your insight."

Fitz left the study and found his cousin in the front hall, ready to leave. The two returned to Darcy House and spent the remainder of the day wiling away the hours in companionable activities, joined by Georgiana and her new companion, Mrs Annesley, for supper and entertainments afterward in the music room. As he sat listening to his cousin play the pianoforte he thought of Mary Bennet and all the beauty she missed out on because of not being able to hear. He dearly wished he could express to her what it felt like to listen to a lark as it sat outside his window in the morning, or hear the notes of a song as they were expelled from his heart through to his fingers and out onto the ivory keys of a pianoforte. Did she remember such sounds from her childhood? A small smile graced his features as he thought of the excitement in her eyes as they spoke briefly of her balloon ride, wishing he could have experienced it with her.

When he retired late that evening he dressed for bed then sat in front of the fire with the book from Mr Gardiner in his hands, remembering the words he promised the protective guardian: *'I only wish to make Miss Mary as comfortable around my family as she is around yours'*. It was enough of a reason to not have to answer anything more to her uncle, but he knew there was more reason than that deep within him. He wanted to know her, understand her, and he could not do so if he could not even speak with her properly.

In his hands he held the key to fulfilling that desire. The leather was well—worn and smooth, showing clear signs of having been read many times. As he opened the front cover he saw a small note from Elizabeth to Mary. He could tell it was written by a child, and he smiled at the obvious affection between the sisters. He turned a few more pages and found the author's explanations of the book. Skipping a few more pages ahead he began to see drawings of hands and arms showing the different signs along with the words they meant. Along the sides he found notes and other sketches and he immediately recognized them as Miss Mary's handwriting.

He thumbed through the book and when he reached the back he found an alphabetical listing of the signs shown within. Looking through the list, he chose a word to learn and turned to the appropriate page. Resting the book on his knees, he tried to form his hands into the proper position, but it was much more difficult than he thought it would be. Sighing in frustration, he found another word and tried that one as well. By the third attempt he thought he did a passable job, so he moved on to yet another sign. By the time he retired an hour later he felt a sense of accomplishment at having successfully signed two words. Now if only he could remember them in the morning.

Determined to know something of these odd signs before he saw Miss Mary again, he spent as much time as he could spare over the next fortnight learning a new phrase every evening.

Fitz found himself with little time to visit the Gardiners again with Darcy, though he was told of the many visits by both of his cousins–Darcy with great enthusiasm, and Georgiana with a tremor of scorn in her voice. He had a feeling she was not happy with Darcy's choice.

Bingley became a regular on Darcy's trips around Town with the sisters in tow. Fitz heard of their trip to the Royal Menagerie and to the Repository of Art, their numerous trips to Hyde Park, and the many days of shopping Darcy enjoyed with Miss Bennet and Georgiana. His cousin was planning a trip to the theater soon. He was still trying to decide which play they would enjoy best, and Fitz was hoping to be free to accompany them when the date was determined. Soon it was and invitations were issued for the Gardiners and Bennets to join them. Fitz was not surprised by the enamored look on his cousin's face when the note was returned accepting the invitation to visit the theater and return to Darcy House afterward for supper.

r Darcy to see you, madam," the butler announced then retreated.

Edith Darcy hastily put her tea cup down and stood to greet her nephew. "It is good to see you Fitzwilliam. If I had known you were coming I would have had cook prepare your favorite lemon tarts."

He smiled and kissed her cheek before taking the seat beside her. "That is not necessary, Aunt Edith. I do not expect such preferential treatment."

"Well you are my *favorite* nephew," she teased.

"Aunt, I am your only nephew."

She poured him a cup of tea, "Somehow I think you would have been my favorite even if I had another. So what brings my *favorite nephew* to my house today?"

Darcy took a small sip of his tea then set it back down. "You know perfectly well why I came today."

"Yes, well, I always feel that a gentleman should be able to give voice to whatever opinion has formed his mind. It helps establish it in his heart."

Darcy felt a tug at his heart. Other than with his cousin, he had not yet verbalized his newfound and quickly growing feelings for Miss Bennet. Somehow he knew this was an important moment in his life. Finally he asked, "What did you think of her?"

"*Her?* Just which *her* are we speaking of? I counted three eligible young ladies on our trip to the Gardens, and while I have my opinions, I would not wish to be wrong," she said with a straight face, though Darcy could tell she was enjoying every moment of this conversation.

"Aunt, you know of whom I speak. Please do not tease me so."

"Fitzwilliam, dear, you really must not take everything so seriously." She took a sip of her tea then cleared her throat, "I was very impressed with *your lady*. I know she is not what your mother's relations would prefer, but I am not as choosy. Miss Bennet was perfectly amiable and I could find nothing amiss with her."

Darcy could not help the smile that creased the corners of his lips when his aunt referred to Miss Bennet as *'his lady'*. "I knew you would tell me the truth. Thank you, Aunt Edith."

"Your father always spoke more harshly of my husband than I felt was necessary, and I know George would have been against your Miss Bennet, if for no other reason than she is your match in every way. He never did understand the dealings of the heart, even when it came to his little brother. Your father was a good gentleman, please do not think I wish to disparage his memory, but there is a reason my heart was drawn to my dear Edwin instead. The two could not have been more different, and perhaps it was because of how they were raised, but George always saw Edwin's place in the family as secondary to his own in every way. We may not have had Pemberley, but Edwin was not destitute by any means. We lived a very comfortable life at Havendale and I am happy to have been beside him all those years."

"I never did understand my father's staunch opinions. He often spoke of Uncle Edwin as *just the spare* even though the family holdings set him up in his own home quite nicely. In some ways I am very grateful Georgiana was born a girl. I doubt my father would have had much to do with her if I had a brother instead."

"Speaking of Georgiana, how is she?"

Darcy sighed and rubbed his eyes wearily as he sat back in the chair. "Oh, Aunt, I do not know what to do with her. She has changed so much in the last year, and I am at a loss as to what will change her back to the sweet child I have always known."

"Unfortunately, my dear, I do not think you can change her back. She is of an age to be responsible for her own mind and her own decisions."

"For now Fitz and I decided to hire another companion—this one more scrutinized than the last, of course. Mrs Annesley will be good for Georgie, but it has been quite the challenge to convince her."

"Well," she patted his hand affectionately, "you just have to do the best you can. You do know, if you ever need a break, you can always send her to live with me, do you not?"

"Thank you, Aunt Edith. I do not wish to burden you, but it may be just what she needs. We will see how she is having Mrs Annesley for a companion, and I will keep your offer in mind. Perhaps the next few months will bring a change to our family. My marrying might be just what my sister needs."

Edith raised her eyebrow at his declaration, "I see. So just when do you think this *change in status* will occur?"

"If I had my way it would be tomorrow, but I do not wish to frighten her."

"A summer wedding at Pemberley would be nice." she suggested.

"Yes, perhaps," he said with a small smile.

The two talked for a few minutes longer, Edith telling of her plan to have a ball. Darcy was not known for his enjoyment of such activities, but he could not deny that he looked forward to asking Miss Bennet for a dance or two, perhaps even three if he was brave enough to face the disapprobation of the drawing rooms.

Mary sat with Elizabeth as they worked on an embroidery project together. She was not at all comfortable with the idea of going to the theater. Large crowds made her nervous, and while Mr Bingley was an amiable gentleman, he was not very solicitous of her *particular* needs. This worried her greatly. Mr Darcy was usually distracted with Elizabeth, though he did speak with Mary some as well. Who she really preferred to escort her was Mr Darcy's cousin, but his schedule was very busy and he rarely had the opportunity to visit. *Oh I do hope he is able to go with us to the theater,* she thought.

She saw movement at the door and looked up to see Mr Darcy, Mr Bingley, and Colonel Fitzwilliam following the butler into the room. She stood, her cheeks becoming pink at her thoughts just before the trio walked in. She caught the colonel looking at her, his wink making her cheeks flame to an even darker crimson.

A walk was suggested. The sisters went to gather their things, meeting two of the gentlemen at the front door. Mary wondered where the colonel had gone, but took Mr Bingley's arm when he offered to escort her.

They were nearly to the entrance of the park when the colonel, having been detained speaking with Mr Gardiner about the book he borrowed, caught up with them. He walked beside her, silently watching her as Mr Bingley jabbered on about something. Mary only caught some of what her escort said as he moved around too much for her to read his lips easily. When they reached the pond and Bingley seemed to be intent upon continuing their walk, Fitz stepped up suggesting Miss Mary might need to rest after such a laborious jaunt.

Bingley profusely apologized to Mary and the three sat down on the bench, Bingley continuing to talk, nearly without a stop for breath, as Darcy and Elizabeth slowly walked around to the other side, where they stopped to gaze out over the water.

Elizabeth's eyes were drawn across to watch her sister as she sat on the bench between the two gentlemen, Mr Bingley obviously holding most, if not all, of the conversation. "Is your friend always so amiable?"

"Only where others allow him to be." She looked at him quizzically, so he continued, "His money comes from trade, so some in the *Ton* do not wish for his acquaintance. When he finds a person to whom his situation does not matter, he can be quite amiable."

Elizabeth began to bite her lower lip, not certain if she should ask what she dearly wished to know.

"I know you want to ask me something, so please do."

"It is rather inappropriate of me to be asking, but I worry about my sister."

"Having a sister myself, I understand completely. I will not judge you, Miss Bennet. What is it you wish to know?"

She turned back to look across the pond once again, "Do you think your friend is drawn to my sister?"

Darcy returned his gaze to the three on the bench, watching Bingley's face for a minute in silence before he answered, "I do not know, but if you wish it of me, I will find out?"

"Oh no, please do not trouble yourself, sir. It was wrong of me to bring up such a subject and I would not have your friend offended by my unseemly behavior."

Darcy turned back to the lady on his arm, his eyes catching hers as he quietly answered, "I do not think so of your question, and I know how to enquire of my friend without his knowing what I am about. You and I are similar in some ways, Miss Bennet, and I understand the bond between two siblings who have been left alone in the world. You only wish Miss Mary to be happy and safe, just as I wish for Georgiana."

Tears began to gather in her eyes as she remembered her family. Removing her hand from his arm, she walked to the water's edge and looked out over the small ripples the wind made.

Darcy was confused. *What did I say to offend her?* When he noticed her wipe at her cheek, he realized just how upset she truly was. "Miss Bennet, I am sorry if I have offended you in some way?"

"No, no, it is not you—it is just..." she sighed deeply, her voice cracking when she spoke the last word, "...*memories.*"

She started to reach into her reticule for her handkerchief when she saw one held out to her from the gentleman who was once again at her side. "Would you like to sit here for a few minutes?"

Elizabeth accepted the cloth and dried her eyes, sitting down beside the water underneath the shade of a tree's wide branches. Mr Darcy sat beside her, his long legs, even bent up to allow his arms to rest on them, were still longer than hers stretched out straight. A small smile formed at the corner of her lips as she closed her eyes, remembering a scene with her father very similar to this many years ago. When she opened her eyes again she saw him staring at her.

"Please tell me what you are thinking?"

Her cheeks pinked and she looked down to her hands folded in her lap. "I was just reminiscing about my father. When I was five he took me fishing, and I remember sitting beside the water with him just as we are here."

"What was he like?"

She sighed, "He was a unique mix–strong in so many ways with a quiet and quirky sense of humor, and yet so weak and fragile as well. Mary reminds me of him. When tragedy struck our family, taking my mother and my youngest sister from us, my father hid away in his study. Sorrow overtook every aspect of his life. He lost his joy after my mother died."

Darcy spoke for the first time of his own past, "My own father was unaffected by my mother's death. He wore his mourning band and avoided society for the proper time, but otherwise he carried on as usual. It angered me how calloused he could be, not even shedding a tear for her."

"How old were you when she...?" Elizabeth found she could not complete her sentence without being overcome with more tears.

"I was twelve. She was ill before she had Georgiana and did not recover from the birth. A fever took her from us just two weeks afterwards. My cousin came to live with us a few years before, but my mother still longed for another child. When Georgiana was born my mother was so very happy. She never even had the chance to hold her though. My father thought whatever malady my mother suffered from would be passed on to my sister, so he insisted the nurse take her away immediately. I stayed by my mother's side, to the consternation of my father, until her last breath." The corner of his lip turned up just slightly as he remembered his most beloved mother. "She told me of her desire to see us grow up and marry; how happy she would be to see grandchildren running around Pemberley." His face once again grew dark as he continued, "It was not meant to be however, and she lost her will to fight whatever malady overtook her. I remember watching the procession from a perch in the trees, with Fitz by my side, as my father refused to allow either of us to join them."

"Our neighborhood was scandalized by my father's actions. He allowed all four of his girls to walk with him when my mother and our baby sister were laid to rest. He and my Uncle Philips nearly came to blows over it, but my father still allowed us to attend."

"You have never mentioned another uncle before. I must say, I thought the Gardiners to be your only family?"

Elizabeth took a deep breath, trying to keep the tears from her eyes as she quietly said, "My mother had two siblings–my Uncle Gardiner was the youngest, and my Aunt Philips was the eldest. After my mother's death, my aunt, who lived but two miles from us, tried to do as much as she could for her nieces. She was never blessed with children, so we were well spoiled by her. My eldest sister had her coming out and my aunt planned teas and card parties the likes of which the neighborhood would talk of for weeks." Elizabeth smiled as she remembered her aunt, but her demeanor drastically changing as she continued her story. "My father and two sisters were taken from us in a house fire nearly four years ago and that is when Mary and I came to London to live with the Gardiners."

"Your other uncle could not take you in? If your Aunt Philips was so close to all of you, it would seem best for everyone if you were allowed to stay there in the neighborhood in which you were raised instead of having to come to London."

"My Uncle Philips, along with two other gentlemen from the nearby town, never made it out of the fire when they tried to rescue my father and sisters. We were on the post carriage the next morning and passed my Uncle Gardiner as he went to burry the family. My aunt was so consumed with grief over losing two of her beloved nieces, her brother-in-law, and her dear husband, I fear she died of a broken heart. She only lived a month longer than her husband."

Darcy did not know what to say. His family had suffered tragedy, but it was nothing compared to the grief he could see in her eyes. He slowly reached for her trembling hand, engulfing her small fingers in his as they sat silently watching the ducks swim across the pond, ripples from their movement making the water rise and fall so smoothly. If only the ripples of the past were as smooth, it would be so much easier for one to put it behind them.

Elizabeth took a deep breath, squaring her shoulders and lifting her chin as she forced a small smile onto her lips. "It is at times like this that I try my best to remember what my Aunt Philips so often said–*think of the past only as its remembrances bring you pleasure."* She turned to her companion and with a quirk of her eyebrow, she replied, "Mr Darcy, I fear we cannot possibly leave this conversation as it is. We must now speak of something, otherwise I will forever remember this day as a dreary one."

His own features brightened by her changed demeanor, "That would indeed be the greatest of tragedies as I wish to remember this day forever."

She blushed, looking down at where he still held her hand in his.

Darcy said, "I am looking forward to our trip to the theater."

"As am I! It is not often we have the opportunity, and the production is one of my favorites."

"Have you seen this troupe then?"

"No, but I have heard of them."

The two continued to discuss the play they were to go see in just a few days.

Fitz had spent just about every night learning to sign, but when it came to actually using the words he had practiced in the mirror, he could not bring himself to speak to Miss Mary. So here he sat next to her on the bench, listening to Bingley talk non-stop, about what, he could not even say.

He looked across the pond and saw his cousin sitting on the ground next to Miss Bennet, the two speaking of what looked like a very serious matter. Fitz turned back to Miss Mary and realized she too was watching her sister. All of a sudden she sucked in her breath and her face went pale, her eyes transfixed on her sister. Fitz put his hand gently on her arm and she broke from her stare, looking to him. "Miss Mary, are you well?" he quietly asked.

She swallowed hard and nodded, then relaxed a little and looked down at her trembling hands in her lap.

I will have to ask Darcy what they were discussing, Fitz thought. He dearly wished to know what made her react so strongly. He was amazed at the deep need within himself to bring comfort to the lady beside him. It was even pushing him to learn signs he could not yet bring himself to use to his advantage.

They sat there for a few more minutes until he saw Darcy and Miss Bennet stand and begin making their way towards them again. He stood, this time able to offer Miss Mary his arm before Bingley even knew they were ready to leave. With his shoulders held high and his chest puffed out just a little more than usual, he walked back to the Gardiners. The gentlemen remained for tea then took their leave, Bingley going to his brother's house and Darcy and Fitz returning to Darcy House together.

A few hours later the two were playing pool, Fitz lining up his shot, when he asked, "Darcy, what were you and Miss Bennet speaking of today at the pond?" He saw his cousin's demeanor and knew he would not get an answer without pushing harder. "I do not wish to pry, I was just curious. Miss Mary saw something her sister said and had a rather harsh reaction to whatever it was."

Darcy leaned his hands against the table as Fitz stood straight, looking at him. "We were speaking of our parents."

"You *both* spoke of your parents?"

Darcy nodded.

Quietly he replied, "So this is serious."

Darcy nodded again, no words coming out and his face showing neither displeasure nor joy.

"Are you prepared to ask for her hand?"

"I am."

"You know my side of the family will not approve."

"Do *you* approve?" Darcy asked sincerely. Fitz did not say anything, so he continued, "I am a man of great means and have relied on my own mind for many years, but it would be nice to have my family's opinion, and seeing as you are as close to a brother as I will have, I just thought…"

Fitz slowly walked over to his cousin. Putting his cue stick on the table he patted Darcy's shoulder, "My only wish is to see you happy, and if she makes you happy, then I will stand beside you no matter what the rest of the family says."

"Thank you."

"And with that, I will bid you good night." He then left Darcy alone.

Darcy retired as well, but, unable to sleep, he sat up reading his father's old journals. They read more like a text book from school than the words of an individual telling his story. His decision was made within his heart already, but reading the journals made Darcy realize just how solemn his life had become. He needed joy and happiness, and he knew Miss Bennet was where he would find that for the rest of his days. Now he need only find the opportunity to ask for her hand and hope she too felt as he did about the future.

Chapter 9

ary sat with her journal in hand, ink stains evident on the fingers and thumb of her left hand as she silently read the words she penned just a few minutes before. She found, many years ago, a great release when she wrote her feelings down on paper, and tonight was no different. It was one of the most difficult nights of her life, but what helped her get through the struggles she faced was knowing Elizabeth was so very happy on the arm of Mr Darcy.

To her disappointment, Mr Bingley was his usual, amiable self, so she could not put the blame for this disastrous evening on him. It was her—*all her*. Because of her own physical deficiencies she needed an escort who could guide her through the obstacles presented by being out in society, and Mr Bingley, though he was gentlemanly in every sense of the word, did not understand her needs enough to be of much assistance. She knew he did not understand the struggles she faced when being out in public, and that alone was enough to make her wary of going to the theater in the first place, but she acquiesced against her better judgment. It was clear she was not meant to be there, and especially not on the arm of one of the *Ton's* most eligible bachelors. Mr Bingley might have ties to trade, but his income and his friendship with Mr Darcy made him quite the catch. That he was a nice looking did not hurt his position either. He knew just about everyone in attendance, and Mary was introduced to more people tonight than she ever remembered meeting in her entire life.

The crush of the crowd everywhere she turned made her want to find the nearest door and run back home, but she overcame her deepest fears and stayed, clutching to the arm of her escort so as not to get lost. The chaos of the lobby soon gave way to the bleakness of the play itself. She had read Shakespeare's play before, but the sheer tragedy as it was acted out before her made her uncomfortable. It might have been different if the play had a happy ending, but the suicide of the two main characters was not to her liking.

What made her even more nervous were the looks she received as Mr Bingley once again led her through the crowds upon their exit from the theater. All eyes turned to the two sisters, very alike in looks, and Mary knew they would be the talk of every drawing room on the morrow. If there was one thing Mary hated more than anything, it was to be fodder for gossip.

With a deep sigh, she closed her journal, setting it down on the table beside her bed. She had hoped writing of her feelings would help clear her mind of the events of this evening, but it did not. She looked over at her sister who sat on her own bed holding tightly to the pillow clutched in her arms, a far—away look in her eyes. Mary walked over and sat down, garnering Elizabeth's attention. She was shocked to immediately be pulled into a tight embrace.

When she finally let go, Elizabeth signed, "Oh Mary, the most wonderful thing has happened to me this evening! It was such a magical experience–the theater, and Mr Darcy even found one of my favorite plays! He was so solicitous of my being on his arm and he introduced me with such pride."

Mary curled her feet underneath her, settling into their usual manner of sitting face to face so they could easily speak. "I can see you had a good time tonight–I am very glad."

"But that is not the best part of the evening," Elizabeth quickly signed back. "I am to be married!"

"Really? Oh Elizabeth, how wonderful!" Mary hugged her older sister again. When she pulled back both had tears in their eyes and they began to giggle at the display of emotions. "You must tell me everything."

"After supper tonight, when he offered to show me a case of his mother's collectibles…" And so the story unfolded.

"It is right over there," Darcy indicated to Mr Gardiner. The uncle gave a nod of approval and turned back to continue his discussion with Mr Bingley while Darcy lead Elizabeth over to the case.

"What a lovely collection." She fingered the birds and made mention of the lifelike characteristics of a few of the larger pieces. When he said nothing in response, she looked up at him. He was staring down at her, and when their eyes met Elizabeth felt her heart begin to pound.

Darcy's plan to ask tomorrow in the Gardiner's garden went awry when he suddenly blurted out, "Will you take my hand?"

Elizabeth was confused as such a request. "Yes, of course, sir."

He shook his head, trying to make sense of what he wanted to say. "I did not mean… that is." He took a deep breath and reached for her fingers, "I meant, will you take my hand in marriage? Will you stand beside me all the rest of our days on this earth? Will you face life's tragedies and triumphs with me?"

She certainly did not expect to hear those words come from him this evening.

He stepped a bit closer, lifting her fingers to his lips. "Miss Bennet, I find I have lost my heart to you, and I hope you feel the same. I have certainly felt you have encouraged me in my regard, and I do not wish to frighten you at such a question, but I find I cannot wait any longer. Will you marry me?"

The room around them began to spin and she felt him reach out to steady her. She then felt her aunt at her side.

"Elizabeth? Are you well?"

She looked around in confusion. "What? Oh Aunt, I am well."

"It is getting late. Perhaps it would be best if we take our leave," she said, turning to get her husbands attention. When he did not seem to notice, she turned back. Noticing the color was back in Elizabeth's cheeks, and she was once again steady, she smiled, "I will give you a moment, then we must leave."

"Thank you, Aunt." Elizabeth watched as her aunt walked away, then she turned back to the gentleman beside her. "Sir, I know not when it happened, but I can assure you I feel the same."

He once again reached for her hand, "You do? And will you..."

She smiled, "Yes, of course. It will be an honour to stand beside you the rest of my days."

Darcy could hardly contain the joy he felt inside, but since the others were just a few feet away he thought it best to bring her hand to his lips for a soft kiss on the back of her glove. "I know how much your sister means to you, and please know that in offering for you, I know it would please you to have her by your side. If you think she would like Pemberley, she is welcome to join our household as well."

It was all he had time for, as their privacy was interrupted and the visitors all took their leave. While helping her on with her cape, he was able to tell her of his intention to visit her uncle tomorrow, and he would forever remember that pink that rose in her cheeks when his whispered breath touched her ear. She gave a simple nod, and within minutes they were gone.

Mary could not help the tears that began to fall down her cheeks as Elizabeth described the scene, "I am so happy for you!"

Elizabeth pulled a handkerchief off the bedside table and handed it to Mary, "Please do not cry–if you cry I shall surely start again, then we will both have swollen eyes tomorrow."

Mary giggled, drying her eyes. "We cannot have that, now can we?"

Taking a deep breath and grasping her sister's hand, Elizabeth continued, "There is one other thing I wished to tell you. Mr Darcy made a point of saying that when we marry you will be welcome in our home as well. Oh Mary, please say you will come with me when I marry? I cannot imagine living apart from you."

"What would Aunt and Uncle say?"

Elizabeth reached for her sister's hand, "If you wish to come with me, they would be happy to let you."

Mary smiled, "Of course I wish come with you." Remembering what the colonel had said about Pemberley, she knew how much she would love it there.

The two spent the next hour discussing in great detail what Elizabeth felt and her hopes for the future. Mary finally returned to her own bed, falling into a deep sleep almost immediately. Her dreams were of a wonderful life with a loving husband and children all around, but when she awoke in the morning and the reality of life once again came into focus, she was disappointed that it would never come to be. She readied herself for the day and tried to forget her own grim future, instead focusing on the happiness of her beloved sister Elizabeth.

Mary and Elizabeth were both tired as they sat in the drawing room awaiting Mr Darcy's expected visit to their uncle. Their aunt was upstairs with the little ones when a letter arrived for both of them. They eagerly opened it, reading the invitation to attend a ball given by Mr Darcy's aunt in almost two weeks' time.

Aunt Maddie came into the drawing room just as the ladies were excitedly reading their invitation. Looking it over when Elizabeth handed it to her, she smiled. "We must send your acceptance immediately."

"Please do not include me, I do not wish to go," Mary stated.

Maddie walked over and sat beside her niece, "Mary, I know how uncomfortable you are in public, but we cannot offend the Darcys by refusing such an invitation."

Mary bit her lip as she thought of all she wished to express to her aunt and her sister, but she knew even as close as they were to her, they would never truly understand her discomfort. With a small nod of her head, she gave in, assuring them of her attendance.

"Wonderful," Maddie said as she stood. "Come—we must answer this invitation and go to the modiste immediately to have new gowns made for each of you."

"That is not necessary…" Elizabeth started to say, but was interrupted by her aunt.

"I will not be gainsaid in this. You will both have new gowns, and that is the end of it. You cannot expect to wear one of the gowns you currently have in your closet to a function such as this. We can well afford a little expense for your first ball."

The invitation was answered and the sisters dressed for their trip to the shop. Elizabeth was a little disheartened to possibly miss Mr Darcy's promised call, but she knew her aunt was right. If their dresses were to be completed in time they must be purchased immediately.

A few hours later, Mary stood uncomfortably in the back room, bolts of cloth all around her and every surface of the table covered in various patterns. The pushy lady came back into the room, and while Mary could not hear her voice, she knew it must be screeching just by the look on Elizabeth's face. The lady pulled Mary's arms out straight from her sides and began to measure, writing down notes as she went along and continuing her intense conversation with Elizabeth. There seemed to be a problem with a particular pattern, and the modiste was determined to have her way. Finally Aunt Gardiner put her calming hand on Elizabeth's shoulder and stepped in, finding a compromise between what the two ladies wanted in the dress.

Mary was pulled down from the stool and Elizabeth's turn to be measured quickly took precedence. Mary watched as the three ladies continued to talk of specific fabrics, some being held up to each of the girls' faces to see if they would work. In the end it was decided what each would wear and the three left with a sense of accomplishment at the day's outing.

They returned home and were taken aback when they saw the colonel pacing in the sitting room.

"Colonel," Mrs Gardiner replied, "we did not expect to see you today. Have you been waiting long?"

He bowed, "Mrs Gardiner, Miss Bennet, Miss Mary, it is a pleasure to see you all again. I came to call with my cousin."

"Oh? Where is Mr Darcy?" Mrs Gardiner looked around the room.

"He is speaking with your husband at this time, madam."

"You did not wish to join them, sir?"

He looked at Elizabeth, a small smile lifting the corners of his lips as he said, "My cousin needed to speak with him alone so I offered to wait in here for your return."

Maddie saw the look between the two and focused on her niece's cheeks as they turned a bright pink. *Ahhh*, she thought to herself, *it seems Mr Darcy has finally made his decision.* She turned back to the others, "We are glad to keep you company then, sir. Please excuse me while I check on my children and arrange for some tea."

When her aunt left the room, Elizabeth spoke, "Colonel, would you like to join us outside in the garden?"

"Yes, of course," he said, putting out both of his arms to escort the sisters out the door and down the stairs to the bench beneath the shade of the oak tree.

When they sat, Elizabeth looked at the colonel, "Is something amiss?"

"What makes you think so?"

"Colonel, I saw your face when we entered the drawing room. You were pacing, and somehow I doubt it was from nerves over your cousin's discussion with my uncle."

Fitz looked at her, carefully assessing her demeanor before he finally replied, "My father saw who my cousin escorted last evening at the theater and came to visit Darcy this morning. He let it be known how he feels about this match."

Elizabeth took a deep breath, the words she was about to say cut short when she noticed Mr Darcy entering the sitting room. She excused herself from the two others and joined him, both sitting on the sofa to talk.

"What have you decided?" Elizabeth asked, her eyes barely showing how frightened she was at what he might say.

Darcy was immediately filled with compassion and wrapped his arms around her, resting his cheek on her hair as she relaxed in his embrace. "Oh, *my Elizabeth*, please do not doubt my feelings. I love you, and no matter what my family says, we will marry."

Fitz sat beside Miss Mary, both watching the couple inside. When Darcy drew Elizabeth into his arms, he turned away, giving them privacy. Before he could even think of what he was doing, he signed to her, "How are you today?"

Mary's eyes brightened and she smiled as she signed back, "You are learning to sign?" Fitz was confused by the unknown gestures, and Mary drew out her paper and pencil from her pocket, writing what he did not understand.

Fitz reached into his jacket and pulled out her well—worn book, "Your uncle allowed me to borrow this."

Mary blushed at the gesture, "You are doing very well, sir."

He grinned, "I am just trying to increase my charms, madam." The smile on her face made his heart beat wildly. "You will also have to teach me how you tell from people's lips what they say."

The two continued to talk, Mary teaching Fitz a few new signs that would help them communicate better in the future, as well as explaining how to read lips. They eventually began to talk of the trip to the theater the evening before, Fitz apologizing for not being able to join them. He could tell Mary did not have a pleasant time and he dearly wished he would have been free to escort her.

"Are you going to Mrs Darcy's ball?" he asked.

Mary sighed, nodding her head, though she did not seem happy with the decision.

"I am as well. May I be the first to ask you for a dance?" Realizing what he said, he quickly replied, "That is... if you *can* dance."

Mary chuckled aloud and shook her head, writing down, "No, I cannot dance."

Fitz felt his throat constrict when he heard the sound that emanated from her when she chuckled. Until now he had not heard her voice, though Darcy said she did speak verbally sometimes, mostly just among her family. The joy he felt in that simple resonance was enough to take the sting of not getting to dance with her away. "We will just find another activity then, and I must insist we sit together during supper," he said with a smile.

Mary nodded in acceptance and they continued to talk until Darcy and Miss Bennet joined them, the Gardiners arriving just a few minutes later with the promised tea. They all spoke for a few minutes about the incident with Darcy's uncle, but it was quickly put to rest when Mr Darcy declared his intention to marry where his heart led and that he did not care about what his family thought. His enthusiasm to speak of his wishes for the ceremony to take place at his home, Pemberley, was all Elizabeth needed to hear to assuage her own trepidacious feelings over the harsh words spoken by his family.

The two cousins were invited to stay for supper, and they were happy to accept. It was decided over the course of the evening that they would stay in Town long enough to all attend Mrs Edith Darcy's ball in a little less than two weeks. Darcy and his sister would then leave for Pemberley the following Monday, followed by the Gardiners and Bennets a week and a half later. Elizabeth was not completely pleased with this decision, but her aunt insisted she would need as much time to shop for her trousseau. It was with a heavy heart that Elizabeth agreed to this plan. The colonel, in an attempt to lighten the mood, offered his services in escorting the family to Pemberley. Darcy offered the use of his second carriage and Mr Gardiner readily accepted, thanking him as it would have been a tight fit in only their own equipage with the servants coming as well.

When Mary told her aunt and uncle of her intention to remain with Elizabeth at Pemberley, they both gave their approval. In truth, they expected it the minute Mr Darcy's intentions were brought to light.

The wedding would take place on the 22nd day of June, just over a week after the bride's arrival at Pemberley, then the Gardiners talked of their intention to visit the Peaks while they were in the north. It was decided that Mary and Georgiana would join them on their tour, giving the newlyweds a little time by themselves, then the two would be returned to Pemberley and the Gardiners would come back to Town. The colonel, concerned with how his young cousin would react with Darcy's marriage, volunteered to accompany her on their tour of the Peaks. The Gardiners understood his concern and were eager to add him to their party as well.

With their many plans set into motion, the two cousins left late that evening.

"I am truly happy for you," Fitz said as they rode in the carriage through the streets of London.

"Thank you," Darcy said through the stillness surrounding them. "I was thinking... I know we have always said we would stand up for the other if we were still a bachelor when the other got married, but I do not want my decision to come between you and your parents. Perhaps it would be best if I ask Bingley to stand beside me instead."

From the tone in Darcy's voice he could tell how heavily this weighed on his cousin's mind. "I thought Bingley was to leave for Scarborough the day after the ball?"

"He is, but his business will take no longer than a week to complete, and I am sure he will be able to join us at Pemberley in time."

"What of his sister? I am certain you do not want to include her in your plans for a small ceremony."

"Since Bingley is going to Scarborough on business, Miss Bingley will be accompanying the Hursts' to Bath," he answered.

"Ahhh, so your plans are well under way for the perfect situation," he joked. "I understand your decision, and appreciate the sentiment, but if Bingley cannot make it, I will gladly stand up beside you."

"I do not want to give your father cause to cut you off for good," Darcy started to say.

"My decision is made Darcy, so there is no talking me out of it. I appreciate the sentiment, but I will not allow you to marry with just anyone standing at your side. If Bingley cannot be there, I would be honoured to fill the position."

He was glad for the darkness of the coach as tears began to fill his eyes. In a voice thick with emotion, he thanked his cousin, then was glad when the discussion turned to all Darcy would need to accomplish with his solicitor before he left for Pemberley.

When they arrived back at Darcy House, they stood in the hall at the foot of the stairs. Darcy asked, "Will you be able to get leave?"

"I have plenty of time saved up and with such an inducement as your wedding I doubt my request will be denied."

Looking around to ensure they were alone, he added, "I was a little worried about Georgiana accompanying the Gardiners on their tour of the Peaks, but with you along I doubt she will cause any mischief."

"That was precisely why I wished to join them." He patted his cousin on the shoulder, "Every newly wedded couple deserves some time alone. I am glad to do what I can for you in your time of need." With a slight bow of his head and a simple exchange to sleep well, Fitz went upstairs to his room, exhausted from the emotionally draining day. He fell asleep with a smile on his lips as he remembered the feeling of Miss Mary's hand on his as she showed him how to form a few signs earlier in the day. Whether he wanted to admit it or not, he was slowly losing his heart to this lady.

Chapter 10

he next two weeks passed slowly for Mary. Mr Darcy visited nearly every day, sometimes bringing with him his sister or his friend, Mr Bingley, but not his cousin. The newly engaged couple were often in the garden or requesting to go for walks, and while Mary was glad to oblige them, she could not keep up with their pace and often found herself sitting alone while they continued on without her.

When Mr Bingley came with Mr Darcy he would amiably talk the entire time. Unfortunately, he still did not understand that he had to face her so she could read his lips, but at least she was not bored. When Miss Darcy accompanied her brother however, Mary saw in her quiet demeanor and steely eyes someone she could not trust. Not knowing if she should warn Elizabeth, she kept a careful watch of the girl for anything specific, but so far there was nothing more than just an uncertain feeling when she was around the younger girl.

While she was extremely happy for her sister, she was also a bit saddened with the reminder that she would never marry. For many years, despite her aunt's assurances to the contrary, Mary had known she would never marry, and she accepted this as the path for her life. However, to watch so closely a couple as in love as Mr Darcy and Elizabeth, she could not help but feel a pang of jealousy and wish to one day be so loved and cherished by someone as well.

Mary's reverie was interrupted by her sister poking her head in the door. "Are you ready to prepare for this evening?" she asked eagerly.

She could not help but smile at her sister's exuberance, and soon the two girls, with their maid's assistance, were dressed in the finest dresses either had ever owned. Elizabeth and the maid were just about to start on Mary's hair when their aunt knocked at the door. The maid answered and Maddie came in with two posies of flowers in her hands.

"These flowers were delivered, one for each of you," she said as she gave each of her nieces their appointed bouquets, Elizabeth's being her favorite flowers, blue and yellow violets, and Mary's being a mix of pink and yellow blossoms.

Elizabeth immediately pulled the card out of hers and ran her finger lovingly over the now familiar script of her intended. She walked over and sat on the bed to read the small note in private.

Mary lifted the petals to her nose, smelling deeply the sweet aroma, "Why would Mr Darcy send me flowers as well?" she asked her aunt.

"I am sure he cares for you as his own sister and wishes you to have a wonderful time as well at your first ball," Maddie answered her niece.

Maddie stepped over to Elizabeth and Mary looked down at the flowers and saw one single pink *Persian Turban* right in the middle of the bouquet with a small, hidden note attached to its stem. She smiled as she pulled the paper out, expecting it to be from Mr Darcy. To her surprise, it read:

I greatly look forward to our supper set this evening and discovering just which charms you will choose to dazzle me with once again. My greatest wish–though I must warn you, it is quite scandalous–is that perhaps you will allow me to teach you to dance? See, I told you it was scandalous.

Waiting with anticipation for your answer.

Sincerely, R.F.

Her heart began to beat quickly and she smiled at the gift he gave her–a ranunculus, meaning *'you are radiant with charms'*. *He remembered the conversation we had before about flowers and their meanings,* she thought. She quickly put the note into her reticule before her aunt and sister came back, the blush on her cheeks still clearly evident to herself, though Aunt Maddie and Elizabeth did not seem to notice as they both began to arrange Mary's hair.

When they were nearly finished, Aunt Maddie asked, "Would you like to put some of these beautiful flowers in your hair?"

"Oh no, I would feel silly doing something like that," Mary answered back, her cheeks flaming once again.

"Oh please do, Mary," Elizabeth pleaded. "I will wear some in my hair as well if that will make you feel better?"

With two pairs of eyes beckoning her to acquiescence to their idea, she finally gave a silent sigh as she nodded. *What will he think when he sees me with these flowers in my hair? Oh I cannot believe I could ever be so brazen! My aunt would never have suggested it if she knew who these were truly from. Oh, I must tell her,* Mary thought as the two ladies behind her finished weaving them into her curls, the larger ranunculus being placed in prominence beside her hair comb. By the time they pulled her up to stand in front of them she once again lost her nerve to say anything about the sender of the posy.

Elizabeth's hair was similarly arranged with her own flowers, and soon the two were ready to leave. Maddie left the room to check on her children once more and the sisters descended the stairs to await the others. They were halfway down when Edward, Mr Darcy, and Colonel Fitzwilliam came out of the drawing room. Elizabeth's eyes were drawn to those of her intended, but Mary saw the look of pride on their uncle's face before he turned away to hide the tears they held as well. She walked down the remaining stairs beside her sister, their aunt quickly catching up with them as they donned their capes and gloves, then all six left for an evening they would never forget.

Mary nearly lost her footing on the steps outside when, Colonel Fitzwilliam, signed to her, "Your hair is lovely this evening, Miss Mary." His hand caught her elbow saving her from certain disgrace, though her cheeks were emblazoned with embarrassment.

The cool night air hit her hot cheeks and all she could do was nod to him as she continued on to the carriage. He sat across from her in the confined space, his eyes never leaving her own. *Somehow I have a feeling tonight will be very different than the theater trip,* she thought to herself. It almost seemed as if he could read her thoughts as he smiled and dipped his head to her.

Sarah Johnson

When they arrived at the ball, Mr Darcy and Colonel Fitzwilliam exited the carriage first. Edward asked Mary if she was comfortable with the colonel escorting her and she assured him she was. He reminded her of his unused second arm if she needed him, then he kissed her hand and exited the carriage, helping his wife down and stepping back as the other two gentlemen helped his nieces.

Elizabeth's heart raced–this was her first public appearance as the intended of Mr Darcy, and the only one before they were to leave Town for Pemberley. He felt her hand trembling on his arm and placed his other hand on top of hers, squeezing her fingers slightly. Elizabeth calmed immediately, matching his pace as they walked through the large doors and were greeted by their hostess.

"Do you think she will be well?" Edward asked his wife.

"Yes dear, she will be fine, just as I have told you. She even assured you herself in the carriage," Maddie quietly said to her husband as they watched the two couples start to mingle amongst the crowd already in attendance.

"I cannot help it. It is my job to worry, and they are like my own daughters," Edward replied.

"Yes, they are as dear to me as our own children as well. We know and trust Mr Darcy, and soon he will be Elizabeth's husband. This is not a situation we are as accustomed to ourselves, but he and his cousin are obviously well acquainted with the intricacies of the society that surrounds us."

"Yes," he nodded, "if it were not for Mr Darcy we would never even be on the invitation list to a Ball such as this." His eyes scanned the room once more, settling finally on the beautiful lady on his own arm. "Come my dear," he said, "I intend to dance every set with you this evening."

She giggled, "You know that is not possible, sir. I am already promised to Mr Darcy, Colonel Fitzwilliam, and Mr Bingley for three sets, but I do not mind giving you my supper set."

"Oh no, I will have your first set as well," he said as he whisked her over to the line starting to form in the middle of the room.

"Fitz, so good to see you here this evening," the colonel heard from behind him.

Mary felt his arm stiffen under her hand as he turned them around, not addressing a gentleman who was staring at her.

"May I have the honour of being introduced to your companion?"

The look in his eye made her stomach knot immediately.

"Absolutely not; I will not have you plying your charms on her this evening. I have been given the task of escorting her and I do not intend to leave her side, so go find another lady to pursue with your worthless declarations."

The man bowed to Mary, but she was unable to tell what he said as his head dipped down. The next thing she knew the colonel was leading her away without so much as a nod to the other gentleman. They quickly made their way to Elizabeth and Mr Darcy, the colonel whispering something to his cousin before he turned back to her. "Let us go and check out the other rooms, Miss Mary," he said with a slight smile, though he held his shoulder much more stiffly than he had before the exchange.

Mary was introduced to several others as they made their way through the house, but the colonel's obvious protective stance beside her kept anyone from asking for a dance or requiring her to speak with them. A simple curtsy was all that was needed in each situation. Mary chuckled inwardly at the stern glances the colonel was giving others, thinking he looked more like a Colonel in the Army tonight than he ever had before.

They made their way to the refreshments table and procured two glasses of punch, then found a quiet place next to the wall where they could watch the dancing. After their glasses were emptied and the colonel seemed to be back to his normal self, Mary looked around to be assured she would not be seen, then she signed, "Who was it to whom you would not allow an introduction?"

He took a deep breath, slowly letting it out before he answered her, "My brother, Viscount Milton."

"He is soon to be my sister's cousin, so why not allow it?"

"He only wished to embarrass you in the crowd, and believe me when I say you will not run into him if Darcy has any say in the matter. He is not allowed in any of Darcy's homes," he explained.

"Why?"

"Let me just say he is not an honourable gentleman in comportment, and he and Darcy had it out a few years ago. Darcy does not slight him in public, but everyone knows the two have nothing to do with each other." He became very serious all of a sudden, looking deep into her eyes as he quietly said, "My brother is a known profligate and gambler, with a long line of mistresses and ruined ladies in his wake. If you are ever in a room with him, please do me a favor and leave immediately. I would not have you injured because of him."

She nodded, thanking him for the warning, then the two returned their gazes to the dancers, watching the lively couples as they bounced down the line then back again. Mary found herself enjoying this evening much better than she thought she would, and most of the thanks had to go to her companion for the evening, Colonel Fitzwilliam.

"You know," he teased, "hearing is not necessary to dancing. I am amenable to teaching you if you are curious?"

"No, I think not, sir. I would truly embarrass myself." She blushed as she remembered his offer in the note as well. "Perhaps if we were alone... that is, not here in this crowd..."

He smiled, "I look forward to the endeavor and will hold you to that when the situation is appropriate, Miss Mary."

Mary's cheeks blushed a deep red. She was grateful when nothing more was said about her dancing. The second set of dances came and went, and soon the colonel was obliged to return her to her uncle's side and dance with his cousin's intended. It was a country dance and they partnered two other couples in their group, both enjoying the fast pace of the steps.

"You seem to be enjoying yourself this evening, Miss Bennet," he said as they spun around in a circle.

"Yes, exceedingly so, Colonel. How is my sister?"

"She is doing well."

"Good. I was worried for her comfort. I know she did not enjoy our night at the theater," the worry she felt made her voice tremble a little.

"Yes, we have discussed that evening at length, and I can guarantee you she will not have a similar experience tonight," he said with a smile.

"Well I do thank you, sir."

"It is my pleasure," he said as the dance came to an end. With a bow, he put out his arm and led her through the crowd and back to the others who waited where he left Miss Mary. Bingley joined him, his sister trying to clutch Mr Darcy's arm in her quest to capture the most eligible bachelor of the *Ton*, but she was denied the pleasure when Darcy excused himself and Miss Bennet from the group to speak with his aunt.

Mr Gardiner stayed with Mary for one more dance as the colonel was obliged to dance with Miss Bingley and Mr Bingley asked for Mrs Gardiner to accompany him. Mary watched from her position, noticing that the colonel was just as amiable with Miss Bingley as he was with her. Her heart clenched with the thought. Over the last few months his warm demeanor and friendly nature had put her at ease and made her think that he may affectionately of her, but it was clear now that this was just how he was with everyone.

Though the thought stabbed at her heart, she knew she could not allow it to hurt. She had lived her life knowing she would never marry, and a few weeks of fanciful thinking would not end that resolve. With a new determination she decided being friends with the colonel was for the best. She could do that. She could control whether her heart fell in love or not, and she would not allow herself to do so.

"Are you having a good time?"

Mary realized the dance was over and the colonel now stood in front of her again. She took a deep breath, smiled, and nodded, then accepted his arm as he once again led her through the crowd.

When the last strings of music ended and the dancing shoes were once again taken off, the flowers released from their hair, and their dresses hanging for the maid to sweep, Mary thought back over the evening. She could not help the smile that crossed her face. She had more fun this evening than she ever thought she could experience, and her new resolve to think of the colonel as a friend was just what she needed to free her mind from the possibility of hurting him with a rejection. After all, a rejected suit is much easier to get over then the disapprobation society would give him for the rest of his days for choosing someone as she to marry. No, they were not meant to be anything more than friends. She laid her head on her pillow and found a peaceful sleep, happy to finally have a friend other than her sister.

Sarah Johnson

M r Darcy made it a point to write to his intended every day, including before he left so she would receive something from the first day onward. He had flowers delivered as well, and Mary noticed they all seemed to have deep and affectionate meanings. She had a feeling the colonel was helping his cousin with this part of the plan. *Would someone one day send me flowers*, she wondered, then her heart began to beat wildly and her cheeks blushed as she remembered the posy she received just before her first ball.

Two days before they were to leave, the sisters sat in the park next to the duck pond when the colonel walked up and greeted them. He explained his purpose in coming was to give Elizabeth a gift from his cousin, then he pulled something from his pocket and held it out to her–a book with a flower placed at a certain spot inside. She excused herself to walk around the pond alone so she could read the marked poem.

Mary smiled as she watched her sister.

Fitz touched her arm to garner her attention, then when she turned to him, he asked, "Are you all packed and ready to go to Pemberley?"

"Yes; I look forward to it."

"It is a lovely place. You must not let its size intimidate you."

"Is it truly so large?"

He chuckled, "When I was a boy and it was raining, we would often play games where we had to hide. Once, when I was around eight, I was distracted by Mrs Reynolds announcing that Cook had some fresh biscuits in the kitchen, so I did not find Darcy. He finally left his hiding spot a few hours later and we never could talk him into playing that game again."

She tried not to laugh, but she could not help it, "How terrible!"

"Oh, the messes we got into at Pemberley and the stories I could tell, but it looks as if your sister has finished her letter," he indicated Elizabeth walking back towards them.

Mary stood. "Thank you; I will always think of the things you have told me of Pemberley as I explore its rooms."

"You may need to draw a map," he teased.

Elizabeth rejoined them and then Fitz walked with them back home. After finalizing the particulars of their travel plans with Mr Gardiner, he took his leave, giving Mary a small wink when he bowed to her. She could not help but chuckle inwardly at such behavior, though she also hoped he did not treat all his friends the same. She could not imagine him doing the same to Miss Bingley.

As he returned home he thought of the way Miss Mary was acting around him lately. It was different than before. It was almost as if she was more comfortable, just as if they were friends. *Is that what she wants? Maybe I assumed she felt more than she did and am just now realizing I was wrong?* She did say once that she knew she would never marry, but he just assumed it was the words of a hurting young lady who had never been given special attention. As his mind began to wander again in that direction, he scolded himself. *I cannot afford to offer for her, so it really does not matter how she treats me. She is a friend, and that is all she will ever be,* he told himself.

Though he tried to not let it affect him, he felt a pain at the realization that he was giving up a good chance for love. By the end of the evening he had talked himself into the decision, and now it was so set in his mind that he knew even the weeks of being around her at Pemberley and as he accompanied her family on their tour of the Peaks, would not cause him to allow his heart to hurt. He would be his usual friendly self, and he would enjoy the time with her and her family, but he would not love her. He could not choose to love her, but he could still be her friend.

Fitz thought his decision would be hard to live with, but instead he found it was freeing and allowed him to get to know Miss Mary in a way he never could have if his heart was dictating their interactions. He found he liked this new venture of just being her friend.

They were on their second day of travel when the weather began to become dark. Edward decided they would stop for the night earlier than expected, and he was just sealing his letter to Darcy telling of their unexpected delay when Mary sat down near him at the table in the corner of the sitting room. "Are you well, my dear?"

She nodded.

"You were pensive these last few weeks, but since leaving Town your mood has improved. Are you sure you do not want to talk about anything?"

"I do have a question, Uncle," she signed. "How did you know you wanted to marry Aunt Maddie?"

"Well," he began, "we actually grew up together and we began as just friends and playmates. One day though, that all changed. I was watching her across a field as she picked flowers, and in that moment I just knew I loved her. I was in the middle before I knew it had begun."

"Is that what love feels like?"

"No, my dear, but it is a good start to the bonds of love that last over time." He stood, pulling her up with him, "Come my dear. Your aunt insists we eat downstairs in the dining room this evening after the children have had their supper, and I know you will need to change. I do too," he said as he looked down at his traveling clothes. "I had best hurry if I am to check on the horses with the colonel." He tapped his hand with the missive he held, "I must also have this delivered to Mr Darcy so he does not worry over our late arrival." He kissed her cheek, then smiled as he went to dress.

Mary changed as well, then after the children ate their supper, she and Elizabeth accompanied their aunt to help the children prepare for bed. Mary assisted Juliana with wrapping her hair with rags while Elizabeth changed baby Joseph. Upon her stepping away from the toddling child, he found the wash basin, soaking his nightgown as he splashed around in the mess. When Elizabeth reached for him, he ran across the room only to be scooped up in his mother's arms. Elizabeth watched as her aunt tickled the child, then lovingly changed him once again. She hoped to one day be the kind, caring, and patient mother her aunt was.

Soon the children were all ready and Aunt Maddie sat down on the bed with her back to the headboard. The sisters gave their cousins a kiss and a hug, and the children cuddled all around their mother. She ran her hand through Henry's hair to calm his always jumpy legs, and began telling them a story. Elizabeth and Mary quietly left their aunt to her nightly ritual with her children.

They entered the sitting room, and Mary asked her sister, "Did Joseph get you wet as well?"

She chuckled, "He soaked himself mostly, but I do need to change before we go downstairs to dine." She turned to go into her room.

"Elizabeth?"

She turned back around, "Yes?"

"One day, would you tell me about your proposal?"

She smiled, "I already did. Do you not remember?"

"No, I mean would you tell me how you felt when he proposed?"

Elizabeth walked back over and took her sister's hand, leading them to the table in the corner of the room. When they were both seated, she signed, "What do you wish to know exactly?"

"What does it feel like? How did you know you would be happy for the rest of your life?"

Elizabeth closed her eyes, a small smile playing across her lips as she began to sign, "When he reaches for my hand, I come alive inside. When he steps away from me, I know there is something missing. It is difficult to describe, but I would say it is like floating. Nothing looks too difficult to face with Fitzwilliam by my side. We have known loss many times over, but I have never felt this kind of connection with another that I feel with him. We are bound in a way I cannot even fathom, much less put adequately into words."

Mary embraced her sister, "Thank you."

When they pulled apart, Elizabeth asked, "Did that answer your question?"

"No, but I have a feeling I shall not truly understand unless I am ever in love."

Elizabeth left the room to change, looking back to her sister from the doorway. What she saw was a grown lady; no longer the little sister who always needed her protection. In a way it saddened her, but she knew it was necessary to step away from that role now that she was to take her husband's hand in just a few short weeks.

Mary pulled her journal out and began writing of the day's adventures and of their good fortune in having two carriages at their disposal for the long journey.

…Henry did not do well in the confined space of the carriage for the second day in a row so the colonel let him ride with him on his horse for an hour, leaving him with many descriptions of all they passed in that time when he finally returned to the carriage. I do not remember much of my life when I was five years of age, but I often wonder if I too had such fanciful tales of mundane accounts.

Just as yesterday, the colonel chose to ride beside us, but I was able to speak with him a few times when we stopped. He is becoming such a good friend. Last evening he even read aloud from a book he brought with him, practicing the signs he was working hard to master. I must say, I was suitably impressed with his efforts. Very impressed indeed.

She had just sanded the drying ink and closed her journal when the two gentlemen came into the sitting room, talking amiably together of the expected tour of the Peaks. Edward saw his niece's slight blush and apologized for interrupting her.

"I was just finishing, Uncle," she explained, happy to see Elizabeth join them as well from their shared chamber.

"If you three will excuse me for a minute, I must kiss my children before they are all soundly asleep," Edward excused himself.

Fitz removed his rain soaked gloves and coat, hanging them by the fire to dry. "Hopefully this weather will clear up quickly and allow us to continue on tomorrow."

Mary walked over to the window, joining Elizabeth as she drew back the curtain to look outside. When she turned back and saw the colonel looking at her in expectation of her saying something, it made her smile. *He truly is a friend,* she thought as she signed back, "Maybe it is just a summer shower?"

"Perhaps," he replied. "They are common at this time of the year."

"Do you stop here often when traveling?" Elizabeth questioned him.

Fitz looked around the charming room, "Here? No, I do not remember ever stopping here before. It is a nice Inn though. Darcy and I usually make it much further by the end of our second day of traveling."

"You have only ever traveled to Pemberley with your cousin then?" Mary asked.

"Though I dearly love Pemberley, I rarely have the opportunity to travel there. My duties keep me bound for other shores or near London, and my parents' estate, Croome Court, is in Worcestershire so the route is not the same as going to Pemberley straight away."

"So you grew up in the West? Is that near Wales?" Mary asked, curious to learn a little more of him.

"Yes, very near actually—within a day's journey—but I would not say I grew up there. I spent most of my youth at Pemberley."

"Oh? Why is that?"

"You have met my parents," he said honestly. "I have never seen things the way they do, and we had a bit of a falling out when I was younger. My aunt and uncle saw fit to allow me to live with them until I was of an age to join the Army." Not wanting to answer any more questions about the rather awkward relationship he had with his own parents, he drew the conversation back to his cousin's estate. "Within Pemberley's borders are held such wonders that you will be awed and amazed at the loving way it warms its way into your soul.

It truly is a magical place. I dare say it is the most beautiful estate I have ever visited."

"The picture Mr Darcy has hanging in his home in Town in breathtaking," Elizabeth replied.

"Yes it is." Fitz knew this next part would pique Mary's interest, so he smiled as he said, "My Aunt Anne was known far and wide for her flower gardens."

"It sounds lovely–I cannot wait to see Pemberley," Mary replied.

"You not only get to see it, you get to live there," he lifted his eyebrow jovially.

"Yes, it will be very different for me." she agreed.

Fitz turned to Elizabeth, "I know your aunt is from Derbyshire, but you have never mentioned having traveled there before now. Is this your first time?"

"Yes, she spent several years as a child in Derbyshire, but her family moved to... that is, she moved away from there to where I grew up... when she was just thirteen. That is when she met my uncle," Elizabeth stammered.

He noticed her nervousness over speaking of where she grew up, so he decided to change the conversation once again to all they would see on the rest of their journey and on their tour of the Peaks. The Gardiners soon joined them and the five went downstairs to dine.

Edward watched his niece carefully as they dined, seeing a small sparkle in her eyes when the colonel took the chair next to her at the round table. He had a feeling the questions she asked earlier were Mary's way of trying to learn her own heart when it came to this gentleman. Having been assured already that he would not raise her expectations, he allowed more lenience than might be prudent. Perhaps it was time to speak with the colonel again about how he felt.

When they returned upstairs everyone retired, sleeping soundly and waking refreshed and ready to complete their journey. The colonel chose to ride inside today, happy to tell stories to the curious Henry who had taken a great liking to him.

It was nearly dusk when they pulled into a long drive that would eventually lead them to the manor house. Fitz watched as the Bennet sisters' faces shone with much joy at the sights surrounding them. When they came over a hilltop and

Sarah Johnson

Pemberley House came into view, Elizabeth sucked in a breath, the words "It is beautiful," falling quietly from her lips.

Mrs Gardiner grasped her niece's hand, squeezing affectionately, "I would never have believed my own niece would one day be mistress over all this."

"It is too much," Elizabeth said with tears in her eyes.

When they finally stopped Elizabeth saw her intended standing beside the entrance. The gentlemen stepped down from the carriage and she recognized the hand that reached for hers. As they waited for the others to descend they shared a semi—private moment, both extraordinarily happy to be together once again. When Elizabeth greeted Miss Darcy, the girl turned her nose up and looked away, refusing even the simplest of acknowledgments. Darcy and Fitz both saw her actions, then looked at each other, knowing they must discuss some things when they were alone.

Darcy took a deep breath, then turned away from his sister and led his guests inside, allowing Mrs Reynolds, the housekeeper, to show them to their respective chambers to change for supper.

Mr and Mrs Gardiner were amazed at the care that was taken with the placement of their children. Their own chambers were connected to the nursery, and Mr Darcy's staff was ready to care for the little ones at a moment's notice, giving their own nurse a chance to rest after such a long journey.

Their nieces would have two rooms across the hall from them for now, but Mr Darcy assured them that on the morrow they could each view the rooms in the family wing which were chosen for them. The mistress' chambers would need some attention as it had not been decorated in nearly thirty years. The paper was old and faded, and in some places it was peeling off the wall. Wanting to give his future wife the opportunity to choose her own furnishings, he did not attend to it when he took over Pemberley after his father passed away.

The room chosen for Mary was decorated by his mother, but it too was in need of some attention. Wanting Mary to feel at home here at Pemberley, he decided to leave the decisions for her room up to her as well. Mr Darcy explained that he had already spoken to the shop keepers in the town of Lambton just five miles away, and they were all anticipating the new mistress' orders for furnishings, wall coverings, and various accoutrements for the area's largest estate.

Fitz was glad to finally be back at Pemberley. Having spent many years here, he was most comfortable within these familiar walls. Nothing had changed in all this time–his room was just as he remembered. Hoping to speak with his cousin alone, he quickly changed and went downstairs, finding Bingley with his cousin in the billiards room.

"Bingley, I did not expect to see you here yet."

He bowed in greeting, "My business was concluded in a timely manner and I arrived at Pemberley yesterday."

Knowing this was not the time to speak with Darcy, he accepted the offered drink and the challenge of a game while they awaited the others.

Supper was served in the family dining room, a decision which upset Georgiana even more, though Darcy was over catering to her whims. This was his estate; their guests were soon to be his family. He wanted them to feel just as welcome here as they had made him feel in their own home. He could at least be proud in watching Pemberley's staff display their best for the soon—to—be new mistress.

As soon as the meal was completed, Fitz excused himself to walk his young cousin up to her room, and speak with her about her display earlier while they were alone. He returned to the others only a few minutes later, not giving any indication to them of the anger he felt rising on the inside of him at Georgiana's threatening words.

The Gardiners excused themselves after just a half hour, citing fatigue from the journey and their need to check on the children in the nursery. They insisted their nieces accompany them. Mary quickly found sleep while Elizabeth was plagued with so much anxiety over finally being here at Pemberley that it was nearly dawn before her eyes finally closed in slumber.

After Bingley retired, the two cousins were left alone at last. Darcy poured a drink for Fitz and received his usual nightly cup of tea from Mrs Reynolds before dismissing her. He settled into a chair across from his cousin, wearily leaning back into the chair's wings, "I hope your journey was easy enough?"

"Other than our delay due to the rain, it was without incident. I take it the last few weeks have not been as easy on you?"

"No, they have been very trying. Georgiana has made every day into a battle, and her refusal earlier to even greet my guests cannot be ignored."

"I agree."

"What can I truly do other than send her back to the school where this idea of her superiority has been allowed to grow?"

"I am at a loss. I tried speaking with her myself, but she just came at me with reason after reason for why you should not be marrying Miss Bennet. Her last statement has me worried though; she stated she will protest your marriage, even if that means missing the ceremony herself"

"Yes," he rubbed his eyes wearily, "I have heard all her arguments over the last few weeks, including that one." He made a face at the taste of the tea.

Fitz stood, "Come; anything is better than watching you drink that nasty swill. We will confront her together; now."

"Now?" Darcy stood reluctantly.

"Why not? Have you anything better to do, or would you rather put it off until she disrupts the flow of activities that will lead to your wedding day?"

He drank the rest of his tea in one gulp and placed the cup back on the table, "Now will do."

Darcy knocked, his cousin at his side while they waited for Georgiana's door to be opened.

The maid opened it just a crack, "Yes, sir? Do you need something?"

"I wish to speak with my sister."

The maid stepped away for a minute, then was back, "I am sorry sir, but Miss Darcy is not available to see you. If you came back in the morning…"

"Not *available* to see me?" his voice was stern and implacable when he barged in through her door. The maid wisely moved out of his way in time to not be injured by the door. Fitz walked in right behind him, dismissing the maid and closing the door. He stood by the door, only wanting to offer his support if Darcy needed it.

"Wha... what are you doing in my... *my room?*" Georgiana stammered as she tried to hide the letter she was reading–an old one from her dearest George.

"I will not be gainsaid, Georgiana! Pemberley belongs to me–every inch of its land, and every room in this manor, including this one. You will not continue to act as you are now. If you cannot accept the fact that *I am marrying* Miss Bennet, then it would be best for you to accept the fact that you will soon be returning to school."

"No... *please, Fitzwilliam!* Please do not send me back to that school," she begged, tears welling up in her eyes. "I cannot take their taunting. I will do anything you ask, just please let me stay with you." She was now sobbing so hard her whole body shook.

He was still unsure whether her tears were real or those of an act. He stood with stiff shoulders as he quietly but firmly said, "Considering what caused us to pull you from that school, I doubt they would accept you back. No, if we decide to send you away again, it will have to be to another place. Believe me when I say, if you do not start acting in a more appropriate manner immediately, I will see you sent off before my wedding even takes place."

"I am... sorry... Fitzwilliam," she said between sobs. "I promise... to be more... amiable."

"See that you are," he said with more softness to his tone. "I only want what is best for you Georgiana, you do know that, do you not?"

"Yes," she sniffled.

He sat down on the edge of her bed, pulling her into a tight embrace, "You are all I have left of my family, but when Elizabeth takes my name and steps beside me as my wife, we have the chance to continue the Darcy family on to another generation. That is what both of our parents wanted for us." He released her and stood back up to leave. Stopping next to Fitz at the door, he turned back, "Please do not make me send you away–it would hurt me more than you know."

"I promise I will try," she said, drying her eyes once more.

"That is all I ask. I know things will be different, but please give Elizabeth a chance." They both left the room. Darcy leaned heavily against the door when he pulled it closed behind him.

"Will this truly be a change of heart?"

Darcy sighed and looked down at his feet, his shoulders slumping in a way Fitz had not seen since his Uncle George's funeral. "She promises to be more amiable, but I fear it is just the threat of sending her to another school that made her agree to try." He sighed, "Did you hear what she said about being taunted while there? I wonder if that is what led her to act as she did and sneak away? More than that though, I wonder what she is hiding from us now?"

"I do not know, but I do know one thing," Fitz grabbed his cousin's shoulder, "you should not have to deal with this right before your wedding."

"Yes, but she was left in my care."

"And mine, Cuz. Now that she knows we will both stand up to her, let me take care of everything else. Your mind need not be so disagreeably engaged at this time. I will handle Georgiana," Fitz promised. "Starting tomorrow, I will remove whatever obstacle I can from your shoulders. I will speak with Mrs Annesley about her duties over the next few weeks."

"Thank you... for everything. I know what you have given up to offer me support in my decision to marry Miss Bennet."

"It was not a difficult decision to make. My father is full of vanity, my mother is spiteful and jealous, and my brother is a rake. I would say the choice to stand by *you* was quite easy indeed. Now," he said with a smile, rubbing his hands together, "I believe you owe me five cigars for my ensuring your intended received her gifts every day, and if I am not mistaken, Mr Gardiner has provided you with a new stash?"

Darcy allowed a small smile to pull at the corners of his mouth, "Yes he has. They are in my study."

"Lead the way, and I might share one with you tonight," Fitz said as they both went back down the stairs.

Chapter 12

itz raced across the fields on his horse, Bingley following not too far behind, each hunched over low with a look of determination on their faces. Bingley's mount almost pushed ahead until something caused him to fall back. Fitz rounded the tree that marked the end of their race and he doubled back to find his erstwhile friend.

"That blasted… no good… why did I wear it anyway…," Bingley was grumbling loudly as he stomped around in the bushes.

"What happened to you? I thought you had me there for a minute, then all of a sudden you were gone."

"I lost my blasted hat!"

"I told you it would slow you down," Fitz jumped down and began to help him look for it. "Ahhh, there it is," he said, pointing about ten feet up into the branches of a tree.

"How did it get way up there?" Bingley huffed as he hurriedly climbed the tree to retrieve it.

"You amaze me with your ability to climb so easily," Fitz called up to him.

"Ahhh, this is nothing to the trees I used to climb as a boy. My aunt's home in

Scarborough had the best one, and I could often be found hiding there from my sisters. If you think that is impressive, you should see me scale a wall. I had much practice in school as I was constantly locked out of my room by a few of my classmates. When I became friends with Darcy, everything changed." Bingley jumped back down to the ground, dusting off his hat before he put it back on his head, pulling it down low so it would not come off again. "Perhaps on the way back we had better not race."

Fitz chuckled and mounted his horse again.

As they rode along, Bingley said, "Darcy says you may be going back to the continent again?"

He groaned aloud, "My cousin speaks too freely sometimes."

"Do not judge him too harshly–it was the night before you all arrived, and he was a bit out of sorts with Miss Bennet's delay, so I may have plied him with a bit too much to drink."

Fitz chuckled, "He has always been easy with his words when he is in his cups. So what other family secrets did my cousin reveal?"

"Hmm… not much, just that you are as stubborn as a mule, but I already knew that."

Fitz laughed. "Yes, well, we cannot all be a puppy like you, now can we?"

Bingley nearly fell off his horse he was laughing so hard. "I remember your last night at Eton well–we decided you were the mule, I was deemed the puppy, but I cannot remember what Darcy was."

"I believe it was the ostrich, for his tendency to want to hide in plain sight."

When the horse snorted and tossed his head, he decided it would be best to not be riding, so he slid from its back, "We must walk if we are to continue this conversation. It would not do to fall and injure myself because of laughing too hard."

Fitz dismounted as well and they continued to talk of school days and how much life had changed for each of them over the years. Darcy and Bingley had lost their parents, and while Fitz' were still alive, he had a relationship with them that was not understood by many. Bingley was one of the few. Eventually their conversation turned to the Bennet sisters, and after discussing the betrothed couple, their thoughts naturally drifted to Miss Mary.

Curious what Bingley would say, Fitz asked, "What do you think of her?"

"I enjoy being around her," he said. "There is just something about her that draws me to talk with her."

"Yes, she is quite friendly when you get past her hard outer shell. At times it can be so infuriating, but her determination and inner strength makes her so animated once she trusts you."

"No... no, I do not think that is it. It is something else. She is just so... calming and sweet."

"Sweet? Well, I guess so."

"You do not think she is sweet?" Bingley asked.

"It is just not the first word I would use to describe her," Fitz explained.

"I have been thinking lately about settling down, and Miss Mary has garnered my attention. With her uncle's position, I do not think she would disparage my connections to trade like most of the *Ton* would."

Fitz felt his throat close up tighter with every word that came out of Bingley's mouth. His heart beat louder and louder, to the point that he could not even hear Bingley any longer. All he heard was the thump, thump, thump of his own heart. *You have no say in her life,* he tried to tell himself. *She is just a friend. I wish her to have a good life, and if she can do so with Bingley, then I should be happy for them, but I cannot bring myself to even consider it an option,* he thought. *She deserves to love and be loved,* he kept reminding himself as he tried to focus once again on what Bingley was saying. As much as he tried, he just could not force himself to be happy that Bingley had decided to pursue Miss Mary.

They were soon back at Pemberley and Bingley wandered off to do something. Fitz was unsure what he had said, but he really did not care either. Needing to clear his head, he set out on one of the walking trails that wound around the gardens. Wanting to be alone, he decided to make his way through the maze to the fountain at the center. He got turned around a few times, but by the third try he remembered the correct combination of turns to reach his intended destination.

When he came around the last corner he stopped immediately. Miss Mary sat on the edge of the fountain. He stood there watching the picturesque scene as it played out in front of him. Though her back was to him, her face was turned so he could see her features. Her eyes were closed and her lips showed a simple smile as her fingers delicately traced over the surface of the water, making tiny ripples that lapped quietly against the sides. The mist from the spray was caught in the wind and he felt the cool breeze wash over his dusty face. The wind carried with it a scent he knew to be what she wore and a faint sound of humming. *Does she remember what music sounds like,* he wondered? It took everything in him to turn away, but he knew he must. He hid behind the brush and watched her for a few more minutes, then, not wanting to meet with anyone else, he returned to his room where he knew he would be left alone until time for supper. After all he heard Bingley say today, he knew he must fortify his own heart before this evening when he would be forced to watch Bingley try to court her attention.

Bingley stood at the foot of the stairs when Mary came down to join the others for supper. "Miss Mary, may I escort you to the dining room?"

She smiled a little and nodded her head, then took the proffered arm, walking beside the gentleman as they joined the others coming out of the sitting room.

"Are you feeling well?" Elizabeth asked her sister.

She nodded yes in answer.

"You do look a little flushed, Miss Mary," Bingley said as he led her to her seat, taking for himself the one right beside her.

Fitz looked at her face. She actually looked a little pale to him; far from the flushed looks he had seen on her in the past. Looking away abruptly he scolded himself silently, reminding himself that she was just a friend. If Bingley wanted to pursue her, and if she was amenable to his suit, then he should not step in the way. After all, it was not as if he had the option of doing the same. As long as she was happy, he could live with that decision.

The meal went by slowly for Mary. Mr Darcy and Elizabeth were barely able to pull their eyes from each other. The Gardiners were quiet this evening. Miss Darcy did not speak, but the way she looked at her brother and his intended could not be mistaken for anything but disdain. Colonel Fitzwilliam spent the entirety of the meal either looking intently at his own plate or staring down his young cousin when he felt she was out of line. Mr Bingley talked with her, but she was not able to answer him in anything more than a nod or shake of her head as he did not know how to sign. Every time she tried to catch the eye of someone else, they were looking away, so she spent the entirety of the meal wondering why Mr Bingley chose to bestow such attention upon her.

When the normal time for the separation of the ladies came, Mrs Annesley stood, excusing herself and her charge and insisted Miss Darcy follow her without complaint. One look at Fitz told Georgiana this was his decision and she had better do as she was told.

"I think we can dispense with the formalities of a separation," Darcy suggested. "May I escort you, my love?" When Elizabeth took his arm, he smiled broadly.

Fitz chuckled at the unusual sight of his cousin smiling. He saw Bingley offer his arm, once again, to Miss Mary, and he followed behind the two, trying not to think too deeply about it. His decision had been made.

When they arrived in the drawing room, Mary sat beside her aunt on the sofa. *Why is Mr Bingley paying such attention to me all of a sudden? In the past he was amiable, but it almost seems as if he is now pointedly focusing on me. Could he be trying to court my attentions?*

Fitz saw her discomfort and, knowing he needed to act more as a true friend would, decided to take some of Bingley's attention off Miss Mary. "Bingley, I hear you are looking to lease a property in the country this year?"

"Yes, I am hoping to have my decision made by Michaelmas so I can take up residence," he said with his usual smile.

"Do you have any prospects?" Mr Gardiner asked.

Bingley set his tea cup down on the table so he could gesture with his hands. "I have a few properties I am to look into, and I am hopeful one of them will be to my liking."

"If you do not mind my intrusion, sir, where are they located?" Mr Gardiner asked.

"Oh, no sir, I do not mind at all," he said back to Mr Gardiner. "One of them is in Yorkshire, and although I am assured it is the most beautiful of places, it is quite the distance from Town."

"Yes, that is still a day's travel north from here," Darcy added. "Beautiful country though, especially the southern areas around the White Peaks." He turned to the others, "Will you enjoy some of that county as well on your tour, sir?"

"No, we will be staying in the Three Shire Head area," Mr Gardiner answered. "With four little children along on our tour we wanted to limit our travel, and that area offers everything we desire."

"I do wish I could join you," Bingley replied, "as I have not seen the Three Shire Head since Darcy and I left Eton." He turned to his friend, "Do you remember that trip?"

"How could I forget? It was the worst holiday adventure I have ever experienced." He turned once again to Mr Gardiner, "Believe me, sir, you should be grateful the rains have not been very heavy this year. I think we walked more than rode that year, and I cannot tell you how many jackets my man had to give away to the bone and rag man because they were ruined beyond repair in the muddy embankments on that journey."

"I hope the weather holds out for all of us on our journeys these next few weeks," Fitz smiled across at Miss Mary when she looked at him.

"You mentioned three properties to view? Where are the other two?" Mr Gardiner asked Bingley again.

"One is in Kent. Did you not travel through there just last year?"

"Yes—yes we did." He was not sure how much Bingley knew of Darcy's struggles with his sister, so he tried to focus on something else. "In fact, that is where Mr Darcy and my niece first met. We stayed in Ramsgate for some weeks around Eastertide."

"Oh, that is right—my friend here goes to Kent every year at that time to visit his aunt."

"Yes, well, that might have to change in the future," Darcy said as he squeezed his intended's hand.

Feeling the tension in the air, Fitz cleared his throat, "Where is the third property?"

"It is in... Hmmmm... let me think now. Hampshire, or Hertfordshire... no, I believe it was Herefordshire." He looked at Fitz, "You grew up near Herefordshire, did you not?"

"Yes, my parents' estate is in Worcestershire."

"It is a pity you are not traveling with me then as I am sure you could show me some of the lovely countryside there," Bingley said jovially. "I greatly look forward to having guests–in fact, if I am able to find a property for this Michaelmas season, let me invite you all to join me in the country. It would be much more fun if my best friend and his extended family were to join me for shooting, fishing, and of course, other social events sure to be pleasing to all."

Darcy looked at Elizabeth, "Well, we had not thought to..." He stopped when he felt her hand squeeze his.

"We would love to join you, sir. You have been a dear friend to my intended, and I am certain he will wish to continue the acquaintance once we are married."

"Yes, yes of course I do," he stammered. "Just let me know when you finally find the place, and we will plan a visit. I must attend the Harvest Celebration here at Pemberley just after Michaelmas, but after that our schedule is free until Christmas." He saw Elizabeth's smile of approval and squeezed her hand in return. He did not even think of the insult he would have unintentionally given his friend without Elizabeth's gentle persuasion. He was grateful for her presence in his life.

"I will send you a note as soon as the papers are signed, and will look forward to hosting you for a change," Bingley replied, then he turned to Mr Gardiner. "You and your family are invited as well, sir."

"This being our second holiday of the year, I really cannot afford to be away from my businesses again unless it is absolutely necessary."

"Yes, of course–I understand." He then turned to Fitz, "If your orders leave you time to visit, you are welcome to come."

"Thank you; I will keep that in mind."

Sarah Johnson

Bingley's mind, as was usual, jumped from one subject to the next without so much as a breath between them. "Miss Mary, I have meant to ask you about these hand motions you use. Are they difficult to learn?"

Elizabeth answered for Mary, "They are not too difficult, sir."

"Perhaps you could teach me a few then, Miss Bennet?"

"Yes, of course." Elizabeth stood and spent several minutes teaching Bingley a few simple signs and how he could use them in phrases. He tried several times, but could not form his fingers properly.

"I find it easiest to do this for that particular sign," the colonel said as he formed his fingers properly to show Bingley.

"You know how to sign, Fitz?" Bingley asked.

"I am learning," he said verbally as he also signed for Mary's benefit.

"How in the world did you become so good? I cannot seem to make even the simplest gesture properly."

"It took many hours of practice in front of the mirror before I was comfortable enough to sign in front of anyone," he explained.

Mary blushed. She did not realize just how long and hard he had practiced.

Bingley sighed, but was determined. He walked away from the others, looking oddly at his own hands as he paced around the room, trying to form the few signs he was shown while the others continued to speak amongst themselves.

"Was that right?" Bingley asked Miss Elizabeth.

She walked over to him, away from the others, "No, no, curve your fingers more," she showed him.

"Oh... right." Then he walked around a little more.

"He will never get this," Darcy whispered into her ear.

"You know him better than anyone–do you really think so?"

He shook his head no just as Bingley stepped up to them again.

120

"Did I get it that time?" he asked, showing her the sign again.

"Perhaps signing is just not for everyone, Mr Bingley," Elizabeth suggested.

"I will prevail, just give me time." He once again tried to form the word. "Was that right?"

Darcy saw that his friend was clearly separated from the others in the room, so he could not help but tease him. "*Bingley!* I cannot believe you would say such a thing," he said in a quiet yet harsh manner. "There are ladies present!"

"OH! Oh, excuse me, I did not realize... that is... I am very sorry." He looked to the others further away and whispered to his friend, "Do you think they saw what I said?"

"I do not think so."

"Capital! Capital! I think I will give this up for now," he said finally as he once again went to sit near the others.

Elizabeth tried not to laugh aloud, but the smirk on her intended's face told of the joke he pulled on his friend. "That was very wrong of you, sir! The poor man will never again want to sign the word *'shoe'.*"

Darcy chuckled, "You must allow me to have my share of fun, my love."

Elizabeth tried not to burst out in laughter as she sniggered, "That was badly done, sir—badly done indeed." She drew her hand up to cover her mouth as she was having a hard time keeping a straight face.

Darcy reached for her fingers, drawing them to his lips for a sweet kiss to the back of her hand. "I am sure Bingley will find a way to repay the gesture, but I could not resist the temptation. He has always been a bit gullible."

Elizabeth smiled widely, "I just cannot imagine that the gentleman I sit here with tonight is the same one who burst into my uncle's house in Ramsgate insisting I speak with him. You are so very different."

"I do not think so. In character I am as I ever was," he replied.

"I think Pemberley brings out the best in you, my love."

"Pemberley brings out the best in you as well, Elizabeth. My heart swells with pride to know that in just three days you will stand beside me as the mistress of this grand estate and of my heart."

The two lovers were interrupted when Mr Gardiner asked for some time to speak with Mr Darcy on the morrow to finalize the contract before the wedding. With a nod of acceptance, Darcy was ready to turn his attention back to his intended, but her uncle had other plans and wished to retire, requesting his nieces accompany them upstairs. Elizabeth receiving one last kiss on the back of her hand and a smoldering look from her intended before she locked arms with her sister and they followed their uncle and aunt up the stairs and to their rooms.

Darcy watched his intended walk away, grinning when she turned back once more from the stairs. "Well, gentlemen, shall we have a smoke?"

"I think I will go on up as well," Bingley replied, leaving the two cousins alone and bounding up the stairs. He easily caught up with the others before they reached the top, and he put his arm out to Mary, who reluctantly linked her arm through his.

When they reached their rooms, the sisters gave their final greetings and each retired alone.

Elizabeth dressed for bed as she thought of all her heart desired. *Three days–just three days and I am to be married. I hope these last few days pass quickly,* she thought as she crawled into the huge bed, curling onto her side as she pulled the counterpane up high, falling quickly into a deep sleep nearly immediately.

Mary was too anxious over the happenings of the evening to sleep peacefully, so she spent the next hour pouring her heart and soul out onto the pages of her journal. Why was Mr Bingley paying her such attention? Why had she not realized before now how long and hard the colonel studied to be able to speak with her in sign? So many questions left her heart reeling and her journal pages full.

As she closed the book, she sighed heavily. It was fitting to end this part of her life with the final pages of the book. She would have to go to the nearest village and purchase another one soon.

Fitz watched as the others ascended the stairs, his heart falling just a little when he saw Miss Mary take Bingley's arm. He turned away and followed quietly after Darcy, taking a cigar when it was offered, then sitting in the chair by the open window, glad for the cool night breeze.

"So…" Darcy sat across from his cousin, "you practiced for *hours* before you even spoke a word of sign to anyone?"

Fitz rolled his eyes, "I had hoped you did not catch that statement."

"Oh, I think everyone caught it, including Mr Gardiner. Does he know how ambitious you are?"

"He is the one who lent me the book of signs." Fitz puffed out a ring of smoke.

"Hmmm…" Darcy did just as his cousin, trying to make his ring larger in their unnamed battle. "Hours you say?"

"Oh come on Darcy; just say what you wish to say. Scold me or tease me, just get it over with so I can enjoy my cigar in peace."

He put his hands up in surrender, "No more; I promise."

"Yes, well, I could tease you in return, you know. I have heard quite the tale from your intended about some of the events of these last few months, and I must say it is a little different than you have told me yourself. Proposing on a whim like you did, with her family looking on? Just what were you thinking?"

Darcy chuckled, "I was merely thinking of my own happiness and did not care if the whole world looked on when I asked."

"For your sake, I am glad she did not deny you."

"Deny me? Never!" He drew in a long puff, letting is out slowly in a long stream of smoke. "You do not think she ever would, do you?"

"It is not for me to say, but from how you described your first meeting, perhaps it is best that you waited until she saw your better qualities before you poured your heart out to her."

"At least I can say I have a lady on my arm. What of you?"

"I cannot afford to marry, you know that."

"I know nothing of the sort, only that my father wanted to see to it you were well cared for and wished to give you a property that would allow you to marry where you desire, but you are too stubborn and refuse even my help in the matter."

Fitz stood, snuffing his cigar in the ashtray. "I will not have this discussion again. Good night Darce."

He watched Fitz leave the room, then whispered to himself, "If you will not accept my help one way, I shall have to try another."

Chapter 13

r Darcy, I do not feel comfortable with these terms. Are you certain?" Mr Gardiner asked as he sat stunned in Mr Darcy's study.

He nodded, "I am."

"I just... that is... please do not take this the wrong way, but you are too generous, sir."

"Mr Gardiner, I do not feel it is too generous at all. In fact, this was a lower figure than I originally wanted, but my solicitor urged me to not put myself in a bind. As my wife, Mrs Darcy will be watched closely by the *Ton*. I intend to give her every avenue at my disposal to make her position in society as remarkable as possible," he explained.

He nodded, "I understand. I do not see things the way you do, obviously, but I do understand your sentiment." He continued to read down the papers, his finger tapped the ink in a few places where he stopped to think, though he did not say anything. Flipping to the next page, he stopped and went back to the previous page, reading the passage again. Finally he looked up, "Sir, I may not be at liberty to admonish your frivolity with your wife, but I must give my concerns over your gift to her sister."

"My own sister has a dowry of £30,000 and has the funds from an estate on my mother's side of the family. Eventually that estate will be given to her when she marries or becomes of age, but until then it is overseen by my steward and the proceeds are put towards seeing to my sister's welfare for the rest of her life. I have only carried out what my father before me set up for his own children." He shifted in his seat before he continued, "My parents were good people; my father taught me to be fair in business dealings as well as with my tenants and staff, but it was Elizabeth who taught me to see the value in those whom the *Ton* looks down upon. I will be forever grateful for her spirit in putting me in my place when we first met. As such, I feel it would be unfair to treat her sister any differently than I do my own. I know it is not equal to my sister's dowry, but I insist upon the amount of £20,000 be added to what she has already, as well as the property I have laid out in the papers. As with my sister, the monies from the property will be put aside for her to use if it is ever necessary. If she marries, I wish it to be part of her dowry, and if she does not, then when I am gone, she will have a place to live without having to worry."

Mr Gardiner saw the agitated state of the man across from him. This was not the Master of Pemberley he was speaking with, it was the orphaned young man of eight and twenty years who knew all too well what it was like to be left alone in the world. He understood what the Bennet sisters had gone through more than anyone, and he loved them enough to do everything in his power to provide for their future–both of them. Mr Gardiner's eyes filled with tears at the realization that this young man cared more for his nieces than their own father.

With a deep breath slowly released through his parted lips, he slowly nodded, "I thank you, sir–with all my heart, I thank you."

"Your gratitude is not necessary, Mr Gardiner."

"Perhaps not, but I will give it all the same. Thank you for caring for my nieces as no one else ever has."

"They have had you caring for them these last few years, sir," Darcy said modestly.

"Yes, but I am their uncle. You are a stranger to them, and yet you have chosen to accept both of them willingly into your family. For that I am most grateful. You truly are a good man, and I dare say your parents would be very proud of who you have become."

Darcy stood and began to pace, his heavy footfalls muffled by the plush rug underneath his feet. "My father was a good man. He was always fair, and raised me to be such, but he was also a very cold man who did not give his affections easily. My mother had a heart of gold, but she was the product of her upbringing as well. As the daughter of an earl, she had very high expectations for who her children would one day marry." He turned back to face Mr Gardiner. "Sir, I know this will sound harsh, but I am glad my parents are no longer alive as I know neither one of them would be accepting of Elizabeth in my life."

Mr Gardiner stood, going over to stand beside Mr Darcy, "You are nothing like your parents, and I will be proud when you join our family in just two days. Now let us sign these papers so as not to delay the ceremony."

Darcy smiled just a little, the creases in his forehead disappearing, "Thank you, sir."

The papers were signed and the two were glad to celebrate with a cigar for each.

"Sir," Darcy said, "Will you keep the particulars of this contract from your nieces? Please?"

"It is your money, son. If you wish them to know what you have done with it, then I will not stop you, but neither will I tell them in your stead."

"Thank you. I would not wish to offend the memory of their own parents."

"Understood, but I will caution you to speak with Elizabeth after you are married. To keep this from her would not be wise. As a man married many years now, I would say keeping the peace is easiest when you are completely honest about all your dealings."

"Thank you, sir. I will tell her, but not until we are married."

Edward drew in the sweet taste, then slowly let the smoke out. "My wife's concerns about Mary will be greatly assuaged by your generosity."

"Is there anything more I can do to make Miss Mary feel at home here at Pemberley?"

He chuckled, "No, no; you have done so much already. She will find much joy in choosing the decorations and furniture for her chambers, and since our arrival Mary's personal maid, Mabel, has been well accepted among your staff."

"If having a familiar face around will help Miss Mary, then I am glad to add her to those whom I already employ."

"When Mary first came to us we had a difficult time learning to communicate with her. I am sure you can appreciate the challenge since you and your cousin have both been trying your hand at signing over the last few months."

"Yes, indeed; it is quite the challenge."

"Mabel was already in our employ, but when the girls came to live with us, she and Mary formed a bond. She easily picked up on the signs she was taught, and within just a month Mary came to us asking if Mabel could be her personal maid. After a trial period to determine if she was qualified for the job, my wife was happy to agree to the plan, so I could not say no to such an idea. I must say she has impressed me with her abilities."

"I have had little interactions with her, but Mrs Reynolds has had nothing but good things to say of her. She seems to get along well with the staff."

"Mary will never tell you, because she is too modest to say so, but it means a great deal to her that you have allowed Mabel to join her here. Thank you." He stood, "And with that, I must leave you to find my wife. We have an appointment amongst your wonderful flowers while the children have their rest."

With that the two gentlemen parted ways.

Maddie felt it was necessary to have a private discussion with Elizabeth before the wedding, which was in just two days' time. She regretted not being available to take Mary to Lambton, but upon finding that Mrs Annesley was to take Miss Darcy there, she asked if Mary could join them as well. The companion was happy to accommodate, and Mary soon found herself sitting in the carriage, across from the two ladies.

When they arrived, they stepped from the carriage and Mrs Annesley told the driver they would be back in an hour, then they proceeded down the street.

Miss Darcy was to pick up a hat at the milliner's shop, and the book shop was just before it.

Georgiana was not happy with the arrangement, but she knew she could not risk upsetting her brother right before his wedding. It took everything in her not to want to do something humiliating to Mary Bennet while they walked down the streets.

Just as they rounded the corner they saw Fitz coming out of a store. "Oh, good morning ladies," he bowed. "I did not know you were coming into Lambton or I would have accompanied you."

"Miss Darcy and I are to pick up her hat, and Miss Mary is in search of a new journal," Mrs Annesley explained.

He smiled at Mary, "If you do not mind, I must go to the book shop as well. Would you care to join me?"

She nodded, signing, "Thank you; yes."

Mrs Annesley said they would return shortly, then ushered her charge down the street towards the milliner's shop. Georgiana could not help but notice the smiles both given and received between her cousin and Miss Mary. Was there, perhaps, something there? Were they sweet on each other? She could not have that, so she would have to find a way to discourage them from forming such an attachment. Knowing Mary was to live at Pemberley, she knew she could take the time necessary to ensure the deaf girl knew that her place was not to ever marry. After all, who would truly love someone like her? The thought of her cousin being taken in by her made Georgiana's stomach churn in disgust. She would not allow such a union.

Fitz picked up the book Darcy sent him to find and walked over to where Mary was inspecting the journals. He tapped her arm and when she looked up, he asked "So, what do you think of Pemberley?"

"It is quite lovely." She turned the journal in her hand over, feeling the soft leather. Putting it down, she picked up another one and began to flip through the pages.

"So… Mr Bingley seems to have taken to signing," Fitz said, trying to see what her reaction to Bingley would be.

Mary chuckled a little, "He is trying, which is an admirable quality."

He was a little disheartened to hear such a compliment from her, but in all honesty, it was true. Bingley was an admirable chap, and if the two could make it work, he knew he would have to find a way to be happy for them.

Mary interrupted his thought when she put her hand on his arm to get his attention. When he looked up, she signed, "Which do you like best?"

Fitz looked at the two journals lying out on the table. One was quite ornate with its purple dyed leather and intricate scrollwork. He picked it up, impressed with the quality of the binding and of the pages within. He placed it back down and picked up the fawn colored one beside it. This one was more rugged looking without all the scrollwork punched into the leather, but it had a quality about it that he liked. He could see many a memory being written down within its pages.

He removed his glove and closed his eyes as he ran his hand over each book. When he opened his eyes again, Mary was looking oddly at him.

"Why did you do that?"

He smiled as he pulled his glove back on, "I have found I see things quite differently after meeting you, Miss Mary. I am drawn to things I would have never considered before, like the soft touch of the leather of this simple one compared to the stiffness of the more ornate one. Both are bound adequately as to ensure a quality product, and I know which I prefer, but the choice is up to you. Will you choose the warm and soft touch, like that of an old friend, or will you choose the flashy and vibrant one that also sits before you?"

Mary tilted her head slightly. She had a feeling what he was saying had more meaning than just the books laid out on the table. Without thinking twice about her decision, she picked up the fawn colored book, placing the purple one back with the others. "Have I chosen wisely Colonel?"

He smiled. "I believe you have, but truly it is only what fits you best that matters, is it not?"

They each made their purchases, then Fitz took the two brown paper wrapped packages and held out his arm to her.

Mary felt the joy of being at the side of someone who understood her so well and hardly saw the disapproving glances Miss Darcy gave her as they all returned to Pemberley in the carriage.

Fitz excused himself, citing his need to see that his horse was taken care of. He untied the reins from the back of the carriage and with a bow to the ladies, went to the stables.

He was surprised to find Miss Mary standing by the fence watching the horses in the field when he was through. He walked up beside her, tapping her shoulder. She turned, and he signed, "May I be of assistance?"

She smiled slightly, "You have my book, sir."

Looking down at the two books he still held in his hand, he chuckled, "So I do." He held it out to her.

"Thank you." She turned away and walked back towards the house, intent upon her first entry being about the two gentlemen who bewildered her more with each passing day. She smiled as she began to form the words in her head already that would later flow from her quill.

Sarah Johnson

Chapter 14

Elizabeth awoke on the morning of her wedding, the sun having barely risen over the horizon. She curled into the settee that looked out over Pemberley's lands, taking in the beauty of the view and the smells of summer as the wind gently blew in through the open window. She closed her eyes and wrapped her arms around her legs, basking in the beauty that surrounded her.

A gentle knock at the door brought her out of her reverie, and she had barely turned around when she saw Mary peek her head in the room. Motioning for her to come in, she scooted over so her sister could sit as well, drawing her arm around Mary's shoulders as their heads rested against each other. Elizabeth sighed aloud, but no words were spoken. The two needed the silence to engulf them, as today was a very big day in both of their lives.

Half an hour later Mrs Gardiner met a maid in the hall just outside her niece's room. Taking the flowers their host sent for his intended, soon to be his wife, she entered Elizabeth's room to see the sisters curled up by the window, both fast asleep. She smiled at the image they created. It was one any parents would have remembered all their days. She realized how much she thought of them as her own daughters. She had looked forward to this day for many years. Knowing the love Elizabeth and Mr Darcy held for each other made today bittersweet. Their nieces would forever leave their care, and though she was happy for them, she felt a pain of sadness at the emptiness in her own home.

She put the flowers on the table and went to wake her nieces with a motherly kiss to their cheeks, then preparations for the day began in earnest. The ladies were soon dressed, their hair coiffed, and their accessories on when Mr Gardiner came to knock on the door. Mary and her aunt left, saying they would see them at the church.

Mr Gardiner walked over to Elizabeth, placing a kiss upon her cheek. He stood back and took in the sight in front of him, smiling at her. "You are quite the lady, Elizabeth. I dare say Pemberley will be the better for having you as its mistress."

Elizabeth reached out for her uncle's hand, "Do you really think so, Uncle?"

"Truly; I have seen the determination and strength you possess, and now you are able to do much good for so many others." He squeezed her hand. "Come, it is time we go for our special ride."

"Oh, no, Uncle, I can walk. It is but a half of a mile to the church."

He shook his head, "Mr Darcy insisted we use the open carriage. He said it would not do to have you six inches deep in mud for such an important day. So ride we shall do, my dear."

Elizabeth laughed as she followed her uncle's lead down the stairs and outside to the waiting carriage. The ride to the church was short, and Elizabeth was glad for the quiet her Uncle gave her in those few moments before her life would forever change. When they arrived, she noticed a carpet set out for them to step down onto. She chuckled, "He is quite gallant, is he not?"

"That he is." Edward kissed her cheek one last time, took his place at her side and put his arm out. When she nodded he knocked on the doors to signal their arrival.

The large wooden doors opened and they stepped from the sunshine into the dark church. The stone façade made it a bit chilly, and when Elizabeth's eyes were finally able to focus in the dim conditions, she could see her intended staring at her. With a deep breath she took the first step towards her destiny.

Mary and Mr Bingley stood beside the couple as the vows were exchanged, then the register was signed signifying Elizabeth's change in status from orphaned daughter of a simple country gentleman to the wife of one of the *Haute Ton*'s most illustrious personages.

Mrs Annesley's appointment during the wedding and the celebration breakfast afterward was to curtail any plans Miss Darcy might have in disrupting the events of the day. It proved not to be an issue though. Georgiana was happy to socialize with the neighbors who were in attendance, and nothing unseemly was said to or about either of the Bennet sisters or their family.

This gave her the opportunity to observe the others in the wedding party. Miss Mary—*now Miss Bennet*—was often seen holding her youngest cousin at the side of either her aunt or the colonel. There was a spark in the eyes of both she and the colonel when they looked at each other, and Mrs Annesley thought there might be something more taking root between the two, but she would never venture to say such aloud. Perhaps she would see this friendship grow on their trip to the Peaks over the next few weeks.

Mr Bingley was quite the wonder to behold. He was a sociable gentleman by nature, and he amiably went from one group to the next until he had spoken with nearly every person in attendance. He paid attention to Miss Bennet for a few minutes, but there was no connection between the two like she saw with the other gentleman.

The revelers were soon gone, and before they knew it, it was time for them to leave as well. Everyone changed into their traveling clothes, the trunks were loaded onto the carriages, and they all gave their farewells to the newly wedded couple. Though there were some tears, most of the day would be remembered as one of happy memories being made and celebrating the family that was now threaded together by the joining of these two individuals.

Bingley traveled with the Gardiners for the first day, departing from their company the next morning. He was excited to find the estate he would settle into for at least the next year, possibly even longer if he liked the neighborhood.

Fitz found he could better handle his own rising feelings when they were not around Bingley. Between keeping a watch of his cousin, giving the necessary attention to the Gardiner children, especially Henry, and deepening his friendship with Miss Mary, he hardly noticed the days going by.

Fitz saw Mary standing away from the others as they looked over the sharp hills all around them. He walked over to her, quietly waiting before he finally asked, "You do not seem impressed with the landscape?"

She sighed, "As beautiful as this is, I much prefer flowers and gardens to the wild nature around us now."

"Yes, I can see that about you. I noticed yesterday that you did seem more interested when we visited Three Shire's Head. The waterfalls are splendid, are they not?"

"Yes they are." Before she even thought about what she was saying, she signed, "The sound of rushing water is one of the last sounds I heard before..."

The tension immediately grew. He faced her, his own words barely above a whisper as he finished her statement, "The last sound you heard just before your accident?"

She nodded her head then looked down at the ground.

Fitz gave her a minute alone and stepped over to speak with her uncle. "Mr Gardiner?"

"Yes?"

"I think Miss Mary—oh excuse me, *Miss Bennet*—is in need of a small respite. Perhaps I could accompany her down there to sit?" he pointed down the hill to a small outcrop of rocks upon which she could rest.

Mr Gardiner looked to his niece, seeing she looked a little out of sorts. "Yes, yes of course. We will not be long." When Fitz turned to walk away, he called out, "Oh, and Colonel?"

"Yes?" Fitz turned back.

"Amongst family, I doubt she will care if you depart from propriety for such a minor detail. *Miss Mary* will do."

He chuckled at the smile the colonel gave before he gave his thanks and turned away.

"What was that, Edward?" his wife asked.

"He knows not how far his heart has taken him."

She looked where her husband indicated, "Neither of them do."

"Indeed," He turned back around just in time to catch Henry's hand before his precocious son decided to roll down the large, rocky embankment.

Fitz put his arm out to her and Mary accepted his escort down the hill. Though Fitz was prepared to sit on the ground, when Mary moved over giving him enough room to share the rock, he could not resist the urge to be so close to her. When he pulled a small notebook and pencil from his pocket she looked at him in curious fascination. He wrote something and handed it to her. "I have wanted to ask you something for a while, but if you are not comfortable with the question, I will understand."

She could not help the swell in her heart when she realized he carried that notebook so they could communicate better. "I am well, sir–truly, I am. What would you like to know?" she answered back.

She tried to smile, but he could see it did not reach her eyes. He wrote again, handing her the notepad and watching as she read his question. "I was curious if you remember certain sounds, and if so, what?"

The corners of her mouth turned up just slightly more than before, and this time her eyes brightened as she wrote, "I remember the sound of birds chirping outside my window, and the voices of my family, especially Elizabeth's laugh."

"Yes, her laugh is... unique."

"Unique?" she chuckled, "That is one way to put it. My sister Jane always laughed with a little squeak to her voice, but Elizabeth was much louder."

"You have never mentioned your sister Jane before now."

"No, I do not talk of my family often." She sighed, then wrote back to him, "It is only recently that I have begun to focus more on the happy moments in my past and not just the tragic times. As my Aunt Philips used to say, *'think of the past only as its remembrances bring you pleasure'.*"

"When so much has happened against you in life, that is hard to remember," he offered.

"True, but as I have grown older I have realized just how important it is to the life I now live. Remembering the tragedy of the past only takes the joy out of today."

He smiled, "Yes it does. Still, you must have regrets? What is one thing you would like to hear again if you could?"

She took a deep breath, slowly letting it out. The moments she had told no one of—when she fell beneath the ice and when she saw her mother and youngest sister—came to her mind. "I have thought often of what it would be like to hear the voice of someone special–just to hear '*I love you*' *again* would be my greatest wish."

"Is there anyone in particular from whom you wish to hear such words?"

She felt her cheeks burning. "Just someone to love, whoever that may be."

"I thought you were determined to never marry?" he said with a smirk.

She was feeling a little uncomfortable with the direction of this conversation, but happy that her companion was such a dear friend. "Perhaps one day I will meet someone willing to do whatever it takes for me to hear those words."

"Yes, perhaps you will."

They sat in amiable silence for a few minutes more until the rest of their party joined them again, then they all continued on their walk.

"Mr Gardiner," Fitz said as the two men fell in step behind the others, "I thought perhaps tomorrow we could rent some mounts and ride to a local garden to spend the day. I know my cousin would enjoy the freedom of riding, and I believe your wife mentioned just last week how long it has been since she was able to enjoy a jaunt about on a horse. We could even have a picnic?" He pulled a brochure from his pocket and handed it to Mr Gardiner.

Edward looked over the list of local sites as he answered, "Yes that does sound excellent. Where is this garden?"

Fitz showed him on the map. It was within just two miles of the inn where they were staying, and they offered trails to ride or walk, as well as mounts and open carriages. They could easily have the inn prepare a basket for their picnic.

"Yes... yes, that does sound delightful–a break from the wild surroundings of the Peak District." He lowered his voice, leaning a little closer, "In all honesty, I much prefer gardens to these hills any day, but my wife has looked forward to visiting this area her entire life and I could not deny her the pleasure."

He chuckled, "I understand completely sir. My young cousin is enjoying herself as well, though she would never tell you herself."

"She is very quiet," he observed of Miss Darcy, who walked beside her companion.

"Yes, she is much like my Aunt Anne; sometimes a little too much so."

Remembering what Darcy told him of his parents, Edward knew exactly what the colonel meant. "I hope she will prove to be decent to my nieces, but if there is a problem I do not doubt you and your cousin will have it well in hand. Bringing up a child can be difficult, especially at some ages, but as my two nieces before you prove, it is well worth the challenge."

"Challenge is a good word for it. I know she is a good person, but sometimes I wonder if we will be able to change what sending her away to school has taught her," Fitz said.

"If not, then it is she who will miss out on the love she could have from two worthy individuals. Do not worry yourself because of that choice, sir–it is her decision to make. All you can do is set the stage for her to excel and see what she does, guiding her when she strays too far off course."

"I have a feeling she is on that path already, sir."

"I see things quite differently, Colonel. I see before me a young girl whose parents are no longer alive and who is struggling to find who she really is. You have provided a companion who is excellent in her advice, and my nieces will now be in her life as well. If there is anything they are good at, it is showing love to those who are in need of it, and your cousin certainly needs it. Things may be difficult for a while, but I dare say in a year, what you see before you will be quite a different image."

"I hope so; I truly do." Remembering why he had stepped back to speak with

Sarah Johnson

Mr Gardiner, he said, "So what do you think about tomorrow?"

"My wife just mentioned to me this morning that we have become too lax with the children's rest time in the middle of the day, so perhaps after a morning open carriage ride and a picnic, the children could return to the inn with their nurse and we can go for a ride. How does that sound to you?"

"It sounds perfectly acceptable to my tastes, sir, and I know my cousin will be amenable to such plans. Does Miss Mary enjoy riding as well?"

"My niece has not had the opportunity for several years, but I doubt she will have any trouble remembering what she knew. She used to be quite the enthusiast, but my brother insisted she moderate her ways after her accident."

"I am sure she will do well on the trails then," the colonel replied.

It turned out to be the perfect plan and everyone in their party enjoyed the day's events. Mary was able to learn a few tips from the colonel that would serve her well in the coming months, as well as give him a pleasant memory when they must part ways again.

The days passed slowly for some and quickly for others, but eventually Mary and Georgiana returned to Pemberley and the colonel and the Gardiners went back to London, leaving the now expanded Darcy family to settle into their new lives.

Mary's equestrian skills improved and she could often be found riding along the trails around Pemberley, though she avoided the paths Miss Darcy frequented. Mr Darcy insisted Mary take a servant with her, otherwise he put no restrictions on her activities. Her sister, on the other hand, insisted she not ride in such a manner as could cause injury. Although Mary would have preferred to be given the freedom to ride as she wished, she understood the sentiment and followed her sister's directives, thinking to herself how very much like their father Elizabeth was.

Elizabeth, after having spent the first few weeks alone with her husband, stepped into her role as mistress of the estate in every way she could when the others returned to Pemberley. It was sometimes overwhelming, but her husband was always there to lend a hand where he could. It was a month fully before she began to understand how Mrs Reynolds, the housekeeper, kept everything running so well for so many years.

Darcy was just starting to become comfortable with the new changes in life when he noticed his wife seemed to not be herself. She was more tired than usual, and he could tell she was losing weight. Feeling she needed to be relieved of some of the duties she performed, he talked with her about his concerns. He thought she might become agitated because of his suggestion, so it shocked him when she demurely agreed then went to her chambers for a well needed rest. He thought she must have been terribly ill to give in as she did, so the doctor was called to see to Mr Darcy's concerns about his wife.

It was with much joy the couple learned they were more than likely to have a baby join the family next spring. The doctor could not say for certain until she was further along, but all the signs pointed to the possibility. Darcy was happy for their lot, and the news helped quell his fears over his wife's health.

The general air of Pemberley and the surrounding area was ripe with anticipation for the future heir to come soon to the obviously besotted couple. Rumors of the doctor's frequent visits only added fuel to the stories talked about in the neighbor's sitting rooms, but for the first time in his life, Darcy did not mind being the subject of their gossip. He could clearly see the changes his wife was undergoing, and the thought of his child growing inside her thrilled him greatly.

Mary also saw the anxiety that came over Elizabeth in the weeks since their return. She was relieved when Elizabeth confided that she might be with child, and especially touched when Elizabeth told her they were keeping it a secret from all others. Mary was delighted at the prospect of becoming an aunt, and promised to not tax her sister too much. She spent her days exploring the house and grounds, avoiding Miss Darcy when she could, and becoming enchanted with the gardens, just as the colonel had insisted she would.

With the help of Mary's personal maid, Mabel, the staff at Pemberley were quickly learning what needs Mary had and how they could help her feel welcomed. The maid became a constant companion at times, explaining things to the other servants or communicating with Miss Mary on their behalf, and a routine was easily established that eased many a difficult situation.

The cook was happy to oblige their new mistress and her sister with providing Elizabeth's favorite dish with supper or Mary's favorite jam when scones were served, and Mrs Reynolds saw to it that the staff did not stare at the odd sight when Mary would sign to others around her. She herself even began to learn some signs. The sisters' devotion to each other was evident for all to see, and the staff were all happy to do anything they could for the two.

Georgiana was walking through the halls one morning when Mabel nearly ran into her, the sewing box she held spilling all over the floor. "Watch where you are going, you insolent girl!"

"I apologize, Miss," she bowed, then she placed Miss Mary's dress on a nearby chair and bent down to pick up the contents of her box.

Georgiana saw Mary's dress and walked over to it. Looking back to ensure the maid was not paying her any mind, she quietly ripped the ribbon on the hem and around one of the sleeves. Then without a second look she continued on to the sitting room.

Nothing was ever said to her, so she was not certain if the deed was even discovered. Then one day she noticed Elizabeth and Mary descending the stairs, and Mary wore the dress. The ribbon had been replaced and it looked none the worse for her actions.

Her brother walked up behind her and addressed his wife, "There you are. I wondered if you had returned from Lambton yet." He turned to Mary, "What a lovely dress."

"Yes, I have always told her this is my favorite," Elizabeth replied. "We just returned not even an hour ago and Mabel was able to replace the ribbon with this new one we found this morning. What do you think?"

"It is quite lovely. Do you not agree Georgiana?" He turned and stared at her with that look that told her she had not gotten away with anything.

She looked down at the floor and sullenly replied, "Yes, lovely. If you will excuse me, please, Mrs Annesley is waiting for me."

On another day Georgiana overheard Mrs Reynolds giving instructions to a maid. "Make sure you sharpen the pencils and put paper in all the rooms, as both the Master and Mistress want them easily available for Miss Mary."

She was incensed with the addition of such tasks to the servants' other duties. *Everyone has more work to do because of that awful girl!* Over the course of the next week, Georgiana managed to drop the pencils to the floor, break the pencil tips, and spill water on the paper in just about every room. She delighted in seeing Mary stooping to reach the pencils that had fallen under the table. *The floor is the right place for her kind!* Mary could feel Georgiana's harsh looks, but did

not dare say anything for want of causing undue stress to her already ill sister–
it was an accident, after all.

The next week while they were in Lambton for her weekly shopping trip,
Mrs Annesley insisted they stop at the stationer. When the clerk asked if he
could help them, she replied, "Yes, thank you. Miss Darcy wishes to purchase
the finest lot of paper you have in stock, and she will be paying for it to be
personalized with the initials *M.E.B.* as well. We wish to make this a very
special gift for someone, so no detail is to be overlooked."

"How delightful," he replied. "My sister has just made some scented waters if
you also wish to purchase one of those to sprinkle on the paper."

"Yes, that sounds just lovely."

"Right this way," he said as he led them over to the counter where several
sample bottles sat.

She picked them up and began to smell the contents. "Oh, this is my favorite,
what do you say, Miss Darcy?"

Georgiana leaned over and sniffed the water, then nodded. Mrs Annesley
handed it to the clerk, who went to fill the order.

Mrs Annesley leaned close to her charge and said quietly, "Do you think you
will have enough money left over to purchase that new bonnet you have had
your eye on, or shall we just go back home from here?"

Georgiana sighed. Nothing went unnoticed by the others. Not the nasty
remarks of Mary's unworthiness she made under her breath, nor the small
pranks she played, such as hiding the book Mary was reading or taking all her
pins so she had to wear her hair down one day until her maid could replace
them. Each time, her brother found a way to make her pay restitution for
the items, and she was beginning to think she would never have another new
bonnet the rest of her life. It was with this realization that she had no choice
but to end the mischief aimed at Mary Bennet. Her brother was besotted with
his bride, and they both expected courtesy and good manners from everyone.
In return, all the tenants and servants alike showed their love of the two sisters.

Georgiana was not happy, but her desire to stay at Pemberley and not be sent
to school was enough to keep her insolence in restraint after that. She rarely

interacted with anyone else unless her brother insisted, choosing instead to spend her days studying in her rooms, riding about Pemberley, or playing the pianoforte.

Unbeknownst to her, Mary loved to be in the room right next to the music room. She could feel the vibrations from the pianoforte through the closed door, and would sometimes spend hours standing there with her hand or her cheek pressed lightly against the wood. This was the closest she had come to hearing music since before her accident, and she relished the opportunities when they were presented to her.

It was with eager anticipation of the still uncertain future, and amidst the chaos of a perpetually sick wife, that Darcy received the expected letter from his friend Bingley. Upon opening it, he tried to decipher the writing, but it was nearly impossible. In Bingley's haste and excitement over the news he wanted to tell, he had jumbled and blotted the words to the point that Darcy could make no sense of what was written within.

Finally in exasperation he threw the missive down on his desk and went back to consoling his wife. He told her of the letter, and they talked of their upcoming visit to his estate, but Darcy could not tell where this estate was located or even what the name was. He promised his wife he would take care of the details, and with her condition not seeming to want to ease, she gratefully agreed to let him. Between Darcy and his steward, the letter was finally deciphered, or so they hoped. A letter was written in response and plans for their journey were decided upon and put into action.

Pemberley's Harvest Celebration was to be held two and a half months after the wedding. The particulars of this annual event were left to the mistress, and though she was not feeling her best, she did not want to disappoint the neighborhood. Mary helped where she could, as did her husband and surprisingly, even Georgiana offered her assistance, but the daunting task of overseeing each detail fell to Elizabeth alone. This kind of schedule made her already tired body even more depleted, and by the time the Harvest Celebration was completed she was more than ready for a much needed break. She did not look forward to the days of traveling in a rocking carriage, but to finally arrive at Mr Bingley's estate and be able to relax for two months sounded like heaven to Elizabeth.

October brought with it cooler weather, beautiful colors in nature all around, and the expectancy that comes with a long journey ahead. Mrs Annesley received word of her niece beginning her confinement and of the young lady's desire to have her there. So it was decided the family would travel to Mr Bingley's estate without the companion, and she would join them when they returned to London in a few months' time. They all gave their farewells and left Pemberley for their destinations.

The Darcys traveled slowly, stopping when the bumpy road became too much for Elizabeth. Georgiana did not care to ask why Elizabeth was so ill lately. Secretly, she hoped it was something that would take her out of their lives for good. Having a mother and cousin who were of poor constitution, and never having been exposed to an expectant lady, it did not occur to her that her sister—in—law could be with child. She greatly looked forward to arriving at their destination as Miss Bingley was to keep house for her brother, and she knew she could find someone with which to commiserate about the woes which befell her dreary life.

After four days of travel, they were finally to arrive at their destination today, and Mary looked forward to it tremendously. Elizabeth, exhausted from the journey, lay with her head nestled against her husband's shoulder, his arm wrapped around her to keep her from falling off the seat. Mary sat opposite them on the same bench with Georgiana, looking out the window for most of the ride.

It was when they entered a small merchant town that Mary became agitated. She recognized the streets. Closing her eyes and rubbing them slightly, she opened them again and looked out the window. Yes, she definitely recognized this town. She remembered often walking down this very road as she and her sisters went to visit their aunt and uncle. Her heart began to beat furiously and her palms began to sweat. She looked to the others in the carriage, but they did not seem to notice anything amiss. Did Mr Darcy not know where they were or what significance it held to her and her sister? How could he not?

Mary closed her eyes and hoped they were just passing through, but when they turned down an even more familiar road just outside of town she could no longer keep from looking out the window once again. They were far enough away to not see the details, but it was clear that the damage from the fire four years ago left no lasting mark on the place she had called home for fifteen years. She sat in stunned silence as the carriage ambled on down the road, to where, she did not know.

146

The knot in the pit of her stomach did not ease as they eventually turned towards the estate that bordered Longbourn. Did Mr Bingley lease Netherfield Park? *Surely fate could not be playing such a cruel joke on me right now,* she thought.

By the time they were stopped in front of the large edifice she did not even know what to think. After her accident the Bennet sisters were not allowed to wander about the area, so they had never actually seen Netherfield Park, but she could not say that now as it clearly stood right in front of her. She felt someone touch her elbow and mechanically let them lead her inside, not even realizing until they were at the front door that it was Mr Bingley, their host. She entered the front hall and the staff was there to take her bonnet and spencer. She saw Elizabeth groggily removing hers as well, then watched as she followed the housekeeper up the stairs. It was obvious to Mary that Elizabeth did not recognize where they were. Not knowing what to do, she followed the others and was soon shown to her room.

She sat heavily on the bed not even noticing the beautiful room around her until the maid finished unpacking her trunks then asked if she was needed for anything else. Mary changed out of her dusty traveling frock then dismissed the maid, telling her to please give her excuses as she was not feeling well and would not be down for supper. The maid left and a few minutes later returned with a tray of soup, but it sat untouched on the table as Mary curled up in the soft bed and went to sleep.

She hoped to wake up and realize this was all a dream, but somehow even as she slept she knew the inevitable would be realized when she opened her eyes once again. Nightmarish dreams plagued her all night, and she tossed and turned so much she woke up the next morning tangled in the bed linens. Unfortunately, she recognized the room as the one she was trying to forget when she went to sleep. Her gut wrenched and she barely made it to the chamber pot before she found herself sick with anxiety.

Sarah Johnson

Chapter 16

arcy," Bingley bowed to his friend when his guests walked into the dining room. "Mrs Darcy," he bowed again. "I pray you slept well?"

Darcy led his wife to a chair, pulling it out for her then taking the one beside her as he answered their host, "Thank you, we did."

Elizabeth poured two cups of tea, handing one to her husband as she received the plate with toast on it from him. She smiled at the knowledge that they were in such a routine that they could predict what each would do.

"If you or your sisters need anything, please let me know." He accepted the nod of thanks from Darcy, then continued his meal as he talked. "I was looking forward to joining the neighborhood at services this morning, but I did not want to leave my guests alone."

"Perhaps we can join you next week, Mr Bingley," Elizabeth replied.

"Capital, capital, I hope you can. I also hope you will join me on Tuesday evening. The neighborhood is to have an Assembly, and I have been assured there will be room for all my guests to attend."

Darcy looked at Elizabeth, his eyes quietly questioning her. When she smiled and gave a short nod, he turned back to their host, "We would be glad to join you."

Bingley's face lit up, "I always say there is nothing like a country dance."

Darcy smirked, "I used to regret your dragging me to every dance you could persuade me to attend, but with such an incentive as dancing with my wife," he reached for her hand, squeezing her fingers, "I do believe even I am looking forward to Tuesday."

"Perhaps one day I too will find someone to provide me incentive to improve myself in some way in which I am lacking," Bingley joked.

"I would be grateful if someone could help you improve upon your writing. You do not know what problems arose from trying to read the directions to this place. I was not even certain which shire it was in at one point."

"Well you seem to have found Netherfield despite my inadequacies," he replied with a smile.

Elizabeth's hands stopped halfway to her mouth with the tea cup. "Netherfield?" She put the now shaking tea cup back down.

"Yes, Netherfield Park," Bingley beamed as he looked around the well—appointed room. "Isn't it lovely? I have never had the pleasure of staying in Hertfordshire before, but I am finding the weather to be very pleasant indeed."

Darcy looked over and saw the color rush out of his wife's face. He picked up her hand, noticing it was cold. "Elizabeth? Are you well?"

She was dazed. "We must leave... I... I... we cannot stay here." She stood, rushing through the door. She nearly stumbled on the bottom stair, but her husband reached her side in time to save her from what could have been a disastrous fall.

"Elizabeth, what is the matter? Why must we leave?"

She tried to pull away, but his arms held firmly around her and she lacked the energy to fight him. He ushered her into a nearby empty room and closed the door, drawing her to his chest as she began to cry. It was several minutes before she was composed enough to pull away. Darcy led her to a seat and sat next to her, "Please tell me what is wrong?"

"Is it true? Are we in Hertfordshire... at Netherfield Park?" she asked, tears once again trying to overtake her eyes.

"Yes, of course we are. Did I not tell you where we were going?"

"I do not remember," she mumbled, looking down at her hands clutched together in her lap.

"What is it, my love," he said, barely above a whisper. "Please tell me?"

Elizabeth took a deep breath and slowly let it out, her eyes closed as she tried to find the right words. "Netherfield is... that is... we are but three miles from where I grew up."

Darcy felt as if he was punched in the gut. "You lived here? How can that be? Fate could not be so cruel," he said, trying to doubt what she said for the simple fact that the reality was so vividly harsh if it was true.

"It is true. My family lived at Longbourn, very near the town of Meryton in Hertfordshire, and Netherfield is but three miles away. The two estates share a border along Longbourn's west side," she explained.

Darcy was beginning to realize it was true and he reached over to draw his wife into his arms again, "We do not have to say if it is not your wish. We can be gone before midday and back in London before nightfall, and I know Bingley will not be offended if we tell him why we must depart."

Elizabeth sat quietly thinking for a few minutes before she finally said, "I think we should stay."

"Are you certain?"

"The past for me was not completely filled with sad memories, and if I run away those are all I will remember. I need to stay and focus on the happy memories here as well." She looked up into his eyes, a sweet smile appearing on her lips, "Also, I would love to show my husband where I grew up."

Darcy chuckled, "I would love to see whatever you are willing to show me."

They returned to their host and apologized, explaining the situation. When he said he would understand if they chose to leave, Elizabeth informed him it was not necessary. Elizabeth excused herself to check on her sister. Mary should have been up by now, and if her own reaction to finding out where they were was any indication to how her sister would react, then there was a good possibility she already knew.

Elizabeth did not hear any noises coming from inside Mary's room and when she opened the door she saw her sister curled up in the window seat hugging a pillow to her chest as she solemnly looked outside. She walked over and sat down, pulling Mary into an embrace, and they both began to cry.

The tears eventually ceased and the sisters sat there for a long time just quietly taking in the reality that faced them. Elizabeth finally signed to Mary, "When did you know?"

"I recognized the streets when we came through Meryton."

"And you did not tell me? *Oh, Mary—I am so very sorry.* You know you can tell me anything. Just because I am married now does not mean you must suffer in silence."

"I may be younger than you, but I am not a child anymore Elizabeth," Mary replied.

"You are correct, you are not, and in the past I have treated you as such at times. I apologize." She hugged her again, then pulled back to say, "I want to stay here at Netherfield for the time we were to visit Mr Bingley, but if you wish to return to Town, I will speak with Fitzwilliam."

"Honestly, I do not know what I want."

"Well, you are welcome to stay of course. Mr Bingley invited us to join him on Tuesday evening for the local Assembly, and I wish to go with Fitzwilliam, but you do not have to join us. If you just want to remain at Netherfield, then do not feel you must leave the grounds."

"Thank you. I do not wish to go to the Assembly, but I also do not wish to go to Town alone either."

"You could stay at Darcy House, or I am sure Uncle and Aunt would love to have you visit them?"

"No, I will stay here... for now at least," Mary replied.

"If you change your mind please let me know. Everything will be well—I just know it will." Elizabeth encouraged Mary to dress for the day saying the gardens awaited them. The sisters then spent the rest of the morning together talking of old memories, both happy and sad, and letting their words heal the hurts their hearts still felt so tenderly.

When everyone gathered that evening after supper, Miss Bingley and Mrs Hurst fawned over Georgiana's pianoforte skills, as they had been doing all day while she practiced. It was just the attention the girl wanted and she was finally happy to be in company with others who would appreciate her.

"Sir William Lucas," Bingley bowed to the neighbor who had invited him to the Assembly this evening.

"Mr Bingley—capital, capital! So glad you could make it tonight," he greeted them happily. "I see you have brought some guests with you."

"Yes, please allow me to introduce my brother and sisters—Mr and Mrs Hurst, and Miss Bingley." They each barely deigned to acknowledge the portly man in front of them. "My friend Mr Darcy and his wife will be joining us as well, but they were delayed. I am sure they will be along shortly."

"Welcome, we are glad to have you, and I will look forward to meeting your friend when he arrives as well. May I introduce you to my family?" he asked.

"Yes of course."

"Right this way, sir." Sir William led them through the revelers beginning to gather for the evening's entertainments. When they finally arrived near the fireplace, Sir William stood next to a congenial lady as he turned back to Bingley and stated, "May I present my wife, Lady Lucas, and our daughters, Mrs Collins and Miss Lucas." He indicated the three ladies. "Unfortunately my son—in—law was unable to be here tonight."

The younger of the two ladies sniggered behind the fan she used to hide her display, and Bingley could not help but wish to ask what led to such amusement. Her bright blue eyes sparkled when they met his, but at her sister's simple movement beside her the young lady comported her features once again and smiled at his. Bingley could not help the fascination he felt for her. There was something about her red hair and sparkling eyes that drew him to her lovely features.

Realizing he had yet to answer, he turned back to Sir William, "I will look forward to meeting him another time." He then introduced his own family that stood behind him. They barely disdained the acquaintance, then turned and wandered off. He was certain Hurst would find the port quickly and his sisters would stand along the edge of the dancers speaking only amongst themselves of the degradation of being in such a place for the remainder of the evening. He sighed audibly, thinking to himself, *it is a sad day indeed when one looks forward to having Darcy arrive to liven up the situation.* When he turned back, he noticed Miss Lucas looking oddly at him as if she was trying to puzzle something out. He decided he would have to find out what amused her so when he had the chance. "Miss Lucas, may I request the honour of partnering you for a turn–if you have anything available, that is?"

She gave him a simple nod and smiled, "Yes or course, sir."

After it was determined which set would be his, Sir William insisted on introducing him to the rest of the neighborhood, so he reluctantly took his leave of the young miss until the time came for their dance.

They were near the door when he saw the Darcys enter. "There you are–I was beginning to worry," he said to his friend. "Sir William Lucas, may I introduce you to my friend Mr Darcy, and his wife, Mrs Darcy."

The older man turned around and bowed, "Mr Darcy, it is indeed a pleasure to make your acquaintance, sir. And Mrs Darcy," he then lifted his eyes and recognized Elizabeth standing in front of him. The smile drained off his face as well as the color and he looked as if he would fall over. Then suddenly a flash of what appeared to be anger overtook his features and he replied harshly, "Excuse me," then turned away and was gone, with no excuse given for such treatment.

Elizabeth swallowed hard and looked down, "I should not have come."

"Everything will be well–he was just not expecting to see you on my arm," Darcy assured her. "Now, you promised me a dance, and I do not intend to leave until we have scandalized the neighborhood with three sets together."

Elizabeth smiled sweetly as her husband led them to the floor where everyone lined up and the dance began. She felt as if she was being watched, but it was not until about halfway through the first of the set that she realized the number of eyes focused on her. She started seeing whispers behind fans and some even turned away in a huff when she passed. She turned her attention back to her husband and tried to ignore the knot forming in her stomach.

When they were finished, Darcy led his wife back to Bingley and spoke with him for a few minutes. They walked around throughout the next set, Bingley speaking with all his new neighbors amiably while the Darcys just followed him. Elizabeth's place on the arm of such a prominent gentleman did not earn her any respect in this neighborhood though, and the shunning she received was enough to cause them to leave after just two sets into the evening.

Bingley was aware the situation was uncomfortable and agreed with his friend that it might be best if the Darcys returned to Netherfield Park. He thought it best that he stay with his sisters and brother at the Assembly in hopes of keeping the rumors at bay when his friend left. Miss Bingley questioned him about the Darcys returning early, but Bingley simply said Mrs Darcy was not feeling well, then before she could question him further, he excused himself to find the lovely young lady with whom he was to dance the next.

When he came upon Miss Lucas, he held out his arm, "I believe we have this set?"

She took it, smiling as she replied, "I have looked forward to it, sir."

Bingley leaned a little closer as he quietly asked, "I am curious what caused such amusement earlier when we were introduced, but I dare not ask such a thing of someone I hardly know."

She chuckled, explaining, "My brother—in—law, while a fine gentleman for my sisters needs, is not known for his dancing skills. I hope your own skills are not as lacking, sir."

They reached the line forming and he led her to her place, then turned facing her, "Your toes are safe with me." When he stepped back into position Bingley smiled at the simple honesty of this young lady before him.

Darcy knew his wife was upset over such treatment as she received this evening, but he did not know what he could do about it. He did not understand why they would treat her so. Later that night, when he and Elizabeth were cuddled in their bed, he urged her to talk with him about the subject that rarely came up — her past.

Elizabeth told of Mary's accident in detail, saying how the perception of her family changed at that time, but never to the point that she was shunned. Mary was certainly shunned by some, but others still accepted her in their society. Mr Bennet's own peculiarities kept him from society for the most part, so the sisters went to Meryton only when they were visiting their Aunt and Uncle Philips.

Finally Elizabeth reached the part of her story that had always been the hardest for her to speak about, but eventually the story unfolded of the night the rest of her family perished.

"Mary and I would sometimes sneak out on summer evenings and go swimming in the pond close to the house. My father knew of this and never said anything, but we continued to hide our activities from our other two sisters. Jane would never have given her consent at such a brazen act, and Kitty did not care much for outdoor activities. Mary and I bonded over times such as these and I would not trade them for the world."

Elizabeth shifted her body, curling more into her husband's arms as she continued. "One night, after our swim, we both returned home and changed into dry clothes. I was famished, so I told Mary I would sneak down to the kitchen where I hoped to find something left from supper. I had some bread and cold meat prepared on a tray and was on my way back to our room when I noticed a flickering light in the room that used to be my mother's chambers. Sometimes my father would go and sit in there. So I placed the tray on the floor and opened the door to tell him good night. I was shocked to find the room ablaze and my father just sitting in the chair asleep. I ran to him and tried to wake him, but he would not move."

Darcy felt her body stiffen and he pulled her a little closer, rubbing her back in small, soothing circles.

"I did what I could to drag him to the hallway, but I knew I could not get him down the stairs safely. I then went to get my sisters. Jane and Kitty shared the room right next to our mother's and when I reached it, it too was nearly consumed in flames. Again I pulled them into the hallway and then ran up the stairs to the nursery where Mary and I preferred to sleep."

"We both tried to help our family to safety, but Mary was having trouble breathing so I had to get her out. The only way she would leave was if I promised to go back in. The neighbors were arriving by the time we stumbled outside, and we told them where the others were. Three men volunteered to go in after them while a fourth took us to our Aunt Philips' house in Meryton." Elizabeth wiped at the tears now running down her cheeks. "None of those who volunteered to retrieve my family made it back out. When the fire was finally quelled all three of them, as well as the rest of my family, were found near the top of the stairs with a part of the ceiling collapsed on top of them."

Darcy did not know what to say about the tragedy itself. He could not imagine losing so many loved ones at one time, but he did not want her to focus on that for now so he decided to ask her about the neighbors. "You said your uncle and two others from the neighborhood went in to get them?"

"Yes, my Uncle Philips is who saw the smoke in the clear night air and alerted the residents of Meryton, who then converged upon Longbourn to do what they could to help. Sir William Lucas urged his eldest son not to go into the burning house, but he would not listen and led the charge to get my family out alive. Mr Goulding was one of my father's chess partners, so he felt a personal need to save them as well. My Uncle Philips only went in because with three trapped within he thought another was needed to retrieve them all safely. He was always wary of fires, but he faced his fear for our family–and he did not make it out."

"I can better understand Sir William Lucas' reaction this evening if the last time he saw you was the night he lost his eldest son." They lay in silence for a minute before he kissed her forehead, "Elizabeth, you did all you could to save them. You cannot blame yourself for what happened."

"I know, but what if we had not gone swimming that night? It was my suggestion–I had to beg Mary to go."

"If you had not gone swimming you would have been in bed and would not have seen the flames. You could have all perished in there that night, but your bravery saved Mary's life and your own. I am sure no one expected a girl hardly fully grown to be strong enough to carry three of your family members out on your own." He dried the tear streaks running down her cheeks and kissed her lips, "I am grateful you survived, otherwise I do not even want to imagine what my life would be like without you."

Sarah Johnson

Chapter 17

he next morning Elizabeth was up before the sun came over the horizon. She had tossed and turned all night long, dreams plaguing the few hours of sleep she did get. Not wanting to disturb her husband, she dressed warmly and went outside to take in the fresh, autumn air. Her feet carried her through the gardens and towards the farm lands that lay beyond. Before she knew it, the fence bordering Longbourn came into view. She stepped up onto the stile and crossed, sitting on the other side just as had so many times before. Although she was not allowed to go onto Netherfield's lands, she would often sit here and look out over Longbourn's fields, usually daydreaming of what life would have been like if her mother and baby sister had lived. She imagined such wonderful fantasies, but now that she was older and married she knew life would not have been as blissful as she imagined. Not wanting to worry her husband who would soon be up and looking for her, so she sighed heavily and stood to make her way back over the stile to Netherfield's side.

"Elizabeth?"

She turned at the familiar voice and smiled, "Charlotte! I did not expect to see anyone, especially here."

"I saw you last night but did not get to speak with you before you left," she explained, walking closer to the stile, but still keeping her distance.

"Yes, I was not feeling well so we did not stay long. I am sorry I did not see you."

Charlotte's face did not hold a smile and her hands trembled at her sides. "To tell you the truth, I did not wish to see you last night, so I avoided the room when I saw you within."

Elizabeth did not know what to say to such a confession, but she knew she had to know, so she finally asked, "Why? Why were you avoiding me?"

"My husband and my father are important members of this community and neither of them would have wished me to speak with you. I thought you might be out this morning so I purposely walked this way in hopes of seeing you."

Elizabeth rushed back down the steps and ran to her friend, pulling her into an embrace. Charlotte reciprocated and the two took much comfort in their lost friendship being restored. When they separated Elizabeth asked, "You are married?"

Charlotte smiled only a little, "Yes, I married Mr Collins three years ago."

"Mr Collins? *My cousin*, Mr Collins?"

"Yes, Mr William Collins. I do not know if you would have heard, but his father passed away just a few months after taking possession of Longbourn. My husband took over and I am now the mistress. We have one daughter and, as you can tell," she turned sideways showing off her protruding belly, "we are to have another child around Christmas."

Elizabeth smiled and reached for her friend's hand, squeezing her fingers in a loving manner, "I am so happy to hear Longbourn has someone like you. It has lacked in many ways for years because of not having a mistress, and my own father's penchant to avoid society did not make him the best of masters."

"My father said you are married as well?"

"Yes, I was married just three months ago to Mr Darcy. We live in Derbyshire, but Mr Bingley is a close friend of my husband's and we came to visit with him before we return to Town for Christmastime."

"Last night you looked very happy when you were dancing. Was that your husband?"

"Yes," she smiled. "He is a wonderful gentleman. You must come and meet him. Perhaps you can join me for tea later today? Mary is at Netherfield as well and I know she would love to see you."

"No," Charlotte shook her head, "I cannot go there. I am sorry, but I cannot be seen with you. It would not please my husband or my father, and I must not anger the neighborhood."

Elizabeth's face fell as she heard the pain in the words spoken. "Charlotte, in truth, we left last night because I was being shunned. What happened? Why am I being treated like this by the society in which I grew up?"

Tears welled in Charlotte's eyes, "Do you not remember that I lost my own brother that night–the dearest person in the world to me?"

"I lost my family as well so I know what it feels like to lose someone so close to you. It might help us both if we take comfort in the friendship we have had since we were young." Elizabeth again renewed her invitation, "Please come and visit me?"

"No, I cannot. I do not wish to ever see your sister again after what she did!"

"My sister? What has she to do with this?" Charlotte started to turn to walk away, but Elizabeth rushed forward, stopping her. "Talk to me–I do not understand."

Charlotte began to weep, her body trembling with the force of the emotions expended. Elizabeth led her over to the stile and helped her sit on the step, then waited patiently until Charlotte was composed again.

"Will you tell me now?"

"I am so sorry... I just cannot... I cannot face the person... who... who caused my... my brother's death."

"Caused your brother's death? Charlotte, whatever do you mean? Mary did not cause that fire," Elizabeth said in shock.

"But... but... everyone said she did. The whole neighborhood... it was discussed for... many months." Charlotte was beginning to cry again and could not stop herself.

Elizabeth pulled out her handkerchief and placed it in her friend's hand, "Mary did not set that fire. I do not know who would say such a thing, but I know she did not–she could not."

"I am certain you are wrong, Elizabeth." Charlotte replied. "Mrs Hill herself said... said that Mary was not... in her chambers when she checked on her that night."

Elizabeth closed her eyes as the realization came to her. She felt weak and leaned heavily on the stile. "Hill was right, she was not in her chambers that night–she was with me. We went swimming at the pond and returned late. I went down to the kitchens to get us something to eat and when I returned upstairs I saw the light coming from my mother's chamber. My father would often sit in there. When I opened the door to tell him good night the flames were engulfing the entire room." Her voice was shaky and it dropped to a near whisper as she continued, "I think it might have started because of the candle being set too close to the bed curtains."

Charlotte saw the anguish on her friend's face and placed her arm around her shoulders, "Oh Elizabeth, I am so very sorry. All these years I blamed Mary. The whole neighborhood blames her."

"I am sorry for anyone who has suffered because of the events of that night, but no one has lost more than my sister and I did. We would not have done anything to cause such grief in our own lives, or that of our friends. You must believe me, Charlotte."

"I do... I do believe you. Perhaps my telling the neighborhood what really happened will soften them to your presence here." She squeezed Elizabeth's hand, "I will do what I can, but I cannot promise anything. My father and Mrs Goulding are both very prominent in the sitting rooms of Meryton and they will not be won over easily by anyone, even me."

"Thank you for trying; that is all you can do."

Charlotte stood, "I... I am sorry, but I cannot visit you at Netherfield. I will try to walk out every Wednesday morning though if you wish to meet here again?"

Elizabeth smiled, "I will be here each Wednesday as the weather allows."

The two left, Charlotte to dress for morning calls to the neighbors and

Elizabeth to tell her husband about her early morning walk. He was just as heartbroken as she was to learn what the neighbors thought of Mary. They both agreed she did not need to know they were being shunned. Elizabeth doubted Mary would leave Netherfield anyway while they were here, so it was not as if someone would come here to purposely treat her badly. The neighbors would avoid Netherfield, and Mary would be none the wiser.

Darcy wrote to Fitz, telling him about their trip and how the visit was going so far. He told of Mary's seclusion to the estate but did not include the information Elizabeth found out this morning.

Later in the day, when Fitz received the letter, he decided he needed to visit Netherfield and be assured his family was well. Really it had more to do with Miss Mary than his cousin, but he was not willing to admit that just yet. He spoke with his commander about taking some time off and it was decided he would deliver some papers to Colonel Forster in Meryton, then he was free for three weeks.

Fitz left his commander's office with a lightness to his step–he would see Miss Mary again in just three days.

 "Oh, there you are Miss Bingley." Georgiana came into the drawing room. She sighed heavily as she sat primly on the edge of the seat nearby.

"Is there something the matter, Miss Darcy?" Caroline asked when she heard the woeful sighs coming from the girl.

"Oh, it is nothing, Miss Bingley. Please do not let me interrupt your activities."

She now set her embroidery aside, lifting the girl's hand in hers, "No, no. It is clear that something is amiss, and as the mistress for my brother I must know how to assist you."

She knew just how to manipulate Miss Bingley into getting exactly what she wanted. Sighing heavily once again, she replied, "My companion was unable to travel with us and my brother has been so busy with his wife that I hardly have the time to see him. I thought, if only I could go to the town nearby, perhaps I could find a small trinket or book he might like. However, it seems I am forever doomed to stay here within these walls as there is no one to go with me."

Even though Caroline could not stand the young girl in front of her, she put on airs nicely and replied, "Why, that is no great problem as my sister and I were curious to visit the local establishments as well. Perhaps you could accompany us?"

Georgiana drew her hand up in a semi—shocked way, her acting skills clearly on display still. "Oh, would you do that for me? Why, I must thank you, Miss Bingley. I never would have thought of such a scheme myself."

"It is no trouble–no trouble at all. Come, we shall find my sister and be off at once."

Mrs Hurst was found and soon the three ladies were transported to Meryton in Bingley's carriage. Miss Bingley was not impressed with the furriers and refused to stay any longer in such a place, so they quickly walked down the street to the next shop. The book shop was not large, but Georgiana did find something small to purchase for her brother. Even though that was not her intended reason for coming, she had to make it look as if it was. Her real destination was the milliner's, where the three went next. They found the shelves full of bonnets and hats that Georgiana longed to wear, but again Miss Bingley was not interested in staying there.

"Perhaps you can go to the other shops and come back for me?" Georgiana suggested.

"Yes, we can do that," Caroline said, looking at her sister.

Mrs Hurst was not completely at ease with this decision, but other than looking askance at her sister and jingling her bracelets, she did nothing. The two left the shop promising to be back in a quarter of an hour for the younger girl.

Georgiana was in a dream world–oh how she loved hats. The other accoutrements ladies of society accumulated–reticules, fans, handkerchiefs, vinaigrettes, and other such items–meant nothing to a wonderfully designed bonnet. She lovingly ran her fingers over the velvets and silks on each masterpiece. The colors of each were well thought out and Georgiana did not remember seeing such mastery of artistry even at some shops in Town.

She made her way around the shelves slowly, finally coming to the few bonnets on display in the window. The bright blue silk ties drew her attention and she lifted it to the light to see how it shone. Something caught her eye and she looked out the window towards several officers on the other side of the street. One with his back to her looked very familiar. His stance and the way he tilted his head ever so slightly — even the color of his hair and the manner in which it was pulled back and tied reminded her of someone. She would know him anywhere–*George Wickham.*

She drew her breath in when the man in uniform turned around. *Yes, it is George! What is he doing here, and in a uniform? He must have joined the Army.* She stepped closer to the window, hoping he would see her. He looked across the street in her direction, the twitch of his eyebrow, so familiar, making her heart beat wildly. She was sure he saw her as he always looked at her in that way in Ramsgate.

The jingle of a bell drew her attention and she looked to the door, seeing Miss Bingley and Mrs Hurst return to the store.

"Oh Miss Darcy, you would not believe the shops here–not one can match those on Bond Street, or even Cheapside," she cackled in that annoying laugh of hers.

"Oh? I am sorry you think so," she replied nonchalantly.

Caroline walked over and picked up the blue silk ribbon Georgiana had been admiring, flicking it out of her hand after looking at it for a few seconds. Her nose in the air and a general appearance of haughtiness on her face, she said, "I cannot think of anyone who would wear these colors. Come, there is nothing worth our time here in this shop."

Georgiana looked back out the window and noticed the group of soldiers was still standing there, but George was no longer with them.

As they walked to the carriage she looked all around, but he was nowhere to be seen. She kept watch out her window the whole way through the small town, but she did not see him again. She would have to investigate further.

The following day she talked Miss Bingley into returning to Meryton, hoping she would see George again. Just as she hoped, Miss Bingley was so distracted by the products that she did not pay much attention to the people congregating in the streets.

Georgiana saw George standing with some of the locals. She continued down the street next to Miss Bingley, and when they were close enough, she cleared her throat. He looked at her–oh how her heart soared when his piercing eyes met hers and that smile appeared on his lips. She fluttered her eyelashes when he tipped his hat to the two ladies. When they were finally to the milliner's shop once again, Georgiana asked if she could meet Miss Bingley at the tea shop in half an hour. She agreed and walked away, leaving the young girl, once again, on her own.

Georgiana walked down the street looking for him, but she did not see him. Just then she heard a noise and turned to look down the alley between two buildings. There he stood, his distinguished red uniform and polished buttons shining brightly. Her heart beat wildly as she rushed to him, following him further back from the street so they would not be seen.

"I did not expect to see you here in Meryton," he whispered very near to her ear.

"My brother's friend, Mr Bingley, has leased Netherfield and we are visiting him." She reached her hand up to cup his cheek as she smiled, "Oh George, I thought I would never see you again after my brother dragged me away from you on that terrible day in London!"

He drew her palm to his lips, kissing it several times before whispering, "My affection is not so fickle. If not for your brother, we would be married right now and I would not have needed to join the Army to find my way in this world."

"So you *have* joined?" She stepped back, keeping his hands in her own as she looked him over, "The uniform gives you a very illustrious look. I think I like it."

He lifted his eyebrow in a flirty manner, "I think I like that you are here. We must meet again–how long will you be in the neighborhood?"

"Our plans are to stay for two months then we will return to Town."

"Well then we must find some way to communicate." He thought for a minute, "Hmmm, Netherfield you say?" At her nod he continued, "I think I can get a note to you through a maid named Becky. I have seen her a few times... when the housekeeper sends her for supplies at the butcher. Do you know of her?"

"No, but I will find her."

"Good. When you know you will be visiting Meryton or out on a ride alone, let me know through her and I will meet you." He looked down the alley to ensure they were still not seen. Assured of their privacy, he drew her closely to himself and kissed her with all the passion he could garner.

Georgiana was so taken aback at his lips, once again, on hers that she closed her eyes to revel in the moment. When she opened them again, he was gone. She smiled and hugged her arms around herself, "He loves me–I just knew he did."

She slowly made her way back to the street and found the tea shop where she was to meet Miss Bingley. She was a little early, so she stood off to the side. Some local ladies entered and were talking about a scandal–something about a fire years ago. She did not pay much attention until she heard one lady say, "Say what you will, but that girl should have been put in an institution years ago. No matter what Mrs Collins claims, I know Mary Bennet set the fire that led to the deaths of six people, three of which were her own family."

The two ladies continued on as they looked at the items on the shelves. Georgiana could not believe what she had just heard–Mary Bennet! She immediately began trying to figure out how she could best use this information to hurt the Bennet sisters. *Oh but I cannot make it so obvious to Fitzwilliam. I do not wish to be sent away, and he has already threatened to do so. Miss Bingley... that is how I will pass this information along. I need only mention what I heard out of concern for our own safety as Mary Bennet is staying at Netherfield. She will inevitably choose the perfect time to tell the others. If there is anything in which Miss Bingley excels, it is being spiteful. She cannot pass up any gossip, and has no guilt in using what she can to her own best interest.*

Miss Bingley joined her and the two purchased some tea before they left. On the ride back to Netherfield, Georgiana told what she heard, saying how frightened she was to learn such news. The false shock and nearly present tears helped to garner Miss Bingley's support, and she said she would take care of the situation herself. Georgiana even went as far as to say it would not be necessary, but of course Miss Bingley insisted it was for the best. Georgiana was happy knowing she would have her revenge upon the Bennet sisters and it would not even be from her own mouth.

After questioning her maid, Georgiana was able to determine which maid was Becky, and with some subterfuge, she was able to speak with the girl, introducing herself as a friend of George Wickham's. Becky agreed to pass along any letters between the two, saying she would go to Meryton again tomorrow. Georgiana thanked her and said she would get a letter to her in time, then she went to her room to pour her feelings out in a missive that turned out to be five pages in length. She sealed it but did not use her own ring in the wax, then wrote on the outside, 'G. Wickham'. Placing it in her pocket, she made her way quietly down the stairs and found Becky again to deliver the note.

When she returned to her room it was time to dress for dinner. Tonight she would stay downstairs in the sitting room after the meal in hopes that Miss Bingley would decide to pass along the information she overheard in town today.

As it turned out, it was a perfectly boring evening, and Georgiana retired late, thinking about the love of her life, the man who held her heart in his wonderful hands—*George Wickham.*

Chapter 18

Elizabeth was again not feeling well when she awoke, but as was typical, within a few hours she was ready for some fresh air. Since her husband and Mr Bingley were fishing, she went in search of her sister to see if she wished to join her in the garden. Mary agreed to the need for some exercise and the two were on their way out when Miss Darcy and Miss Bingley came down the stairs laughing together about something.

"Oh, there you are," Elizabeth said to Georgiana. "I was looking for you just a few minutes ago."

"I was with Miss Bingley," she said, putting her nose in the air just a little more than usual.

Elizabeth noticed the gesture and thought she would need to speak with her husband about Miss Bingley's influence over Georgiana. "Well, my sister and I are going on a stroll through the garden and I just wanted to see if you wished to join us?"

Miss Bingley turned her face away, the look of disdain clear on her features as she huffed slightly, "I cannot even believe she is allowed to be in my brother's house–it is a disgrace, I tell you!"

Elizabeth immediately became defensive. "A disgrace? Just what is so disgraceful about my sister?"

Darcy and Bingley walked in the front door at that moment, shocked at seeing Miss Bingley and Mrs Darcy in what seemed to be a standoff, both standing straight and staring at each other with great determination in their eyes.

"What is it? You make such an accusation, yet you cannot tell me?" Elizabeth alleged.

Miss Bingley straightened her shoulders, standing a little taller, "Of course I know of what I speak. She does not deserve to be here. She does not even deserve to be in my good friend Miss Darcy's life at all. What kind of influence can she possibly provide for such a young and impressionable girl as this?" she drew her arm around Georgiana's shoulders. "Why, if my own sister had such a reputation I would have nothing to do with her."

"Caroline!" Bingley was shocked at what she pronounced.

Elizabeth felt her husband come up to stand beside her, but she was not about to let this go. "What do you mean? Just what sort of *reputation* are you implying my sister has?"

"Why, that of a murderer, of course. It is all over the neighborhood how she set the fire that killed her own family and several others who tried to help them."

"Caroline, THAT is ENOUGH! Go upstairs, NOW!" Bingley was furious as he turned to his friend, "I am so sorry, Darcy. I do not know what has gotten into her."

Mary stood frozen. Tears began to well up in her eyes. The next thing she knew her sister was right in front of her, trying to get her attention. She looked up to see what she would say.

"Oh, Mary–you know we do not blame you for that fire."

Mary noticed that, somehow, Elizabeth did not look shocked at this news. *Did she know of these rumors? No–surely if she had, she would have said something; but the look on her face suggests otherwise.* Mary had to know; she had to ask. She closed her eyes and swallowed hard, the lump in her throat growing larger with each second that passed. Finally she opened her eyes again and signed, "Did you know of this? Did you know this rumor and not tell me?"

"I just... that is... we thought it would be best if..."

Mary immediately signed, "I am not a child, Elizabeth! I do not need to be coddled." Before her sister could come up with a reply Mary turned away. "I need to be alone," she signed as she quickly left the house, running as she made her way through the garden and into the wood beyond.

Elizabeth started to follow after her, but Mary had run off so fast she did not see in which direction she went. She stood there in the middle of the doorway with a look of such distress on her face, and Darcy felt so helpless. "She cannot be left alone. What if... what if something happens to her?"

At that moment they heard a voice neither one expected, "Good day to you all." Fitz sauntered over to the group standing by the front door, and was just about to ask what they were looking at when Elizabeth broke out in tears, burying her face in her husband's chest despite the presence of others around them. "What did I say?"

"It is not you," Darcy replied. "Mary ran off."

He immediately became alarmed, "Which direction?"

"She ran through the garden, but we do not know where she went from there," Darcy replied, his hands holding his wife to him.

"I will go after her," Fitz said stoically. He walked over to Elizabeth and put his hand on her shoulder, "I will find her–I promise." He then looked up to Darcy, "Give me some time. If I need help I will signal you."

Darcy nodded.

Elizabeth drew her face up, her eyes pleading with Fitz, "Please tell her I am sorry. I am so very sorry," she burst into tears again.

"I am sure she knows already." With a nod of his head he ran off in the direction his cousin indicated.

He had been searching for nearly an hour when he stopped, frustration overwhelming him as he yelled her name knowing she could not hear him anyway. He heard the sound of a river not too far away. Hoping a drink of the cool water would help calm his nerves, he turned that direction. As he came out of the wood and looked towards the rushing sound of water he stopped immediately. There she was, perched on a rock, looking at the river below. Fitz did not want to frighten her, so he slowly walked up behind her. She did not turn around, so he took a step to stand beside her.

Mary saw movement beside her and looked over, surprised to see the colonel standing there. She tried to smile, but knew he was not fooled. "Why are you here?"

"I would ask the same of you," he replied.

"I just needed some time alone."

It was in that moment when she looked up at him with those eyes so full of sorrow that his heart broke for her and he realized just how much he wished to make her smile again. How much he wished to always make her smile. He knew it was not meant to be though, so he stepped back and leaned against a nearby tree as he gave her the space she needed.

Mary's heart pounded in her chest and she could hardly think of why she was even out here. Instead her thoughts turned to the muscular frame and compassionate eyes of the gentleman that stood just a few feet from her. *Why had he come to Netherfield?* She glanced over at him and felt her heart race even faster. He always looked so charming in his uniform, but what he wore today–a green coat and top hat–made him look even more dashing than usual. She could not help the small smile that came over her lips when he looked at her with those eyes that bore into her soul.

Her smile made his grow even more prominent, and he signed, "Do you want to talk now?"

She could not help the chuckle that came out as she nodded. She could not deny him anything. When that thought flitted through her head she immediately felt the truth of it in her heart–*yes, anything.* He could ask anything of her and she would do it for him. Her cheeks became pink at such a thought and she looked down at her own trembling hands held in her lap. She felt his presence beside her again and she moved over, happy that he chose to sit beside her on the rock.

The two sat like that for a long time, neither one saying anything, but both just absorbing their newfound feelings for the other. Finally Fitz reached over and tapped her arm, making her turn towards him. "Please tell me why you ran off?"

Mary closed her eyes and, for only the second time in their acquaintance, she opened her mouth and spoke to him, her voice cracking as she said, "Miss Bingley said the neighbors believe I set the fire that killed my family... that I am a..." she looked down to her hands as tears filled her eyes, the final word coming out only as a cracked whisper, "—*murderer.*"

He did not know what to say to such a preposterous notion, but it was the next sentence out of her mouth that made his heart truly breaks for her.

"Elizabeth knew. She knew and she did not tell me." She felt the tears cascading down her cheeks and within seconds she was shaking as the sobs escaped her. The next thing she knew the colonel's arms wrapped around her and pulled her into his chest. The world around them disappeared and all she could think of was the comfort she felt in his embrace as she cried as she had not done in years, the tears pouring from her eyes and soaking into his waistcoat.

Fitz could not stop the tears that fell from his own eyes as well, though they were silently brushed away with a quick flick of his hand. He wanted to take the pain away, to tell her he did not see her as others saw her. More than anything, he wished to always be the one she turned to in her time of need, but he knew he could not offer for her. His own situation, was not enough for even his own comfort, much less that of a family. As his arms held her to his chest his heart broke for the love he knew he held, yet could not speak of to anyone, including her.

When Mary finally calmed, Fitz pulled back and offered her his handkerchief. She chuckled slightly as her cheeks became scarlet from the embarrassment she now felt for such brazen actions. It took everything in him not to kiss her right then and there. Knowing they needed to leave, he stood and held out his hand to help her up. When their fingers met, his heartbeat raced even more, but he ignored the feelings welling up within him and drew her hand to his lips for a simple kiss. "Miss Mary, you are the strongest person I know. You have faced such tremendous obstacles in your life, and you have overcome them all. You do not need others to tell you who you are. You know what Miss Bingley said is not true, and those who truly know you are also aware it is not true. Do not let this neighborhood define you."

She nodded, quietly taking in all he said. When his hand took her elbow, she accepted his arm and walked silently back to the house next to him. They parted in the hallway and she thanked him, and then retired for the night saying she had a lot to think about and would not be down for the evening meal.

Fitz went in search of his cousin to let him know of Miss Mary's safe return. He found Darcy in the library. When they were both seated, a drink in hand and a cigar in each of their mouths, Fitz asked, "What happened?"

"She did not tell you?"

"She said very little when I found her," he replied.

"Bingley and I were not there for the whole conversation. We came home from fishing and entered to find my wife and Miss Bingley standing nearly toe to toe and battling it out with words. Miss Bingley said the neighbors believe Mary to be the one who started the fire, then Mary ran off."

He knew that was not all of it. "She said Elizabeth knew and did not tell her."

Darcy reached over to stamp out the cigar, knowing he could not enjoy it at this time. "Yes, we knew of the rumors."

"And you purposely kept this knowledge from her?"

"Yes we did," Darcy answered softly.

Fitz cursed under his breath and stood to pace the room, the cigar that had been in his mouth now lay in the pile of ashes along with his cousin's. "WHY? Why would you treat her like a child? She deserves to know what is going on around her!"

Darcy could see his agitation and knew it would be best if he stayed seated, though he too wished to pace. "I can only say we thought it for the best."

"You thought it for the best? Really? Well it did not work out so, now did it?"

He tapped his foot in agitation, "No, it did not. We were wrong."

Fitz knew something had to be done. "Who started these rumors? What has been done to keep them from spreading?"

Darcy sighed heavily, rubbing his eyes as he answered his cousin, "Elizabeth found out just a few days ago when she spoke to her friend, Mrs Collins. It appears to have been the belief from the beginning that Mary started the fire, but my wife informed her friend of what really happened that night. Mrs Collins promised to try her best to tell others, but she could not promise it would be accepted after all these years. It seems her talking about it has brought the rumors back into circulation. My sister and Miss Bingley heard some ladies talking of it the other day when they visited the shops in Meryton."

"Wait a minute," he stopped pacing and looked pointedly at his cousin. "Georgiana was allowed to go into town with only Miss Bingley as a companion?"

Darcy could take it no longer and he stood to pace the floor as well, "Yes, I gave her my permission when she asked, not think something like this would come of it."

"That... that... *harridan* is the last person Georgiana needs to be around right now," Fitz dropped heavily back into his chair.

"Yes, I see that now. I was a little distracted and did not see what harm it would do, and for that I am beating myself up–believe me," Darcy explained.

"Distracted? Distracted? WHAT could be so distracting that your sister's wellbeing has been all but forgotten?" Fitz now sat, but his posture as a commander was clear.

Darcy knew only the truth would be acceptable. "Elizabeth... she has not been well lately. She... that is... we are to have a child."

Fitz's shoulders relaxed and a smile came across his face, a dramatic change from just a second before. "She is with child? Truly?" At his cousin's nod he immediately stood and grasped his hand as he shook it and congratulated him. "I can now understand what would distract you so much from your sister."

Both men sat back down again and Darcy replied, "Bingley said he will ask Hurst if they will remove to Town with Miss Bingley on Monday. I hope they are willing to do so as I do not feel it is in the best interest of this rumor that we abandon the area so soon."

"No, I agree with you there. It would be best if we stay here for a few weeks at least. We must try to make them see the error in that blasted rumor, starting tomorrow at Sunday services." He shook his head in disgust, "Did she truly accuse Miss Mary of being a murderer?"

He nodded, "Yes she did."

Fitz cursed again, this time more loudly than he intended. "I am sorry, Darcy."

"I understand."

The two sat in silence for a few minutes until finally Fitz stood, "I think it is time I have a talk with Georgiana."

"We have already tried, but your help is more than welcome. She is in her room. I will take you there now." Darcy led Fitz up the stairs and to the door. "I will be just two doors down," he pointed to the correct door. "I need to see tell Elizabeth."

He nodded, "I will see you later."

Chapter 19

itz did not wait for the knock he gave to be answered, mostly because he knew his cousin well. When she did not wish to speak with someone she was apt to ignore their knocks. He instead opened the door and saw her sitting at the small desk by the window. He stepped in, closing the door and drawing her attention. "I think we need to talk."

Georgiana shuffled the papers quickly, hiding the letter she was writing to George beneath a blank sheet of paper. She hoped Fitz did not see anything. Trying to draw attention away from the letter, she stood and walked towards the fireplace to sit, lifting her hand to the other chair indicating she wished him to sit.

"Why Georgiana? Why did you do that to her?"

"I did not do anything. It was Miss Bingley who..."

He cut her off immediately, "Are you going to tell me you did not have a hand in that humiliating charade?"

She could not lie to him, so she just looked down at the hands neatly folded in her lap.

"What has happened to you? The last two years you have changed from the sweet child I once knew into someone I do not even recognize any longer. Why? Why are you doing this?" She did not offer any excuse so he continued to speak. "Does it make you feel better to humiliate Miss Mary like that?" When she did not make any attempt to even look up at him, he continued his plea, "Tell me, Georgiana–does it?"

"She deserves it!" Her eyes jolted up. Filled with fury, she continued, "She has taken my only family from me. Because of *her* I cannot even see my aunt and uncle any longer. *She and her sister* have pushed their way into my life and have taken over everything. My brother even offered to redecorate her rooms at Pemberley to whatever she chose. He has never done that for me! He will give her anything she wishes! She was not born into a family such as ours, and yet my brother has even given away part of the Darcy legacy to give her a dowry."

"What do you mean?"

"Oh, did he not tell you?" She gave him a look of superiority as she explained, "He gave her £20,000 and has signed over to her the whole property and earnings of *Rose Bluff*. It was listed in the marriage contract," she replied.

He felt the fury rising in his chest, but he could not give in to that now. He would confront Darcy later. For now, he had to deal with Georgiana. "And just how do you know these items were in the marriage contract? Somehow I doubt your brother discussed the details with you since he did not even mention them to *me*."

"I... well, you see, I was in his study, and the papers were..."

"You were there without his permission, and you read them. Is that it?"

"Yes... but it is not how it sounds," she tried to say.

He stood, "It is exactly how it sounds, Georgiana." He turned and walked to the door. With his hand on the handle he looked back to her, "If I have my way you will be sent to your Aunt Edith. We will see what your brother thinks, but believe me, whatever is decided, you will have no more freedom to hurt Miss Mary again. Of that I can guarantee."

Fitz immediately left the room, nearly slamming the door in his anger. He could not face Darcy right now, so he went downstairs to see if he could find Bingley. Locating the billiard room when he heard balls clicking together in that unmistakable sound, he entered, grateful to see that Bingley was alone. "I apologize for showing up so unexpectedly."

"Come in, come in. You know you are always welcome, as I told you at Pemberley. Will you be staying with us for a while?" Bingley handed him a cue stick and began placing the balls back in the correct formation on one end of the table.

"Yes, I have some time off and will be here for a few weeks." He leaned down, letting the anger he felt be expelled into the balls that scattered over the table. Unfortunately, none went into the pocket, so he stepped back for Bingley to take his turn.

"My sister and the Hursts will be leaving on Monday. I hope Miss Mary is well?"

"No harm came to her and I was finally able to locate her beside the river."

"I have informed my sister that she will apologize before they leave," Bingley replied as he took another shot and watched yet another ball roll into the pocket.

"Perhaps it would be best if she did not—unless it is coming from true intentions," Fitz offered. When Bingley's next turn did not result in a pocketed ball, he stepped up to try again.

"Yes, you are right. She is still leaving nonetheless, and I hope Miss Mary has not been too affected by Caroline's ill intentions."

"Only time will tell how hurtful her words truly were," Fitz said, taking the last shot and sinking the ball easily.

"Everything will be well, though, correct?" Bingley said, compassion evident in his features.

Fitz's heart wrenched. "Yes, I think so." He cleared his throat at he turned to reposition the balls again. "So, last time we spoke you were thinking of showing Miss Mary your attentions. How is that going?"

Bingley shrugged his shoulders, "After I left Pemberley I did not think much on her, so evidently my heart was just not in it. She is a pleasant young lady, but…"

He smiled at hearing what Bingley said, "I understand."

The two men played a few more games before it was time to change for supper. Miss Darcy and Miss Bingley did not come down to join them, so Fitz and Darcy were surprised to find both Elizabeth and Mary waiting with Bingley when they returned to the sitting room. The meal was expertly prepared, though it was not fully appreciated by those who ate it.

When they returned to the sitting room after the meal, Bingley asked, "Mrs Darcy, do you play the pianoforte?"

"Unfortunately I do not. I used to be able to pick my way through a simple piece, but I have not practiced in many years. I fear I would be a rather dull entertainment this evening."

Fitz looked over, "Darcy may want to string me up for saying so, but my Aunt Anne saw that we both played well enough to be considered accomplished."

Elizabeth smiled and turned to her husband, "Do tell, sir—I did not know you held such talent for the instrument?"

He smiled, "My cousin greatly exaggerates my abilities. He was a much better student than me, and I have not played in many years."

Bingley patted the colonel on the shoulder, "Well, it looks as if we must leave the entertainment up to you this evening."

Fitz looked to Mary, "Only if Miss Mary will turn the pages?"

She nodded and joined him on the other side of the room as he shuffled through the music sheets. When he found one he thought he could remember well enough, he sat down and stretched his fingers, then began. He indicated when to turn the page and Mary did it expertly as he made his way through the piece. At one point he saw her press her hand up against the top of the instrument and he wondered what she was doing. When he was through he bowed to the applause the others gave, then he turned back to Mary, asking, "Are you well?"

"Yes; please do not concern yourself on my account. I am stronger than some think me to be."

"Of that I do not doubt. I did not expect you to come down tonight though."

"I cannot hide away from my troubles. If I did, what life would I lead?"

"Very true. Will you join me in another song?"

She smiled, "Yes, of course. You played that masterfully."

He cocked his head and asked, "How could you tell?"

"My cousin is learning to play and I have found that if I place my hand as so," she put her hand lightly on the wood, "I can feel the movements of the piece."

"That is interesting. Can you tell when I hit a wrong note?"

She chuckled, "No, it is not as clear as hearing with my ears, but I do enjoy the experience as much as one in my situation can."

Fitz pulled another piece of music from the stack and replied, "I am constantly amazed at the world in which you live." Laying out the pages on the stand, he winked at her, "This one is much faster, so are you ready?" At her nod he began, enjoying the smile on her face as she once again placed her hand against the wood and *listened* to the piece in her own way.

When the music ended, Elizabeth insisted it was time they retire, so the two ladies left the gentlemen and went upstairs. They arrived at Mary's door and Elizabeth stepped inside with her, closing the door. Elizabeth reached out to embrace her sister, then when she released her, she signed, "I must apologize. You were right–I had no cause to keep such knowledge from you. I truly am sorry, Mary. You are all the family I have left, and I only meant to protect you, but I can see very clearly in front of me that you are fully grown and able to take care of yourself as well."

Mary signed, "I too must apologize for running away from you as I did. I am sure you were worried for my safety."

Elizabeth smiled, "We have both learned something from today, and that is what matters most. You know you can talk with me about anything, do you not? My being married now does not change that."

"I do know, but it is always good to hear anyway."

"While we are confessing our all to one another, there is one more thing that has been kept from you, and I cannot in good conscience continue to do so."

Mary was curious what could cause her sister the obvious distress she displayed, and she nodded in response then awaited whatever it could be.

"When my marriage contract was signed by our uncle, my husband insisted on you receiving a sizeable portion, so he has set aside £20,000 to be added to what our mother left us. He also did not wish to ever see you without a home, so he has also given you a property that is not necessary to the Darcy holdings. He says it is worth about £4,000 a year, and the proceeds from it have been transferred to our uncle until you are of age or choose to marry."

Mary was shocked with such news. She started to say something a few times, stammering out finally, "He is too generous…"

Elizabeth reached for Mary's shaking hands, "I do not want this news to frighten you. Fitzwilliam only wishes to see you properly cared for, and though it is a large amount, he insisted it be yours."

She took a deep breath, squared her shoulders, and said, "Will you thank him for me?"

"Yes, I will do just that. I am sorry we have kept it from you this long."

"I can understand why you did, but it means a lot that you have now told me. Thank you." She kissed her sister's cheek, "Good night Elizabeth."

"Good night," Elizabeth said, then left and she went to her own room to await her husband. When he entered a few minutes later she was already dressed for bed and was sitting at the mirror brushing out her hair. He took the brush from her and finished the job, then as she plaited her hair he changed into his nightshirt and they both climbed into bed.

Elizabeth lay with her head on her husband's chest, "Have you discussed with your cousin what should be done with your sister?"

Darcy's hand reached over and he began to caress his wife's slowly growing abdomen. "We could send her to stay with my Aunt Edith."

"Yes, that is always an option. It might be best at this time."

"I agree–you do not need this kind of stress. I will speak with Fitz tomorrow and write to my aunt."

"Will you tell Georgiana?"

"No, I think it best we keep this information from her until it is necessary. She will not be pleased with our decision."

"No, but she has not made this easy on you."

"I was not thinking of me," he pulled her closer and kissed her slowly, drawing her into the passion that slowly built between the two.

The following morning Elizabeth dressed and went to check on Mary. When she opened the door, she was surprised to see her sitting at her mirror, already dressed. Elizabeth walked up behind her and dismissed the maid, waiting until the girl closed the door before she signed to her sister, "Did you sleep well?"

"Adequately," she answered before she reached for her bonnet.

Elizabeth's hand reached over to stay Mary's, "You do not have to go."

Mary's voice cracked as she looked her sister in the eye and said, "Please, Elizabeth, do not treat me as a child. It is clear I cannot run away from this. I have never been known to miss Sunday services without good cause, and I intend to go this morning."

When Elizabeth released her hand, Mary placed the bonnet on her head and tied the ribbon into a bow. She then reached for her cloak, draping it over her arm as she turned to leave the room. "Are you coming as well, or will I face them on my own?"

Elizabeth could not help the feeling of dread that overtook her, but with a determination, she replied, "Of course I am going with you. I would never wish to leave you to face any situation alone."

The others were waiting for them in the front hall. Bingley informed them that Caroline had yet to awaken, and Mr and Mrs Hurst offered to stay behind with their sister. Miss Darcy did not wish to go either, but after her brother insisting and her cousin saying he would pick her up and take her to the carriage himself, in her nightgown no less, she acquiesced to their request to dress and be downstairs in time. She refused to look at Elizabeth and Mary as they joined the group.

Darcy walked over to the mirror where his wife was affixing her own bonnet on her head. He leaned close to her ear and whispered, "I take it she is determined to go?"

"Yes. Perhaps it is for the best."

"It might just be," he said, lifting her hand to deposit a kiss on the back of her fingers before she pulled her gloves on.

While the couple had a private moment, Fitz held out Mary's cloak, draping it over her shoulders. Stepping in front of her so she could see his lips, he said, "I am glad you have not changed your usual habits just because you are here."

"Thank you, Colonel," she replied.

He offered his arm to her, "Everything will work out—you will see. And if the day does not go as I hope, you still have my friendship."

"With you beside me, I know I can face the neighborhood today." She blushed when she realized just how such a statement could be taken, but he did not seem to mind.

They all walked out to the waiting carriage. Darcy was busy handing Georgiana in when Mary took the opportunity to sign to her sister, "I wish to visit our family's graves after the service."

Elizabeth closed her eyes and took a deep breath. She was not quite ready to face the headstones of her family that would confirm, for eternity, their absence from this life, but more importantly she would not let Mary face them alone. "We shall go together."

Mary gave a simple, heartfelt nod of appreciation, and then took the hand held out to help her into the carriage. The short ride was quiet. Georgiana sulked at being required to attend and the others readied themselves for what they knew would be a difficult situation of support for one of their own. When they arrived, the gentlemen helped the ladies down and Bingley stepped beside Miss Darcy to offer his arm so the much larger frame of the colonel could escort Miss Mary into the service. He knew just how intimidating the Army commander could look, and today might be just the day to utilize whatever means they had at their disposal.

Noticing his wife's agitated state, Darcy asked, "Elizabeth, are you well?"

She swallowed hard, then quietly said to her husband, "We wish to visit the headstones afterward."

"Are you certain?"

"No, but I will not let her stand there alone, and she is determined."

Remembering well the day he first went to visit where his own parents were laid to rest, he understood completely the gravity of such a decision. He gave her a simple nod, "Whatever is required of me, you need only ask."

She squeezed his fingers, "You are sweet to offer, but I doubt there is anything you could do that will make this any easier on either of us."

"Perhaps there is something," he said. "Give me just a moment." He walked over to the footman, speaking quietly with him, then, with a nod, went back to his wife's side.

"What was that about?"

"You may ask questions which I shall choose not to answer."

She chuckled, "My, aren't you being a tease today." Realizing his mission was to lighten the moment, she whispered, "Thank you."

"It is the least I can do." Then turning towards the group, he met Mary's eyes and asked, "Are you ready?" At her nod, he held out his arm to Elizabeth, "Then let us join the service."

A few people lingered outside, but most had already arrived and were finding their usual seats when the Netherfield Park group entered. Reverend Carter stood at the back door, his tenure of only two years as rector in the neighborhood making him completely unaware of who had just entered his church. He was happy to greet Mr Bingley and be introduced to the others of the Netherfield party. When the visitors walked away to find their seat, he turned to greet Mr and Mrs Collins as they came through the door, not giving any special notice to the silence that now permeated the room.

The bell tolled and Reverend Carter walked to the front. Facing the congregants, he asked them to all stand, opened his prayer book, and bowed his head to lead them in the opening prayer. When he was done, he motioned for the choir, who began the first song of the morning's service.

He noticed a congregant was becoming quite irate, wondering what the man meant when he leaned over to his wife and loudly pronounced, "I will not stay if *she* is to be admitted within this church!" The man then forcefully pulled his wife's arm, hurrying his family along behind them as they exited the building, slamming the door in their wake.

Not knowing what to say, the rector cleared his throat and motioned to his wife, whose lovely voice he looked forward to hearing every week from the choir, to begin their selection again. They were just about to start singing when a second congregant left the church as well. A third family was on their way out the door when he finally silenced the choir and looked over the ashen faces of everyone else still there. He noticed no one occupied the benches near the Netherfield Park party, and yet all their eyes were drawn to them.

Not knowing what to do, he addressed the local magistrate, "Sir William, if you would be so kind, please tell me what is going on here? Why are so many leaving this morning?"

Sir William Lucas' face filled with anger and his voice was gruff when he answered with vehemence, "*She* killed my son and several others in this neighborhood, including her own family, and you graciously accept her into your church? No sir, Reverend Carter—I will have no part of this service if she is to be included amongst your congregants!" He too turned to leave, urging his family to join him. When Mr Collins turned as well to follow his father—in—law out, he grabbed his wife's arm. Charlotte silently mouthed, "I am so sorry," as she passed Elizabeth and Mary on their way out of the church.

Reverend Carter was taken aback, but, trying to return reverence to the sacred service, he once again motioned for the choir to begin their selection of music.

Darcy reached for his wife's hand, squeezing it in silent support as they shared a hymnal. Fitz felt like storming out. How these people could spout Christian beliefs and yet treat someone as sweet as Mary as they did, he could never understand. A movement beside him made him look at Mary. She stood tall, her shoulders held high and a slight smile on the corners of her lips as she mouthed the words to the hymn being sung. She was the very image of strength and elegance in the midst of such turmoil. With a deep breath, he too squared his shoulders and joined the choir in praise.

Georgiana held her nose higher. This was just the kind of reaction she had hoped to see this morning. What she did not expect were the stares she too received from those who continued to leave. Many even shunned her as they walked by! She was shocked! How could they treat her so? In stunned silence she stood frozen beside her brother.

By the second song all the other congregants, save the party from Netherfield, had left. Even the choir members collected their instruments and music sheets and quietly walked out of the church. Mrs Carter refused to acknowledge such rudeness and instead continued to sing along with the few who were left. When the song was finished, Reverend Carter turned to his wife and reached out his hand to her, asking her to come to his side.

Bingley honestly did not know what to say. For once in his life, he was truly speechless. When the rector and his wife walked up to them, he was glad Darcy spoke, as he did not think he could have put three intelligent words together after such a spectacle.

"Sir, I must offer our apologies. We meant only to join you in worshipping this morning, not cause a great upset."

He led his wife over to the group, "No, it is I who must apologize for such a cold welcome from my parish. Be assured, if you desire my services while you are visiting our neighborhood I will gladly attend to you."

"We thank you, sir," Darcy said as he turned to lead his family down the aisle. He stopped at the door and turned back to the rector. "If you have time on the morrow, perhaps you could come by Netherfield?"

"I will do just that," Reverend Carter replied.

"If you do not mind," Darcy replied, "My wife and sister wish to pay their respects to their family before we leave."

"Yes, of course; take all the time you need," the reverend said, then he turned and followed his wife out of the church.

The group walked out through the large, wooden doors. The grey skies seemed to mirror the bleakness they each felt on this cold autumn day. Elizabeth linked arms with Mary and they made their way towards the headstone they knew well, that of their mother and sister. When they were younger, the sisters would all visit as often as they could, placing Mrs Bennet's favorite flowers there in remembrance. Returning today brought back a flood of emotions barely kept in check.

The others watched from a distance as the two leaned down to clear away the creeping buttercup and Herb Robert that had grown up around the single stone that marked the graves of both, then the sisters reached their fingers out to trace the familiar etchings in the limestone—*Frances Gardiner Bennet* and *Lydia Bennet*. Elizabeth also ran her finger over the carved angel her father insisted be put beside his daughter's name.

Darcy strode quickly back to the carriage, exchanging a coin with the footman who presented him with a bundle of freshly picked wild asters. Where he found them in such haste Darcy did not care. He divided the bundle in two and returned, walking past Bingley, Fitz, and Georgiana and on to the sisters. He gently placed a hand on Elizabeth's shoulder, and when she looked up at him he handed her one of the bundles. He then leaned down and kissed her on the forehead before giving the other bundle to Mary and returning to wait with the others. When Mary signed 'thank you' to him from afar, he gave her a simple nod of understanding.

Georgiana huffed at his actions and turned away, marching to the carriage to wait.

Bingley placed a hand on Darcy's arm to stay him. "I will wait with her. Your place is here." Then he went to stand beside the carriage door until the errand was completed.

After a moment in silence, Elizabeth and Mary placed flowers in front of the grave and moved to the next much larger headstone. Their Uncle Edward told them of the arched design, with columns on each side, that he had chosen when he came to make arrangements for his family members to be buried. Elizabeth remembered his description perfectly and she smiled slightly to know what she thought it would look like was a true representation. It was clear no one visited this headstone, as it, too, was covered in the same creeping buttercup and Herb Robert. They lovingly cleared the invasive plants away.

The first name to appear below their fingers was that of their father—*Thomas Bennet*. Mary stood with her hand on the hard, cold limestone, her eyes closed to the world around them until finally Elizabeth grasped her fingers. They looked at each other and, with a nod, both placed the blue flowers in front of his name and moved on to their sisters—*Jane Bennet* and *Catherine Bennet*. Elizabeth smiled at the angels etched between the two names. She remembered well her insistence to her uncle that the headstone have these figures, and that they match the one her father had placed beside Lydia's name.

Memories flooded their minds, quiet respect and sadness pervaded the beating hearts, and tears filled the eyes they thought could cry no more. Darcy and Fitz saw their distress and went to their sides immediately, offering a dry handkerchief and comforting each sister as they all shed tears for the lost loved ones in their lives.

Elizabeth and Mary thanked the cousins and, with a deep breath and a renewed strength, they stepped to the two nearby headstones bearing the names of their beloved uncle and aunt, *Henry Philips* and *Martha Gardiner Philips*. Once again they removed the weeds that had grown up all around, and lovingly placed some flowers there, then they turned to leave.

Mary saw, out of the corner of her eye, the name of Benjamin Lucas. She reached out to touch Elizabeth's arm, nodding towards it. With a determined sigh, Elizabeth joined Mary and they walked over to it. There were no weeds or vines growing around this headstone, and Elizabeth suspected the fresh flowers on the ground might have been placed there by Charlotte. They each added some of the wild asters to then, then found Mr Goulding's headstone, giving him the same respect due him for his ultimate service to their family.

With the task finally completed, Darcy and Fitz led the sisters back to the carriage where Georgiana sat with the corners of her mouth turned up at, hinting at the pleasure she took in Mary's pain. She glared at them in silent exuberance as the others took their seats. Bingley knocked on the roof with his walking stick, and the carriage jolted into action.

Georgiana said with a smirk, "It was such a lovely service this morning, was it not?"

Fitz turned to her with fury in his eyes, "That is enough! We will not hear one disparaging word from you or I will personally turn you over my knee and give you the whipping you deserve."

Her jaw dropped in shock and she turned to look at her brother.

"I will not stop him," Darcy said coldly, taking his wife's hand in his own.

She sniffed and crossed her arms over her chest as she sat back in the seat, refusing to look at anyone. When they arrived at Netherfield she exited the carriage and stomped up to her room, not to be seen again the rest of the day.

Mary disappeared into the garden, finding a bench at the back where she could sit alone to ponder the feelings coursing through her today. She had not been there five minutes when Fitz came upon her, sitting beside her without saying a word. Mary appreciated more than anything that he did not pressure her to talk; he just sat with her in silence.

The rest of the day passed slowly, the mood of the house being far from what any of them desired, but neither were they prepared to ignore the events of the morning's service and the memories evoked with the two sisters paying their respects to their family. It became very clear to Elizabeth that these people she had grown up with as neighbors would never accept Mary. She thought about whether they should continue here or go back to Town, but she was not certain which was best. One thing Elizabeth did know was that she would have to talk to her sister–she would have to let Mary be the one to decide whether they stayed or left. It was not easy to let her make such a decision, but it was what was necessary.

Chapter 20

itz was coming down the stairs when he saw the butler answer the door. He recognized the visitor as being the rector they met briefly yesterday at church, so he stepped up to greet him.

"Reverend Carter, I met you yesterday," he bowed. "I am Colonel Fitzwilliam."

"Yes; yes, of course," he handed his hat and coat to the waiting butler and bowed to the colonel. "I came to speak with Mr Darcy. Is he available?"

"He and Mr Bingley were just going over some estate business, but I doubt my cousin would mind the intrusion; right this way," he said as he turned to walk down the hall towards Bingley's study. When they entered, he said to the two men bent over a ledger at the desk, "We have a visitor, gentlemen."

Darcy looked up and, upon seeing the familiar face of the rector, he stood to greet him properly. Bingley stepped up beside him as well. Greetings were exchanged all around, pleasantries were expended with, and the men were soon seated and ready for the conversation they all knew was coming.

Darcy began. "I am very sorry for the disruption to your service yesterday."

"No, no–it was not your fault. I do not hold you, *or your family*," he said with great emphasis, "responsible for the neighborhood's false ideas espoused so easily yesterday."

"I am surprised to hear such words, considering you have not yet spoken with us about the events which led to such accusations of my sister," Darcy replied.

"It seems the sitting rooms have been abuzz with much talk this last week and I have been none the wiser. My wife, however, has heard quite a few tales and felt it best that I speak with Mrs Collins, so together we paid a call on her before I came here."

He nodded, "Then I am sure you have been informed quite accurately of the events which have transpired. Mrs Collins spoke with my wife just last week and has tried to do what she could to tell others of the true events of that tragic day, but I suppose she has not been very successful."

"No, I would say not. She was quite upset over yesterday's church service. My wife has agreed to assist in her quest to alter the general opinion of the neighborhood, so perhaps things will change soon."

Fitz spoke up, "I am surprised you have been here, what was it? Two years?" The rector nodded his head, and Fitz continued. "Two years–it is quite a length of time for you to not have heard these rumors before now."

"I was very lucky to have been chosen for such a position. As I am sure you are well aware, it is unusual to find such at my young age. The last rector died suddenly though, so I did not have the occasion to speak with him before I took over the parish. As you can well imagine, this event was put behind the town of Meryton for several years, and it is only your return which has caused it to become fodder for the sitting rooms once again," the rector answered. He then turned back to Darcy, "Truly, I apologize for how your family has been mistreated. I hope you will stay in Meryton for a while longer, but I would understand if you feel you must leave. My wife was quite taken aback with watching from afar as you visited the headstones of your family yesterday. Such a tragic tale. It has touched her so deeply she wished me to inform you of her personal vow to see to their upkeep in your absence. They will be properly cared for from now on. Any time you are passing through and wish to stop to pay your respects, please feel free to do so and to visit us for tea if you have the time."

That was almost too much for Darcy, and he choked out, "Your wife is all that is good." He cleared his throat and took a deep breath, then solemnly continued, "We appreciate all you have done. My wife has spoken with her sister, and Mary insists we stay—for now. I know she has enjoyed the country air and gardens while we are here."

"Perhaps the situation will be resolved soon. I hope so, at least," the rector replied, then he stood. "If we can do anything else to help, please do not hesitate in approaching me or my wife." He then took his leave of the cousins, following Bingley out of the study and back to the front of the house.

When Bingley returned he was surprised at the tension in the room. Darcy and Fitz sat in silence, the former going over the ledger once again and the latter just staring at him with an odd look on his face. It was almost as if he was irate, but Bingley could not think of a reason Fitz should be upset with Darcy. He shrugged it off and sat back down at the desk to finish the task at hand, not even noticing when Fitz left them alone just a few minutes later.

Rain fell that night and continued for several days. After two days of being inside with limited opportunities to do more than just pace the halls of Netherfield, Bingley suggested to Darcy and Fitz that they practice the new boxing techniques Fitz had recently learned.

The furniture in a small, unused sitting room were pushed out of the way, the carpet rolled up, and soon the three men were facing off against each other as Fitz showed the new moves. Half an hour had passed with the three alternating in rounds when Bingley was called upon to settle a dispute between two servants. He excused himself, leaving the two cousins alone.

Fitz had still not talked with Darcy about what Georgiana revealed to him regarding Mary's dowry, and the longer he let it eat at him the angrier he became. As the punches were thrown and the two cousins went round after round against each other, the tension built in the room. Darcy knew all too well the look in his cousin's eye, but he did not know from what it stemmed. He blocked jabs and defended himself, but the seasoned soldier was no match for him and he could soon taste blood in his mouth from one powerful swing.

"What is wrong?" Darcy said with a grunt as he threw a jab that was easily blocked.

"Wrong? Now *why* would anything be *wrong?*" Fitz answered through gritted teeth.

"You have been avoiding me, except in the company of others, for days now," Darcy continued to block the barrage coming at him. "What did I do?"

Fitz scoffed, "Oh, nothing of import, you just let your good sense fly right out of your head, and for what? So you can be seen as the savior of all once again? I can see the headline in the papers–*Fitzwilliam Darcy Saves the Day!*"

Now Darcy was completely confused. "What are you talking about?"

Fitz continued to throw hard punches, "Why did you... do that to her. You have set her up... to be taken advantage of... and I do not understand... your logic, Darcy."

He stepped back and threw his arms up, "WHAT exactly did I do?"

Fitz stepped forward again, each accusation he gave punctuated by another jab. "You gave her more money... than anyone of her status would have for a dowry. On top of that... you gave her *Rose Bluff*. WHY Darcy? Why did you do that to her? She does not deserve... to be hunted by the voracious wolves... of the *Haute Ton*,... *like my own brother,*... just because she now has the resources... they want so badly to attain... for themselves."

Darcy was shocked at his cousin's words, but he would not let him win this battle. "Her uncle and I came to the agreement easily, so what is it to you," he came at him with another jab.

"I do not want to see her hurt."

"So you are now her protector?"

"I did not say that..."

"What are you to her then?" He could feel the slight shift in their positions, so he threw a few more punches that finally put Fitz completely in the defensive. "Why does it matter to you? Does Mary not deserve to one day wed?"

"Of course she deserves it, but at what cost? How many fools will she be exposed to in your quest to marry her off?"

"That was not my intention," he grunted out. "I had to do it."

"WHY, Darcy? *WHY?*"

Darcy lunged forward, his words now coming with as much force as his fists. "If you care so much... then why not admit it to someone?... Admit that you care for her." Fitz stopped in his tracks, but Darcy's assault did not diminish. "Admit that you would marry her if not for your... *blasted* pride. The very same pride... that has kept you from... accepting *Rose Bluff* from me... years ago… as my father intended."

Fitz did not see the last two punches that came at his face, Darcy's left fist connecting with his lip while his right landed squarely on the side of his eye just a second later. A sharp pain assaulted him and he heard his cousin say through the haze, "I gave it to her because you would not allow me to give it to you directly. If you are unwilling to admit your own feelings, to yourself and to her, at least I know she will be provided for her entire life."

Darcy saw that his fists had connected, as well as his words, so he took a step back, breathing heavily from the exertion. "Fitz, you know I love you like a brother, but sometimes you can be the most impossibly stubborn person. I only hoped my gift would open your eyes to the possibilities life could hold for you."

Fitz looked at his cousin, his left eye starting to throb and swell already. He felt a trickle of blood at the right corner of his mouth and he swiped at it with the back of his hand. *He brings up a good point. Why? Why am I doing this to myself? Why am I doing this to her?* He stumbled backward until his sweaty back hit the wall, then he slid down to the floor. He held his head in his hands and finally allowed himself to admit his own heart's desire. "*I love her,*" he said, barely above a whisper.

Darcy walked over and bent down next to him, handing him a handkerchief for his lip. "I am glad to hear it, but really, she needs to be the one you tell, not me–*yet.*"

Fitz could not help the dazed look on his face as he stared at his cousin.

Darcy stood and walked over to the chair that held their shirts, tugging his own over his head and hastily pulling on his coat. He then threw Fitz his shirt and smiled, "Perhaps it would be best if you were dressed though."

Fitz could not help but laugh. "Thanks," he said as he stood and pulled the white lawn over his head, a smear of blood from his lip now evident on the front. He reached up to wipe at his cut lip with the handkerchief once again. "I mean it Darce—*thank you.*"

"For what?"

"For being *my brother* and not giving up on me."

Darcy walked over and patted him on the shoulder, "What are *cousins* for?" He reached out and embraced Fitz in a show of brotherly affection. "I guess you have someone with whom you need to speak now?"

Fitz wiped the blood now starting to dry on his lip, then hastily hung the cravat around his neck as he replied, "I am not like you. I refuse to ask for her hand in such a hasty manner. No, this will take some planning. Would you happen to know if there is a circulating library in Meryton?"

"Yes, Elizabeth has mentioned wanting to go, but we have not yet had the opportunity."

"Hopefully they will have just what I need. Thanks."

Darcy stopped with his hand on the doorknob, turning back to his cousin, "I am sorry for the bloody lip and black eye."

He shrugged his shoulders as if it were nothing, "I am certain Bingley can spare some raw meat, and I carry arnica liniment and witch hazel in my trunks for just such occasions as this."

"So you get into fights often then when you travel?"

"Often enough; it is the life of a soldier—although usually the liniment is for my opponent."

Darcy chuckled and left his cousin, heading upstairs to get cleaned up.

Fitz looked around the room. Somehow the rain outside no longer dimmed the views around him. The wallpaper shone a bright, sunshine yellow, whereas before he saw it more as a drab mustard color. He chuckled at himself—the room had not changed a bit, but he had.

With a lightened step, he went upstairs. He had the handkerchief pressed against his lip and was paying little attention where he was going when he rounded the corner and ran into Mary. Reaching for her elbow, he righted them both, then apologized.

She was shocked to see such a sight before her. The colonel stood there in only his stockings, breeches and shirtsleeves, his cravat hung loosely around his neck and his coat draped over his forearm. What shocked her the most was the bleeding lip and swelling eye. She reached up, her fingers barely touching his hot skin as she verbally said, "What happened? Was this because of *me?*" She was frightened he had been in a fight with one of the locals due to the events at church on Sunday.

"You?" He chuckled, "No… no, I can honestly say this was all on me."

"Who would do such a thing?" she said, shocked.

"My cousin. He thought I needed some sense knocked into me, and, now that it is done with, I could not agree more."

"Does it hurt?" she asked as she lightly caressed the swelling skin next to his eye. A movement further down the hall caught her attention and Mary realized she was touching the face of the gentleman in front of her. Her hand lowered gently to her side as her cheeks became bright pink.

Fitz replied, "Darcy and I grew up nearly as brothers, and sometimes a few punches are just what we need to set to right our solid friendship. Did you never fight with your sisters?"

Mary chuckled, "No, I cannot say we have ever had reason to cause harm to one another, though we have occasionally thrown a pillow or two at each other."

He smiled, wincing at the pain. He brought the handkerchief back to his lip, "Pillows would have been a gentler touch, but I doubt they would have had the impact I needed to find my resolve."

"Just what *have* you resolved to do, Colonel?"

As much as he wished to take her in his arms right there, he did not want this moment to turn into something more–he had plans for his proposal, and this was not it. So he looked down at his attire, shrugged his shoulders, and answered, "I have resolved to get cleaned up before I become fodder for the maid's room this evening. If you will excuse me," he bowed, then turned to continue on to his room as Mary watched on, confused with his answer. When he was gone, she continued on her way, trying to determine just what he could have meant.

Fitz found that, once his mind was made up, he quite enjoyed the presence of his dearest friend beside him even more. He hoped she accepted him easily, but if she did not he was determined to win her love in time.

The evening meal and entertainment was pleasant enough, though Georgiana excused herself as soon as she could. Something was going on with her cousin—Georgiana just knew it. He was acting so strangely this evening that she hardly recognized him. He walked into furniture—twice. Several times, when she tried to speak with him, he completely ignored her. Once he even walked away when she was in the middle of talking. She caught a few glances he gave to Miss Mary, and that worried her. He would never raise the expectations of a young lady without due cause, but tonight he was clearly flirting.

As she made her way up the stairs and down the hall to her chamber, she heard a small noise.

"Psssss…psssss"

With her candle in hand, she slowly made her way to the noise, surprised to see the maid Becky hiding next to a table. When she was close enough, the maid lifted her finger to her lips, indicating to Georgiana not to speak, then held out a letter. She took it and turned it over, recognizing the seal immediately. When she looked up again the maid had already disappeared, so she quietly went to her room, dismissing her own maid as soon as she was dressed for bed, then sat against the headboard of her bed, snuggled within her pillows and blanket, to read her missive.

> Dearest G.,
>
> I regret that I cannot put your name, for I dearly love to speak it, but I cannot risk this being found by someone other than you. The last letter I received from you was nearly found, so please be careful. Perhaps it would be best if you burn this letter and any others you may have in your possession as we cannot risk your brother finding out that I am so near you.

When your last letter arrived I was surprised at the length you had written, but after reading it I am no longer shocked at you, but at your brother. What a tale you have laid out for me of your life since we were last together in the spring. I cannot believe your brother would lower himself enough to marry a woman such as Miss Bennet, but it seems he is not above falling in love as well.

Unfortunately, love is not what is keeping us apart. It is the simple matter of my not being able to afford such a wonderful lady on my arm since your brother has cheated me out of so much of the inheritance I was due. I can well live without the money, but my heart aches at not having you beside me. If only I could be assured of having access to your money once we marry. Perhaps... no, I could never ask such a thing from you. Forget I even brought the subject up. If fate means us to marry then even your brother does not have the means to keep us apart.

I have been successful in finding a career for which I feel I was ideally formed, and that your brother can have no say in. I will continue to save every spare bit I can, and when you are of age and we are finally able to marry, we will have enough put back that we will not have to rely on your money.

Oh my dearest, I miss you tremendously. Do you think you will be able to sneak away into the woods one fine afternoon? If the weather and my commanding officer cooperate with such a plan, I will be waiting for you in the wood at the back of the gardens on Saturday. I hope to see you, and I promise more pleasurable pursuits than talk of us not being together and the financial strain your brother has caused me. Saturday–do not forget.

I am always yours,

G.

Georgiana closed her eyes and held the letter to her heart, a smile forming easily on her lips as she said his name silently in her head–*George!* It was as if they were meant to be together–George and Georgiana. She was convinced it was what her father wanted; after all, her father always told her that they were both named after him. If her father were still alive she knew he would not keep her from the love of her life. Somehow she would find out what George refused to ask of her–she would discover if her brother and cousin had changed the terms of her dowry. In her sneaky way, she once heard them discussing the possibility, but she had no particular knowledge if they decided to or not. She would find out, and she would assure George on Saturday that even without that money, no one could keep her from him.

She read through the letter once more before she folded the pages and carefully tucked them into her hiding place. She refused to burn such wonderful words! No one would find them in her trunk. Her brother was not even aware of George's presence nearby, and her maid had no reason to need it until they packed to leave, so for now she felt the letters were safe.

Georgiana yawned as she blew out the candle and climbed under her covers, going to sleep nearly the instant her head lay on the pillow. She dreamed of her brother walking her down the aisle of a church, happily kissing her cheek and giving her hand to George as they exchanged vows before the minister. It felt so real when he took her in his arms and kissed her so gently. She awoke to reality, but she would not give up her heart's desire. She *would* one day marry George Wickham.

Chapter 21

itz rose early, as usual, and stood at his window looking outside for a long time. For the first time in his life he knew what his future would hold—or at least, what he hoped it would hold. Even the uncertainty of the moment could not dampen his enthusiasm.

Sitting down at the writing table, he pulled out some paper and sharpened some quills, then laid them out in his usual fashion and uncorked the bottle of ink. He set about the task of writing to inform his commander of the decision to sell his commission. It took a few tries to get the wording right, and he was glad when he finally produced a legible copy to send on its way. When he pressed his ring into the red sealing wax he felt a great weight lift from his shoulders.

He and Darcy had several detailed conversations, and it was decided that even if Mary did not accept his offer immediately, Fitz would still resign his position. Darcy was insistent upon his staying with them until his situation was settled, especially with the great risk of Fitz being sent back to the continent in just a few short months.

Fitz placed the letter in his leather case along with the papers he was to deliver to Colonel Forster today. He called his man to help him dress. For the last time, he pulled the bright red uniform over his shirt sleeves, clasped the brass buttons, and looked in the mirror. Everything he saw in front of him would be no more after today. With a heavy sigh he picked up his leather case and hat, then descended the stairs and exited into the garden.

When he saw Mary sitting by herself on one of the nearby benches, he turned towards her. "Good morning," he signed when she looked up to see who approached.

She smiled broadly, "Good morning." She could not help but stare at him—especially in his uniform.

Fitz sat down beside her, placing his leather case on the bench between them, then said, "I hoped to see you this morning before I left. I have something of import to tell you."

"Oh? What is that, Colonel?"

"My cousin has finally persuaded me to do what I knew was right all along. I knew several months ago of the possibility of my going back to the continent early next year and, although I have enjoyed being a soldier, I cannot continue to put my own life in danger any longer. I have been on several campaigns already, and I know the risk I would take in going again. Darcy finally convinced me to sell my commission."

"You will no longer be in the Army? Where will you go?" She did not know what she thought of such news.

"Darcy insists I stay with them for now, and I am happy to oblige," Fitz said with a smile. "I have some plans which I hope will make my future very bright."

Mary could not help the relief she felt that he would not be going back to the Continent. "You will be staying then? You will not have to leave again?"

He reached his fingers just slightly towards her hand, stopping himself just short of such a breach of propriety. "No, I will not have to leave again." Mary closed her eyes and swallowed, trying to still her rushing heartbeat. When she opened her eyes again Fitz was watching her carefully. She gave a small smile, "I am glad."

"Are you?" he asked quietly. "You wish me to stay?"

202

"Yes."

He nodded and then stood, "I have one last bit of business, and I will be back later, but I wish to speak with you about something. Maybe we can take a walk when I return?"

"I would like that," she replied.

He stood and bowed, then left on his errand, happily whistling a tune as he rode to Meryton. His meeting with Colonel Forster was over with quickly and went better than expected. The man was a very competent commander and the two colonels talked for nearly an hour about the different campaigns they had been in over the years. Fitz was surprised they had not met before, given the many places and battles they had in common.

The local colonel had a personal messenger leaving with some mail bound for London today, and he was glad to offer his services in delivering Colonel Fitzwilliam's letter to his commanding officer. Even more good news for Fitz was that the colonel's nephew was in the Army and had served long enough to purchase the rank Fitz was looking to sell. Colonel Forster promised to send his nephew a note with the messenger, and was certain they would be able to meet within the week to work out the details.

With even more bounce to his step, Fitz now walked down the streets of Meryton. He had plenty of time to stop at the library and a few shops, as his horse needed a new shoe and was now at the blacksmith's shop.

He passed the milliners and saw a hat in the window that he was certain Georgiana would like. He would have to tell Darcy. Just as he was turning towards the library, he caught the back of a man who turned off the street. He was a soldier, dressed in the usual red uniform indicative of the militia that was quartered here. There was something oddly familiar about him though, and it made Fitz stop for just a minute. He could not remember where he had seen the man before, and with only a glance at his back he thought perhaps he was wrong.

He did not find what he needed in the library, but after searching the shelves at the book shop right next door, he was able to find a used copy of a book about flowers and their meanings–just what he needed. He purchased it and thanked the shop owner, then made his way back down to the blacksmith's.

As he waited for his horse's shoe to be finished, he stood with his back against the fence, one foot cocked up on the railing. He thumbed through the book, coming across a few entries that may be of use in his plight.

The sound of a young lady giggling across the street made him look up. Once again he saw the familiar soldier he had seen earlier. He was flirting with a young girl with bright red hair. As the soldier turned, Fitz recognized his profile immediately. *George Wickham!*

Not wanting to give away the fact that he was here, he turned and leaned over the book. The two paid him no mind and walked on down the street, Wickham continuing his flirtations to the eager young lady. When Fitz was alone again he went to check on his horse. Finding the task completed, he rode back to Netherfield to speak with his cousin immediately.

He quickly found Darcy and Elizabeth sitting in the library. "I hate to interrupt your privacy, but there is something of import which I must discuss with you," he said when he came in the room.

Elizabeth started to stand, "I will just leave you two alone then."

"Actually, I am certain your husband will want you to hear this as well," Fitz said. When she sat again, he closed the door and pulled another chair closer to the sofa on which they sat, whispering when he finally spoke. "I was in Meryton just a few minutes ago, and you will never guess who I saw in the middle of the street, flirting with the local young ladies."

Darcy knew his cousin would only speak so of one man. His face flushed in anger as he said through gritted teeth, "George Wickham!"

"I see you feel as I do about this information," He looked back at the door to ensure they were still alone. "Do you think Georgiana knows he is in the neighborhood?"

"How could she?" Darcy replied.

"Well, she did go to Meryton without us last week," Elizabeth said quietly.

Darcy sighed heavily, "Miss Bingley. *Oh God!* How many times will that one bad decision come back to haunt me?"

"Do not be so harsh on yourself, Darce. You know *she* is responsible for this mess, *not you.*"

Elizabeth reached for her husband's hand, squeezing his fingers lovingly. "Fitz is right–this is not your fault."

Darcy did not want to hear it right now, so instead he asked, "What do you think we should do? Question her?"

Elizabeth spoke up, "No, I am certain she will just lie to you if you ask her straight out."

"I agree with Elizabeth," Fitz said. "I think if she does know we may find evidence of it in her room." He turned to Elizabeth, "Could you distract her for an hour so we can search through her things? Perhaps a walk in the garden?"

"I doubt she would be willing to walk with me. Do you have any other ideas?"

"I think she can be persuaded," Fitz replied with a sly look. "Come," he stood, "I think it is time we have a few words with Georgiana." He led them all up the stairs and knocked loudly on his cousin's door. When she answered, shocked to see them, he said simply, "Georgiana, we have not seen you outside of your room lately, and we all feel it would do you good to take a long walk in the garden with Elizabeth."

"But, I was just about to…" she started to say.

He interrupted her with a stern look, "If I hear anything further it will be daily directive. Now change your shoes and be downstairs in five minutes."

She reluctantly turned and closed the door once again.

When he turned back to Darcy and Elizabeth he noticed the shocked looks on their faces. "What?"

"Do you think this will actually work?"

"There is only one way to find out–you have five minutes to prepare yourself and meet her in the hall, *Mrs Darcy.*"

Darcy turned to his wife and kissed her cheek, "Thank you."

Elizabeth slid her hand almost unperceptively across her slightly swollen abdomen as she took her leave of the gentlemen.

When Fitz turned back to Darcy he could not help but laugh at the smile on his besotted cousin's face. "You caught that little gesture?"

"Yes; I am surprised you did as well."

"If I did not already know your secret I doubt I would have noticed anything."

Darcy became solemn once more as he replied, "If I cannot even properly rear my sister, how will I ever be a suitable parent for my own child? This situation is showing me more and more just how unqualified for such a position I truly am."

Fitz leaned in closer to his cousin, lovingly patting his shoulder, "Do not place the blame on yourself–this is all Georgiana's fault. *All of it*–do you hear me?"

"I hear you, but I cannot say I agree."

"Well, for now, that answer will have to do. Come; we will hide around the corner until she leaves."

They hid from view until Georgiana went downstairs, then they quietly crept into the room, checking the dressing room for her maid. When they were certain they were alone, Darcy replied, "I will search in here and you search in there. What exactly are we looking for?"

Fitz began to turn over the papers on the desk, "Anything–a note or letter, perhaps a handkerchief, a button–anything that looks out of place amongst your sister's things."

"A button? Who would give a lady a button?"

"When I saw him he was wearing the uniform of the local militia. It is not unusual for soldiers to give a lady they are courting a button from their uniform."

"Oh–that makes more sense then. I wonder how he was able to enter the militia?"

Fitz shrugged, "Probably won it in a card game. He was always lucky in cards."

"Yes, unless he was drunk."

Fitz pulled a small trunk out from under the bed and pulled on the lid. "This is locked. Do you happen to have a key?"

"Yes, in my room. I will be right back." He left and quickly came back with a key, giving it to Fitz as he knelt down beside the trunk. When the lid was opened and they saw several letters in the otherwise empty trunk, he could hardly believe it. He reached for one and opened it, recognizing the scrawl immediately. "I think I am going to be sick," he quickly stood and went to the dressing room. The last time he had felt such dread was when he discovered Georgiana missing in Ramsgate.

Fitz followed Darcy, pouring some water in the basin and giving him a cool cloth, then he went back to gather the notes and lock the trunk again. He put them in his coat, then went to retrieve his cousin, taking him to his own room to recover and discuss what they found. The two pored over each letter, finding a few clues in them that led them to believe the two had been secretly writing since Ramsgate. One missive mentioned a maid named Becky and Darcy made note of it to follow up with Bingley.

By the time Elizabeth returned, Fitz had put the letters back in the trunk, and the two were awaiting her in the library once more. They told her what they found and the three of them were able to come up with a plan. Darcy wrote to his aunt, Edith Darcy, explaining the situation, and if all went well, Fitz would return to Town within the next week to deliver Georgiana to Mrs Darcy. They talked of a few contingencies in case they had to leave early.

When they were done, Darcy said he needed to speak with Bingley about the maid mentioned in the letter, so he excused himself.

Elizabeth was leaving the room when Fitz said, "Elizabeth, if you have a minute, I wish to speak with you?"

"Of course; what is it?"

"It is about your sister... Miss Mary." He felt his throat grow tighter, so he cleared it and continued. "I... that is... I know it is not usually done as such, but I wish to receive *your* approval to ask for her hand... in marriage."

"You are right, it is not usually asked of a sister, but I appreciate the sentiment. Let us sit and we can talk about this, shall we?"

Sarah Johnson

Chapter 22

Mary sat on the large swing that hung from a tree at the back of the gardens. She looked out over the fields beyond the gate, her mind wandering back to the words Fitz had used earlier when they spoke briefly. *'I have some plans which I hope will make my future very bright.'* Just what did he mean? What plans did he have, and more importantly, how did she feel about those plans possibly taking him from her again?

He is not here for me, she kept telling herself. He is only a friend. He does not wish to be more, and he deserves to have a wife one day. Perhaps one day soon. She could not help the sadness she felt when she thought of him being married to someone else.

Her toes barely reached to the ground, pushing the swing ever so gently in the cool autumn breeze. I must be happy for him, no matter what these plans are, she told herself. He wishes to speak with me when he returns, so for today I still have my friend.

Mary's thoughts continued and time slowly slipped by. She did not even realize how long she had been outside until she looked up and saw the light beginning to fade in the sky. She was just about to stand when she felt a presence behind her and a familiar hand come around her shoulder, presenting her with a small bundle. She chuckled at such a gift and reached up to take the flowers from him, bringing the bright pink ivy geraniums to her nose. She breathed in the fragrant sweetness and smiled. She was just about to turn around when she realized what other items the bundle held as well. The geraniums meant *'bridal favor'*, and they were surrounded by linden leaves, which stood for *'conjugal love'*. Tied around the bundle was a vine of ivy, meaning *'fidelity in marriage'*.

When what she held in her hand was realized, Fitz stepped around the swing. He reached for her empty hand as he dropped to one knee in front of her, drawing her hand to his lips and depositing a simple kiss there before releasing it again. He looked deep into her dark brown eyes and signed, "I have held you in a special place in my heart since my cousin told me of you before we even met. Then we became acquainted and that feeling quickly grew into a very special friendship. Being away from you the last few months has made me realize just how in love with you I am. I know such a path is truly frightening for you, and I understand all the obstacles in my way to such happiness, but I cannot go through life without you by my side. Please tell me you feel the same? Please marry me?" He then pulled out of his pocket plaited strands of straw, holding it out to her.

'Agreement'. Slowly her hand reached up, her fingers lightly running over the woven texture. She looked up into his bright blue eyes and could not help the tears that welled up in her own. "You love me?"

"How could I not?" He replied. "You are the most fascinating lady I have ever encountered. Your mixture of strength and vulnerability is ingrained into my heart, and I cannot go another day without you by my side." He lifted the plaited straw between them, "So will you agree to marry me?"

Mary reached out to take the strand from him, giving him a simple nod.

Fitz slowly reached both of his hands up, taking her face in them as he drew closer to her mouth. When their lips touched it felt like fire kindled between the two and he could not break the bond they now shared. He felt Mary's hands reach around his neck and her fingers tangle into his blonde hair as she pulled him closer ever so slightly. The kiss was slow and passionate, and when the need for air finally became too much for both of them, they separated. Fitz kept her face in his hands and rested his forehead against hers, looking deep into her eyes. No words were needed–her eyes told him how much she returned his love.

The gentle motion of the swing broke the moment and they realized their need to return inside before it became dark. Fitz stood and reached out his hand to her. When she took it and stood, he drew it to his lips, depositing a kiss before winding it around his arm and leading her through the garden and back inside. Fitz was excited to see the smile on Mary's face and the simple pleasure in her eyes. When they parted at the stairs, he eagerly went to find his cousin and inform him of the good news.

Mary nearly floated up the stairs to dress for the evening meal. She chose a simple white gown with a bright pink ribbon tied around her waist, the pink being repeated on her sleeves and on the hem of the dress. The ribbon matched so closely with the color of the geraniums the colonel had given her that she had asked her maid to weave a few of the flowers into her hair. The curls atop her head were encircled with a braid, and the geraniums woven within. Mary could not help but smile at the sentiment with which she had chosen such frivolous accoutrements tonight. *Will he notice?*

When her sister came into her room she was seated at the dressing table, the straw plait in her hand as her fingers ran across the surface. She looked up into the mirror when she felt her sister's familiar arms wrap around her.

"You look lovely," Elizabeth said. "He will be dazzled by your beauty."

Mary turned around, signing, "You know?"

"Yes, he approached me earlier today. He said he knew it was not usually done, but he felt he must ask for my approval before he would speak with you," Elizabeth signed. "When I saw you talking so easily with him that day in the park many months ago, I knew you two would find the love Fitzwilliam and I have found. I am so very happy for you!"

Mary pulled her sister into a tight embrace as tears flowed from the eyes of both. When she finally let go, she told Elizabeth the details of the proposal, showing her the flowers and telling of their meanings. By the time they heard the chime of the clock indicating they should go downstairs, both had shed many tears and spoken of the love neither one ever truly thought they would find.

Elizabeth inspected Mary's hair, affixing one geranium that had come loose. "He will love it."

Mary blushed, "I hope so."

"Of course he will," Elizabeth said with conviction. "Now come—we have two gentlemen awaiting us downstairs." The two stood and left the room, joining the men and Georgiana already in the drawing room.

Fitz was mesmerized when Mary walked in the room. She was glowing. He stood from his seat and walked over to her, taking her hand in his as he bowed and kissed the back of her fingers. He noticed the others were giving them a little privacy, and he grinned at his intended. When her cheeks became pink, he signed, "The rosiness of your cheeks and the flowers in your hair only add to the beauty you already possess."

Their moment was interrupted when Mrs Nichols entered, announcing that the meal was ready to be served. Fitz gladly led his lady to the dining room, sitting close to her in hopes of the small touches he wished to bestow upon her during the meal. He soon realized that her being left handed was a blessing indeed, as he was able to hold her right hand in his left under the table without anyone being the wiser—*or so he thought.* Nothing was unseen by Elizabeth, but she understood the need for such stolen caresses and would allow the breach in propriety for now.

The two were also observed closely by Georgiana, who had not yet been told the news of their engagement. By the end of the evening she was more furious than ever. She came to the conclusion that the two would marry, and she had a feeling her cousin was doing so just to acquire the piece of property she thought would one day be hers. As soon as the meal ended she excused herself from the company and retired for the night.

When she was dressed for bed and her maid dismissed, she pulled the trunk out from under her bed and opened it, reaching for the letter on the top. She opened it and read the first line, becoming a bit confused. *I thought this one was at the bottom?* She picked up the other letters, shuffling through the stack until she found the one she wanted, then put them away again, not giving another thought to her discovery.

She sat at the desk for the next hour penning a missive to George with several ideas of how she could sneak away to join him and they could finally be married. Then she sneaked down the back stairs to the place she would hide her letters for the maid to deliver them. She knew the maid's schedule would take her to Meryton tomorrow, and she hoped George would write her back soon, as she was becoming exasperated with being separated from the love of her life. Sneaking back to her room once again, she could not help but wish for George's arms around her.

She sat in her bed late into the night reading through the love letters she had collected from him over the last few months. Finally, exhaustion overtook her and she went to sleep, dreaming of a life she dearly wished she could have with her love.

When it came time for everyone to retire, Fitz asked Darcy and Elizabeth if they would mind him walking Mary to her room. Darcy, now in a position of power over his cousin, smirked as he answered, "I think that would be a decent idea. I am sure my wife wishes to walk Mary to her door as well, so we will make it a group effort."

Fitz rolled his eyes, but he knew he would get no time alone with Mary tonight so he put out his arm and smiled when she wrapped her hand around it. As an annoyance to his cousin, Fitz walked as slowly as he could.

Elizabeth held onto her husband's arm as they made their way up the stairs. Being more than a few paces behind the newly engaged couple, she knew she would not be heard if she whispered, so she leaned closer to her husband, "You know he will pay you back for such a stunt."

"Of course he will; I expect nothing less."

She chuckled, "As long as I do not have to pay for it as well."

Darcy stopped walking at the corner of the hallway, giving the couple ahead of them time at Mary's door alone. He turned to his wife and drew his arms around her expanding frame, his hands loving the soft form. "I know all too well what he wishes, and I have no problem giving my cousin time to woo his intended, but I take my job as her protector very seriously."

Elizabeth smiled, "Are you going to be this protective of our own daughter." Her hands wove around his neck as she played with the dark curls that lay there.

Darcy slowly lowered his face, their lips nearly touching, "I love it when you talk of *our children*."

"How many do you wish to have?"

Darcy pulled away just a little to peek around the corner, happy to see that his cousin was keeping to an appropriate distance. When he turned back to his wife, he smiled, "I always wished for a house full of children. I was a single child for 12 years, and Pemberley was very lonely. Even when Georgiana was born the house still seemed so empty since she was so much younger than me. Fitz's presence there when he was younger helped give us the bond we now possess, and I dearly wish that for my own family." He saw her thinking, so he quietly asked, "How many do you wish to have?"

"Well, as you know, I grew up in a much larger family, but it was always me and Mary alone in the world. My mother and youngest sister died when I was only five, and after that my father secluded himself in his study and left the rest of us to our own devices. I have always wondered what our family would have been like if such tragedy did not strike."

Darcy took her hands in his and rested them both on her abdomen, "Elizabeth, whether we have just this one child or a dozen, you and I are not our parents. If tragedy strikes our family... not that I want it to, but if it does, we will not react as our parents did by pushing our own children away. It is not who we are. We both know to live each day as it is given to us, and I expect our days, no matter the size of our family, to be filled with laughter and joy." He let go of her hands and drew his arms around her in a tight embrace, she resting her cheek on his chest.

When they felt it necessary to release each other, Elizabeth quietly replied, "Thank you Fitzwilliam. I cannot but agree with you about our household."

Darcy took a step backwards and brought both of her hands to his lips, depositing a kiss on the back of each, then smiled, "I think they have had enough time alone."

She chuckled, "Yes, quite so."

He wrapped his wife's hand around his arm once more as they rounded the corner and walked up to the couple.

Fitz saw them coming and drew his intended's hand to his lips giving a chaste kiss, though the look in his eye was anything but chaste. He then looked to his cousin, "Darcy, Miss Mary wishes to go for a ride tomorrow and I have offered my services in accompanying her, if that meets with your approval?"

"The weather today was quite nice," Elizabeth answered, "so perhaps it would be a good day for us to take a picnic and explore the trails around the area?"

Darcy looked to his wife, "Are you certain you wish to ride? I know you do not enjoy the activity."

Elizabeth just smiled broadly, "What I enjoy is being with my family, and I will be well enough riding, though we may have to take it slow."

Mary signed to her sister, "Only if you promise I can ride across one field at top speed?"

Elizabeth reached for Mary's hands, squeezing them, "I promise, as long as you promise not to get hurt."

Fitz chimed in, "I will, of course, offer my services in accompanying her across the field."

"Of course you will," Darcy replied. "Hmmmm..." he thought, "I am certain Bingley and Georgiana will agree to such a plan. Perhaps it will be a day of fun and celebration."

Fitz took Mary's hand once more, looking deep into her eyes, "Any day with Mary by my side is cause for celebration."

The gentlemen took their leave of the ladies. Elizabeth slipping into her sister's room with her, to speak for just a moment, before she too retired.

As they walked towards Fitz's room, Darcy asked, "Are you certain you wish to go off the property?"

"No, perhaps it would be best to stick to Netherfield's lands. With Bingley along it should be easy to determine just when we should turn back."

Darcy thought for a few seconds before he replied, "We will need to tell Georgiana of your plans soon."

"Not until after I speak with Mr Gardiner. I do not need this getting back to my parents before I go tell them myself."

Darcy nodded, "Yes, I can see how that could turn into a very harsh situation for you. If I can do anything…"

"I will let you know."

"Until tomorrow," then he took his leave and went to his own room to await his wife.

Sarah Johnson

Chapter 23

itz came bounding down the stairs with a light step, surprised to see Bingley in the hall. "Isn't it a bit early for you?"

Bingley drew his hand over his face as he sighed heavily, "Yes, but there was a matter I had to see to personally this morning. I tell you, Darcy is much better suited to being the master of an estate than I will ever be."

Fitz now stood beside him in the front hall. "Believe me, of that I know all too well. Nothing compares to the size of Pemberley."

Bingley's eyes grew larger, "Yes, Pemberley would certainly send me into apoplexy. Is it too early for you to join me in a drink?"

Fitz shrugged, "Does that offer come with a cigar as well?"

"Yes of course," Bingley smiled.

"Then lead the way, my good man, lead the way."

When the two were seated in Bingley's study, Bingley nursing a drink and Fitz puffing happily on his cigar, Fitz finally broke the silence. "So tell me, what is it that has you wishing for such strong spirits so early in the day?"

"I followed the maid this morning and found that she was, indeed, delivering a message to Wickham. Who it was from I know not, but I am sure you can easily guess who I think it is. So my day started with my having to dismiss the girl without reference and come up with a reason to give the housekeeper when I returned. With everything else going around the neighborhood, Darcy and I thought it best to keep this from even Mrs Nichols. She was not pleased with my decision, but she would never risk her own employment to say as such to me."

Fitz sighed heavily, "I am truly sorry for the upset my young cousin has caused to your household."

"As long as she is safe—that is all that matters."

"Well, for now she is. Hopefully within the week she will be on her way to the north with Mrs Darcy and Mrs Annesley, then we can be more easily assured of her safety."

Bingley stood and went to pour another drink from the sideboard, slowly sipping it. "What is it about that cad that draws ladies' interest? Do they not see that he is nothing but a rake?"

"I am sure you have heard the many rumors about my own brother over the years, and I have often wondered the same about him. Unfortunately, both he and Wickham were born with good looks and charming smiles, and the ladies do not see the deceptiveness of their schemes until it is too late. I know for my brother it is all about the conquest; the chase. Once he has his prize he no longer sees a need to continue and he breaks the poor lady's heart, leaving her to the contrition of society. Perhaps Georgiana has not yet seen this side of Wickham, but he is just the same as my brother. Neither can be trusted."

"Of that you are correct—neither can be trusted." Bingley drank down the last of the drink quickly.

Fitz walked over to the sideboard and removed the glass from Bingley's hand before he could pour another, then turned towards the door. "Let's get some food in your stomach before you regret how quickly you consumed that liquor."

Bingley nodded his thanks and the two removed to the dining room to break their fast.

Later that morning, Georgiana was looking everywhere for Becky, the maid, when Fitz found her.

"What are you doing, Georgie?"

"Oh, nothing of import... just... exploring," she stumbled through the words.

Fitz put his arm out to her with a smile, "Well, let me persuade you to go upstairs and change–we are to go riding!"

She tried to gracefully decline, "Oh, no, you should go without me."

"Nonsense! I know how much you enjoy the exercise." He then led her upstairs and promised to be back soon to escort her downstairs. Knowing Wickham's plan to meet with Georgiana in the back of the gardens, the gentlemen plotted a course that would keep them far from that area.

The afternoon was enjoyable for the group of six–just what they each needed. Mrs Nichols prided herself on the basket she had the cook prepare; cold meats and cheeses, boiled eggs, fruits and nuts, and everyone's favorite dessert–gingerbread. Cider from the recently harvested apples was the perfect complement to the foods provided.

When everyone had eaten their fill, they lounged on blankets laid over piles of crunchy, autumn leaves beneath the wide branches of a nearly bare tree and listened as Elizabeth and Darcy took turns reading a book of poems aloud, Elizabeth signing for her sister's benefit. Then the racing games began. Elizabeth was to be the judge, and she eagerly waved her handkerchief high over her head as the horses and their riders bounded across the fields. Mary was a quick study and with all the tips she had received from the colonel, as well as the hours she rode around Pemberley, she and Georgiana proved to be equally proficient in their equestrian skills. They each won one round against the other. When it came time for the gentlemen to race, it was no contest–Fitz was the fastest in each round. Darcy's own excellent skills had never matched the fervor of his cousin.

By the time the party arrived back at Netherfield they were all ready to retire early. After such a cold welcome last week, they would not try to disrupt the church services again this week. Though it was not what Mary truly wanted, she knew it was necessary to concede to reading her prayer book in her room until they returned to Town and she could once again join the congregants of their parish church.

Caroline Bingley was incensed at her brother for sending her back to Town, and at his guests for treating her as they had. Thanks to whatever Charles told their sister Louisa, even she had been ignoring much of what Caroline said since returning to London.

Caroline lounged on the fainting couch in her room, her feet covered with a light blanket and her fingers twirling a lock of her hair as she thought of what she could do to get back into their good graces. Nothing came to mind. *Absolutely nothing.*

The maid brought her tea and, as Caroline was pouring, she heard a knock at the door. "Enter," she called out, not surprised to see Louisa come into the room.

"Are you feeling well?" Louisa asked. "You have not been your usual self since we came back to Town."

Caroline sat up straighter and put a false smile onto her lips so as not to give anything away, "I am feeling fair, Louisa."

"May I join you then?"

"Yes, of course," she said as she began to pour her sister a cup of tea, adding milk just the way she liked it and giving it to her with practiced ease.

Louisa talked, but Caroline was not much in the mood for listening, so her mind wandered back to her previous thoughts. For years she held out hope that Mr Darcy would marry her, making her the mistress of one of England's finest estates, but that did not happen. Instead he chose to marry an orphan with no worthy connections. He and his cousin were taken with the Bennet sisters, that much was clear to see. Then there was Miss Darcy. The young girl was a schemer and Caroline knew all too well how much the girl manipulated those around her to get exactly what she wanted. Caroline knew she had been used by them all, and she could take the censure from her brother no longer. She was older than him, and yet he treated her as if she was not even of age yet.

As her mind continued to wander, she looked for ways she might bring pain to the lot of them. Still nothing came to mind.

". . . She said she could not believe the distress her family was under because of that rake! Can you just imagine, Caroline? It is good for us that our brother is not like so many others," Louisa said. "Caroline? Are you even listening to me?"

"What? What was that? Oh, yes, of course I was listening. Such a rake... yes, yes." She seemed distracted still, but Louisa went on to talk more while Caroline went back to thinking of how she could get back at the Bennet sisters for taking what was already claimed as hers.

Suddenly a thought came to her–*the Countess Danver!* She would never allow the marriage to continue if she knew what Caroline now knew of Mary Bennet. Mr Darcy would be forced by duty to his family to send his wife away, and then she could easily slip into her place to be paraded around on his arm once again. After all, he was her brother's best friend and they had been intimate acquaintances for many years.

Louisa drank the last of her tea as she continued talking, "... I told her we would call upon our return to Town, and today is her day to be in, so we can leave as soon as you are dressed."

"Pay a call? No, no, I have plans already, Louisa. I must pay a call of my own this afternoon, so I cannot join you."

Louisa stood, "If your plans cannot be changed, then I will give Miss Spencer your regrets in not being able to join me."

"I am sorry, but they are very firm–I cannot change them today," Caroline replied, standing as well.

"Then I will not keep you," Louisa said as she quit the room, leaving Caroline to dress.

The perfect dress was chosen, her hair was fashioned in the most pleasing array of curls, and soon Caroline was on her way to visit the countess. When she arrived she awaited the maid who accompanied her as the girl knocked on the door. Her card was given, and soon she found herself standing in the hall. She remembered the grandeur of the home from her last visit. She then followed the butler up the stairs to the sitting room where the grand lady sat.

"Miss Bingley to see you, madam," the butler said as he led the visitor into the room.

The countess looked at her for a long moment before she finally gave a small nod and the butler left the two ladies alone. "Miss Bingley I am not usually in the habit of accepting a call from someone I have only met twice in passing."

Caroline gave a low curtsey, "I do appreciate your seeing me, as I have news from your family. They are currently visiting my brother, and I just returned from his estate this week. There is something I thought you would be quite interested in knowing."

She again stared at the visitor for a long minute before standing and directing Miss Bingley to join her on the sofa. "I have but a few minutes, as I am expecting other callers today. What is it you wish to tell me?"

Caroline smiled at being asked to sit in such a grand house. Never before had she been accepted by someone of such rank. She smiled sweetly, and began, "My brother has leased an estate in Hertfordshire, and as I said, I have just this week returned from that country. Miss Darcy is such a lovely young lady and I am happy to say that we were often in company together while I was there."

"I am glad to hear my niece is doing so well."

"I am, however, displeased with some things I have heard of Mr Darcy's new wife and her family, and I knew such distressing news must be conveyed to your family immediately. It is very shocking indeed." She then went on to recount for the countess the rumors she had heard of Mary Bennet and the events which surrounded the death of her family.

The countess was indeed shocked, and she thanked Miss Bingley for bringing such news to her attention.

Caroline soon took her leave and made her way back through the house to leave. She was just descending the stairs when she heard someone address her.

"Miss Bingley? It is good to see you again."

She did not recognize the gentleman who spoke from the hallway below.

"Viscount Milton," he said as he bowed. "We danced at the Edgerton's ball last year. Obviously I did not make such a memorable impression upon you as your beauty did upon me, madam," he said in the most charming voice.

"Oh, yes, now I remember. It is a pleasure to see you again, my lord."

"You were calling on my mother?"

She looked up the stairs then back to him, "Yes, I had some news to convey to her."

He smiled, his captivatingly good looks clearly on display still as he replied, "I hope it is not that you are now engaged."

Caroline smiled sweetly, "No, not yet." She looked around them. Seeing no one else, she leaned over the railing of the stairs just a little closer to him as she whispered, "It had to do with your cousin, Miss Darcy, and my desire to see her taken care of properly."

He took the opportunity to step closer to the lady, her décolletage on perfect display from where he stood in the hall. He held out his hand, "Oh? Would you care to expound upon that statement?"

Caroline was flattered at such treatment, so she took his hand and let him lead her down the rest of the stairs and to a nearby room.

When the door was closed she started to tell him of the rumors, but he quickly stopped her by stepping closer and drawing his finger lightly down her cheek. "I must be truthful with you; I did not ask you in here to listen to such rumors. I leave the parlour gossip to my mother."

Caroline found herself slowly stepping back a few paces, soon realizing she stood between the viscount and the closed door. Her stomach churned in anticipation, but she did nothing to leave the room. Instead she just stood there, almost in a trance, as the viscount stepped even closer. She felt his fingers on her cheek once again and noticed him lean slightly closer when they both heard a noise in the hallway. They froze as the butler answered the door and led someone up the stairs, leaving the hall silent once again.

Milton's deep voice finally broke the stillness. "I hope the dance we shared in the past is not the only one with which I am to be graced? Are you to attend any functions while you are in Town?"

"We have been invited to the Beaumont's ball next week, but have not yet returned our answer."

He leaned just a little closer, "I will be there as well. Perhaps, if you are free, we could dance the first?"

"The first?" She was mesmerized by the moment. "Yes, of course; it is yours."

"And the supper dance?"

"You wish to dance with me twice?"

His voice became gruff even though he continued to whisper, "I wish much more than that, but it is all we are allowed in such company."

She smiled, "I will look forward to partnering you twice then."

He leaned in even more, slowly hovering over her as his lips drew so close to hers that she could feel his breath. Caroline closed her eyes and let him lightly pull her into his embrace as his lips finally touched hers. When he let go she was so spellbound by the feelings tumbling around inside her that she did not realize he had left the room.

She opened her eyes and lifted her hands to her cheeks, trying to cool their obvious redness. When she was finally composed, she peeked out into the hall and did not see anyone. Quietly making her way back to her carriage, she eagerly returned home and sent her answer to the Beaumont's invitation on its way, hoping Louisa would not mind her making such plans. When she retired that evening, all she could think of was the fascinating viscount and how much better suited he was for her than she ever thought his cousin Mr Darcy would be.

Early Monday morning brought news for both Darcy and Fitz. Aunt Edith sent a request to have Georgiana join her until the family returned to Pemberley for the winter. They would need to have Georgiana to her in Town by Wednesday as she was to leave early Thursday morning. After speaking with Fitz, Mary and Elizabeth about their thoughts, it was decided they would return to Town on Wednesday.

Fitz received a letter as well, his being from the soldier Colonel Forster knew who wished to purchase a commission. He proposed they meet any afternoon the colonel had available. A letter was sent in return saying he would be in Town by Wednesday and giving details of when and where they could meet.

Elizabeth wished for one more meeting with Charlotte before they left, so the Darcys' carriage pulled through Meryton several hours after Fitz had left on horseback. Charlotte was sad to see her friend go, but the two were determined to find a way to write to each other. With no mutual friend it would prove to be a challenge, but they each came up with several ideas they would try over the next few months, hoping one of them worked well enough to keep the knowledge of their letters from Charlotte's husband and family who did not approve of their continued friendship.

It was decided that Georgiana would not be told of her own trip to the north with Aunt Edith until Darcy delivered her to their aunt's house after they arrived in London. He would also divulge the two secrets being kept from her at that time—that of his own child expected to come in the spring, and of Fitz's marriage to Mary.

Georgiana seemed sullen on the trip back to Town, and Darcy had a feeling she knew he was aware of Wickham's presence nearby, but nothing was ever said, so he could not be certain.

When they arrived at Darcy House, Darcy helped Elizabeth and Mary down, then he climbed back into the carriage, addressing Georgiana firmly, "We are to visit Aunt Edith."

"Perhaps it would be best if we change from our traveling clothes first," she offered.

Darcy knocked on the top of the carriage, "There is no need; she expects us to arrive immediately upon our return to Town."

"Oh," was all she said before she turned to watch the activity outside the carriage as they made their way through the crowded London streets.

When they arrived and Darcy helped his sister down, Georgiana noticed her trunks were being taken from the carriage by the footmen. "What is going on, Fitzwilliam? Why are they removing my trunks here?"

He did not answer her. He only followed the butler into the house and through the familiar hallways in silence, stopping at his aunt's sitting room door. Aunt

Edith greeted them with a hug and invited them to sit. After tea was served, the housekeeper was dismissed and Darcy closed the door, ready for the storm he knew was to come next.

Georgiana was still confused as to why she was here. "Fitzwilliam? What are you not telling me?"

Darcy took a slow drink of his tea and turned his harsh gaze to his sister, "I believe it is *I* who should be asking such a question of *you*. What are *you* not telling me, Georgiana?"

She stumbled in her answer, "Me? What... what do you... mean?"

"I know Georgiana, so there is no need to put on an act. Because of you, Bingley had to let a maid go without reference. Because of you we have had to leave Meryton earlier than originally planned. Because of your continuing lies I can no longer trust you."

Aunt Edith spoke up, "I have agreed to take you home with me for the winter. Mrs Annesley will be joining us later today, and we will leave early tomorrow morning."

Georgiana jumped up, "NO! YOU CANNOT! I will NOT go with you!"

Darcy restrained her flailing arms easily and looked deeply into her eyes, "You have left me no choice, Georgiana. I have given you opportunity after opportunity to change the course of your life, but you continually choose to chase after a rake and a profligate who only wants your money."

"NO! HE LOVES ME!" She could not help the tears that welled in her eyes and ran down her cheeks.

Darcy felt her relax so he let go of her arms as his aunt stepped up to embrace her, "No, my dear, he does not love you. He loves money. Anything that will get him what he desires, he will use to his advantage. You deserve better than that in a husband."

"Aunt Edith is right, Georgie," Darcy quietly replied, his sister now shaking as tears wracked her body.

Edith turned to her nephew, "I will handle this; you go back to your wife and get settled from your trip."

226

"Are you certain? What about the other matters?"

She nodded and quietly said, "I will tell her. Your place is beside your wife."

Darcy kissed his aunt's cheek and left, his heart breaking at the sight of his sister in such distress. He did just as his aunt suggested and returned to Darcy House and his wife, drawing strength from her encouragement.

That evening all three of the inhabitants of the supper table were quietly eating their meal when Fitz arrived. He bounded in the room with a grin on his face, "You are now looking at a *former* Colonel in His Majesty's Army!"

The mood in the room improved immediately with congratulations given. Mary squealed when Fitz grabbed her up in his arms and swung her around in his excitement. Then, sitting her back on the floor, he told them all of his meeting.

Darcy and Elizabeth looked at each other, giving the couple a moment of privacy.

Fitz could not stop smiling. He then kissed her cheek and helped her sit again, taking the seat next to her. Mary could not help but laugh at his child—like exuberance.

Darcy offered a toast to his cousin's new status as a civilian, and the rest of the evening was spent in much better spirits than their afternoon had been.

The next day Fitz would call on Mr Gardiner to ask his permission to marry his niece, then Darcy and Fitz would both call on Lady Danver to apprise Fitz's parents of the news. Fitz thought he should do this alone, but Darcy would not hear of it. He insisted on going with his cousin. Even if he would not admit it to his cousin, Fitz did appreciate having Darcy's support.

Sarah Johnson

Chapter 24

After a fitful night of sleep, Fitz set out for Brunswick Square at the earliest appropriate hour. When he arrived at the Gardiner's residence he was informed that Mr Gardiner was at one of his warehouses, so he rode on to Cheapside to find him. He was impressed with the size as he followed an employee through the stacks of shipping crates and up the stairs that led to the office.

Fitz thanked the man and watched as he walked back down the stairs and continued on with his work. After taking a deep breath, Fitz knocked solidly on the door, entering when he was bid so by the familiar voice inside.

"Good morning, sir," he bowed.

Edward Gardiner stood and smiled, walking forward with his hand outstretched to shake his visitor's hand. "Colonel, it is a pleasure to see you today. Please have a seat." He indicated the chair beside the desk, ensuring Fitz was comfortable before sitting down himself. "I have not seen you in several months now."

"Yes sir; not since we traveled together through the Peaks after my cousin wed your niece. It is always nice to see you though."

"I know you are kept busy with your duties, and I am grateful you have taken the time to pay a call," Edward replied.

Fitz shifted in his seat, wishing he could stand to pace. "Actually, I am here on a matter of business."

"Oh? What business would bring a colonel to my door?"

He cleared his throat, "It is more on a personal basis, not as a colonel."

Edward thought he had a small idea of why the slightly younger man in front of him could be here, but if he were correct then he would not make this easy. "You have intrigued me, sir. Please continue."

Fitz's knee bounced in a nervous state as he began the speech he had practiced for days. "Mr Gardiner, it has been a great pleasure of mine to be intimately acquainted with your extended family since the spring. My cousin and your niece make a wonderful couple and I dare say they will one day make incredible parents."

Edward interrupted him, "Are you saying my niece is with child?"

"What?... Ummmm..." Fitz could feel the heat rising in his cheeks. "I did not mean to imply… I just meant... when they are ready to say..." He quit talking immediately. *Darcy is going to kill me for telling their news*, he thought to himself.

"Yes, of course." Edward tried not to chuckle at the obviously flustered man. "Perhaps it is time we talk with our niece."

His cheeks turned scarlet, then he took a breath and tried again with his own plight. "Sir, it has been my pleasure to know your family."

"Yes, you stated as such already."

Fitz nodded, trying to get back on track with his speech. "These past few months I have come to accept something I have chosen to ignore before now." He took a deep breath and quickly stated the rest. "I have come to ask for your niece Mary's hand."

Edward did not move. He was leaned back, his arms resting across his chest as he steepled his fingers in front of his lips. His demeanor gave away nothing of the joy he felt on the inside. He knew how cruel this would be, but he could not resist the opportunity to tease the clearly rattled colonel. "As far as I am aware, my niece has no desire to ever marry. She has stated such many times over the years, and I doubt a handsome face could convince her otherwise so quickly."

Fitz felt his throat swell. He could barely breathe. "Sir, I can assure you of her acceptance of my suit."

Edward sat forward, "Oh? When exactly have you seen my niece since we parted ways?"

"I have been visiting Bingley's estate for the last week and a half."

"And in a week and a half you have come to this arrangement?"

Fitz could hardly stay in his seat now, "Sir, I know you take great pleasure in this conversation, but I can honestly tell you if you continue on much longer without giving your consent I very well might need a bucket."

Edward could not help the laugh that escaped his lips. He leaned forward and patted the younger man's shoulder, "All right, I will stop teasing you and give you my answer. I have seen you both with that look in your eye, and I am happy to see you have finally come to your senses. If she will have you, then you have my permission to marry my niece."

Fitz jumped up, eagerly shaking the man's hand as he thanked him for his time. Mr Gardiner pulled out two cigars, offering one to Fitz. The men talked for another half an hour, Fitz telling Mr Gardiner of selling his commission easily and his new status in society. When the time came for him to take his leave, he promised to pass on a request for the residents of Darcy House to visit Brunswick Square for supper on Saturday evening.

As Fitz rode through the streets of London, slowly making his way back to the Mayfair district where Darcy House was located, he could not help but smile at all he passed. He chuckled at two little girls in a park who were in a squabble over a doll, their nursemaid stepping in to quell the fighting. One couple nearby tried to hide their amorous embrace behind some bushes, and he could not help but think of Mary and his desire to do just that with her. The crisp autumn air filled his chest, invigorating him on his excursion. The only thing that could take the joy of the moment from him was the knowledge that he and Darcy would be visiting his mother this afternoon to apprise her of his recent decision to sell his commission and marry someone of whom his parents would never approve.

Fitz and Darcy stood before the door to the Earl and Countess Danver's house. Fitz could not stand still and continually fussed with his waistcoat, "I would be more comfortable telling my parents of selling my commission and my plan to marry if I were in my uniform, but instead I have to be in this blasted coat and cravat." He pulled at the tight material around his neck.

"Whether you are in your uniform or not, you are still the same man with the same authority over his future. Do not forget that," Darcy encouraged.

The butler answered the door and led them to the sitting room where the countess was receiving callers this afternoon. She stood as they were announced.

"I did not know you were back in Town, Darcy," the countess replied, giving him a kiss on his cheek. She then turned to her youngest son, "And you! I know not why you have kept yourself away for so long. I pray your duties have not been too taxing of late?"

"I have been kept rather busy," Fitz replied, sitting beside Darcy where his mother indicated.

The countess took her own seat looking like the queen herself receiving visitors to her court. They exchanged pleasantries usual to the sitting rooms all around London as they waited for their hostess to complete her preparation of the tea. She finally poured it for the two cousins, handing them each a cup. Fitz was just clearing his throat to begin when another visitor was announced. They all stood as Lady Beaumont, Lady Danver's dearest friend, was announced. Greetings were exchanged and they were soon seated again, Lady Beaumont, as was her usual way, taking over the conversation.

"I am surprised to see you, Mr Darcy. I was unaware of your return to Town."

"We arrived just yesterday, my lady," he answered.

"Yesterday! My," she looked at her friend, "you have not wasted any time in paying your dear aunt a call then. I am certain she appreciates your eagerness to see her as soon as may be."

"Why, yes, of course. I could not wish for a more considerate nephew. He has always been so intimate with our family." Lady Danver knew this was not true, but she would use every opportunity presented to her to further her place in society.

Lady Beaumont turned now to Fitz, "My husband tells me your regiment will be leaving again early next year. I do pray you will be safe in your travels."

Fitz tried to answer, "Yes, I believe they will..."

The lady drew her hand to her heart in an exaggerated flourish as she turned back to her friend, "Oh I cannot imagine being in your situation, my dear. My own sons are, luckily, not drawn into this dreadful war which seems to never end. I cannot imagine having one of them leave me so often for—what is it, his third trip to the continent?"

"Yes; how dreadful each of these trips has proven to be for me," Countess Danver was putting on quite a show for her friend, waving her handkerchief and patting the corners of her perfectly dry eyes.

"You are very blessed to have had your son return to you. We will all pray for his safety once again."

"Actually, I will be perfectly safe..." Fitz started to say, but was again interrupted.

"Now, now, I know you only wish to impede any distress for your mother, so we will change the subject."

Fitz sighed. He knew he would never be able to tell his mother anything with Lady Beaumont here, and as the two were good friends, it was likely she would be here for quite a while with his mother.

"Mr Darcy," Lady Beaumont now turned back to the other gentleman, "I have been privileged to hear your aunt mention often of your recent marriage."

"Yes, my lady. We were married a few months ago."

"Pemberley, I am sure, is more than ready for a new mistress, and dare I say a new heir soon?" She smiled and turned to her friend, "I cannot tell you how wonderful a new babe can be for a family." She clasped her hands together and drew them to her chest, "It is a feeling like no other to see the next generation, and I am grateful daily for having my grandchildren so near." She gave a contented sigh, then turned back to Darcy, "But sir, I was surprised to hear from your aunt that your wife was not known among our society. Wherever did you meet her?"

"No, I do not believe she has made your acquaintance," he offered, trying to stop the direction he knew this conversation was going. "We met when she was on holiday in Ramsgate with her family."

"Am I also correct in that you have not yet been to Town with your bride before now?"

"Mrs Darcy and her sister, Miss Bennet, have lived here with their relations for the last few years, so we felt the need to stay in the country immediately following the wedding," he answered.

Fitz saw his mother's jaw tighten and her shoulders stiffen at the mention of Mary, but she said nothing.

"Bennet... hmmm, Bennet... I cannot say I recognize that name. You say they have been here in Town the last few Seasons?"

"Their father kept his family from much of society, so I doubt you would know of him. He held land in Hertfordshire. When tragedy took their family from them, my wife and her sister came here to stay with relations."

Lady Danver now played with the lace half—gloves on her hands, trying not to show too much disdain, though she felt it rising in her chest.

Lady Beaumont was shocked to hear such news of the ladies' family. She drew her hand to her chest, "Oh my! What a tale. It is settled then–your wife must be introduced to our society, and I will personally do so this evening. I am certain you would not deny me the pleasure of escorting your wife around my ball this evening, would you, sir?"

He looked to his cousin, who only lifted his eyebrow in amusement. Turning back, he tried to decline the invitation, but was interrupted once again by the persistent lady.

"Nonsense, my dear–I will not take no for an answer. I will expect to see you and Mrs Darcy there, as well as Miss Bennet. Your sister is not yet out, is she?"

"No, she is not." He looked to Fitz, then back Lady Beaumont, "I am not certain we are available at such short notice," he tried to say.

She leaned over and patted his hand, "Your wife has yet to be introduced to anyone, and as this is the largest ball of the Little Season, it is the perfect opportunity. Now that we know you are back in Town and are calling on others," she said, lifting her hand to indicate Lady Danver, "you simply must come." She nodded in determination, "We will expect you and your lovely wife, as well as her sister, at nine this evening."

"Well, I am not certain my wife has something appropriate to wear as we just arrived," he tried to get out of it again.

"Oh my! Do not tell me Mrs Darcy does not have *something* she could wear to such an occasion. It would not do your reputation well to have your wife in rags, sir."

He mumbled, "That... that is not what I meant."

"I am sure you do your best as a husband, unlike some of our set who are chintzy over the tiniest charge for necessary accoutrements." She looked to the Lady Danver with a knowing look.

Darcy's aunt blushed slightly under such scrutiny of her husband's known habits.

Lady Beaumont turned back to Darcy, "No, no, you must come! I insist."

The clock chimed in the background and he knew the time for their call had come to an end. When they stood, Lady Beaumont addressed Fitz, insisting on his presence at the ball this evening as well. Neither one gave any indication they would attend, but they both knew there was no getting out of it.

They took their leave and both climbed back into the carriage. "You know your wife will not take too kindly to such an underhanded scheme?" Fitz said with a smirk.

"Yes, I know." Darcy rubbed his face wearily and leaned back into the cushioned seat. "While Lady Beaumont is quite assertive in her insistence, she is also correct. Elizabeth must be introduced as my wife, and there is no better time during the Little Season than at the Beaumont's ball."

"Well then, let us dig out our dancing shoes and convince our ladies what fun we will have," Fitz replied.

Darcy chuckled, "I think convincing Elizabeth will be easier than convincing Mary."

"You might be right there," Fitz replied. "Do you mind if we stop somewhere first?"

"What are you thinking?"

"I think if we show up with the perfect blossoms in our hands we may have an easier time of convincing them."

Darcy smiled, "That is very true. To the flower shop it is," he said as he opened the door to inform the driver, then they were off.

Mary was delighted when Fitz came back from visiting her uncle with the good news of his approval. Now, as he and Darcy were visiting Countess Danver to apprise her of the news, she and Elizabeth sat talking of their plans over the next few months, including their planned visit to the Gardiners on Saturday.

Elizabeth was insisting upon Mary getting a new gown when the two gentlemen returned, each bearing a small bundle of flowers. Mary blushed when Fitz took her hand and kissed the back before giving her the blossoms– oak leafed geraniums, meaning *'true friendship'*, and a few lemon geranium leaves mixed in. Their meaning of *'unexpected meeting'* piqued her interest and she looked at him questioningly.

Elizabeth asked, "Did it go so well as to put you in such a gay mood?"

Fitz took the seat nearest Mary, "Actually, I was not able to speak with my mother on the matter as she had another visitor–Lady Beaumont."

Darcy sighed. "Yes, and there is something else we must apprise you of, my love," he said to his wife. "Lady Beaumont is to have a ball this evening, and she insists we attend. While I would normally not have a problem denying her request after just arriving in Town yesterday, she was correct in saying I will have to introduce you to society as my wife, and this ball is the perfect opportunity to do so."

Fitz saw Mary tense at the talk of a ball. He reached for her hand, gently squeezing her fingers.

Elizabeth smiled, "So we are to go to a ball tonight? Is that what you are trying to tell me?"

"Only if you wish it?"

"I see no reason not to go. As you say, I will need to be introduced, and that *is* why we have come back to Town instead of staying at Pemberley, so I see no need to put off the inevitable." She smirked at her husband, "I only hope to fill my dance card adequately as I dearly love the exercise."

Darcy stood and bowed to her, "Madam, may I take this opportunity to ask for your first set?"

"Why, of course, sir," she teased as he kissed the back of her hand.

"And your supper set as well?"

She giggled, "Yes, of course."

He leaned closer as he whispered, "I dare not ask for your last set, but perhaps when we return..." he did not finish as he once again drew her hand to his lips, this time for a slower, more intimate exchange.

Fitz turned to Mary, giving the other couple a moment of privacy. "You need not be worried–I will stay by your side the entire evening."

"You know you will have to dance at least once," she replied.

"Not at all; unless it is with you?"

Mary blushed, remembering the note he sent her many months ago before he escorted her to her first ball. He had said that his dearest wish was to dance with her, but not being able to hear the music made such an activity nearly impossible for Mary. "Perhaps one day, but not with so many others around to witness my clumsy attempts," she answered.

He smiled, "I will one day have my dearest wish fulfilled, of that I am certain. Until then, I can wait with the promise of it being satisfied sometime in the future."

Elizabeth stood and reached for Mary's hand, "Come," she said, "we have great deal to accomplish if we are to be presented on the arms of these fine gentlemen tonight." The sisters walked out of the room and up to their rooms.

"My wife is the most gracious lady I have ever known," Darcy said in complete admiration as he watched his wife walk away.

"Yes, she is quite the catch," Fitz smirked. "I will be forever thankful she caught your eye, as it allowed me to find my heart's desire as well."

Chapter 25

It was clear from the moment they stepped out of Darcy House that they were back in London. Mary could feel her chest tighten with the familiar fog that eerily hung over the city as she was handed into the carriage. Though she did not wish to ruin everyone's evening, she was not feeling her best.

She could just make out the face of her intended across from her with the small tendrils of light from the carriage lamps. His eyes bore into hers with an intensity that made her blush. She turned to gaze out at the city that unfolded around them. Though the sights they passed were not those of Brunswick Square, where her relations had lived for the last few years, there was still a basic familiarity in the streets and people she viewed through the window. London, truly, was an interesting and diverse city.

When they passed the elegant homes of Mayfair and turned down the prestigious Park Lane, the carriage slowed to await their turn in the long line that had formed. Mary could not help but chuckle at the ridiculous headdresses of some of the ladies as they were helped from their carriages and led inside the stylish home standing six stories above them. She looked back to Fitz who winked at her. It was at times like this that she would swear he could read her mind.

Soon it was their turn to escape the protection of the comfortable box and join the other revelers who, before them, had already paraded into the home and given their respects to the host and hostess, before fading into the crowded ballroom.

Mary stood as near to her sister as she could, her hand grasping Elizabeth's until it was necessary to let go and remove her cloak. She allowed the maid to help her change her traveling shoes and replace them with the soft material of slippers that would not stand up to much more than one night of wear. When she stood to join the others she saw the familiar outstretched arm of her intended and looked lovingly up into his eyes as she smiled and wound her hand around his outstretched arm. She trusted him; completely trusted him. With a peaceful sigh, their eye contact was broken and they followed the Darcys through the line. Both ladies were presented to their hosts, and Lady Beaumont eagerly greeted them both. She leaned over to whisper something to her husband, but Mary did not catch what was said. Then the lady wound Mrs Darcy's arm through her own and began to walk up the stairs, Darcy following after them just a pace behind. Fitz gave a small nod to their host, then they too joined the others traversing the stairs to the elegant first floor, where they dancing would be held.

Mary was excited—more so than she ever thought she would be in a situation such as this. She walked through the crowd, stopping when Fitz did, and stood quietly as Elizabeth was introduced with pride. When she was introduced, she did not feel the familiar dread in the pit of her stomach. Instead she curtsied quietly and gracefully, as if she had been accustomed to doing so all her life. As was customary whenever they went somewhere unfamiliar to Mary, Elizabeth answered the queries so Mary would not be required to speak. It was clear Fitz was learning this technique as well, as he often engaged the others in conversation that only required an occasional nod or smile from her. She had a feeling the comfort she felt this evening came mostly from the gentleman who stood by her side, but she too had grown much more at ease with society over the events of the last year and with the help of her dearest friend.

They made their way through those assembled until Mary felt the familiar thumping in the floorboards that let her know the music was signaling the beginning of the dancing to come. Darcy and Elizabeth excused themselves, leaving Fitz to stand with Mary as they made their way to their places in the lines that formed down the center of the long room.

Fitz tapped Mary's arm, and when she looked at him he asked if she would like a drink. She nodded her head and looked back to the activity surrounding them as the dance began. Fitz went to find the refreshments table, bringing back a drink for each of them and the two stood by the fireplace talking of the people around them. Mary pointed out Miss Bingley, and Fitz was surprised to see that her partner for the opening set was his own brother. *Hmmm*, he thought, *how curious? I must warn Bingley about his sister's reputation if she accepts too much attention from Milton.*

The dancing continued as the hours passed. Elizabeth was the talk of the evening and found herself dancing nearly every set. Luckily she had already reserved the supper set for her husband. The two were quite the sight to see, both excellent in their execution of the necessary steps. What drew the onlookers most though was the love that shone from their eyes as they danced. No one ever expected to see Fitzwilliam Darcy smile with such alacrity, yet his wife seemed to draw it out of him.

When the set ended the crowds began to descend the stairs once more to the second floor, where supper was to be served. The two found Fitz and Mary already seated at a long line of tables and they sat down across from them. Elizabeth quietly mouthed to Mary asking if she was having a pleasant time, to which Mary gave a smile and a nod. She truly was enjoying herself.

The white soup was eaten and the dancers' spirits were bolstered for the final three sets of the evening. Fitz was not required to dance, so he remained by Mary's side the entire evening, turning them away from any of his family members when he saw them nearby. His goal was to completely avoid them all evening, and so far he had accomplished it with practiced ease.

With only two dances left, Mary began to grow fatigued. The combination of the lateness of the hour and the ill effects the London air had on her health finally grew too much for her. Not wanting to disturb her sister's obvious enjoyment, she tried to ignore the growing tightness in her chest. The music began again and she found herself enjoying the moment, though eventually she could not help the yawn that escaped her lips behind a well—placed fan.

Fitz did not miss it though, and leaned over to ask, "Would you like to rest a bit? Lady Beaumont is my mother's dearest friend, and as such, I happen to know this house very well. There is a sitting room on the main level that I am certain is empty."

Mary nodded, accepting his arm as they made their way through the crowd and down the stairs. When she was seated on the sofa in the small room, Fitz signed, "I will be right back with a drink." Then he left.

She looked around the room. It was quite beautiful, though she could never picture a room in her own home looking as elaborately decorated as this one was. Lady Beaumont had a particular style that Mary could never fully appreciate. Seeing a vase of dried flowers on the table by the window, she stood and walked over. Her fingers naturally rose to touch the hard buds. She closed her eyes to draw in their sweet fragrance.

Suddenly, she felt that someone was behind her. She expected to see Fitz, but when she turned she saw another familiar face instead–his brother, Viscount Milton. Mary froze, not certain what she should do.

Milton was well into his cups and could hardly stand straight when he saw Fitz go down the stairs with Mrs Darcy's sister on his arm. He was curious where they were going, so Milton excused himself from the lady who was clinging to his arm. When he saw his brother once again ascend the stairs, this time alone, he quietly went down to the main floor and began to look for the lovely brunette who was obviously left alone. When he opened the sitting room door, he saw her standing over a vase of flowers next to the window, her eyes closed as she drew in their sweet fragrance. Closing the door quietly, he stepped closer to her and spoke, "My, my, what have we here?"

At that moment, Mary turned around.

Milton leered at her and took another step closer, "Now why would my brother be in here all alone with you?"

Mary read his lips, but she did not say anything in return.

He continued to ease closer to her. "I have not had the pleasure of being introduced to you, though it has not been from lack of trying on my part. I must say, you and your sister do make quite the impression. You are both lovely." His eyes raked over her figure as the slurred words were formed.

She felt sick to her stomach and thought of the warning Fitz had given her many months before about this man. 'My brother is a known profligate and gambler, with a long line of mistresses and ruined ladies in his wake. If you are ever in a room with him, please do me a favor and leave immediately. I would not have you hurt because of him.' She stepped around him to leave the room

242

but Milton's hand grabbed her arm forcefully enough to make her wince in pain and turn toward him, her back now to the door.

"What is wrong? Did my brother warn you not to be caught in a room alone with me?" He saw the answer in her eyes and laughed. "I thought so. Well let me tell you something—*no one* can stop me when I want something, *not even my brother.*"

The next instant Mary felt the viscount's hand release her arm as his body fell to the floor with such force that she could feel the boards move under her feet. She turned and saw Fitz standing there with his hand in a fist. He immediately grabbed her hand to lead her out of the room, "Come, it is time we leave."

They found Darcy, and Fitz leaned into his cousin's ear and whispered, "We must leave."

"Why? What is wrong?"

"Mary just needed to rest for a minute so I led her to the lower sitting room, then left to get her a drink. When I returned I found... that is... *Milton*—he tried to..." he could not say the words, but his eyes turned to Mary.

Anger immediately rose on Darcy's face, "We will meet you in the cloak room." When Fitz walked away with Mary, Darcy turned to retrieve his wife, once again at the side of Lady Beaumont. He gave his regrets that they must leave before the final set, then led Elizabeth away, explaining quietly to her what had taken place. They descended the stairs and Elizabeth turned towards the cloak room. "I will be right behind you," he said, continuing on down the hall.

When Elizabeth saw her sister sitting on the fainting couch, distress clearly visible on her features, she sat beside her and drew her arms around her shoulders in a loving embrace.

"Where is Darcy?" Fitz asked.

"He said he would be right behind me."

Fitz knew that could not be good, so he excused himself, though he doubted the two heard him or noticed him leave the room. He quickly walked down the hall towards the sitting room where he had left Milton. He heard shouts from within and knew what he would find when he opened the door. What surprised him was that it was not just Darcy and Milton, but his own parents in there as well.

"Fitzwilliam Darcy, you let go of him this instant!" Lady Danver pulled on her nephew's arm in vain.

Darcy did not even flinch at her order as he held tight to his eldest cousin's cravat and jacket. "I will only ask you once more Milton — *WHAT* did you do to her?"

The earl stepped up, "Boys, I will not allow a scene here in the middle of my friend's ball."

Darcy turned to his uncle, "I am no longer a boy and do not need to be addressed as such by anyone, *even you*. Mary is *my wife's sister* and she is under *my* protection. As such I have a right to know what he did to her."

Fitz stepped up to stand beside Darcy and stared at his brother. Milton's eyes grew glassy with fear when he saw the look on both of their faces. "I didn't mean it," he began to stammer, "I was just having some fun."

Fitz leaned closer as his voice rung out, "If you EVER touch her again, you will not live to see another day!"

Lady Danver placed her hand on her youngest son's arm, "Now, Richard, that is not necessary. Your brother did nothing wrong. *She* should have never even been here tonight."

"She was invited by Lady Beaumont and has every right to be here."

She took on an air of superiority, "We both know she was invited only because it would be rude of my friend to specifically leave her out of the invitation, but we all know just where someone such as she belongs."

The earl echoed his wife's sentiment, "Darcy might allow her into his home, but she will never be allowed in mine. The Fitzwilliam name will not be sullied by her ilk."

Fitz felt the furry rising even higher with every word his parents uttered. "I went to visit you this morning to apprise you of some news, and as it happens, I was unable to discuss it with you because of your other caller. However, I feel it is best that you know now. I have resigned my commission and will soon be married. We were thinking of a ceremony with our families in attendance around us, but I now wonder if perhaps it would be best if we marry quietly and leave Town for good."

Lady Danver spoke again, "Well, I must say, I am a bit shocked, but I see no reason to leave Town so abruptly. You must bring your intended by to see me. I will be available to you tomorrow."

"You have made it clear that she is not welcome in your home," he said as he looked at his father, "and I take that personally."

Lady Danver was incensed with the shocking news. "WHAT? You are engaged to... to... *THAT HALF—WIT?* No! Absolutely not; I will not have you shame our family further than what Darcy has already done by such a connection!"

The earl spoke "You cannot be serious! I have already found a bride for you and her father and I have been discussing the details of a spring ceremony at our estate in Worcestershire. She comes with a sizable dowry and a small estate."

"A bride for me?" He scoffed, "I doubt you care so much for my happiness. No, I will not marry the daughter of one of your *associates* just so they will promise to forgive a debt you owe them." At his father's surprised expression, he looked at both of his parents and continued, "I see I had it right. Let me make myself very clear right now. I will marry *who I choose* and *for the reasons I choose*, without regard to you or your wishes. If you need to pawn someone off on one of your sons, try doing so to Milton here," Fitz took his brother from Darcy's grip and shoved him towards his father. "At least that would be fair in some way; after all, it is this thatch—gallows' gambling and profligate ways that have put Croome Court in such a state as to need such a large increase of funds."

"Richard! How could you say something so crass about your brother," Lady Danver helped Milton stand and lovingly patted his hand.

"Oh, who is offended at insults now? Am I not to respond when you called my intended a half—wit? She is anything but, and to say such about her says more about you. At least in my brother's case, he has worked hard to earn such a reputation." He pointed his finger at his brother and growled, "DO NOT come near her again!"

Fitz immediately turned and stomped out of the room, followed directly by

Sarah Johnson

Darcy. They located the ladies and left for Darcy House before any of the others in the room were composed enough to join the ball again.

The carriage ride was quiet and Elizabeth sat beside her sister, their hands clutched tightly together. When they arrived at home, she excused them both and went upstairs to retire. Elizabeth left Mary with her maid and went to her own room to dress for bed. When she was ready, she made her way back to her sister's room and found Mary sitting alone on the bed, just staring at nothing in particular as she brushed her long hair.

"Here, let me help you," she signed. She took the brush from Mary's hands and pulled the coverlet back, helping her sister get settled. Elizabeth climbed onto the bed herself and positioned a pillow behind her back as she leaned against the headboard. She pulled Mary's head to her lap and ran her fingers through her sister's dark curls, slowly feeling the tension leave Mary's body.

Fitz and Darcy sat silently in Darcy's study, both trying to forget the events that brought an abrupt end to their evening. Fitz was very much in his cups when Darcy called for his man to help him upstairs. He was sure his cousin would sleep the night away, but he did not envy him the headache he would wake with on the morrow.

When Darcy went to find his wife, he discovered the two sisters curled up together. Both were asleep, their arms entwined as they held tightly to one another, Elizabeth's other hand gently laying on her expanding stomach in a protective manner. He smiled and reached his hand out, laying it on top of hers for just a minute. Then he released her fingers and pulled the counterpane higher and kissed Elizabeth's cheek, leaving the two to sleep soundly as he retired alone.

Fitz did wake to a pounding headache, and when the grogginess cleared a little he remembered why he drank so much last night. He took care of his needs and called for something to sooth his head. Darcy's housekeeper sent her vile concoction of tea with some unknown ingredient, and though Fitz could hardly stand the smell, he swallowed the tepid tea. The taste lingered. He eventually started to feel the headache ease. He did not care what it was, as long as it helped ease the pounding behind his eyes, he would swallow the swill with gratitude.

When he lay down again, he found himself growing weary and quickly fell back to sleep. Waking hours later, he felt much better, though he was still not back to his usual self.

The clock on the mantle told him it was well into the day, so he dressed with the intention of apologizing to his intended for sleeping so long. He thought it would be nice to do something together today.

As he readied himself and allowed his man to shave his face, he thought of what they could do that Mary would enjoy. He had narrowed it down to a ride in the park or a stroll to a book store when he was finally dressed and ready to face the rest of the household.

He expected to find the other three residents in the sitting room, but he found only his cousin, alone and in his study busily working his way through a large stack of correspondence.

Darcy glanced at the clock when Fitz came in the door, "I cannot say I have ever seen you sleep away the day like this; it is nearly four o'clock."

Fitz sat in the chair opposite Darcy and ran his hand over his still weary eyes, "I must have had quite the number of drinks last night as I do not remember much beyond coming back to Darcy House."

"Yes, you did your best to empty my supply."

"I thought my head would explode before I drank that vile tea your housekeeper sent up. I do not know what she puts in it, but I am ever grateful for that foul stuff."

"For years you have teased me for drinking her concoction every night, but I see you are finally starting to see its benefits," Darcy replied with a smirk.

Fitz sighed heavily, "Yes, though I still say it is revolting."

Darcy shrugged and went back to writing, "One gets used to it when the benefits are so numerous."

"So where are the ladies? Do not tell me they have gone shopping?"

Darcy placed his quill back in the holder and looked at his cousin, a grim expression on his face.

"What is wrong? Where are they?" When no answer came in the few seconds of silence, he sat up straighter, "Where is Mary?"

Darcy stood and went to the sideboard, poured two drinks, then turned back and handed one to his cousin. Fitz put it down on the desk with a heavy hand, pushing it away, "Isn't it a bit too early to start today?" When Darcy drank his down in one gulp, Fitz could not help but stand and, in agitation, ask again, "Where is she? *What has happened?*"

Darcy sighed heavily and answered, "She has gone to stay with her uncle and aunt for now." Fitz turned to leave the room but Darcy caught his arm, "She was not feeling well this morning, but she insisted on going."

Fitz cursed loudly and slammed his fist down on the corner of Darcy's desk, then picked up the drink and swallowed it quickly as he sat back down and held out the glass for his cousin to fill again. When the glass was returned to his hand, he once again emptied it just as quickly.

Darcy sat back down heavily. "We are to go there tomorrow evening for supper."

Fitz nodded slightly, though the knowledge did not ease his mind. He then stood, "I need to get out of the house."

"Are you going to Brunswick Square?"

"No," he stated flatly. "I do not wish to force my presence upon her; as you said, we are to go there tomorrow."

"Where are you going?"

"I do not know; I just need to get out of here. It feels as though the walls are closing in around me. I will be back in time to leave tomorrow."

Darcy nodded and watched as Fitz left his study. He put what he was working on away and went to find his wife to apprise her of his cousin's reaction to the news.

Chapter 26

itz was tired when he arrived back at Darcy House, but he was determined to put on his best clothes and attend to Mary this evening. As he climbed the stairs wearily he heard his cousin come into the hall below. "Do not worry, Darce, I will be ready in time to go."

Darcy quickened his pace and was now standing at the base of the stairs, "Actually, our plans have changed. My wife is already with her. I was awaiting your return before I go back myself."

"You have already been there today?"

"We received word this morning that Mary has taken on a small fever, so we went immediately."

Fitz flew back down the stairs and called to the butler to have a fresh horse readied.

Darcy interrupted, "There is no need; my carriage is awaiting us. Perhaps it would be best if you change first though."

Fitz looked down at his grimy riding clothes, then turned and took the stairs two at a time in his haste. "Give me five minutes."

Darcy nodded to his cousin and called for the carriage to be pulled around to the front. Soon they were seated opposite each other as they made their way through the streets. Fitz could not help the agitation that built up in his body, and soon his foot was tapping up and down on the floor.

"It is nothing to worry about," Darcy tried to assure him. "It is merely a trifling cold."

Fitz turned his gaze from looking out the window back to his cousin, "I should be by her side and I am not. How would you feel if it was Elizabeth?"

Darcy nodded, quietly saying, "I would feel much the same."

Fitz looked down at his hands. "I should have talked with her when we came in from the ball, but I did not have the chance before she retired. I should have gone to see her yesterday, but instead I spent my day in bed because of drinking too much and then roaming around the countryside, trying to forget the abysmal way my family has treated the woman I love."

"It is not your fault. You knew they would react strongly to any lady they did not choose for you."

"Yes, but I did not expect them to claim so vehemently that she should be in an asylum. I certainly did not expect my parents to allow my brother to do as he wished with your wife's own sister."

Darcy could see the anger rising in Fitz's face. "Your parents have long ignored Milton's behavior, and their reaction to Mary has always been that she belonged in an asylum. They stated as much the night they first met her at my house all those months ago."

Fitz sighed heavily, tears beginning to form in his eyes. "If anyone deserves to be loved, it is Mary."

The rest of the ride was spent in silence, Darcy allowing Fitz to gain more control of himself before they arrived at the Gardiner's home. When they finally pulled up to the familiar facade, they alighted from the carriage and Fitz bounded up the steps to knock quickly on the door.

Edward Gardiner dismissed the footman and answered the door himself. He greeted the two gentlemen, turning to Fitz when he said, "Perhaps it is best we speak in private."

250

Fitz nodded and followed the slightly older man through the halls to his study at the back of the house. When Gardiner offered him a drink, he shook his head, "No thank you."

"Have a seat," Edward said, sitting in one of the chairs beside the fire. He smiled a little, "I find I do not know what to call you, as I have always referred to you as *'Colonel'* before now."

"My cousin calls me Fitz and my mother calls me Richard–either will do."

"Fitz it is then. I know you must be anxious to see my niece, but she will not be down this evening."

His face fell. "I had hoped to see her, even if she is not feeling well enough to join everyone downstairs."

"I will inquire if she is up to a visitor, but I can make no promises."

Fitz nodded, "Thank you, sir."

Edward sighed heavily as he began what he knew would be a very difficult conversation. "I first wanted to speak with you about what my niece has been through."

"I am very sorry about what happened at the ball. My brother is a cad and I should never have left her alone..."

"No, no, that is not what I meant. Mary has had a hard life, and you do not fully understand what she has had to face all these years. Darcy told me of your brother, and he has assured me that neither he nor you will allow the viscount to be around her again. That is not what I was referring to though." He shifted in his seat, leaning forward and resting his elbows on his knees as he folded his hands together. "My niece has been told by some of society for many years that she is worthless. Many people in her own neighborhood have ignored her, disparaged her, and shunned her, treating her as if she is not worthy of even the most basic of concerns. She has chosen very few people to which to open her life, and I am grateful for you being one of those few. But you have to understand that acting out in anger is not what this situation needs. Mary knows not everyone will accept her, but what she needs most of all is to be protected and loved. She needs to be treated as any lady would wish to be treated by her intended. Do you understand what I am saying?"

Fitz thought in silence a moment before he answered, "I think I do. You are saying it would be best to ignore what has happened and just go on with our lives as we wish?"

"Yes, exactly," he replied.

"I cannot say it will be easy, but I understand why it is necessary."

"You have only been around my niece for a few short months, but she has dealt with these kinds of situations most of her life. I had a hard time at first as well, but with time, I learned it is best to just ignore what does not affect your daily lives."

"It saddens me that my family has reacted so harshly to this news of my betrothal, but my cousin wisely pointed out on our way here that they would have reacted thusly with anyone who was not their particular choice."

"I never had to face my parents' derision in my choice of wife as they passed away before I was married, but I understand how hard this must be for you."

Fitz sighed heavily, running his hand over his weary eyes. "My parents and I have not seen eye to eye in a very long time, and I cannot say I am completely surprised at the situation. It is just painful to have to face such treatment now. It makes me wonder, if they feel this way about Mary when her loss of hearing was clearly from an accident, what would they have thought of me if I had returned injured from battle? I was lucky enough to go through two campaigns without so much as a scratch, but many of my fellow soldiers returned with missing limbs or vision and hearing problems. What if…"

"Yes it is difficult, and I do not envy your position, but you cannot let yourself get off into what if situations."

"You are correct; I must just put this behind me." Fitz had to smile slightly, "I do think, sir, that the inducement is well worth the cost."

Edward stood, "Yes it is. Now, let us go and speak with my wife about how Mary is feeling." When they were about to exit the study, Edward turned back to Fitz, "Oh, I have one other thing to speak with you about before we join the others."

"Yes? What is it?"

"We feel it is best if Mary stays here with us until she is wed. We would not want to force the Darcys into being responsible for chaperoning you both at all times, and as you are living with them as well..."

"I understand completely, sir. And thank you."

"You are thanking me? For what?"

"Caring so much for her."

"Mary is easy to love."

Fitz smiled, "Yes she is."

When Mary awoke, a very faint but particular smell of frankincense and cloves greeted her. She knew before she opened her eyes that Fitz was nearby. *What will he say? Will he be upset with me for coming back to my uncle's home?* She lay very still hoping he would leave, but it seemed she would not be so lucky. Finally she began to move and opened her eyes, looking around the familiar room and finally to the gentleman at her side. He put his book on the side table and took her hand in one of his, placing the back of his other hand lightly on her forehead.

"Your fever is nearly gone now."

Her voice cracked as she asked, "You are here?"

Fitz looked deep into her eyes and replied softly, "Where else would I be?"

She did not know what to say to such a loving statement, so she said nothing as he continued to hold tight to her fingers. Her body ached and she wished to stretch more than anything, but she did not want this moment to end. Almost as if he read her mind, he stood and kissed the back of her hand, then excused himself from the room, leaving her to the care of her maid, Mabel, who sat near the door.

When she was dressed in a fresh nightgown and her hair was brushed and plaited neatly, Mary once again climbed back into her bed. She sat up against the headboard and pulled the counterpane up high, relishing in the scent of lavender that lingered on the fresh linens. She smiled at the memory of helping

Elizabeth make sachets of dried lavender to use in the closets throughout the Gardiner's home. Her reverie was interrupted when Elizabeth entered the room with the housekeeper, Mrs Walters, in tow.

Setting the tray down on the table, Mrs Walters shooed Mabel from the room, making sure she took all the old bed linens with her, and then returned to Mary's side and began to place more pillows behind her back. She looked at her directly so Mary could easily read her lips, "Now, I have brought you some broth, and it will do you good to eat as much as you can. We will have you feeling well enough to court your gentleman properly very soon."

Mary could tell Elizabeth was trying not to laugh at the housekeeper's insistence, and it made her smile all the more. She sat up straighter, appreciative of the extra pillow behind her back, and laid the serviette across her lap, allowing Mrs Walters to stir the broth until it was cool enough. When Mary had eaten what Mrs Walters felt was a sufficient amount, the housekeeper excused herself, leaving the sisters alone.

Elizabeth sat beside her on the bed. Mary slid over and blushed slightly as she asked, "How long was he here with me?"

"He refused to leave after supper last night. Fitzwilliam and I went home and returned this morning to find him still by your side as when we left him. Aunt Maddie said he did sleep a few hours in the room next door, though he was back at your side before the sun was up this morning."

Mary nodded, not sure what to say. Her fingers gently ran over the back of her hand where she still felt the effects of his kiss before he left the room. When she saw her sister's hand gently rest against her slowly expanding abdomen, she asked, "Have you told Aunt and Uncle yet?"

Elizabeth smiled, "Yes, we told them last evening. They are so very happy for us."

"I knew they would be." They sat in companionable silence for a while longer until Mary felt her eyes growing weary once more. Elizabeth slid out of the bed and helped her get into a more comfortable position, then she left to allow her sister to rest once more.

When Mary awoke again a few hours later, Fitz was once again at her side, this time his fingers were entwined with her own and he was not reading. Instead five year old Henry sat upon his lap, fast asleep. Fitz's light blonde hair and blue eyes were in contrast to the bright red hair of her little cousin; otherwise they were the picture of affection she always dreamed of seeing in her own father. She could not help but smile as she thought of him with their own child one day.

Fitz saw that Mary was awake and he shifted Henry in his arms. The boy began to stir, stretching and yawning after his invigorating nap.

"I am surprised you were allowed in here," Mary signed to Henry when he looked at her.

He replied quickly, "Oh, Mama sent me in here to sit with you."

Fitz chuckled, "Yes, he was charged with the task of keeping me busy. It seems he tried to help your aunt a little too eagerly with her threads this morning."

Mary looked at Henry disapprovingly, "You know you are not allowed in your mother's sewing box."

"Yes, but it was a most important task," he quickly explained. "I needed some red and blue threads to tie together your birthday gift."

Fitz smiled, "Oh? Is someone's birthday coming soon?"

Mary blushed, "It is in early December—the sixth."

Fitz looked back to Henry and ruffled his red hair, "I think you and I need to make some plans. Perhaps we can give your cousin a few minutes of privacy while we talk of this special date, then we can return and trounce her in a game of droughts. How does that sound?"

Henry began to bounce joyfully, "You will help me? Oh, how wonderful! I will show you what I have so far." He stood and began to pull Fitz from the chair and towards the door. When they reached it, he turned back to Mary, "We will be back," and then they were gone.

She laughed at the display, though she was grateful for a few minutes alone. Mabel helped her with her needs, and by the time the two conspirators returned, Mary was dressed and feeling well enough to go downstairs to join the rest of the Gardiner family for tea.

As they sat apart from the others in two chairs positioned near the open doors that led out to the garden, Fitz watched his intended. Her cheeks no longer held the bright coloring that indicated a fever, and her pale skin was now back to a more natural look. Her dark brown curls were bound in a simple plait that lay across one shoulder, and when she looked at him, her dark brown eyes never stopped telling their own story. What they showed now was uncertainty.

"Are you feeling any better?" Fitz asked.

"Much better; thank you," she said as she drew her shawl around her shoulders. "I did not expect to see you today."

Fitz looked around, determining that the others were not paying any attention to them. He leaned forward, his face coming that much closer to hers as he silently moved his lips for only her to read what he said. "You mean everything to me; of course I wish to be at your side."

Mary's eyes began to fill with tears and she reached up to wipe them, finding that Fitz held out his handkerchief to her. She chuckled at how quickly he had anticipated her need. "I was not certain how you felt, especially since you were not awake yet when Elizabeth told me about what your parents said."

"Is that why you decided to come back here to your uncle's house?"

"Yes; I did not want to make you have to choose between me and your family."

His heart nearly broke. "I will always choose you–*always*."

"I was not certain since you were still abed."

"For that I must apologize most sincerely. I let my family's reaction affect my actions the night before, and in my anger I had too much of my cousin's fine Scotch to drink, leaving me with quite the headache when I finally awoke late in the day." He reached out to take her hand in his, "I promise to not let myself do that again. I do not want to be anything like my father, and yet I succumbed to one of his vices when faced with their harsh criticism. I truly do apologize."

Mary blushed and looked down at their entwined hands. She squeezed his fingers slightly and nodded her head in acknowledgement of what he said.

"Now, we have a great deal to discuss–such as, when do you wish to marry?" Mary was uncertain what to say and was glad when Fitz continued, "I hope to have the papers drawn up this week, and if it is agreeable to you, wed as soon as the banns are read. How does that sound?"

She smiled sweetly, "I do not desire a long wait."

"We could be wed by the end of November, then we need not be bound to remain in Town any longer than necessary, and by your birthday we could be back in Derbyshire and established in our own home."

"Oh no," Mary signed hastily, "I dearly love Christmastime in London." She drew her hands to her chest, sighing and closing her eyes as she began to sign, describing her favorite time of the year as though magic was contained within her words. "The shop windows display such wondrous beauties to behold, and the bakeries provide the neighborhoods with such delightful aromas. Oh, how I love to help decorate the banisters with boughs and holly, and roast nuts and wassail over the fire. It thrills my heart to purchase special gifts for my loved ones. Then there is caroling and ice skating in the park."

Fitz chuckled, "You make me wish to remain in Town as well, though I cannot say I have ever taken as much pleasure in the season as you seem to do." With a nod of his head, he replied, "It is settled then—we will wait to leave until after Twelfth Night." He looked askance at the others. Finding that they still paid them no heed, he added, "I look forward, most of all, to finding as many mistletoe boughs hung around the house as I can."

Mary blushed at such a brazen statement. "I think I might like being married this year."

He leaned closer and drew her hand to his lips for a kiss, then with a twinkle in his eye and a wink, he said, "I know for certain I will as well."

Their moment was interrupted with the delivery of the checkered game and pieces by a certain little red—headed boy. Fitz gathered Henry onto his lap as they set up the board, whispering their strategy to each other, then the game began in earnest. Fitz watched as his intended thought very carefully about her own moves, often positioning her pieces in such a way as to allow Henry to take them and eventually to win. *She will be such a loving mother*, he thought to himself, his cheeks becoming reddened when she looked up at him in that moment. Their eyes met and neither wished to break the contact, but Henry required their attention. Before Mary went back upstairs to her bed, Fitz took his leave, promising to be back the next day after he completed what was required for the banns to be called beginning this coming Sunday.

Sarah Johnson

Chapter 27

The weeks leading up to the wedding were filled with enough shopping trips to frustrate anyone, much less Mary who did not enjoy such outings to begin with. However, Elizabeth and Aunt Maddie insisted upon the excursions, so Mary followed along, making decisions about material choices, sleeve length, color combinations, lace, and a number of other accoutrements that were deemed necessary for Mary's trousseau.

Fitz had his own frustratingly intricate details to attend, mainly the marriage settlement. He, Darcy, and Mr Gardiner spent many hours at the solicitor's office and in conference about the contract. The wedding clothes were ordered, the banns were called, and papers were signed. He was surprised to not hear from his parents, especially after the first time the banns were called in the church in which they attended services. He thought for sure they would begin to accept his choice, but, then again, he knew how implacable his father could be when it came to admitting a fault. It was the main reason he had spent his teen years at Pemberley instead of with his own family.

Finally the 26th of November dawned. The wedding was to take place in the chapel where the Gardiners, along with Elizabeth and Mary, had attended Sunday services.

The bride dressed with care with the help of her sister and aunt. Her hair, having been freshly washed with vinegar and cold water, was piled atop her head in shiny, bouncy curls with seed pearl pins scattered throughout. One long curl hung down onto her shoulder.

The wedding dress decided upon was her favorite of all her new gowns. It was a surprise gift from Elizabeth; one which was ordered months ago as a special birthday gift for Mary, whose birthday was just a week away in early December. When Elizabeth received it, she knew she had to present it to her sister early. It was quickly chosen as the dress Mary would wear for the ceremony. The soft white muslin was a simple cut with short capped sleeves around which was embroidered small holly leaves with berry clusters. A larger version of the same clusters ran diagonally down the front of the skirt and encircled the hem, giving it a distinctly festive look. The green velvet cape, lined with a red interior, was a gift from her uncle and aunt. Such luxurious fabrics draped around her shoulders were sure to keep the chill of the stone church at bay.

The carriage ride was short and before she knew it she was standing at the back of the church beside her uncle, awaiting the opening of the doors.

Edward touched her arm and waited until she turned towards him. "It is not many months ago that I stood in this same position with your sister, and I feel just as proud in this moment as a father ever could for a child. If your own parents were here today, I doubt they would feel any differently than I do now. I am so very proud of the lady you have become. You truly are proving that nothing can hold you back from having a happy and fulfilling life at the side of a gentleman who cares so very deeply for you. Your aunt and I love you very much." As he leaned down to kiss her cheek Mary felt a swish of air and knew the doors had been opened, beckoning their walk down the center aisle.

When her eyes alighted on those of her intended, she felt a flutter as her heart began to pound more furiously than ever before. There he stood, his blonde hair and blue eyes in stark contrast to the green coat and red waistcoat he wore. She smiled at the thought that he matched her own gown and cape so nicely. When her uncle placed her hand into the groom's, she knew her deepest desire was soon to be fulfilled. She may never get to hear the words from his lips, but she knew he loved her dearly as it shone from his eyes when he looked at her as he was doing now.

The ceremony was long, as was typical, but eventually it was completed and the next thing she knew, Mary was signing her name for the last time. *Mary Elaine Bennet*, she wrote in the register with practiced ease. She smiled as her eyes focused on the familiar script of the name above hers–that of her husband. *Richard Andrew Fitzwilliam.* She was now married. Her eyes began to fill with tears, and, not wanting to cry in front of everyone, she tried to brush them away without anyone taking notice. Her husband noticed though, and while he made a comment aloud that would draw the attention of everyone away from his bride, he placed a handkerchief into her hand. When she was composed again she wound her arm around his and he led her from the church and into the waiting carriage that would take them across Town and back to Darcy House, where a lavish wedding breakfast awaited them.

Not wanting to frighten Mary, Fitz kept his seat across from her, and they rode in silence. Mary was grateful for the time to get her emotions back under good regulation, and when she looked across at Fitz and he winked at her, she blushed. *He is such a tease, yet so caring as well,* she thought.

They soon arrived at Darcy House and the two followed the other family members who attended the wedding into the house where everyone else was awaiting them. The ceremony itself had been small and intimate, but those who were invited to the celebration afterward were too numerous for Mary to even keep a proper count. She did not realize her uncle's associations and their group of friends from church were so many until today when they were all gathered together in one place–all to offer felicitations to her upon this new phase of her life. She was comforted in knowing that all these people accepted her in their lives in some fashion, exactly as she was. It was a moment of clarity she would forever remember when this realization came upon her. *If only my husband's family would accept me,* she thought. *I must not lose hope. I must believe that one day they will choose to become a part of our lives.*

Her thoughts were interrupted when Fitz tapped her on the arm then signed, "Come; you must meet some friends of mine." She smiled and followed along, delighted to see that he introduced her with such pride. He truly did love her beyond what she could have ever imagined.

When the guests had finally gone and the servants were busily cleaning up what remained of the feast, Elizabeth pulled her sister aside to speak privately. "Mary, there is one last surprise for you today. My husband and yours," she stopped and smiled at such a statement, chuckling when Mary smiled broadly as well. "As I was saying," she tried again, "our husbands have been keeping a secret from us. I was only told this morning, as it has been appointed to me to tell you. Instead of having you stay here with us immediately, it has been arranged for you and your husband to go to a cottage just outside of Town for the next week. I am assured you will return before your birthday, at which time Fitz intends to spoil you with an evening of entertainment the likes of which I could not get him to reveal. Perhaps you will have better luck than I did."

Mary smiled even more broadly, "I have a good idea what he has in mind."

"Do you? Well I shall leave that secret between the two of you then. Oh Mary, I am so very happy for you!" Elizabeth embraced her and could not help the tears that began to fall down her cheeks. She released her and dried her eyes, then asked Mary, "Is there anything we need to speak of before you leave?"

Mary thought of all she had learned of marriage over the last few weeks from both her aunt and her sister. "No, I doubt there are any reassurances you have not already given me. I trust my husband and I know everything will be well."

"You are so much braver than anyone would guess," Elizabeth said as she stood, embracing her sister one last time before they both returned to the others.

The carriage was ready to leave, their trunks already affixed to the back and Fitz standing at the door to hand his bride into the seat. He followed after her and they waved to the Darcys and Gardiners as they drove away.

When they were no longer in sight of Darcy House, Fitz looked at Mary, sitting across from him, and lifted her hands to his lips, bestowing a kiss upon the back of each glove. He then lifted his fingers to her cheek, drawing the back of them along her flushed skin as he asked, "I hope this surprise is not too much for you?"

Mary leaned into his hand and sighed deeply, "No, I will take great delight in the time alone with you."

It was exactly what he needed to hear, and it took everything in him not to take her in his arms at that moment and kiss her senseless. He knew he would never be able to stop though, and it would not be that long of a ride once they were out of Town. He switched seats to be closer to her, happy, for now, to sit by her side.

"Are you upset over your family's decision not to join us today?"

Fitz flexed his arm at the question, but tried to seem nonchalant in his answer,

"No, it really matters not to me what they choose to do."

Mary turned around so she could see his mouth more easily. "What makes you say such a thing? They are your family."

"No, Darcy and Georgiana are my family. My Aunt Anne and Uncle George were more like parents to me than my own have ever been." He sighed deeply, then explained further, "My father and I had a… a difference of opinion, you might say, when I was barely into my teen years. Darcy's parents insisted I stay at Pemberley, and it was at that time that my own parents became so distant to me."

"What led to such a situation?"

"My father wished me to join the Navy at the age of three and ten."

"Is that not the typical age for such a career?"

"Yes, but it was for no good reason other than his own greed. He was promised by a friend that I would make quite the fee if our ship took on pirates, and he was determined to have me on the most profitable ship in the fleet."

Mary shook her head in shock at such knowledge. "Was his greed so strong that he would place your life in mortal danger?"

Fitz looked out the window for a minute before he turned back to her. "My father has many habits that have drained the coffers of his estate, and now with my brother's profligate ways as well, I doubt anything except a large influx of money will garner their approval." He sighed heavily, "I have never been of much use to them except to be the spare just in case my brother did something ridiculous which ended his days on this earth."

Mary took his hand in hers and wrapped his arm around her shoulders tightly as she leaned into his side. "You mean everything to me."

Fitz kissed her forehead, smiling at such a statement. "Thank you."

The two sat in silence, enjoying the sights that passed, until finally Fitz pointed to a small cottage on a hill. It was such a charming place, with its thatched roof and red brick walls, trails of ivy meandering their way up and surrounding the first floor windows. Bright blue shutters stood out in contrast to the green of the ivy and red of the bricks. The gardens that surrounded the small house told of its beauty in the height of summer. She could not help but wonder if it was just as beautiful with a layer of fresh snow on the ground and bushes. It was cold enough to snow, but so far the ground lay in wait of the first covering of the winter. *Perhaps it will snow while we are here,* Mary thought.

She did not realize they had stopped until Fitz stood to step down, helping her as well. The footmen were taking care of the trunks when an elderly lady appeared in the doorway. She welcomed them and introduced herself as Mrs Simpson, the proprietor, then she showed them into the sitting room where she had a warm pot of tea hanging over the fire and a light repast awaiting their arrival. When they were settled she told them of the stew, cheeses, and fresh bread that awaited them in the kitchen, then assured them of their privacy for the rest of the evening. She smiled at the happy newlyweds as she left them alone.

Fitz heard the door close and saw the carriage through the window as it drove away, then he turned his attention to his wife. *Ahhh, his wife.* The thought brought a fanciful smile to his lips and Mary chuckled at his grin.

When they were finished with their tea, Fitz stood and began to clear the furniture from the middle of the room, pushing everything against the walls.

"What are you doing?"

He faced her and held out his hand, "May I have this dance?"

"Here? Now?" She was not sure what to make of such a request.

"You promised me months ago that one day you would allow me to teach you to dance, and I intend to begin our lessons now. You cannot deny the request of your new husband, now, can you?"

With a deep breath and a lift of her chin, she took his hand and stood. "No, I cannot deny your request, though I am curious how you intend to teach me when I cannot hear the music."

He began to position his arms around her as he answered, "You can count, and that is all that is required for this particular step. Now, you place your hands here, and here, while mine go here, then you just follow my lead."

After a few comical attempts and some sore toes, the two were finally able to find a rhythm. Fitz loved the feel of her in his arms, and he was reluctant to stop, but he did not want to tire her too quickly, so he slowed their movements and wound his arms around her, pulling her body closer to his as his lips captured hers in a slow and sensual continuation of their dance.

The passion between the two grew and Fitz knew he must stop, so he reluctantly pulled away. When he saw the look of bliss on Mary's face he embraced her tightly, kissing her hair as he told her how much he loved her. He was surprised to feel her press her cheek into his chest. Pulling back, he asked, "Are you well? Do you need to sit?"

Mary blushed, "No, there is no need to rest."

"What were you doing?"

Her cheeks flamed an even darker color and she turned away from him, walking over to feel the lace curtains that hung over the window.

Fitz stepped up behind her, wrapping his arms around her waist as they looked out into the setting sun beyond. When they had been silently standing there for a few minutes, he leaned around to say, "Please tell me? I promise I will not tease you."

She took a deep breath, then turned around and signed, "It has been my deepest desire just to hear 'I love you', and I found, when you drew your arms around me so tightly, that having my ear to your chest made it seem almost possible."

Fitz reached for her hand, drawing it to his lips and kissing her fingers before he placed her hand onto his throat and uttered the simple words, *"I love you."*

Mary felt the rumbling and smiled. When he pulled her ear back to his chest and repeated the words again her heart began to race. It was the closest she had come to hearing words in so many years, and she was glad to finally have someone who understood her deepest need. Lifting her face and looking back into his eyes, she too replied with the dearest words of affection, only to have her words silenced by his mouth once again descending upon hers. What she thought was passion before was nothing compared to what she felt building between them now. Before she knew it, he lifted her into his arms and carried her up the stairs and into the bedroom. When he kicked the door closed she could not help but laugh. He placed her feet back onto the floor then kissed her so deeply that everything else was soon forgotten.

Sarah Johnson

Chapter 28

ary awoke early the next morning. She lay beside her husband looking upon him with fascination. Never before had she taken the opportunity to stare at him so intently, and yet here he lay before her and she could not pull her eyes away. His eyes were closed, and that was the one feature of his that she loved the most because of their piercing blue color. Now with them closed, she began to notice the other things she had always found fascinating about his appearance. He had a firm jaw line and muscular neck, but it was softened in appearance by his locks of curly blonde hair. He was so very different than his cousin, and yet so much alike. They both had a similar structure to their face with prominent cheek bones, and that nose. It almost seemed out of place, yet it was perfect at the same time.

She did not wish to wake him, so she slipped out of bed and went into the dressing room. She was a little sore, but Elizabeth had given her a salve that seemed to help. Finally she began to brush the tangles from her hair, determined to never go to bed again with it down. After working through many knots she was finally able to run her fingers through freely. Finding a ribbon, Mary braided her long brown hair loosely, tied the ribbon around the end, and then made her way back to the bed where her husband still lay asleep.

When she climbed in and pulled the counterpane up, Fitz began to move. The next thing she knew he forcefully pulled her closer to him, insisting she lay her head back onto his chest. She chuckled and gladly conceded. Sleep would not come, so she thought of all that had changed for her over the last year. She did not even realize her husband had fully awakened until she felt his hand squeeze her fingers, stopping her from playing with the hair on his chest, an action she did not realize she was doing until he stopped her. Her cheeks flamed scarlet.

Fitz lifted her chin so she could see what he said. "I do not mind your touch, I only wished to tell you—*I love you*." He then kissed her on the cheek before replying, "I need to get cleaned up, then I wish to take you on a morning ride."

She smiled. "I will leave you to dress," she said, standing to go into the other room where her trunk was unpacked.

Fitz reached for her hand, pulling her back to the side of the bed, "When I have dressed I will give you a proper kiss. For now, this will have to do." He then kissed her cheek again, his scruffy beard rubbing against her delicate skin. Mary chuckled at the feeling, then leaned down to kiss his cheek as well before quickly leaving the room to call her maid.

When they came down the stairs Fitz smelled the tempting aromas coming from the kitchen. Mrs Simpson was just pulling some fresh bread from the oven when he poked his head into the room. She insisted upon them eating, so they broke their fast before continuing with their plan to go for a ride.

After being in Town for the last month it felt good to get on a horse and fly across the fields once again. Mary would never forget the feeling of freedom it gave her. Elizabeth did not like riding, so she was glad to have a husband who loved it as much as she did. He even volunteered to teach her to jump once they finally returned to Derbyshire and the winter ground was thawed. Mary looked forward to the new adventure that awaited her.

The week they were to spend at the cottage slowly went by, each new day bringing them even closer together. Soon they were watching the trunks be lifted onto the back of the carriage once again. The ride back to Town seemed to pass more quickly than it had when they left, and they were greeted at Darcy House by their eager relatives. Elizabeth whisked her sister away while Darcy suggested Fitz join he and Bingley in a game of billiards.

"Bingley, I must say, I did not expect to see you upon my return," Fitz said as he entered the room.

"No, I would guess I was the furthest person from your mind today." He poured Fitz and drink, explaining his presence as he handed it to him. "I came to trounce my friend here once more before I must leave for the north. Apart from my sister, the rest of my family insists upon being together for Christmas this year, so we are scheduled to leave for Scarborough tomorrow morning."

"Miss Bingley is not too pleased with your decision?"

"No, she is not. She would prefer to stay here where she is certain she will find a husband this season." He rolled his eyes in exaggeration of her charms as he repeated what he had heard Caroline spout for days now. "That is what led me to Darcy's door. I did not realize you would be returning today until the butler announced your arrival."

"It is of little consequence, Bingley," Darcy shrugged as he patted Fitz on the shoulder and took a seat. "I doubt there is anything I can pry from my cousin that your bachelor ears cannot hear as well. He is not one to tell of his exploits too easily."

"Exploits? You must have me confused with my brother. I have never been known to bandy about Town as some do." He sat down, putting his drink on the table beside him. With a smile he replied, "I must say though, Bingley, marriage is highly recommended."

Bingley laughed, "I am not quite ready for that, my friend. Perhaps when I meet the right lady."

"Well, when you do, sweep her off and marry her as quickly as you can. There is nothing like marriage to settle a man's heart." Fitz turned back to Darcy, asking, "Has there been anything said from my family?"

"Nothing that I have heard. We have visited a few of my friends, and their wives have accepted Elizabeth without any difficulties. Lady Beaumont even called on us a few days ago. On several of our calls your recent marriage was brought up, and nothing more than best wishes for your future were given."

Bingley cleared his throat, interrupting the two, "I hate to say it, but my sister has mentioned visiting Lady Danver, and you know the animosity she holds for Miss Mary… er, I mean, Mrs Fitzwilliam."

Fitz could not help but smile at Bingley's blunder. "Well, we shall have a good time of the season with those who wish for our company and friendship, and all others cannot temper our good spirits."

Darcy chuckled, "Said like a man clearly in love."

"And proud of it," Fitz replied, lifting his glass in salute.

The next morning Mary awoke to her husband playing with her hair. She had gone to bed with her hair plaited loosely every night since the second night of their marriage, and yet every morning she would find it down and tangled again. This morning, it seemed, her husband had already worked the tangles out of it with his fingers.

"Ahhh, I was wondering how long you would sleep." He kissed her cheek, his smooth skin telling just how late it was in the day.

"Oh, what you must think of me, sleeping so late like this." She started to pull the counterpane back, but he stayed her hand.

"It is your birthday, and if you wish to sleep the day away then that is what you have the freedom to do."

"One thing I must do today is finish our Christmas greetings and get them sent, so be prepared to lend me a few minutes of your time to sign a few personal ones to your family."

He leaned down and kissed her forehead, "I will do as you wish, but I still see no point in your quest of sending my parents greetings. You know they are only tossed into the fire, do you not?"

"It matters not to me what they do with them, only that we send them. We will do what is right and proper, even if they refuse to acknowledge us."

"That is what I love about you—your compassion for others is astounding." He stood, revealing that he was already dressed, though his boots were lying next to the chair in the corner of the room. "I will leave you to your necessities and will see you downstairs."

Mary began to work her fingers through her hair as she went into the dressing room to call Mabel. She had chosen what she would wear on this special day already, and with the help of her maid she was soon dressed with her hair coifed in a suitable manner.

She descended the stairs and found the others in the dining room breaking their fast. When she entered, her husband stood and took her elbow, leading her to a chair, then he filled her plate from the dishes on the sidebar and placed it in front of her. It seemed even the kitchen staff were prepared to give her anything she desired. Everything looked wonderful, and it was not long before she knew she must stop before she ate too much.

Fitz then insisted they go to the sitting room, where a few small gifts lay wrapped on the table. Mary opened each, thankful for the items each of them had chosen just for her. She saw a brown paper package tied with blue and red thread and knew it would be from her young cousin Henry. Their plan originally was to meet up with the Gardiners and go for a ride in the park, then return to Darcy House for a family supper, but they had received word yesterday that Juliana, the eldest Gardiner child, was ill. It was decided it would be best if they all kept their distance, so the Gardiners would now stay away for a few more days until their daughter was recovered. Mary now looked at the package Fitz held out to her. "Oh, no, I will wait until Henry can see me open it," she said.

Fitz insisted she take it, "He insisted you open it first thing this morning, and I have been tasked with the job of describing in great detail your reaction to his gift."

When she opened the gift, she saw a simple wooden frame with a drawing, obviously done by the five year old. It was of a small red—headed boy giving flowers to a larger girl in a blue dress–clearly it was his rendition of both of them. She laughed at such a heartfelt gift.

"These are for you as well," Fitz said as he pulled out a handful of wildflowers Henry had picked from the garden."

Mary's eyes began to well with tears even as she also chuckled at the dead flowers among those few that were still brightly colored. "He is becoming quite the lad, is he not?"

"I dare say he will be a chivalrous young man when he is older," Fitz replied. "I helped with the frame," Fitz indicated the gift in her hands. "What he had was four twigs held together at the corners with red and blue thread, but as you can see," he pointed to the packaging, "I was able to convince him to use that for decoration instead and we used this leather strapping to hold the frame together."

Mary hugged it to her chest. "I shall treasure it always." She went on to open the other gifts before her.

When she thought she was finally through, Fitz handed her a letter. She wondered at the smile on his face. It was clear he was enjoying this moment. Breaking the wax seal, she unfolded the piece of paper to reveal six tickets. When she looked at them to see what they were for, she was quite shocked. One of the most renowned deaf lecturers was to be in London and her husband had not only found out without her knowing, but had purchased tickets for them, the Darcys, and the Gardiners to all attend tonight's lecture, though the Gardiners would now not be able to attend. She felt tears welling in her eyes and before she could pull her own handkerchief from her pocket Elizabeth handed her the newly embroidered one she had just opened.

Mary felt truly loved and accepted by her whole family. She thanked everyone for their gifts, then the two sisters went upstairs to prepare for the evening's event, descending a few hours later in eager anticipation.

Fitz felt the tension in his wife's shoulders when he placed the cape around them. He leaned closer, placing his own cheek against hers, then whispered, "I love you."

Mary could not help the smile that overtook her features. She loved that he had found a way to let her *hear* those words. Before she could respond though, she was whisked away into the carriage and found herself seated beside her sister. The next few hours were a whirl of activity, but Mary did not feel lost in the crowd as she usually did.

When they returned to Darcy House and she retired that night, Mary thought of all she had been blessed with, from a loving sister to a wonderful family, and now a wonderful husband as well. She just knew her life would turn out better than she ever hoped or dreamed.

The weeks leading up to Christmas were spent with all the typical Christmastime traditions. Edward Gardiner was happy to have the help of the two younger, and much stronger, gentlemen this year when the yule log was placed within the hearth and finally lit.

Fitz was true to his word and found every mistletoe bunch he could, paying the bravest of the servants mighty handsomely to climb out onto branches high above their heads to gather the highly sought after leaves. He then made sure they were strategically placed around Darcy House in such a manner as to give him many opportunities to kiss his wife. It was, of course, a great inducement to the Darcys to also find as many as they could. After all, this was their first Christmas season as a married couple as well.

In the evening the stories of the season were told to the young Gardiner children, some tales becoming quite elaborate and fanciful, just as the emotions this season always brought about in everyone. Many hours were spent around the pianoforte while carols were sung of the Savior's birth. Wassail and nuts were roasted over the fire, and on two occasions Mary talked her family into playing Snapdragon, though her aunt insisted they not play until after the children were in bed. She did not wish to have her precocious Henry pick up on such a game at such an early age.

The ladies spent several days making handkerchief dolls to give out to the children at the foundling hospital. It had become a tradition for them every year after they moved to Brunswick Square, as one of the largest hospitals was very close to them. This year they were able to make more than their usual amount when Darcy showed up with a large stack of newly purchased cloths and insisted on every child receiving a gift.

As the weeks quickly passed, Fitz was glad they had stayed in Town instead of returning to Derbyshire so soon. He could not imagine a more special time than what they had this year with his wife by his side and her family surrounding them.

It was a few days after Boxing Day and Elizabeth and Mary were in the drawing room when a footman entered with a letter for the mistress of the house. As soon as she saw the writing she knew it was from her friend Charlotte Collins. "Oh, I do hope her confinement has gone well," she said to Mary as she eagerly opened the missive.

She began to read quietly.

Sarah Johnson

December 28, 1811

Longbourn, Hertfordshire

My Dear Friend,

Oh what news I have for you—my confinement is ended and I have delivered a son. A son! Can you believe what favour I have been bestowed upon me by the Almighty? My husband is as I have never seen him before. He parades our William around to anyone who visits. The joy upon his face is enough to carry me through a lifetime. It makes me proud to have given him his heir.

I am feeling much recovered, and in fact I went on a walk yesterday. I know this shall shock you, as I was never fond of the exercise, but I found it invigorating.

Unfortunately, the good feelings it produced were not long with me, as I came upon my sister seated on a back bench in our garden. She was upset over something, so I sat to speak with her. The tale she told was heart—wrenching, Elizabeth, and I do not know who else to turn to in our hour of need other than you. I know my family has treated you, and especially Mary, very cruelly, but it is to you I must now turn for our salvation.

Maria is with child, and my father is furious. The scoundrel was a soldier in the militia, but has since removed with the regiment to wherever they will quarter for the winter. I know not where, and Maria will not tell of his name, only that he was not happy to learn of this news before he left. It seems she has borne this secret for over a month, but the time will shortly come when it can be hidden no longer. My father was ready to turn her out of his home and insist she leave Meryton, but my assurance of finding a solution has stayed his hand at least a little for now. She is with us here at Longbourn, but my husband's patience is not easily given in such a situation.

It is with heavy heart I must ask for your help. With my own confinement just ending, I cannot travel with her, and I know of no one else to whom I can turn. I know your husband is from the north, and I thought he may know of a place far enough away from here, that Maria's reputation, and that of our family, can be saved? Please,

274

Elizabeth, you must know of a place my sister can be sent.

If you feel I have overstepped our tenuous friendship, then I apologize. I have no one else to call upon other than you. Please tell me you can help?

Your Friend,

Charlotte Collins

Elizabeth's face went pale as she read the last part of the letter.

The gentlemen entered the drawing room. Seeing the distressed look on his wife's face, Darcy went to her side, "Elizabeth? Are you well? What has upset you?"

The tears began to fall slowly down her cheeks. She pulled out her handkerchief and tried to quell them, but they only intensified.

Darcy pulled his wife into an embrace. "What has distressed you?"

Elizabeth could not bring herself to give voice to the words, so she handed him the letter and watched as he read the shocking news.

Darcy's jaw was firmly set when he turned to his cousin. "Do you remember when we were in Hertfordshire and you saw…" he paused as he turned back to look at the open door. Assured of their privacy, he continued, "… when you saw Wickham in Meryton—did you recognize his companion?"

"I did not recognize her, but I can tell you she looked to be about Georgie's age, this tall," he held out his hand, "and had red hair. Why? What is this about?"

Elizabeth's heart dropped when she heard his description. The girl could be none other than Charlotte's sister. She whispered, "*Maria, what have you done?*"

Darcy stood and handed the letter to Fitz, who in turn read it and gave it to his wife. The silence as Mary perused the missive was palpable. When she finally folded it and held it out to her sister, no one in the room expected the words she signed next, "She will be most welcome to stay at Rose Bluff."

Elizabeth quickly replied, "Oh, Mary, do not feel you are obligated to do so. I am certain we can find somewhere else for her to go."

"I say this not out of obligation. I have been in the position of being judged by society, and whether she deserves to be shamed or not, I will not sit by and allow such treatment of another. I would be happy to have her join us at our home."

Fitz stepped up to her side, wrapping his arm around her shoulders as he said, "I agree with my wife. She will be welcomed in our home. After all, it is not as if she can go to Pemberley. If my suspicions are correct about the child's father, Georgiana needs to be kept away from Miss Lucas. What better place than Rose Bluff?"

Darcy looked to Elizabeth, "It may be the best situation for her. The estate has had minimal staff all these years. Mrs Lewis, as well as Mr Porter, have already agreed to be the housekeeper and butler, and we know well of their loyalty to the family from our time in Ramsgate. The remainder of the staffing needs can be filled from Pemberley's servants, specifically chosen with their discretion in mind, and Rose Bluff is far enough away from Hertfordshire to ensure the Lucas family's reputation is not tainted." He turned to Fitz and Mary, "Are you certain?"

They both looked at the other, each communicating with their eyes alone, then Fitz reached for Mary's hand and drew it to his lips, depositing a simple kiss before turning back to Darcy. "Yes, we are certain. She is welcome to stay with us."

Mary spoke, "My only request is that she not be told I am the mistress."

"If that is what you wish, then it shall be," Fitz replied. "We can place her in the guest rooms on the far side of the house from where we will frequent. With a small staff, it would not be uncommon to have some of the rooms closest to her closed up."

"We must keep this from my sister as well," Darcy said.

"Yes, certainly," Fitz agreed.

"Miss Lucas will need a traveling companion," Elizabeth pointed out.

"We can have Aunt Edith take Georgiana to Pemberley to await us, and Mrs Annesley will then be available to travel with Miss Lucas," Darcy suggested.

"She is trustworthy in keeping silent of the errand, and she will need to be told anyway since she is my sister's companion." It was a sound plan and was agreed upon easily.

"Come; I have quite a few letters to write, and that can best be accomplished in my study," Darcy suggested, "and you, my love," he said as he held out his hand to his wife, "can write to your friend and assure her of our assistance."

The particulars were decided and letters written, discretion being called upon in each one. Mrs Lewis was to choose a minimal staff from among Pemberley's servants and remove to Rose Bluff immediately to prepare it for occupation. It was decided the Fitzwilliams would leave in three days time in order to be established in their new home before their visitor was to arrive. Mrs Edith Darcy would travel on from her estate, Havendale, to Pemberley with Georgiana, freeing Mrs Annesley to accompany Miss Lucas on the journey. Elizabeth wrote to Charlotte, telling her to have Maria's trunks packed and ready at dawn, one week from today, and a carriage would be there to pick her up. The location to which she would go was not revealed, but she did assure her friend that if Charlotte wished to send any correspondence to Maria, she could send it to Pemberley and they would see it was delivered.

So it was that the Darcys and Fitzwilliams were removed from Town before Twelfth Night, each bound for their homes in Derbyshire.

Sarah Johnson

Chapter 29

Maria thought she could cry no more, but every day that passed proved just how misguided such an assertion was. The burning in her eyes was the least of the pain she felt though. Her father had turned her out. He did not care where she went, only that she was far enough away as to assure the family's name remained unharmed by her actions. Charlotte was doing everything she could, but Mr Collins was known to keep a tight rein on his wife. Surprisingly, Charlotte found a friend who was willing to help, and now here the two sisters stood, Maria's trunks stacked by the front door as they awaited the carriage of this unknown benefactor.

Through the thick fog that settled on this cold morning, just as the sun was beginning to rise over the horizon, they heard the carriage as it approached. The driver stopped and two footmen jumped down to attend to the trunks. The door opened, and an older lady descended the stairs and approached, giving them a curtsey.

"I am Mrs Annesley, and I take it you are Mrs Collins?" she said to the elder of the two sisters.

"Yes, I am," Charlotte answered.

"You must be Miss Lucas," she said to Maria. "I am pleased to make your acquaintance." She then turned back to Charlotte and held out a letter, "I am to deliver this to you. There is no need to read it immediately."

"Thank you," she said, placing it in her pocket. The next thing she knew Maria's arms were wrapped tightly around her as the girl began to sob. Charlotte returned the embrace, telling her how much she would be missed. The sudden crying of her own babe in the background made her pull away. "I must attend to William, and it is time for you to leave."

Mrs Annesley's arms wrapped around the girl's shoulders, and with a simple nod to Charlotte, she led Maria to the carriage. Then they were gone. Maria watched as the neighborhood she had always known passed outside the windows. Tears continued to stream down her cheeks. The soaked handkerchief she held tightly in her grip was no longer of much use.

When the last of Meryton finally passed, Mrs Annesley closed the shades on the window and moved to sit next to the girl. "Here," she said as she handed her a fresh linen cloth. "I know this must be extremely difficult for you, but you are not alone. You have friends who love you and wish the best out of this situation."

She sobbed even harder, "My family has turned me out, I know not where I am going, nor with whom I will be staying. Who are these friends?"

"I am not at liberty to say, but they care for your well—being. Now, it will not do to distress yourself like this. Just relax," she said as she reached for the ties to Maria's bonnet, removing it. "You just lay your head down here," she indicated her lap. Maria laid her head on the older lady's lap and a rug was draped across her chilled body. "That's it… now just rest." The gentle hands ran through Maria's red curls, the motions soothing the girl's frayed nerves and within minutes she was calmed and asleep.

The days were cold, the journey long, and when they finally arrived at their destination on the fourth day of travel, both were weary of the roads and Maria was sick from the constant rocking. Mrs Lewis was introduced as the housekeeper and the person to whom Maria need speak with if she required anything. It was explained which rooms would be open to her use and which section of the garden had been established as her private area. A maid named Cora would be her constant companion, and when it came time for the mid-wife to be called, she, as well as Mrs Annesley, would also assist with the birth.

Maria was soon settled in her rooms, the loneliness she had felt over the last few weeks not diminishing with her arrival here. Cora served her dinner and soon Maria was ready to retire. The journey caused such weariness that she was quickly asleep.

Mrs Annesley returned to Pemberley the next day, leaving Maria in the hands of the servants of Rose Bluff until she would return for the girl's confinement. Being privy to the details of last spring, and knowing what her employer surmised about this fallen young miss and who the father of the child could likely be, she was glad to know Miss Darcy was saved from such a fate. Her charge was, at times, difficult to convince of her own culpability in the matter, and she felt it might be best to tell her of Miss Lucas. She would bring it up with Mr and Mrs Darcy when she returned. Perhaps in time they would see the wisdom in introducing the two young ladies. One was in need of a friend during such a difficult time, and the other was in need of a lesson to be learned from such tragedy.

The Derbyshire winter was colder than usual this year. The toll it took on Elizabeth was noticeable. While she grew with child, her habits of walking out every day came to a sudden end and she was confined to pace the halls of Pemberley, usually with her husband at her side.

Georgiana's time with Aunt Edith, and the presence of her companion, seemed to quell her insolence, though she still refused anything more than the basic interaction she must have with her new sister.

Letters between Rose Bluff and Pemberley were regular enough to warrant hiring a delivery boy to go between the two estates. Mrs Lewis' son, James, was the perfect candidate for the position. The boy was eager to be of service, and when he was not going between the two estates, he continued his work in the stables. The ten miles became more difficult with the snow, slowing some deliveries to only once a week. It was on one such week when the missives were stacked high awaiting the boy's return, that Fitz had a thought. He quickly jotted down a note for his cousin, placing it on top of the stack before going to find his wife.

She was sitting in the library reading when he tried to sneak up on her. Anticipating him, she moved just as he reached out from behind.

He stomped around the chaise to sit beside her, "I shall never understand how you do that?"

"It is easy—when you enter the room, I feel your presence. No matter what has my attention, I know when you are near."

Fitz wound his arms around her waist, pulling her into his embrace. "You know just what to say to make me feel completely besotted."

His lips descended, meeting hers in a fury of passion that built quickly, ending only when they both needed air. Fitz reclined on the chaise and pulled her tightly to his chest, running his fingers through her dark curls.

Mary rested her cheek against her husband's chest, the movements of his heavy breathing evidence of their exchange. All her life she had longed for something, but she could not determine what it was. Now after being married these past few months and the small intimacies she shared with Fitz, she knew just what was missing from her life. How she could have thought marriage was not for her, she did not know. This was exactly what she needed. *He* was exactly what she needed.

Fitz saw a small smile play across her red, swollen lips. He tapped her arm, drawing her attention, "What has amused you?"

"Life… marriage… *you*," she answered verbally.

She did not speak often, but when she did he loved to hear her voice. He replied, "How I ever convinced myself I could live without you in my life I shall never know. I will forever be grateful to my cousin for setting me straight."

She kissed the small, faded scar next to his mouth left from that exchange, the roughness against her lips pleasing in a way she could not describe. "I am forever grateful he did as well."

"I know you have missed seeing your sister this last month, and I have devised a plan. I wrote to my cousin asking if my Aunt Anne's sled is still at the back of the carriage house. If it is, I expect he will agree to send it for us to use."

Mary sat up quickly, a large smile now brightening her features.

"This pleases you?"

282

"OH yes! I would dearly love to visit my sister!"

"Then we shall do just that. I expect this storm to pass quickly, and James will surely be able to make his deliveries to Pemberley by tomorrow evening. If the weather holds out, we could be there very soon."

She stood, signing to him, "Then I must pack."

He stood as well, taking her hand and drawing it to his lips, depositing a simple kiss on the back. "It will be good to see our family once again. Hiding within just a few rooms here in our own home is quite daunting at times."

"It is not you who must hide, my love."

"You cannot fool me. I was present when you were verbally assaulted by my young cousin, by my own mother, and then later by my cousin again along with Miss Bingley. I was also there when you were shunned from even attending a church service while in Meryton. You need not try to convince me why you wish to keep your presence as the Mistress of Rose Bluff from our visitor. I understand more fully than you will ever know. Mrs Lewis has established a routine which seems to give us our privacy, but I see how tense you become when you are walking from room to room. This is your home and it should not be this way."

She looked down, "I have encountered situations such as this for long enough to know this is just how it is to be for me."

Fitz lifted her chin so she would look at him, "No, it need not be like this. When we return from Pemberley we will find a more reasonable solution. I cannot have my wife feel this way in our own home." He did not give her time to object before his lips were gently coercing hers into submission. When the kiss was broken, he signed, "I love you."

She smiled, "I love you as well."

"Come, we must attend to our trunks, Mrs Fitzwilliam."

Elizabeth was seated in the drawing room, knitting something special for their baby as she watched Mrs Annesley and Georgiana. They were positioned by the window in front on an easel. The girl had such talent, yet she would hardly receive even a compliment from Elizabeth without turning up her nose. In the month since returning to Pemberley, she had found the best solution was to leave Georgiana's care to Mrs Annesley. If Miss Darcy's presence was requested, the companion was sure to have her charge attend. Today was just such a day. Elizabeth had spoken with Mrs Annesley about spending more time in the presence of her new sister, even if they were simply in the same room doing different tasks. Today Miss Darcy was practicing her drawing, and the unusual winter light from the large window was just perfect.

Elizabeth was lonely here at Pemberley. If it were not so cold, she could retreat into the garden, but at this time of year and in her condition, her husband requested she remain indoors. She saw the logic in his request, though it was difficult to be so alone. As the master of the estate, he spent several hours each day on business, and she did not like to disturb him. So she sat here in silence watching Georgiana and missing her sister Mary greatly.

Darcy walked into the room carrying a letter, "I have heard from your uncle. He wishes to send his love and assure you of their comfort this winter. He also wished me to convey that he has found what made the nursery so drafty, and the children are now much warmer after attending to the window sill."

She moved over so he could sit beside her on the sofa, receiving the kiss he always administered to her cheek. "I thought it was the window last year, but could not be certain. I am happy to hear it has been repaired. Poor Henry was forced to sleep in the coldest bed in the whole house."

Darcy chuckled, "Yes, he told me once about the quilt you made just for him because he was often found crawling into your bed at night."

Elizabeth smiled, her hand moving to rest upon her growing stomach.

Darcy looked across at his sister. Assured of some privacy, he too reached out to touch his wife's belly, locking his fingers with hers. All of a sudden he felt a tiny movement and Elizabeth nearly jumped. "Was that... ?"

"I think so," she replied in shock.

He pulled her closer to his side and moved his hand, hoping to feel the movement again. As if on cue, the babe moved again. "That must feel strange," he whispered.

"It used to feel as if a butterfly was fluttering on the inside, but lately it is becoming stronger."

He smiled as he caressed her belly, "My little butterfly."

Georgiana saw the exchange and rolled her eyes. "I would never act this way in public with my husband."

Mrs Annesley looked over to the loving couple, "When you are old enough to marry, perhaps you will feel differently. This is not a public place, it is their private home. They are clearly in love and looking forward to their growing family. My husband and I shared moments just like this as well."

Georgiana stood, removing her smock, "I am finished for today; this light is no longer adequate." When she passed her brother, she put her nose in the air and kept walking.

"I am sorry, sir, madam. I will speak with her," Mrs Annesley replied as she pulled the drawing from the easel and gathered the supplies.

"There is no need," Elizabeth answered. "Even if she refuses to accept my place here, I still wish to see her every morning. I fear if you say anything she may refuse even that small accommodation."

"As you wish, madam. Perhaps tomorrow we can try the music room?"

"Yes, that would be lovely; thank you."

Mrs Annesley left to catch up with her charge, leaving the couple alone.

Darcy sighed heavily, "This is not working. I do not know what to do, but something must get through to my sister. I see what this is doing to you. You have lost a little of the sparkle in your eye, and it pains me to see it go."

"Do not worry, my love. When the weather warms and I can return to my daily walks out of doors, I am certain the sparkle you love so much will return as well."

"I hope I do not have to wait so long as that," he replied. "Winters here in Derbyshire can be quite long, and it is barely February."

Mrs Reynolds knocked on the open door, entering to say, "Sir, Madam, you have visitors."

"Who could it be in this cold?" Elizabeth said as she stood, her hands going to her hair to ensure it was not out of place.

Darcy stood, kissing her cheek and smiling, "You look lovely. Let us go and see who is here."

When Elizabeth entered the front hall and saw Mary and Fitz standing there, she broke out in an enormous smile and ran to embrace her sister. The two gentlemen exchanged their own, more subtle greetings, and watched as their wives cried and signed faster than either of them could keep up with.

"Perhaps we should leave them to their own devices?" Fitz suggested.

"Yes, I am certain they would both appreciate some privacy." Darcy walked over to them, welcoming Mary and suggesting the two take tea in the drawing room. The visitors coats were removed and the sisters were soon back to discussing all they had longed to tell the other over the last month that letters could not adequately convey while the gentlemen removed to the billiards room for a few games and their own discussion.

Chapter 30

eorgiana was happy to have her cousin at Pemberley again, even if it meant his wife must be here as well. It freed her from the obligations to sit with Elizabeth every day. Mrs Annesley still insisted they attend the entertainments after dinner, and that was enough for her. Most of her time was spent in her own rooms.

It was on one such afternoon, when she was quite bored and Mrs Annesley was mending something in the dressing room, that Georgiana decided to go downstairs. She heard the sounds of balls cracking against one another and saw the butler retreating from the billiards room. Before the door closed she heard her brother say to their cousin, "It is from your father."

Curiosity got the better of her and she sneaked past the door and into the hidden service corridor. She found most of the passages in the lower levels of Pemberley were rarely used, only those surrounding the bedrooms above stairs. She knew the hidden wall panel was covered by a large tapestry, so she opened it just enough to hear what was being said within the room.

"I cannot believe his gall!" Darcy was furious.

"What does he write?"

Sarah Johnson

"Here, you must read this dribble for yourself to believe he would even ask such a question."

Fitz began to read the letter aloud.

> "We have removed from Town back to our home. Your aunt is quite missing the frivolities of the Season and is already planning a few parties and teas for when we return. We would hope you could attend, though we cannot offer an invitation for the whole family."

He looked up at Darcy, "I cannot believe he would invite you and not your wife!"

"Oh, that is the least of it. Continue reading," Darcy suggested.

> "Your cousin Milton has also removed from Town. It is he who I wish to discuss, and why I find myself penning this missive. Upon my arrival, it has come to my attention that Croome Court is not as productive as it has been in previous years, and with the debts we have accrued in Town over the last few months something must be done. I have already told Milton that he must marry. It is, however, imperative that the family line not be tainted, and this is why my main objective was to write to you immediately. The time has come for my son and your sister to marry. It is what your father would have wanted, and I dare say my own sister would have wished it as well, had she lived long enough to give her blessing to such a union. With the financial holdings being tied up in the land, we will require the marriage take place immediately as to ensure the estate not be broken up and sold off..."

Fitz stopped reading and handed it back to Darcy, silence filling the air.

Georgiana felt tears well up in her eyes. She could not believe her uncle would look upon her only as a means to saving his own home. Did he not love her? Did he not care that her heart was given to another? When she heard one of the gentlemen moving about, her attention was once again turned to the occupants of the room.

Darcy wadded the paper up and threw it towards the fire. "It is with a heavy heart I must insist my family part ways with your father and mother," he said to Fitz.

288

"I understand. They have not spoken to me since I made the decision to marry, though my wife insists on writing to them at least once a month. They have never answered her—not even the simple Christmas greeting she sent." With a heavy sigh, he said, "It seems to be the way of things in this family of ours."

"I will not sacrifice my sister. She deserves to find happiness, and I doubt Milton could inspire such feelings in her."

"I doubt he could inspire such feelings in any lady," Fitz said with a smirk.

"Yes, well, if they wish him to marry they will have to find someone else. I am unwilling to give my sister to such devices. Your father was obviously well into his cups when he penned this missive, and I will not allow this to affect my own family." He stood suddenly, "Come, it is time we found our wives. Perhaps it is warm enough for a short walk out in the garden."

"I am sure they would both appreciate the fresh air," Fitz replied as he followed his cousin out of the room.

Georgiana peeked out from behind the tapestry that covered her hiding spot. When she was satisfied that they were gone, she went over to the fire. Seeing that the letter was not completely burned up, she pulled the wadded mess from the coals, smoothing the pages before she put them into her pocket and sneaked back out of the room and upstairs. When she was assured of her privacy, she read what she could of the missive. The words cut to the deepest part of her soul. *How could her family think she was worth nothing but a prize for marriage?*

It was with a downtrodden expression that she joined the others for supper that evening, excusing herself early with the excuse that she did not enjoy playing cards. Darcy was worried and questioned her further, but upon her insistence that she was just not feeling well, he allowed her to retire, stipulating she take some of Mrs Reynolds' tea before she went to sleep. Even the vile taste of the concoction could not deter her from the desire to sleep, so she easily accepted his terms and retired, though sleep did not come easy for her that night.

Elizabeth and Mary sat beside each other at the table. Their husbands entered the room, both nearly becoming sick at the sight of the food on both the ladies plates.

"Must you insist upon eating that so early, my love?" Darcy replied as he kissed Elizabeth's cheek. He sat and nodded for the waiting footman to pour his drink.

"I see nothing wrong with this wonderful dish our cook has provided," she replied. "It cannot be too odd if my sister is eating it," she said with a smile. "Are you certain you will not have some as well?" she asked Fitz.

He patted his stomach and groaned aloud, "Oh, no—I will just join my cousin in some tea, or possibly some coffee?" He looked to the footman who nodded and left to procure the stronger drink for him.

Elizabeth cocked her head and looked at her sister. "Now that I have heard two gentlemen, one of whom, I must confess, I thought would eat nearly anything set before him," she said, looking at Fitz, "it *is* rather odd that you would like this dish so much. Are you feeling well?" She placed her hand on Mary's forehead.

"I feel perfectly well. Why do you ask?"

"Hmmm… I have not seen any other reason to think so, but…"

Mary tapped her sister's arm, then signed, "Elizabeth, you are not making it easy for me to see what you say when you turn away."

"Oh, I am sorry," she signed. "Perhaps we should speak about this later."

Mary was confused, but she agreed and continued on with the meal. When the sisters were both finished, Elizabeth excused them and insisted Mary join her in her chambers for a private discussion. They were soon both settled into chairs, facing each other.

"I wonder," Elizabeth signed, "if you are feeling odd in any way?"

"No, not really. Why?"

"Now, I do not wish to frighten you, but I have heard that every lady is different with their symptoms."

"Symptoms of what?"

290

She reached out to take her sister's hand in her own, squeezing Mary's fingers as she asked, "Have your courses been regular since you married?"

"My courses? Why ever would you ask such a thing…" then it dawned on her just what her sister suspected. Her hand flew as she quickly signed, "Could it be? Could I too be with child?"

"I cannot say for certain, but I do wonder, what with our odd choice of food this morning. Would you like me to call for the doctor?"

"Oh, no—it would only worry my husband."

"Would you rather worry your expectant sister," she said as her hand fell to her expanding midsection.

She knew exactly what Elizabeth was doing, and it was working. "All right," she finally signed, "I will see the doctor."

Mrs Reynolds was called and it was explained to the housekeeper that the sisters wished to keep this call private. She assured them of her silence on the matter and promised to bring the doctor up herself when he arrived.

Within just a few hours their questions were answered and the doctor confirmed that, to the best of his ability at this point, he thought it very possible that Mary was indeed pregnant. He left the two giddy sisters to tell the news to their husbands in their own way.

That evening after dinner, the four of them, as well as Georgiana and Mrs Annesley removed to the sitting room. Darcy, as was his usual request, asked his sister if she would like to play for them. He was shocked when, for the first time since before she was removed from school, she agreed. As she was choosing her music he looked over at Fitz, confusion apparent on his features.

Fitz shrugged his shoulder, then cleared his throat and stood, "I will turn the pages for you, Georgiana."

She gave a simple thank you, then sat on the stool and began to play. Fitz looked over to his wife. She sat with her eyes closed and her hand laid against the wooden surface of the table beside her. In his distracted state he nearly missed the nod from Georgiana to turn the page.

When the others retired for the evening, Mary insisted she and Fitz stay for a few more minutes alone. Fitz offered to play the pianoforte. Sitting on the stool and pulling his wife closer, he insisted she sit on his knee, then he wound his long arms around her and began to play the one song he knew well enough to not look at his fingers. It would have been quite the comical scene if anyone came in, but in such privacy it became an intimate moment between the two. Mary sat with her eyes closed and her back leaned into her husband's chest. The beat of the notes resonated into her so that she could almost hear them being played. When they stopped, she felt her husband's hands wrap around her waist and his scruffy cheek rub lightly against her own as he laid his chin on her shoulder and gave her a kiss.

She knew this was the moment to tell him. Without opening her eyes, she reached her hands out in front of them and signed, "We think I might be with child." She felt him stiffen and she opened her eyes, turning to look into his face.

He reached up to cup her cheek in his palm, his other hand going to his chin as he drew his finger out from it, asking, "Truly?"

She placed her own hand on top of his, moving it down to her abdomen and signed in return, "Truly."

Tears welled in his eyes and he pulled her into an embrace she would not soon forget. When Fitz finally softened the kisses and pulled away, he suggested they retire. Mary stood and held her hand out to her husband. They walked side by side out of the room and up the stairs, each delighted in their newfound feelings of hope at what the future would hold for their family.

The days turned into weeks, and weeks into months. It was soon confirmed that Mary was, indeed, with child. Unlike her sister, she had a much easier time right from the start. Georgiana began to spend more time with the sisters. Darcy did notice, though, that she sometimes displayed a melancholy. On another search of her room no more letters were discovered, and Darcy knew he kept a tight control of the posted letters coming into and going out of Pemberley. Her change in disposition could not be from George Wickham contacting her again. Perhaps it was the realization that she was wrong in her assessment of him? Darcy took his thoughts to his cousin, but neither could come up with a reason. They only determined to keep a close watch on her for now.

Before they knew it, the snow of winter melted away and the first buds of spring began to poke through the barren ground. For two months the sisters had enjoyed each other's company, but it was time for the Fitzwilliams to return to Rose Bluff. Fitz had ridden there a couple of times over their stay to work with the steward on the spring planting schedule, but otherwise they had left their visitor all alone.

Elizabeth understood Mary's reluctance to introduce herself to Maria Lucas as the Mistress of Rose Bluff, but she also encouraged her to say something, if only to allow her more freedom at home. After their harsh reception in Hertfordshire last autumn, she did not expect Mary to concede.

They had been gone for two days when a letter came for Elizabeth. It was quite thick and that worried her. With trembling hands she tore open the seal, ripping part of the last page in her haste. Setting it aside, she scanned quickly through the first page, then the second, getting to the third and final page. With careful positioning she was able to read all of her sister's words, and it was with a joyful heart that she went to speak with her husband in his study.

Elizabeth opened the door and saw him sitting at his desk, his fingers of one hand tapping the wood in a rhythmic pattern as he scoured over maps of the lands. His other hand was raised to his forehead, rubbing circles on his temples with his thumb and forefinger. *He must have a headache.*

When he heard the rustle of her skirts, Darcy looked up. "Oh, I am sorry dearest; I did not see you standing there."

She walked over to the desk, positioning herself behind his chair. She urged him to lean back as her fingers wound into his dark, curly hair. "You need to rest from these maps. You and your cousin were poring over them for weeks, and now here you are agonizing still. Just trust that what has already been decided will do well."

He let out an audible sigh as he closed his eyes, the pressure of her hands working magic on the pounding in his head. "Thank you."

"For what?"

He reached up to grasp her hand in his, leading her around his chair and pulling her onto his lap. "For putting so much trust in my abilities to manage this land. I doubt my father ever would have been so generous."

Elizabeth wound her hands around his neck, resting her forehead against his as she looked him in the eyes. "Fitzwilliam Darcy, you are a gentleman most capable of the task before you. You have been reared to be who you are now, and anyone who would not be proud of what you have become is not worthy of our time and thoughts."

With such encouragement, he pulled her closer, their lips meeting for a few moments of passion. When they finally separated, he laid his hand on her expanded belly, addressing the babe within, "Your mother here has the most luscious lips."

She gasped, "Sir! How shocking! You mustn't speak so to our child!"

His hand continued to rub circles on her belly. "What should I say then? That I hope she carries your dark eyes?"

"My only wish for our child is that it be a healthy babe. I could not bear it if…"

"Our child will be perfect, no matter what."

"I know what it is like to live every day with someone others see as only an imposition."

"You have proven your ability to love the undesirable, and I dare say, even with the hardships you and Mary have faced, you would not wish to change a thing if it meant they led you right here to my arms," he said with a smile so large his rare dimples shown.

She could not help but smile herself, "Yes, in that you are correct. Speaking of Mary, I have received a letter from her."

"Already? They have been gone but two days."

"If you do not mind, this position is causing my back such pains. Perhaps we could move to the sofa instead?"

"I do not mind at all," he replied as he helped her stand. "I will call for tea," he said pulling the rope to call for Mrs Reynolds. When the order had been given and they were finally settled on the sofa with their tea, he asked, "Now, what was it your sister had to say in her letter?"

Elizabeth sipped the hot liquid, then placed her cup down on the table to pull the missive from her pocket, opening it. "The decision of whether to introduce themselves to their guest was taken from them, as Miss Lucas saw them from

294

the garden when they arrived."

Darcy took the letter, reading the portion to which she pointed on the back of the first page.

> "When I was settled in the drawing room, awaiting Fitz for our tea, I was shocked to see Miss Lucas appear in the doorway. Her eyes were red and swollen, and I could see the trembling of her hands. My husband came into the hallway at that moment and invited her in to join us, and amazingly she accepted.
>
> It was a tense repast, but she did not refuse. I dare say she was grateful for the opportunity to see someone besides Mrs Lewis and Cora. She and Fitz spoke a few words, and he introduced himself to her, but otherwise we all sat in silence."

He handed the letter back to her, "What a reception."

"Yes, quite. She goes on to say that the next morning Mrs Lewis asked, on her behalf, if she could break her fast with them. Upon their acceptance, she sat with them, though again few words were spoken. The rest of the letter is more of Mary's feelings on the situation."

"She will do her duty as mistress of Rose Bluff, and will offer what services she can to their guest."

"Yes, she will, of that I can be certain. She may not have wished to be in this position, but if there is anything my sister thrives at, it is being the best person she can be when forced into impossible situations."

"I have faith in her ability to handle the situation with grace. They may even bond over the shared experience of both being with child," he suggested.

"I hope so."

Darcy put down his tea cup, stood, and held out his hand to his wife, "Come; I fancy a walk in the garden with my favorite lady."

She took his hand, accepting his assistance with standing, then wound her arm around his and they left the room.

Sarah Johnson

Chapter 31

he months wore on, their days filling quickly with outdoor activities of many sorts. Now that the sisters could visit more easily, they saw each other more frequently. Some weeks it was shopping while other weeks it was a picnic. When their husbands could join them, they did, though most of the time they were busy with watching over the new land developments at Rose Bluff and Pemberley.

Elizabeth invited Georgiana on any outing she had with Mary. Sometimes she surprised them both and joined them, though it was not with any regularity. She may not have been trying very hard, but it was evident she was at least trying a little. Darcy was disturbed by his sister's continuing melancholy though and had already contacted Aunt Edith to see if Georgiana could stay with her for a few months after the baby was born. She needed much more attention than he and his wife would be able to give her with a new baby around.

Maria Lucas became quite the companion for Mary. The two often walked in the garden and sat together in the drawing room. The rumors of the fire were never spoken of by either, but the camaraderie they had easily overshadowed any uneasiness each felt in the beginning of their friendship, especially after Mary confessed her own expectancy to Maria. At times it was quite comical to Fitz what odd combination of food the two would come up with next.

After some weeks, Maria confronted Fitz when he was alone, insisting he tell her why she was with them. He told of her sister's letter and of his wife's insistence that she stay with them. When Maria questioned whether Mary felt guilty over the death of her brother, she was told the true tale of that awful night so many years before, when both girls had lost their loved ones. Knowing the truth, she was better able to accept the friendship Mary was willingly offering to her.

Easter holiday came and went, and the next big event would be Elizabeth's confinement. The month of May began with all eyes carefully watching the obviously very pregnant Mrs Darcy. Each week the local gossips spoke of her presence in church services. A few of the local gentlemen had a betting book going on whether the babe would be a boy or a girl and when it would be born. Though they would never admit it in public, a few of the ladies convinced their husbands to make some wagers for them as well. Every week that passed more people were disappointed that the day they had chosen for the birth of the heir of Pemberley had passed. Anticipation built to the point that Elizabeth stopped going to the shops for the simple reason that she did not wish to hear, yet again, the observations from all that she had not yet had the babe.

When the time finally came and the midwife was called to Pemberley, the entire neighborhood waited with bated breath on the news to be announced. A footman delivering some letters to be posted was nearly run over by the ladies coming out of the milliner's shop when they recognized his livery. He told them he knew nothing yet, but the entire way back to Pemberley he felt as if he was being followed.

"Joseph? Is there a problem?"

He heard his master's voice and was relieved. "No, s'r. 'm sorry sir. Jus' comin' from Lambton."

"You were walking rather oddly. Is there something amiss?"

"Nothin' to wor'y ya wit', sir."

"Very well," he said with a nod as he continued on to the stables. His wife was not the only one giving birth at this time–his prized mare was as well. Having spent his day pacing the floors of his study, he was willing to endure anything to stop from agonizing over what might be taking place above stairs with his wife and child. He followed the noise coming from the back stall and was not at all shocked to see his cousin in the thick of things, his coat tossed aside onto the stone wall of a nearby empty stall.

"There you are," Fitz said, moving over so Darcy could enter the stall.

"I see things have not changed. You still fancy getting your hands in on anything to do with horses."

Fitz chuckled. "Let me get washed up and I can keep you busy."

"Actually, I thought I might be useful out here."

"You do know this gets messy, do you not?"

"This is not the first birth I have seen, Fitz."

"Peering from the fence as a colt is born in the middle of the field is not the same as being in the thick of it." When his cousin glared at him, he shrugged his shoulders, "If it will keep you occupied for a time, then who am I to tell you no. You might want to remove your coat and waistcoat. I doubt the mare will care whether it is silk, and I dare say your valet would not be pleased if it must be replaced."

Darcy chuckled as he unbuttoned and removed the items, folding them neatly and laying them over next to his cousin's coat. "What can I do," he asked as he rolled up his shirtsleeves.

"Wash up," the head groom called out from the other side of the stall. "O're there," he pointed to a table where a bowl of water, a cake of soap, and some linens were laid out.

"My hands are clean," he said in his Master of Pemberley voice.

"S'r, beggin your pardon, but n'one comes in 'ere wit'ot washin' up first." When the Master did not move, he continued, "Me record wit' births speaks for itse'f, sir. 'Tis my way wit' e'eryone."

Fitz patted his cousin on the shoulder, "He has an excellent point, Darce. My hands could stand a wash as well," he pulled his cousin over to the table, getting his own hands wet and lathering up before handing the cake of soap to his cousin. He quietly replied, "Whether this does any good or not, it would not do to have you thrown from the stables right now. Best wash up."

Darcy scrubbed his hands, up to his elbows, then the two returned to the stall.

"Thank ye, sir," the groom said with a bow of his head. When the mare gave a whinny, he cried out, "'Tis abo't to get messy, sir."

The next hour was a blur of activity, and by the time the two cousins left the stables, Darcy did not even remember the offense he had felt at the groom's insistence that he wash. They returned to the house and went to change their clothes. Darcy was just coming out of his room when he saw Mrs Reynolds enter the hall, a maid following behind with a bucket of water.

"May I speak with you, Mrs Reynolds?"

The housekeeper turned to the girl. "Go on in with the water. I will be in shortly. Let Mrs Wilson know it is freshly boiled, and give her this," she said as she pulled a cake of soap from her pocket and handed it to the girl. When she was gone, Mrs Reynolds turned back to Mr Darcy. "What can I help you with, sir?"

"Why have you a need for water and soap?"

"Mrs Wilson will not hear of anyone entering the birthing room without having first washed. She says it was a practice taught in a lecture she attended from a well known doctor, and has since begun practicing it with all her patients. She also insists the windows remain open to give the room fresh air. I must say, her practices are rather odd, but Mrs Darcy is insistent upon having Mrs Wilson as her midwife."

Hmmm, he thought, perhaps the groom is correct in his assertion if the medical community is beginning to embrace such a custom for patients as well. He addressed the housekeeper, "If my wife is happy, and she and the babe remain healthy, then maybe there is something to Mrs Wilson's methods?"

"Perhaps. What was it you needed, sir?"

"Just your reassurance, I suppose."

He looked like the boy who had lost his mother all those years ago and the housekeeper felt her heart break at the look in his eyes. "Mrs Darcy is in good hands."

"Will she see me?"

"Sir! The birthing room is no place for a gentleman."

"I just need to see her; only for a minute."

"I will speak with Mrs Wilson—it would not do to upset her."

"Thank you," he answered as she walked away. He paced the hallway until a few minutes later when he saw Elizabeth's door open and Mrs Reynolds nod that he would be permitted in. With a quick stride he was at his wife's side nearly immediately. He knelt beside her, taking her hand in his, "Are you well? Please tell me you are, my Elizabeth?"

A pain came over her and she squeezed his hand as she tried to control her breathing. The midwife came up to the other side of the laboring mother, urging her to take a deep breath and let it out slowly. She then showed Mr Darcy how to comfort his wife by stroking her stomach in a circular pattern.

When the pain had subsided, she replied, "I know it is not the usual practice for gentlemen to be admitted to the birthing room, but I am never one to turn a father away. I have found the mother is usually calmer with him at her side."

"You do not mind my being here then?" Darcy asked.

"No sir, I do not. As long as your wife is doing well, I will not ask you to leave."

Elizabeth smiled, "I must say, I prefer you by my side as well."

He squeezed her hand, kissing her fingers, "Then by your side I shall be."

The next few hours were agonizingly slow for Darcy, who had to watch as his wife's body was riddled with painful contractions. By the time the babe was ready to be born, he was eager to step out of the way and let the ladies take over.

With Elizabeth in the proper position in the birthing chair, and with urging from the midwife to push, Darcy watched as his daughter was born. He was so shocked at the miracle he had been privy to that he was glad to be led to a chair to sit. When his daughter was placed within his arms, he fell in love with everything from her beautiful eyes to her dark curly hair. She began to fuss, her hand waving around, so he reached out to touch her palm, her tiny fingers wrapping around his as she calmed. He smiled at the resemblance she held to his wife. It was as if he were holding a younger version of Elizabeth in his arms. He could not be any happier then he was in this moment with his wife beside him and their daughter in his arms.

When Elizabeth was cleaned up and settled in the bed, Darcy moved to sit beside her where he could hold both his wife and his daughter in his arms together. Mrs Reynolds showed the others from the room and the new family was left alone to rest after such an ordeal.

Georgiana and Fitz sat alone in the sitting room. He could tell she was tired, but she refused to go to bed. Aside from the way she acted, Fitz could tell she cared for Elizabeth's safety. Shifting on the sofa into a better position, he said, "Georgiana, come join me over here. You will be more comfortable."

She was about to decline, but the sofa did look inviting. "Thank you," she said as she sat down, leaning heavily into her cousin's shoulder.

He drew his hand around her shoulders and pulled her head down to rest on the pillow. She easily acquiescence, though she stated, "I do not wish to go to sleep."

Fitz chuckled. *Yes, she truly does care.* "Are your trunks packed for your trip next week?"

She huffed, drawing her arms up to her chest and her feet closer to her body, "Why must I go back with Aunt Edith?"

"Georgiana, we have been over this. We will not go over it again. You are going."

"Well if I must go, at least it is in the summer when I can still ride and be out of doors. Last winter was quite droll."

"Your aunt said in her latest letter that her mare has given birth. She plans to take it to Tattersall's next year when it is weaned."

Georgiana perked up, "Really? How wonderful! Has she named it yet?"

Fitz patted her on hair, "No, she says you are much better at that and she will leave you to find the proper name for this foal."

"What color is it?"

302

He chuckled, "I know nothing more. You will just have to find out when you get there. Then you must write and tell me what name you have chosen."

She looked up at her cousin, "I will do that."

It was several hours later when Mary finally came into the room. She smiled at the sight of her husband asleep against the corner of the sofa, and Georgiana curled up beside him. It was just as she suspected a daughter would be with a father. She walked over behind them and gently kissed her husband's cheek, rousing him.

He smiled when her face came into focus. "Has Elizabeth had the babe?"

"Yes," she signed. "It is a healthy baby girl."

Georgiana began to move and as soon as she noticed Mary's presence, she asked, "How is she? How is my brother? Is everything well?"

Fitz put a calming hand on her arm, "All is well, Georgiana. Elizabeth has had a girl, and they are both doing well."

She squealed and bounced on the sofa in her excitement, "A niece! Oh how wonderful! I am now an aunt! Can you imagine? Aunt Georgiana! Oh it has such a wonderful sound to it, does it not?"

Fitz leaned over and kissed her on the cheek, "Yes it does. Now then, *Aunt Georgiana*, you best get up to bed so you can see the babe for yourself tomorrow."

She quickly left the room, giving a final smile to both Fitz and Mary.

Fitz chuckled at his cousin, then, when he was alone with his wife, he reached for Mary's hand, drawing her around the sofa and down onto his lap. She sank into him, resting her head on his chest in clear exhausted. Fitz reached for her hand and together with his own, he began to caress her expanding belly.

They sat in silence for a few minutes before Mary stayed his hand. "If you continue, I am likely to fall asleep here. Let us retire while I can still walk up the stairs."

Fitz kissed her forehead, then helped her stand and they went upstairs and to their room.

By the time the neighborhood broke their fast the next morning, news of the birth of Miss Rose Amelia Darcy was spread far and wide.

Mary felt relief at being able to be a part of the experience before her own time came. Mrs Wilson was good about explaining exactly what was taking place, and Mrs Reynolds made sure Mary stood in the proper place and was not in the way. They even allowed Mabel, Mary's personal maid, to be present to sign to her mistress when it was necessary. Sometimes being deaf in a hearing world was quite difficult, but Mary was shocked at the ease with which the events of that day unfolded. Later, when she and her husband were sharing their stories of their day, she was happy to find that she no longer feared what was to come for them as well in about five months time.

Mrs Edith Darcy visited Pemberley for the first week of the babe's life, celebrating her arrival with the family at the christening, then she returned to Havendale with Georgiana. Her niece was not happy to be sent from Pemberley, but without any other choice, she acceded to her family's wishes. She did find a small amount of anticipation in being able to name the foal when she arrived with her aunt. The Fitzwilliams returned to Rose Bluff as well, leaving the new family alone at Pemberley.

Maria Lucas excitedly awaited news from Mary about Elizabeth's confinement. She dearly wished to be there, but knew it was not possible. When the mistress finally returned, the two could be seen together, conversing about the birth for days. Mary was able to give Maria some insights she learned from the midwife, and she delivered a letter Elizabeth had written. Although Maria did not look forward to her own confinement with much anticipation, the letter did assuage some of her fears of the process. She also felt better knowing Mrs Annesley was to return for her confinement. The dear lady had made quite the impression on Maria, and she spoke often of the care she provided and love she showed during the days they spent traveling to Derbyshire.

Chapter (32)

itz was working in his study, watching out the window as his wife and their guest sat in the garden enjoying the summer sunshine. The two had become quite the odd pair, Maria even learning to sign so they could speak with more ease. Sometimes, however, they chose to write out their conversation, as they clearly were doing today. He saw Mary write something in her notebook and hand it to Maria, who wrote her own answer before returning it to Mary. Shaking his head and chuckling at them, he looked back down at the papers strewn across the table in front of him. He did not enjoy this part of being a land owner, but he could not be happier to be in such a position, with a wonderful wife with whom to share his life and a child on the way, instead of being out on the battlefield somewhere or possibly even injured or dead.

"Sir?"

"Yes Mrs Lewis?" he answered the housekeeper.

"You have a visitor," she said with a puzzled look on her face. This was the first time they had received a visitor since no invitations were sent because of their guest.

Fitz was taken aback until he saw Bingley step into the doorway. "Bingley!

Come in, come in. It is a surprise, to be sure, but a pleasant one. Mrs Lewis, could you bring us some refreshments?"

"Right away, sir," she answered as she left to do as he bid.

Bingley looked around the room, "I see you are settling in here. You are in need of some shelves," he nodded at the books stacked on several surfaces and the floor around the room, "but otherwise it is quite the cozy space."

"We have recently changed a few of the rooms around, and this one was chosen as my study. The shelves are being fashioned now and should be delivered within the month. As you can see," he pointed to the table at which he sat," I am in need of a desk as well. We are giving quite the custom to the local carpentry shop." He looked around the room, his eyes drawn to the bare windows. "I will leave the finer details to my wife. My cousin is to visit in about a month, and I am certain our wives will have drapes ordered before too long."

Mrs Lewis returned with the refreshments. Fitz quickly shuffled the papers around, clearing a place on the table for the tray, then thanked and dismissed the housekeeper.

"I am sorry I cannot offer you a more comfortable seat," he said, indicating the two chairs at the table.

Bingley nodded, "It will do nicely; I thank you."

The two sat, Fitz leaving the chair facing away from the window to Bingley. He breathed a little easier when he saw movement out the window and realized it was Mrs Lewis speaking with the two ladies. They then stood and walked off to the far end of the garden, out of sight from this prospect. "So what brings you to Derbyshire?"

"I was compelled to come by Darcy, who cannot stop talking of his beautiful daughter, and since you told me before to stop by here any time I was in the neighborhood, well… here I am."

Fitz remembered extending the offer, but it was well before they knew they would have their guest staying with them. "How are your sisters?"

"I just received a letter from Hurst saying Caroline is being courted, and he expects to be approached for a private meeting very soon, perhaps even this week." Bingley leaned back in the chair, "The freedom that knowledge gives me is unimaginable!"

Fitz chuckled, "Yes, I dare say your sister has been quite the burden."

"I tell you Fitz, if she would give up this notion that she is worthy of marrying a peer, my life would be much easier."

"I take it this beau of hers is not a peer then?"

"Who knows? Hurst does not give a name, and honestly, I doubt I would deny anyone's suit, even if it was *your* brother."

Fitz laughed aloud, "Now there is a match I would have never seen coming!"

"We would be like brothers, so it is not as if *everything* would be horrid if that were true."

"Well, in all seriousness, Darcy has heard from my father that Croome Court is in need of an influx of money, so you might want to keep an eye on your sister. Her £20,000 dowry would be quite the lure for my father and brother."

"I will keep that in mind, but really, it is up to Hurst as I am not in Town right now. Caroline is of the age that anything I say would be disregarded anyway." Bingley stood and went over to the window, looking out to examine the garden. "You have quite the view here."

"Yes; my wife's love of flowers is what made me choose this particular room for my study. I can easily look outside to see where she prefers to be when I am required to be in here about my business."

Bingley chuckled, patting his friend on the shoulder, "Oh, ho, you do have it bad, Fitz."

He stood as well, "I only hope you too will one day meet your perfect match."

"Ahhh, now that is something I would like to happen soon."

"You have now decided you are old enough."

He began to pace around the room, looking at different items as he spoke, "I know I am still young, but I am old enough to want to be settled. I hoped with leasing Netherfield Park last year that I would have found a neighborhood in which to remain, but with everything that took place, I just do not see that happening. I have let the lease go. Now I must find another estate, and this area has drawn my attention. I would not mind being within a days' journey of Pemberley and Rose Bluff."

"I know nothing of the estates available around here. Have you spoken with Darcy?"

"Yes, he knew of a couple, which is why he sent me this direction. One is just five miles down the road from here—Buckley Hall."

"Hmm, I had not heard it was to be sold."

"It is not officially on the market yet. The owner was visiting Darcy last week and mentioned his intention to sell. It is not a holding he is bound to keep as it came into his hands from his first wife. She died long ago, and they never had children, so it has just sat there for many years now. He visits only a few weeks of the year, but his wife and children do not join him."

"So your prior knowledge might give you the advantage."

"That is what Darcy was hoping. I am to meet with the solicitor and owner tomorrow morning. I must say, I was hoping to stay here for the night, if it is not a problem?"

Fitz could not see a way to deny Bingley's request without raising suspicion, so he replied, "Of course you are welcome. I just need to speak with my wife and have a room prepared."

"If you do not mind, I would like to stroll through the garden and take a look at this wonderful estate."

"Yes, of course; right this way."

Fitz showed him out, then went to find his wife, who was easily located in the sitting room. He told her of Bingley's visit, apologizing for any burden it would put on her, but she assured him it would not be a problem.

Bingley was happily walking along the garden path, whistling a tune, when he saw a tree branch on the other side of a tall stone wall move. He thought it was just the gardener, but when he heard a feminine voice say, *"Oh, why must you cause me such grief?"* his interest was piqued. The wall was too high to see over, so he called out, "May I be of assistance?"

The tree's movements ceased.

"Madam? I am sorry to have startled you, but I heard you say something is causing you grief. Do you need help?"

Maria sighed loudly. There was no way to avoid whoever this was. "My bonnet is caught on a tree branch, and I cannot seem to get this knot undone to remove it from my head."

Bingley was just tall enough to get his hands in a good position to pull himself up onto the wall. From a sitting position on top, he was able to reach out and grasp the tree branch, though he could not remove the hat from its hold. He looked through the limbs to the young lady below, "How did you get yourself in such a situation, madam?"

"Well," she tried to look up at him, but the bonnet would not allow her to do so, "I was trying to reach a flower, and somehow my bonnet became caught in the tree."

"Oh? Which flower was that?"

She pointed to a vine that grew up the side of the wall, "Right there beside you—the honeysuckle. It looked so lovely growing in such a stark and lonely place there on the wall," she said in a wistful tone.

Bingley looked down to the vine within his reach. "Yes, it is quite breathtaking." Plucking one of the small white flowers he reached through the branches to the young lady below him, "For you, madam."

Maria felt her cheeks flush and reached to take the tiny flower from him. "Thank you, sir."

He tried once again to get the hat, but it was in vain. "I fear it is hopeless. Perhaps it would be best if I climb down there and try to untie your bonnet instead."

"Oh no! I could not ask you to do that, sir. Why, there are brambles all around under this tree, and you would surely catch yourself on them." When he reached through the tree branches instead, she sighed in relief. The last thing she wanted was to be seen in her condition by such an amiable gentleman.

Bingley reached through the branches that held her bonnet captive, and to the ribbons tied next to her left ear. She was right; it was quite the knot. His own attempts to untie it only resulted in her sucking in her breath in pain from it tightening. "I am sorry."

"You do not happen to have a pen knife, do you?"

"I do actually," he said. "I was traveling today and thought it might come in handy, but my trunks were already fastened, so I stuck it in my pocket." He pulled the forgotten item from his jacket pocket and unsheathed it. "Now please hold very still–I do not wish to injure you." He worked the blade slowly under the ribbon, very close to her ear, slicing ever so gently into the ribbon until finally she was free.

When she felt the release as the tie was cut, she took a deep breath. "Thank you, sir. I am forever in your debt."

Bingley sheathed the knife and put it back in his pocket, then turned back to look through the branches of the tree to the young lady beneath. Her red hair was very familiar. "Have we met before?"

"I doubt it. I am not from here."

"Oh? Then what brings you to my friend's garden?"

She quickly reached for her bonnet, ripping it from the branch as she turned to leave. "I thank you, sir."

Before he could say anything else, she was gone. He shook his head, chuckling at the peculiarity of the situation. *I know her from somewhere, but where could it be?*

Seeing the vine trailing up the wall, he plucked one of the buds and brought it to his nose. The honeysuckle smelled just as lovely as it looked. He climbed down from his perch on the wall and continued on his walk with a newfound energy.

That evening at dinner he brought up what happened to his hosts, but they did not offer an explanation of who the young lady was. The next day he left for his meeting, hoping he would run into her again, but he did not.

It was late that evening when Bingley returned, and, the household not expecting him, Maria was dining with Fitz and Mary. When Fitz heard his friend speaking with the housekeeper, he quickly excused himself from the ladies, saying he would see Mr Bingley in his study. He slipped out into the hall and thought he had closed the door in time, but when they were in his study, Bingley's words made him realize he was mistaken.

"I believe I asked you just yesterday about the young lady with red hair whom I met in your garden, and your answer was to avoid the subject. Now I see her once again, eating at your table no less, so you cannot deny the acquaintance."

Even though the words were spoken in a jovial manner, it was the harshest tone Fitz could ever imagine Bingley using. He knew they were caught. He sighed heavily and replied, "She is a guest in our home."

"Why not tell me that when I asked before?"

"I know you want to know with the purest of intentions, but you must understand that I simply am not at liberty to discuss Miss Lucas' situation."

Suddenly he realized where he had seen that red hair before. "Miss Lucas? From Meryton?"

Fitz realized his mistake, again all too late. Frustrated with himself, he spun around and poured himself a drink, swallowing the burning liquid in one gulp.

Bingley came up beside him, patting him on the shoulder, "Just what have you gotten yourself involved in here, my friend? Is it truly so bad that you cannot tell me?"

"No, Bingley, I cannot tell you." Fitz still had his back to the room and he did not realize Bingley had left until he heard the door down the hall open up and his friend give a greeting to the ladies. He rushed from the room and entered the dining room just after him.

"Miss Lucas! I knew I recognized you yesterday, but I could not remember where we had met. It is a pleasure to see you again, and here in my friend's home."

Maria looked to Mary, then to Fitz, not knowing what to do. Tears welled in her eyes and she stood and bolted from the room.

Fitz closed the door quickly and turned to Bingley, "You must leave her be. She is in no condition to see others like this, and as you can tell, she is quite emotional."

It took a few seconds, but Bingley realize that the girl who ran from this room was with child. He did not see it yesterday, as she was mostly hidden from his view by the tree branches, but it was clear today that she was expecting. "She was sent here to be hidden away by her family."

"In a way; her father would never agree to such a scheme, but she had nowhere to go and Mrs Collins wrote to Mrs Darcy…"

He understood now. "I am truly sorry if I have upset her. Please offer my apologies."

Mary nodded at his request and excused herself to check on Maria, leaving the two gentlemen alone. She went upstairs and knocked on the girl's door. When the maid let her in, she dismissed her and went to sit next to the distraught girl. She embraced her and the two sat as such for a while.

When she had finally calmed, Maria let go and signed, "I am sorry for bringing such shame to your home."

"Oh, no, my dear, it is Mr Bingley who offers his most sincere regrets. He only wished to continue the acquaintance and did not realize it would upset you."

She lifted the handkerchief to dry her eyes and smiled a little when she said, "He is a most amiable gentleman. I cannot place the blame on him. He came upon me yesterday when I was in the garden and my bonnet became stuck in a tree. He helped free me, and then before he could offer a proper greeting, I ran off." She reached over to the nightstand and picked up the honeysuckle flower he had given her, fingering the drying petals. "If only I had not…"

Mary reached for her hand, squeezing the shaking fingers with her own, "You are not the first to make such a mistake. I know it is difficult to not know what the future will bring, but look around you. We will not turn our backs on you. Whatever comes will come, but we will stay right here beside you."

"Why? Why do you do this for me after all my father has said and done to you?"

"I have always found my strength comes in knowing what God would have me do, and doing it. One of my favorite passages in the Good Book is found in Luke chapter 6.

> 'But I say unto you which hear, Love your enemies, do good to them which hate you, bless them that curse you, and pray for them which

despitefully use you. And unto him that smiteth thee on the one cheek offer also the other; and him that taketh away thy cloak forbid not to take thy coat also. Give to every man that asketh of thee; and of him that taketh away thy goods ask them not again. And as ye would that men should do to you, do ye also to them likewise. For if ye love them which love you, what thank have ye? for sinners also love those that love them. And if ye do good to them which do good to you, what thank have ye? for sinners also do even the same. And if ye lend to them of whom ye hope to receive, what thank have ye? for sinners also lend to sinners, to receive as much again. But love ye your enemies, and do good, and lend, hoping for nothing again; and your reward shall be great, and ye shall be the children of the Highest: for he is kind unto the unthankful and to the evil. Be ye therefore merciful, as your Father also is merciful. Judge not, and ye shall not be judged: condemn not, and ye shall not be condemned: forgive, and ye shall be forgiven: Give, and it shall be given unto you; good measure, pressed down, and shaken together, and running over, shall men give into your bosom. For with the same measure that ye mete withal it shall be measured to you again.'"

Mary looked directly in the younger girl's teary eyes when she said, "I am doing just as it says–blessing your father who has cursed me. Treating you as I myself would wish to be treated. I will not hold you in judgment or condemnation, for it is not my place to do so. It is my place to love you and to show you mercy.

Maria wiped the tears that ran down her cheeks. "Thank you. It is through you that I have learned what compassion truly is."

"I am not the only one who cares for you–we all do."

"Yes, I know, but you and your family are a rarity in our society. I know I will have to be hidden away from everyone for a long time. It is the punishment I must bear."

"Only if you wish it." Mary saw Maria look back down to the flower still lying in her palm. "If it means anything to you, I would trust Mr Bingley with the knowledge of your situation. He will not tell anyone."

"Are you certain?"

"Yes. Every family has their secrets, and Mr Bingley has been privy to a few in my husband's family that could have brought ruin to them all, and yet he has honoured their friendship above all else," Mary explained.

Maria blushed, "He is a good man."

Mary smiled, "Yes he is." She then stood to leave.

"Will you please give him a message for me?"

"Yes, of course."

She reached out and placed the flower in Mary's hand. "Tell him I am sorry to have run away from him–twice now–and if he wishes to make my acquaintance again tomorrow, I will await him in the garden."

She smiled at the spark in the girl's eye. "I will tell him. Now you rest."

Mary returned downstairs and found the gentlemen in the sitting room. As soon as she entered the room, Mr Bingley rose and asked after Miss Lucas.

"She is well," she signed, letting her husband translate for her. "She said to tell you she is sorry to have not given you the opportunity to greet her properly." She then offered the small white flower to him. "If you still wish to make her acquaintance after seeing what condition she is in, she will await you in the garden tomorrow."

He reached out for the gift and smiled, grateful for the chance to apologize in person, "Yes, thank you. I will do that."

"Mr Bingley, I only ask one thing of you–do not raise her expectations. She is young and has had her heart broken by both her beau and her family. She has a harsh life to look forward to if she chooses to keep her child, and an even harder one if she chooses to give the babe away. It is a decision she is not making lightly, and I do not wish to see her hurt again."

He fingered the delicate petals, "I promise to keep your reproach in mind. It has been many months since we were last in company, and I only wish to offer my friendship."

"If it ever becomes more than that, please remember all she has been through."

"I will. Now, if you do not mind, I will retire."

Fitz watched as Bingley walked from the room. When the door was closed, he went over to his wife, putting his arms around her expanding waist and drawing her closer. "You are very protective of Miss Lucas. I must say, it is a quality I find quite charming and one I expect to see on display more often when our own child is born." She smiled, her eyebrow arching in a particular manner he had learned to always question. "What is it?"

She spoke softly, "Honeysuckle—its meaning is *'generous and devoted affection'*."

He smiled, "Do you think those two…"

"Perhaps, but we will leave that for them to work out." She leaned up on her toes to place a simple kiss on his chin before she laid her head against his chest, enjoying the slight beat of his heart she could feel against her cheek.

Finally Fitz pulled back, "Come, it is time we retire as well."

Sarah Johnson

Chapter 33

Bingley was to meet with the owner of Buckley Hall again in a week. He offered to go to a nearby inn, but Fitz and Mary insisted he stay with them. He and Miss Lucas met in the garden and he apologized for all he had done, but when his excuse was simply that he wished to renew the acquaintance she could easily forgive his eagerness.

Over the coming week they were often found in each other's company, usually in the garden. Fitz had to laugh at the sight of them. Miss Lucas was the only young lady he had ever met who could talk just as much as Bingley, and amazingly enough, they both enjoyed the constant chatter.

When it came time for the meeting, Bingley left. It was not two hours later when Darcy arrived, surprising Fitz. When they were alone, Darcy pulled a letter from his pocket and gave it to Fitz, watching the reaction as his cousin read it.

"He cannot think he will get away with this," Fitz threw the note into the table and stomped across the room.

"Of course he will get away with it. What proof have we to offer other than the word of a young lady not even of age and in such a condition? Even this letter is not specific enough to force his hand in the matter. I will not offer my sister's own reputation to bring him around." He sighed heavily. "He will not marry without being paid off, and her family can hardly put together such an amount as he desires."

"No, you are right; it is quite the number."

Darcy sat down in the chair, "Has she decided what she will do with the child?"

"No, not yet. She is a confused young girl and should never have to make such a decision as this."

"I can only be grateful it was not Georgiana. She was in the hands of that rogue, and we were lucky to not have the same consequences thrust upon her."

"Yes, well, in that I cannot but agree. I would have given anything to keep Wickham from marrying Georgiana, and here we sit enraged at his refusal to marry Miss Lucas. Perhaps this is a blessing instead."

"Perhaps it is."

"How is Georgiana? Has she behaved since returning from your aunt's?"

He accepted the tea his cousin poured, saying, "She has decided she likes the office of an aunt and has taken it upon herself to teach Rose all she knows of Pemberley House and its history. She is beginning to warm to Elizabeth more, and they have a few cheery conversations a week without issue. I think she prefers to be at Pemberley and knows now that I will send her to live with Aunt Edith permanently if it ever becomes necessary."

"That is good, though I would like her to be back to her old self. Still, it is progress."

"Mrs Annesley still thinks it would do her good to meet Miss Lucas, but I cannot bring myself to agree with such a plan. I do not want someone else to be hurt because of my sister's schemes, and who is to say she will not say something about Miss Lucas in retaliation, just as she orchestrated for Mary last year?"

Fitz sipped his tea. "Hmmm… at first I thought she was not ready for such an action, but now I actually agree with Mrs Annesley. I have a feeling it is the connection to Wickham that has kept Georgiana going so long in this direction, but if she sees the results of such a decision, and is made aware that Wickham is the father of Miss Lucas' child and yet still he refuses to do the right thing and marry her, it is possible she will begin to change.

"Would Miss Lucas even agree to such a meeting?"

"I believe she would," Fitz answered.

A knock on the door interrupted the two, and Fitz answered it to find Bingley standing there, a huge smile on his face. "I take it the meeting went well?"

He followed Fitz into the room, "Very well indeed. We have come to an agreement, and if everything goes well, in about a month I will be the owner of Buckley Hall." He saw Darcy sitting there and went over to greet his friend, "I did not expect to see you here today."

"I had news to discuss with my cousin, but it seems your news is much better than my own."

"Oh? Is there something wrong?"

Darcy did not know what Bingley knew of Miss Lucas or her situation, so he looked to Fitz.

Fitz saw the look and answered, "He is aware of the situation." He then turned to Bingley, "Darcy has been in contact with the child's father, and it is as we feared–it is Wickham. He is refusing to marry Miss Lucas without a large cash settlement and the assurance he can be assigned to any regiment he wishes within the militia. Even if I had such connections, I refuse to use them on such a cur."

Bingley sat and accepted the tea from Fitz. "With such a man, this is probably for the best then."

"In some ways that may be," Darcy answered, "but what is to become of those he has abandoned? Will we be forced to take the child in when it is born? I cannot see letting it fall to the poorhouses of London. What of Miss Lucas? Where will she go? Will her family ever accept her back in their home after all this?"

"We have spoken with her, and she has not made any decisions about the future, but if necessary she can stay with us for a while longer. We do not wish to throw her out, and the few letters she has received from her sister indicate that her father is not willing to have her back at home. He blames her for the ruination of their family."

"It is as I feared," Darcy said. "We should not be held responsible for her–she is no relation to us."

"Whether she is a relation of ours or not," Bingley said firmly, "it is our Christian duty to not turn her out. If I could, I would support her, but you know how that would look." Bingley felt his heart break for Maria. Over the last few days he had become quite attached to her, and he could not see her life being dictated in such a way because of someone who fooled her into thinking he cared for her when the opposite was true.

"What of Georgiana? Should she be told of this," Darcy said, holding the letter up.

"I say yes, Mrs Annesley says yes–it is only Darcy here who is holding out," Fitz explained to Bingley.

"Before the subject of telling Miss Darcy is even decided, ought we not ask Miss Lucas her opinion?"

"Yes, you are correct," Fitz replied. "I do not think it will be a problem though. She can be trusted with the knowledge of who Wickham is to our family, and I dare say she will have compassion on my young cousin that I myself find very hard to have for her these days."

"I will talk with Elizabeth," Darcy said, then he stood. "I must return home. Good day gentlemen, and Bingley," he turned to his friend with a slight smile, "I will be happy to have you as my newest neighbor, Bingley."

With Miss Lucas' time coming closer, Mrs Annesley had recently begun visiting the girl every week on her day off. She was to do so again today. When she descended the stairs she was met by Miss Darcy, Mr and Mrs Darcy, as well as the young Miss Darcy in her father's arms. They were all preparing to go somewhere, and she smiled at the family that stood before her.

"Mrs Annesley," Darcy said, "I am glad you have not left yet. We are to visit my cousin today. Would you like to go with us?"

She saw the look he gave her and knew they had taken her advice to heart and thought it best to let the two young ladies meet. With a nod, she replied, "I would like that, sir. Thank you."

With that they all left together for the short ride through Pemberley's lands, beyond the town of Lambton, and on to Rose Bluff. When they arrived they were led through the house and out into the garden, where greetings were exchanged by all.

"We have a lovely repast for everyone," Fitz said, leading them to a table set up under the shade of a tree. "Our other guests will be with us in a few minutes," he offered when everyone was choosing a seat.

"Other guests?" Georgiana questioned.

"Yes, we have two visitors staying at Rose Bluff, and they will be here shortly. They chose to take a stroll through the garden just before you arrived."

Having been sequestered with her Aunt Edith or at Pemberley for most of the last year, Georgiana was eager to discover who these visitors were. "Do I know your guests?"

"I believe you do," Fitz answered as he held the chair out for his young cousin. "Mr Bingley is here, as well as Miss Lucas, whom you should have met last year when we were visiting Hertfordshire." He turned around, "Ah, perfect timing. I was just telling my cousin who was visiting," he said to Bingley and Maria as they joined the others.

When Georgiana turned to greet them, her eyes immediately went to the expanded mid—section of the girl and her hand went, in shock, to her mouth.

Bingley turned to the lady who held his arm, searching her eyes to see that she was ready for this discussion. When he saw the determination in her features, his heart beat harder in admiration.

With a decided lift of her chin, Maria let go of her companion's arm and stepped up to the table, "Miss Darcy, it is good to see you again. We met last year when you were visiting my family's neighborhood."

Georgiana mumbled, "I… I do not recall meeting you."

"No, I dare say I would not have made much of an impression on you as it was only in the milliner's shop that we saw each other, but I remember it very distinctly. You were pointed out to me before that by a mutual acquaintance, but we hardly exchanged two words with each other that day before you left with Mr Bingley's sisters," she nodded in his direction.

"We could not possibly have a mutual acquaintance," Georgiana replied harshly, looking pointedly at the girl's obvious condition.

"Actually, you do," Mrs Annesley said as she stepped up to take Maria's arm and help her sit. "She is, that is, she *was* an intimate friend of Mr George Wickham"

Chills ran down her body and she could not think. "No… no it cannot be. He did not tell me of any acquaintances except…"

Bingley now stepped closer, "Except the maid Becky?"

Her eyes grew wider and she sucked in a shallow breath.

Darcy now sat beside his sister and reached for her cold and shaking hand, "Georgiana, we have all tried to tell you for well over a year now, and you have not wanted to hear what we had to say. I even questioned bringing you here today, but I see the good that could come from this, and we must tell you all that you do not yet know of Wickham."

She looked around at those faces that surrounded her, still shocked at what she assumed to be the news they would say. She knew she had to hear the words though. With a simple nod, she replied, "What do you want to tell me?"

Darcy took a deep breath, then began. "Miss Lucas has been staying here since we removed from Town after Christmas. She had nowhere else to go and her own family turned her out. We could not see turning such a sweet young lady to the streets, and when we found out about her situation Mary insisted Miss Lucas come and stay here with them." He saw Georgiana look over at Mary with an odd expression, almost as if she was confused by such knowledge. "Georgiana, it has been many months now that we have been searching for the father of this child that is to come soon, and we recently heard from him." He reached into his pocket and pulled out the letter from Wickham. "I know this will be hard for you, but you must read this for yourself." He placed the letter on the table, then let go of her hand, stood, and walked away.

The others followed as well, except for Maria Lucas, who remained seated beside Georgiana. Tears were already welling in Georgiana's eyes, but she knew she had to stay in control. So with a shaky hand she reached for the letter. She recognized the familiar handwriting immediately and her heart sank just a little more. She unfolded the pages and read, gasping when he made a slight mention of her and how he had played her for a fool more than once. His greed was made evident in the requirements he had for marrying Maria. It was obvious he knew he was the father of the child, though he did not make a specific acknowledgment of that. He was quite crafty in his wording. He refused to do anything about the shame it would bring upon the Lucas family if he was not given a dowry equal to that of Georgiana's own, which had been kept from him last year. Seeing the harsh words written about her in his own hand was more than she could bear. The tears that had welled in her eyes now began to pour down her cheeks, and her body shook with intensity. Before she knew it, Maria had her arms around her and was holding her close, letting her cry as she assured her everything would be well.

Georgiana was not aware of anything except that her heart felt as if it were ripped in two. She hardly heard the comforting words or felt the strong arms that lifted her and carried her inside and up to a bedchamber where she could rest. Mrs Annesley stayed by her side, offering as many clean handkerchiefs as was necessary, and letting the reality of the truth sink into the heart of the distraught young girl.

Darcy could not bear to see his sister in such distress, so when he had delivered her upstairs, he left her in the care of her companion, who assured him it was all for the best. He returned to his wife's side. They stayed, visiting with the others for a few more hours, then they went back home to Pemberley, intent upon returning for his sister again tomorrow.

The following day, before he could even call for the carriage to be readied, he received a note from Fitz saying Georgiana had asked to stay there at Rose Bluff for a few more days. Darcy was glad to see they had finally gotten through to her. He had Georgiana's trunk packed and sent it on its way, with a note for Fitz asking to be kept informed of all that happened while she was there.

He was found by his wife an hour later, sitting in the nursery, holding his tiny daughter in his arms, and talking with her about how much he loved her and what he wished for her life ahead.

Georgiana awoke on the second day of her stay at Rose Bluff. She'd had quite the revelation yesterday, and it made her sick to find she had trusted her heart to someone as despicable as George Wickham. With what she now knew about him, she began to question every interaction they had. In every instance she realized he focused on her money. Thinking back to their last meeting in Meryton, she was reminded of how she left wanting to do just what he would not voice. The manipulation was clearly seen now, in light of her new revelations.

Fitz knocked on her door early, but she was already awake. He arrived with a tray of her favorite foods and a compassionate smile. He placed the tray on the table and sat down across from her. "I thought you may want to talk with me."

"I do have some questions," she replied.

"I thought you would. I will answer what I can."

She sighed heavily, "You are nothing like your parents."

He was curious just what she meant by such a statement. When she said nothing further though, he knew he had to ask what motivated it. "My father and I have rarely seen eye to eye on anything in my lifetime. That is why I spent my youth at Pemberley instead of Croome Court. You have been privy to that for a long time though, so I wonder what motivates such a statement now?"

"I… that is… your father's letter to my brothers…"

His hand stopped halfway to his mouth with a piece of toast, dread washing over his face. His hand fell, "Oh Georgie–how did you hear about that?"

She pulled several letters from her pocket, replacing all but one of them. She placed the singed note on the table and slid it over to him.

Fitz reached for it, his hand covering hers. He squeezed her fingers, but she would not look up at him. "Your brother and I would never allow him to take your inheritance from you. We wish you to marry for love."

"What inheritance? As I see it," she said, looking around the room, "it has already been taken from me."

Fitz was confused. He too looked around, not understanding what she meant. "Your inheritance is safe from anyone."

She sniffed, "Yes, you are keeping it well maintained."

Now he truly was confused. "Georgiana, Rose Bluff is not your inheritance. What would make you think that?"

"My brother said to me years ago that even if I married a man without wealth, we would still want for nothing. That my father saw fit to leave a nice place for me."

"And you thought all these years it was Rose Bluff?"

She nodded, looking down at the plate of food still untouched before her.

He had a sudden realization. "That is why you were so upset over my wife's dowry. You thought it was taken from your own." He stood and scooted his chair around closer to her, then sat again and turned toward her. "Georgie, your brother and I would never steal from you. Your own property is safe and your brother sees that it is well maintained."

She finally looked up into his eyes. "Rose Bluff is the only property of which he has ever given mention."

Fitz chuckled, "My dear, you know very little of all your brother possesses—he has been highly sought after by the mothers of the Ton for many years now because of the vastness of the Darcy wealth. What he gave my wife, and ultimately me through her, was only what he has been trying to force me to accept since your father died." He knew he had to explain further. "Rose Bluff was brought into the Darcy coffers by your mother—I believe it belonged to my father's maternal grandmother, so it would not pass to him. It was part of your mother's dowry. It was intended to be given to a second son, but your parents were never so blessed. I left home at the age of thirteen and went to live at Pemberley, and became almost as a second son to my aunt and uncle. The papers were being drawn up to have Rose Bluff given to me upon my marriage or the age of five and twenty, but they were not to the point of being signed, so they were not acknowledged as being part of Uncle George's will. Then your father's sudden death brought an end to that. Your brother has been trying ever since to force me into accepting it, but I was too stubborn to do so, insisting instead that the Army would be my life. After my refusing all these years, Darcy finally decided to go another route and gave it to the lady who he knew had stolen my heart. That is why he did not tell me of Mary's dowry."

It all made sense now, and Georgiana shook her head at her own ignorance. "I am sorry, Fitz–I never meant…"

"I know," he said, patting her hand before he slid back over to eat the nearly forgotten food before it became too cold. "Your dowry was stipulated in your father's will. You are to receive a property called Avonaire. It is in Staffordshire and is about the size of Rose Bluff, though a different style altogether. As you already know, you are also to receive the sizeable amount of £30,000. Your brother chose not to tell you all the particulars because of scum like Wickham who would take advantage of such knowledge. So what is commonly reported is only a portion of your inheritance."

She looked back down at the table. "Evidently Geor… *Mr Wickham*… knew of my full inheritance. He mentioned it several times."

"I do not doubt that–he was often in your father's study and could very easily have looked at the papers detailing everything."

"What else have I not been told about him?"

Fitz knew exactly what she meant. "Georgiana, it is not my place…"

"My brother will not tell me, but I did not expect such treatment from you. If you wish me to make an informed decision of where my heart may lead me in the future, then I must know the whole truth."

She was right. The food in front of him no longer looked as appealing, so he pushed the plate away and leaned his forearms on the table, folding his hands together. With a nod of his head, Fitz began, "Wickham was always a degenerate. He grew up with us at Pemberley and often caused trouble for your brother to have to clean up. Your father never saw his faults though, so he was left to his own devices. After your father's death…" He then went on to describe for her the terms of her father's will, the money left to Wickham, as well as the living he was to one day receive when it became available. When he got to the part of the tale about Darcy paying him in lieu of a position in the church, Georgiana as shocked. She had heard quite a different story from him. Fitz then told of the confrontation the two had when Wickham returned later, insisting he be given the position. Darcy refused, and Wickham warned that he would one day have his revenge. That confrontation took place just two months before Georgiana's new companion, Mrs Younge, was found, and shortly afterward the trip to Ramsgate took place.

"That was all I ever was to him—a means of getting back at my brother."

"Yes."

Tears began to fill her eyes and she burst out crying, "I am so sorry. Oh! What have I done to you all? How could you ever forgive me after such ill treatment?"

Fitz pulled her into an embrace. "We love you Georgiana. Of course we will forgive you. *Shhhh.*" He continued to comfort her until she finally calmed several minutes later.

"Miss Lucas is having quite the time of things," he said to her, "and you can imagine she is lonely. She requested that you stay here for a few days."

"Oh yes, I would like that. Do you think my brother would let me?"

"I will write to him immediately. He was to come for you today, but I can see no harm in you extending your stay a few days."

When he was gone, Georgiana sat down at the desk and pulled out writing supplies, then spent the next couple of hours penning a letter each to her brother, her cousin, Elizabeth, and Mary. She asked for forgiveness from each, promising to be more accepting of them in her life in the future. By the time her trunks arrived, her task was completed, and she went to deliver the ones she could for now, saving the two others for when she returned to Pemberley.

Fitz and Mary both sat and read their letters together, and each was glad to accept her apology. Fitz kept a close eye on her for the few days she stayed with them, and he noticed a marked change in her. She no longer bore the haughty look that so often was seen across her face, and several times she willingly chose to sit beside Mary or join her in activities. She truly was a changed girl, and his heart swelled with pride. *One day she will grow into quite the lady,* he thought.

Georgiana returned to Pemberley with Mrs Annesley a few days later, giving the letters to her brother and Elizabeth almost as soon as she descended from the carriage. Again her apologies were accepted, hugs were exchanged, and Georgiana finally began to see the loving family she had all around her.

Sarah Johnson

Chapter
34

he new month brought with it an air of change. Georgiana now joined Mrs Annesley on her weekly visits to Rose Bluff, and the two young ladies were becoming quite close. Mary often joined them as well, and Georgiana now welcomed such friendships in her life.

The two expectant ladies talked of all that was soon to come to each of them. Maria was still unsure what she would do when her child was born, but she could not help but feel excited for the preparations that were underway all around the house for the Fitzwilliams' child, expected to come later this autumn. Maria tried to teach Mary how to knit, but after many hours of hilarity at her attempts, it was determined knitting was best left to the others. Being left handed, Mary just could not get the proper technique.

Bingley stayed at Rose Bluff for as long as he could, then was required to remove to Town to finish the paperwork needed for the purchase of Buckley Hall. Fitz received a letter nearly immediately from his friend, and it was with great shock that he went to inform his wife of the particulars written within—or those he could make out through Bingley's splotches and splatters of ink. As it turned out, their jokes about Miss Bingley being perfectly matched to Fitz's brother were actually truer than they realized. By the time Bingley arrived, the two had already announced their engagement and the wedding was set to take place in just three weeks. It was to be the last big event of the Season before everyone removed from Town for their country estates.

His father would be happy for such an influx of money. Croome Court would be saved for another generation, unless of course his brother gambled it all away as he was known to do. If Bingley was smart, he would write a marriage contract that did not give the viscount much opportunity to access such funds. Though Fitz did feel sorry for Miss Bingley for being taken in by his brother, he could not help but find humor in the situation. He laughed so hard he nearly fell from his chair–if only Bingley had been here to share in the moment. When he had sufficiently composed himself, he decided this news would be best to tell Darcy in person, so he had his horse readied and went to visit Pemberley to apprise him of this latest on—dit.

Darcy was just as shocked as Fitz had been. They wrote Bingley a letter in return, giving him a few things to include in the contract. When he received their expected reply, he was glad for their advice and made certain what they suggested was written out very specifically in the papers. The viscount was not happy with such wording that would tie his hands to the funds, only giving him access to the interest on them, but the announcement had already been made, and the earl would see to it that the wedding happened. He would not allow his son to make their family the laughing stock of the entire Ton by jilting the bride at the altar. As it turned out, the earl was not happy to learn of his son's inebriated proposal, but it was made in front of others so there was nothing he could do about it that would not bring ruin to his own family. Miss Bingley, though connected to trade, did have the dowry needed, and that became the only thing he cared about with regard to the union.

The three weeks since Bingley left passed slowly for the ladies as they awaited the day when Maria would begin her confinement. Georgiana convinced her brother and cousin to allow her to stay at Rose Bluff for the time being. It worked out well in that it also allowed Mrs Annesley to stay by Maria's side during the last few difficult weeks of her pregnancy.

Bingley's business was concluded quickly, the only thing keeping him in Town now was his sister's wedding. The ceremony was concluded without any difficulties, though there was obviously no love between the bride and groom. It was in that moment when Bingley decided he would not let love pass him by. He already knew he felt something for Maria Lucas that he had never felt for anyone else before, and with everything she had been through, he dared not even hope she felt the same for him. Even if she did not love him, he knew she could grow to if given the opportunity. Love was not a word he had ever allowed himself to use to describe his feelings for her, but the longer he thought on it, the stronger the emotion grew within his chest. By the time the wedding breakfast was over, his heart and mind were set. He left immediately for Meryton.

Sir William Lucas was only on his second cup of brandy, with the nearly full bottle sitting beside him, when his visitor was announced.

Bingley stepped into the older man's study. "It is good to see you again, sir."

He did not even rise to greet his guest. Motioning for the servant to leave them, he said gruffly, "I can see no good reason for you to be in my home, Mr Bingley."

"Sir, I am certain you were not expecting me, but I had to discuss a matter of great import with you."

"Oh, and what could draw a gentleman such as yourself to my door?"

"Your daughter–Miss Lucas."

Suddenly the father took a large drink, swallowing all that was left in his glass. "I will not hear her name said in this house."

Bingley stood taller, lifted his chin, and took a stance he had seen the colonel take on many occasions. "You cannot convince me you do not care for your own child's welfare."

"I know not and care not where she is. Mrs Collins has taken care of sending her away. That girl has made my family suffer grievously. Obviously the rumors of her actions have gone further than I knew if you have come to my door."

"I know exactly where she is, and I have been in her company these last few months at least. Whether you want to hear it or not, I have come to inform you of some judgments you have made on my friends that are completely false."

"Why would I care what you think of me? I have come to my judgment of your friends through an experience you could know nothing of," he spat out in vehemence.

"You mean the fire?"

Silence permeated the air.

"Yes, I know the particulars of that dreadful day. I know all your family has lost with the death of your eldest son, Benjamin. He was a brave young man who stood up in the face of danger and paid the price for trying to save the lives of his friends and neighbors. He is a gentleman I would have loved to meet. I also was there when you snubbed my friend's wife, who had nothing to do with the fire. She tried to save her own family and was only able to get one sister out before the flames were too much for her."

"MARY BENNET is who deserved to die in that fire, not my son! After all, she is the one who set it!"

Bingley stepped closer, intensity coming to his eyes as he lowered his voice, "Miss Mary Bennet, now Mrs Fitzwilliam, did not set that fire—it was an accident caused by a candle set too close to the bed curtains. In his misery over the loss he felt, Mr Bennet would often drink too much and sit in his wife's chamber in misery and melancholy, only later to be found passed out. That time, he placed the candle too close to the bed curtains, and when they caught fire, he was so far into his cups he did not even seeing the raging fire all around him." Bingley looked pointedly at the decanter sitting beside Sir William.

He noticed the look and slid the glass away. As much as he did not want to admit it, the tale did have merit. He still refused to believe it fully though. "You don't know her—if you did, you would know she set that fire intentionally."

"You, sir, do not know her! While you are sitting here in this state remembering the past and all you have lost, she is standing beside your daughter in the final weeks of a pregnancy which will forever change her life."

"WHAT? What are you talking about?"

"Oh, did you not know?" He leaned down closer to the older gentleman's face, "When you tossed your daughter from your home for being taken advantage of by a rake, Mrs Fitzwilliam found out and opened her own home to Miss Lucas. She and her husband have since taken care of her every need, including not allowing her to feel shame for one wrong decision. Have *you*, sir, ever made a wrong decision and then had it held over your head the rest of your days?"

He was so shocked he could not think straight. "No, you cannot be correct… she… she was sent away to the north."

"Yes—to Derbyshire, where my friends reside."

The words of Reverend Carter's recent sermon echoed in his mind. *'He that is without sin among you, let him first cast a stone at her.'* Suddenly the realization came over him and he crumpled down to his knees. "What have I done to my own child? What kind of life is she to live now?" He began to weep.

Bingley bent down beside the older gentleman, placing his hand on his shoulder, "You have the opportunity to make things right with your daughter, and with Mrs Fitzwilliam."

"How is that ever to be accomplished? They will never forgive me."

"Can you forgive Miss Maria for the mistake she made?"

"Yes, of course; she is my child."

"Then what makes you think they will not, in turn, forgive you as well?"

"Would they? Would they both?"

"I believe so. One way to show your daughter how much you care for her future is to allow me to offer for her."

"You… you want to marry my girl? Even though she carries another man's child?

"Yes."

"Even if she gives birth to a son? Would you truly accept the child as your heir?"

"Yes."

Why?"

"Because I love her. Love can overlook a multitude of wrongs."

"And does she love you as well?"

"I must be honest with you, sir—I do not know. What I do know is that we get along well together, and we have grown quite close over the last few months. I would like nothing more than to court her properly and take the time necessary to build our affection, but that time has been taken from us." He looked pointedly at the father sitting before him. "If I am to save her reputation and not consign your grandchild to the life of a bastard, then we must marry before she begins her confinement." He knew what he said was harsh, but he was unwilling to leave this house without the permission needed to marry.

The father looked down at the floor, "Her confinement should begin at any time now."

"Yes, sir."

He thought about it for a minute fully before he looked back to the young gentleman beside him, "What must I do?"

"Return with me to Town. I will purchase a special license and will then make haste to Rose Bluff to speak with her."

He stood back up, "We can leave immediately and be in Town before nightfall."

"What of your wife?"

"You let me deal with Lady Lucas. Once I tell her you are to be married, she will quickly change her tune. She is away for a few weeks anyway, visiting her sister, so by the time she returns, the deed will be accomplished."

The two hastened back to Town, taking rooms at an inn. After the sun fell below the horizon, the two came up with a quick draft of a marriage contract, then Bingley retired.

Sir William sat up late into the night writing a letter each to his daughter, as well as to Mary. The next morning he would give them both to Bingley to be delivered when he saw the ladies. He retired that night with great relief–his daughter would be cared for, and, because Bingley was a new land owner himself, even his grandchild would want for nothing. Above all, it was clear the gentleman had much love to give to both. He could not ask for things to have worked out any better for his family.

The next morning the two quickly found a solicitor to sign the contract, then they visited the Archbishop to obtain a special license. As soon as the father had signed the necessary places on both documents, Bingley was off, bound for Derbyshire.

Two days later a road—weary Bingley arrived at Rose Bluff late in the evening as the sun was setting. When he was informed that Miss Lucas had begun her confinement, though the baby was far from coming still, he insisted on speaking with her. It was only with his personal assurances to Mrs Darcy that he would not cause her any undue distress, and after explaining what exactly his purpose was, that he was allowed to enter the birthing room.

Maria was mostly just uncomfortable at this point. She had experienced a few pains, but they were not enough to think the babe would be born that soon.

When she heard that Mr Bingley had arrived and wanted to speak with her, she was shocked. It was simply not done! A birthing room was no place for a gentleman, especially a bachelor! With Mrs Darcy's assurances, she finally agreed to see him.

When he entered the room and looked around, the other ladies left, giving them some privacy. Elizabeth was the last to go, saying as she left, "We will be right outside if we are needed."

He nodded in thanks. When the door was closed he had nowhere else to look but at Maria, who sat in a chair by the open window, a blanket draped over her legs for modesty. "I know it is unusual to request you see me now, but I could not let you go through this without first asking–will you marry me?"

"Wha… what do you mean? How can that even be possible?"

Bingley stepped towards her, pulling the papers from his jacket. "I cannot allow you to live your life in derision from society because of one mistake in your past–a mistake that can more adequately be called manipulation by another. I care too much for you to see that happen. So on my way back from Town, I stopped to see your father."

She barely whispered, "Papa… how is he?"

Bingley pulled out the letter from her father, holding it out, "He sends his love and wishes you to read this." He then retreated to the other side of the room to give her privacy.

She opened it and immediately began crying with the words of apology and love written within. It was at the end that she saw how much he had changed. He was willing to allow her to marry, but only if she cared for Mr Bingley. If not, he would like her to come home, with her child.

Do I care for him? Well of course she did, who could not with such an amiable

335

gentleman. A better question would be—did she love him? She looked across the room at him and blushed when she felt her heart beat rise. Looking back down at the letter, she once again read her father's words. For months she had wished for them to be said, and here she sat with them right before her. *What do I truly want?*

She once again looked up at him. He had not judged her harshly, as she was sure everyone else would do if they only knew. Not only that, but he offered to marry her and take her child as his own—*even if it was a boy.* What man would do such a thing? *Is he doing this simply because of his desire to help someone in need, or is it because he truly cares… for me?* As much as that gesture meant to her, and her future, she could not answer until she knew what he felt for her.

"Mr Bingley?"

He quickly strode back over to her. "Yes, Miss Lucas?"

"Sir," she said agitatedly, playing with the paper in her hand, "I appreciate the sentiment of what you have proposed, but I cannot make you a slave to my own mistakes. You deserve to marry for love, not for obligations which are not yours to carry."

Bingley lowered himself to his knee and reached for her hand, stilling it. "Miss Lucas, I shall always remember the moment we were introduced and even now I can recount every word spoken between us when I met you the first and the second time. While I do feel a sense of obligation in righting your situation, it is only because of affection that I have offered for you. Miss Lucas… Maria, I find I love you more with each passing day, and I hope you feel the same about me."

She let out the shallow breath she did not even realize she was holding in. His words were just what she needed to hear. "Mr Bingley, I find myself in a situation the likes of which I could have never foreseen, but I would have it no other way if it has brought you to me." She looked up, smiled, and replied, "I find I too have grown to love you very deeply, and I would be honoured to marry you, sir."

There was a silence between the two as they stared into each others eyes. Slowly Bingley brought her hands to his lips, depositing a kiss on each, then he replied, "I will be back in one hour with the parson." He stood and hastily departed, turning back at the door to give her a wink.

The ladies came back into the room with questioning looks on their faces. Maria giggled and drew her hands to her flushed cheeks, "I am to be married in one hour!"

"OH MY! One hour? We have a great deal to accomplish then." Elizabeth looked around. "We cannot have you married in here–it would not be proper."

"Come," Mary signed to Elizabeth. "We will go find Georgiana, and I am certain we will have my private sitting room just down the hall looking lovely enough for a wedding in no time."

Elizabeth turned to Mrs Annesley, "Can you attend to the bride's attire?"

She smiled, ushering them from the room, "Yes, yes, I have it well in hand. We will meet you in Mrs Fitzwilliam's private sitting room at," she looked back at the clock on the mantle, "… ten o'clock."

With a nod, Elizabeth and Mary left to find Georgiana and apprise her of the news.

Sarah Johnson

Chapter 35

itz walked into his wife's sitting room and saw Bingley pacing while the parson was preparing himself and setting the register out on the table. He walked over with a decidedly gay stride, stopping Bingley in the middle of the room with a firm hand to the nervous man's shoulder, "You know, when I said to you that when you found a lady worthy of your hand you should sweep her off and marry her as quickly as you can, I did not expect you to take my advice to heart quite so passionately."

Bingley smiled, "You heard."

"Who in the house has not heard of your plight? Storming in to the birthing room just to bare your soul to your lady love and save her from the derision of the world? I would say you are a gentleman among gentlemen; a knight riding in on a powerful steed." He chuckled and continued, "You will be the kind of savior about which novels will surely be written."

Bingley broke out in laughter, "I know not how you do it, but you always know just how to break the tension in a situation. Thank you."

"Well, in all truth, I had to do something. You were nearly wearing a hole in my wife's favorite carpet, and you will soon find just how expensive it is to furnish a home such as this. That is, if everything went well and you are, indeed, my newest neighbor?"

He nodded, "Yes, everything was completed, and Buckley Hall is now the land holding of the Bingley family."

"Capital, capital." After a moment of silence, he continued, "In all seriousness, Bingley- I cannot imagine Miss Lucas being cared for more than you will do. I can see it in your eyes and demeanor. I doubt she even knows herself how deep your feelings run."

"I think she is too much in shock of the moment to even think of anything like that."

"You are correct." He looked over to where the parson now stood beside the table, "Now, it is time we find Darcy and get ready for this wedding. Do you have a ring?"

"No need to find me—I am right here," they heard Darcy say as he entered the room

Bingley pulled a small box from his pocket, opening it to show his two closest friends. "It was my mother's ring. Caroline did not want it—she said it was too simple for a viscountess to have on her hand. Do you think Miss Lucas will like it?"

Darcy gave him a simple nod and Fitz said, "She will love it."

Bingley smiled, "The stone is small, but it is the same deep blue color of her eyes."

Fitz declared, "It is official—you can now be considered a besotted fool."

Elizabeth and Mary entered to their husbands' laughing. Both smiled, then took a seat. Georgiana was right behind them, with baby Rose in her arms. She too sat down, with Darcy taking the seat between his wife and sister.

Fitz announced, "Well, as the host of this gathering, I must go and lead in the bride." When he passed Darcy he leaned over and whispered, "Keep an eye on him—he may just get sick or forget to breathe, and we do not need any more surprises for this evening."

Darcy covered the chuckle he gave with a well—placed cough, then took his place beside the groom.

Fitz soon returned with the bride, and the ceremony began. She was beginning to feel more than just a little discomfort, and a few times they had to stop for a minute to let her pains pass, but eventually the required readings were read, vows were given, and signatures were scribed.

When Maria placed the quill back into the holder and turned to look at her husband, she was surprised with his next action–that of gathering her in his arms and kissing her soundly, right there in front of everyone.

The smile she gave was soon overshadowed by an enormous pain that nearly made her crumple to the floor. Bingley held onto her through it all as the other ladies rushed to her side. When the pain subsided and they insisted it was time to return to her room, he reached around her, steadying her and taking her hand, "I will help you. After all, I have already broken with tradition and entered where only a lady dare, so what is one more time?"

Fitz chuckled, "You and Darcy are of the same mind, I see."

"Oh? Did you enter your wife's birthing room as well?" Bingley asked as they walked past.

"I was the first person my daughter saw when she opened her eyes," he stated proudly, looking over to the baby Georgiana held in her arms. "I will never forget that look as long as I live."

Bingley looked back to Maria. "If you need me, just call. I will not hesitate to be there for you as well."

She blushed, "I think we will be well, Mr Bingley."

He leaned in and kissed her cheek, "You may now call me Charles." Then without waiting for her response, he led her from the room.

It proved to be a long night for the groom. After riding hard for two days to get back to Pemberley in time, then the emotional toll of the events since his arrival, he was exhausted. He refused to go to bed though, insisting that if his wife was upstairs not able to sleep, then he would not sleep either. The sun finally began to rise the next day and still they heard nothing from the ladies. Darcy was the only one brave enough to knock on the door for some word on how everything was going, and he returned with the news that things were progressing, but it would be a while longer. By the middle of the afternoon Bingley was nearly ready to burst down the door himself from the anxiety of not knowing what was happening, when suddenly Elizabeth entered the room and announced, "She is ready to see you, Mr Bingley."

He nervously asked, "Has she had the babe?"

Elizabeth smile and nodded, "Yes — a beautiful and healthy baby girl."

Bingley flew past her and up the stairs, stopping only to knock on the closed chamber door. When it opened, he bounded into the room and stopped. There, sitting against the headboard, was his wife. In her arms was a baby, her red hair clearly peeking out from the blanket in which she was wrapped. Tears welled in his eyes. Mrs Annesley excused herself, leaving them alone.

He walked over to the bed and leaned down to kiss the forehead of the baby. Then his eyes drew up to those of his wife, and he leaned in a kissed her slowly. When she asked if he would like to hold the baby, he took the small bundle in his arms, then sat on the bed beside his wife.

"What shall we name her?" Maria asked.

"I must say, I was not prepared to provide a name beyond just a surname. Have you not thought of any these last few months?"

She looked down at her hands, the blanket below them being twisted in agitation, "No, I knew I could not keep her, so I did not want to distress myself further by picking out a name."

Bingley reached out to grasp her hands in his. When she looked up into his eyes and he smiled lovingly at her, she felt no shame. He truly cared for her enough to overlook her past mistakes. Bingley pulled her hand to his lips, kissing it. "We have time to come up with a name. For now, we will just call her *my sweet*."

She whispered, "I like that. It fits her."

"Yes it does. Now I insist you rest."

"Oh, no, I could not sleep right now. I do not want you to leave." Her cheeks flamed when she realized just what she had said aloud.

He shifted his position, leaning his back against the headboard, holding the babe in one arm as he drew his wife closer to his side with the other. "I had no intention of leaving. I will stay right here with my two Bingley ladies."

An hour later Mrs Annesley checked on them. Seeing they were both fast asleep and that the babe was beginning to stir, she took her from Mr Bingley's arms. When he looked up groggily at her, she whispered, "I will go and change her; she will be well. You need your rest." He thanked her and nestled down into the bed further, pulling his wife closer, and was asleep again before she left the room.

With so many visitors, Rose Bluff was alive with activity. The limited staff made things interesting, but with some adjustments it was bearable. The Darcys had already brought their own personal staff with them, and the nurse maids were happy to add another little one to their care–when her father would let the new Miss Olivia Bingley out of his arms that is.

Mrs Annesley was once again able to focus her attention more fully on Georgiana, and on one particular day she came upon the somber young lady in the garden. She sat down beside her, "I looked for you in the stable, but they said you did not wish to ride today. Are you well?"

Georgiana sighed heavily, then with tears in her eyes, she turned to her companion, "I know everything around me is well, but I cannot help but think of all I am missing in my life. My parents are gone, my Aunt Catherine has not had any contact with us since before my brother married, and even Fitz's parents refuse to be a part of our lives."

Mrs Annesley handed her a handkerchief. "I have never heard you refer to them as your cousin's parents–they were always your beloved aunt and uncle. Is there something you want to tell me? What has caused such a change?" When Georgiana said nothing, she replied quietly, "Your brother has noticed your melancholy these last few months, and he is very worried. He thought you being with your Aunt Edith would help, but you came home just as sullen. If you cannot confide in me, please, I urge you to do so with someone."

"Who?" she said with tears now running down her cheeks. "Who could possibly understand my loneliness?"

Sarah Johnson

"Mrs Fitzwilliam would understand."

She sighed, "Yes; yes she would."

"Will you talk with her?"

Drying her eyes, she took a deep breath, then replied, "If you think it would help I will speak with her."

The companion reached out and squeezed the fingers of her charge, "Of course it will help. I will go find her."

It was not long before Mary joined her on the garden bench. After the two had sat in silence for a few minutes, Mary tapped Georgiana's arm and signed as she verbally asked, "What do you need of me?"

It was the first time Georgiana had ever heard Mary speak and she was shocked at the soft voice that came out. "I did not know you could speak."

Mary replied with a smile, "I was a perfectly normal child until my accident. I just choose not to speak if I do not have to because it is strange for me–I cannot hear my own voice. I know not whether it is easy for others to understand me or not."

Georgiana gave a small smile, "It does have an odd tone I have never heard before, but I like your voice. It is soothing."

She smiled, "I have never heard it described in such a way before. Thank you."

"How do you handle all you have endured with such grace and determination?"

"I am not used to speaking, so if you do not mind, I will write my answer," she said as she pulled a notebook and pencil from her pocket.

"Yes, of course,"

Mary began to write, and, when she was done, she passed it to Georgiana. "Everyone has a burden they must carry, but one thing I have always relied upon is my faith. God has never abandoned me even when others would have nothing to do with me. He is always just a prayer away."

"But what of others? How do you face such ridicule and not wish to retaliate against them? How do you even face me without wishing to cause me pain for

344

all I have done to you?"

"Others know not everything I have been through. Even Elizabeth understands only a portion. When I was eight years of age and the fever took my hearing, I was alone. I spent several months feeling despondent because of my lot, but I just could not live my life in such a manner. One day I was out walking and one of the neighborhood boys began to pelt me with rocks. They knew I would not cry out, so they thought they would get away with it."

Georgiana replied, "It must have been so lonely."

"It was. I tried to get away, but they had me trapped against a garden wall and I could not get around them. Suddenly Elizabeth came running up, pushing her way through the and to my side, and threatening to box their ears if they threw one more rock at me. She always had such spirit."

Georgiana read of the account, chuckling when she got to the part about Elizabeth. "She is just as strong now as she was then."

"Yes, but she has now realized an important lesson—you cannot confront everyone who wishes you ill."

"Like me."

"The Bible speaks of turning the other cheek, and that is what I have always tried to do. Those who ridicule others are, themselves, crying out for help in some way. Just like you. I knew something was missing from your life all those many months ago, and yet I doubt even you realized yet what it was. Do you know now?"

"All I know is that I am lonely," she said as tears began to well in her already swollen eyes.

Mary pulled out her handkerchief, handing it to her, then wrapped her arms around Georgiana's shoulders and held her tight as she cried. "You are not alone, Georgiana. You have family, and we are all here for you," she said verbally. "*Shhhh.*"

When she had finally calmed and Mary released her, Georgiana asked, "Why? Why do you offer me friendship when all I wished was for you to be out of my life?"

"That is what family does, and are we not family? We are practically sisters, or cousins, depending on which way you look at it."

She smiled, "I have always wanted a sister, or another cousin."

"You have had two sisters here beside you now for over a year."

"Yes, and I have abused you both so grievously," she said with obvious contrition.

Mary reached over to lift her chin so she could look into Georgiana's eyes, "All is forgiven and in the past. We must now look to the future."

Georgiana smiled, "Thank you."

Mary smiled. "Now," she said with a decided lift of her brow, "my husband will not allow me to ride without a companion. Would you care to join me today? We cannot ride as we used to, but a jaunt through the park or around the lake will do us both much good."

"Are you certain you are able to do so safely?" she asked, looking at Mary's pregnant form.

"I am not so very unstable yet, though I doubt I will be able to ride for much longer. In fact, today may be my last ride for quite some months," she replied, placing her hand lovingly on her expanding belly.

"Then I simply must join you," Georgiana said with a smile as she stood, holding out her hand to Mary. When Mary stood as well Georgiana linked their arms together, "On to the stables," she said with a giddy laugh.

Their ride was short, and was more of a walk with the pace Georgiana insisted they keep. The trail around the lake was traversed, then the ladies returned to the terrace to partake of tea.

Georgiana smiled when she saw her cousin walking up behind his wife. Mary knew he was near and turned to greet him. When she turned back and Fitz took a seat next to her, Georgiana tilted her head and asked, "How do you do that?"

"Do what?"

"How do you know when someone is behind you? Or for that matter, how do you do any number of things without being able to hear properly?"

"When one sense is gone, the others compensate. I may not hear with my ears, but I can feel vibrations in the floor, or the way the wind shifts behind me. My eyes pick up on shadows and light more easily and, believe it or not, my neck tingles when my husband is the one trying to sneak up from behind."

"It is truly fascinating. Tell me, when my cousin plays the pianoforte for you," she noticed the pink that rose on her cousin's cheeks and chose to ignore it, "do you hear the music?"

Fitz took his wife's hand in his, spreading her fingers out and laying it against his own, palms together, as he explained, "With the lightest touch to the pianoforte, she is able to feel the notes."

Mary looked deep into his eyes and the two were lost to the world around them for a moment. He understood her so much it made her heart swell with delight.

Georgiana gave them a moment, then when Fitz finally released his wife's hand, she asked, "Do you like listening to music?"

Mary blushed, looking down at her tea cup, "Yes, absolutely. I often listened to you play when we were at Pemberley."

She chuckled, "I thought so. I thought I heard you outside the door one day when I was practicing, but I could not determine why you would be there. I asked the maid and she said she often saw you there."

Mary smiled, "Music is soothing to the soul. I could easily feel the vibrations through the door, so I would stand there with my hand or my cheek pressed against it."

Georgiana immediately had an idea. Her face beamed as she asked, "Would you like me to teach you to play something?"

Mary sat back, "Me? Oh no—I could never…"

"Nonsense! Come," she stood, reaching her hand out to Mary, "we shall make an afternoon of it, and by this evening we will be ready to entertain the others." When Mary hesitated, Georgiana lifted her eyebrow as she had seen Elizabeth do many times before, "I am certain you will need something else to fill your days since you will not be riding again anytime soon."

347

Sarah Johnson

Mary looked up and closed her eyes, then chuckled and, with determination, accepted her husband's help to stand. He kissed her on the cheek and the two ladies repaired to the music room where Georgiana proceeded to teach Mary a simple tune, as well as a compliment to a harder tune they could play together.

Later that evening they performed for the others and received great applause. Georgiana retired and lay in her bed that night, a smile on her face, as she remembered all Mary had said of what her world was like. As much as she had taught Mary today, Mary had taught her as well. She would never see the world the same way again.

Chapter 36

It was another three months before Mary's confinement was to begin, and during that time the Bingleys settled into their own home, the Darcys returned to Pemberley, and the Fitzwilliams continued to do what was needed to ready their lives and home for their own soon coming babe.

They had not been back at Pemberley a week when Georgiana went to Elizabeth and asked if she would join her in visiting the graves of her mother and father. Elizabeth was touched with the sentiment, and, even though it was a difficult request, she gladly accompanied Georgiana to the church.

Elizabeth had only been a few times with her husband, but he came every week on his own. The carriage ride was quiet, and Georgiana held Elizabeth's hand firmly in her grip. The two arrived and descended from the carriage, Georgiana grasping the flowers she had brought from the garden. Then they turned and entered the large church, walking through the chilly building to the alcove that memorialized the previous four generations of the Masters of Pemberley and their families.

The vicar heard someone enter, so he stepped into the sanctuary. Upon seeing who it was, he held back, standing silently at the door as the two ladies paid their respects. It nearly broke his heart when he heard Miss Darcy begin to cry.

Being a father himself, he wished to comfort her. Mrs Darcy had the situation well in hand though, and she held the girl tightly as the tears were expelled. The two then stood there talking quietly for several minutes, then they turned to leave. Mrs Darcy stopped at the door and turned back to look at him, giving a simple nod of thanks before pushing the heavy door open, then they were gone.

The following week he noticed the two ladies joined Mr Darcy on his usual trip. He had been praying for quite a while for Miss Darcy to be ready for such a step, and it seemed she had finally come to terms with her parents being gone. He was happy to see the three each week thereafter on the visits.

The relationship between the three sisters, and their dear friend Maria, grew. The four were often seen in each others company, and when they could not visit, letters were frequently exchanged. The ladies weekly shopping trips to furnish the three estates were a wonder to behold. Georgiana soon found a pursuit about which she could be passionate and the others loved her creative ideas. What used to be just a fascination with bonnets had now grown into a love of decorating that would never leave her.

Darcy surprised his sister with the knowledge that he would fund the redecorating of her rooms, including, at the insistence of Elizabeth, adding a small pianoforte to her private sitting room. The gift was a shock to Georgiana. After all she had done to them, Elizabeth and Mary both continued to love her in ways she could not fathom.

Maria's family began to write to her and soon the separation of their lives came to an end. Though she now lived too far away for frequent visits, she was happy just in knowing her family accepted and loved her. Plans were made for the Lucas family to visit Derbyshire for Christmas.

Bingley often received letters from his sister, and though she constantly talked of how wonderful her life as Viscountess Milton was, he knew she was not truly happy. Who could be, with such a husband as hers? His liaisons and gambling had not ceased, and from everything Hurst told him, the ladies of the *Ton* still did not accept Caroline into their homes unless it was for gossip which only she possessed. While Bingley felt sorry for her, this was exactly what she wanted–a title. She felt it was an even exchange–her dowry for the honour of being a viscountess, and one day a countess.

Fitz was excited to receive a note from a distant cousin on his mother's side announcing that he and his wife now had their second child. He eagerly told his wife the news, excitedly describing his own anticipation of sending out announcements of their own soon enough. Mary just laughed at his child—like exuberance as she came to love a new side of her husband rarely seen by others–that of a father.

After being in the birthing room with both Elizabeth and Maria, Mary was expecting her own confinement to be rather long and difficult. It was shocking to all when news came that Fitz hardly had time to pen a note to the midwife before Mary's pains were coming too close together, and before the midwife even arrived, their son was born. Mrs Lewis had her hands full with keeping the two calm, and with help from Fitz and Mabel, Mary's maid, the healthy Fitzwilliam heir came into the world.

When the news reached Elizabeth, the Darcys rushed to Rose Bluff, meeting the Bingleys as they arrived as well. After seeing that her sister was well, Elizabeth had to laugh at the stories they would one day tell of how often Mary frightened everyone around with her harrowing tales.

The following day Darcy found his cousin in his study writing, so he sat down, looking around the newly furnished room, admiring the carved wood on the shelves and desk, until Fitz was finished.

"What brings you in here?"

"The ladies were discussing bonnets and gowns, and as much as I appreciate the lovely items my wife chooses to purchase, I am simply not that interested in hearing of their minutest detail. So I left them to their devices. I am certain Bingley will be joining us soon as well. He just went to check on his daughter in the nursery."

"Well, if you do not mind, I have some notes of announcement to write."

"Most families do not send such news until at least the christening of the babe," he teased.

Fitz smiled, "Have you seen the size of my son? He is half—grown already!"

Darcy laughed aloud, "He does make quite the impression. He is nearly as large as Rose, and she is five months old now. Have you decided on a name yet?"

"Yes, we will call him *Bennet Andrew Fitzwilliam*," he stated proudly.

"It is a strong name. I am glad to hear you will pass your wife's surname on to your son."

"I am a bit surprised to hear that from you, especially since your entire life you have rankled at the use of your mother's surname for your own Christian name."

He smiled slightly and looked down at his hands, "That was before I heard it fall from Elizabeth's lips. It is a wonder how I ever hated it so. Perhaps we will one day do the same with my son."

"What is this about Darcy having a son? Did I miss some announcement?" Bingley said as he entered the room.

Darcy looked at his naïve friend, "Really, Bingley? My daughter is but five months old. I cannot see us having another one so soon."

He raised his eyebrow at his friend, "Think what you will, but it is known to happen."

"Perhaps, but my wife is in no condition to experience another pregnancy like her last one any time soon," Darcy replied.

"Well, as my wife can surely attest, every lady is different," Fitz replied with a chuckle.

Bingley walked over and sat down next to Darcy, clapping his hands and rubbing them together in an excited fashion, "I believe you owe us a story. How did this all come about so quickly? Were you not the one who said you would never wish to be with your wife when she was in childbirth?"

Fitz laughed, setting his quill aside and capping his ink bottle. He knew he would not finish the notes right now. "Well, it all began right after we broke our fast yesterday morning. My wife began to feel uncomfortable, so I refused to leave her alone in the sitting room. She kept insisted it was just a small ache in her lower back and that putting her feet up would help. So we relaxed together until mid—day. Then all of a sudden she had a sharp pain, and another, and then a third right on top of that. Mrs Lewis insisted I call for the midwife while she took Mary upstairs to lie down, and by the time I sent the note, then went to tell them, it was time for my son to enter the world. It was not my intention to be there with her, but since there was only Mrs Lewis and Mabel, my presence was needed. By the time the midwife arrived, Bennet was here."

Bingley sat shaking his head at such a tale. "It is unbelievable what ladies go through, is it not?"

"Absolutely," Fitz agreed.

"I would not trade with Elizabeth for the world," Darcy replied.

"Well, since you two will be here for at least a few more days, perhaps I can interest you in riding through the fields with me? The harvest was plentiful this year, but I have a few changes I am discussing with the steward for next year, and I would like to get your opinions."

"I doubt I have anything useful to add to the conversation, but I would like some fresh air," Bingley offered.

Darcy stood, "It must then fall to me to teach you two how to be a gentleman."

Fitz laughed aloud, "Uncle George used to say I did not pay close enough attention to my studies, and now that is coming back to haunt me."

"Even being raised to take over Pemberley, it was several years before I was comfortable with my place as Master. Both of you have stepped into your role with much more ease then I ever did," Darcy said as they left the study.

The cold of winter set in early this year and soon after the birth of Bennet Fitzwilliam the first snow fell. While it would not remain on the ground for long, it did delay the guests who were visiting Rose Bluff from returning to their respective homes. No one minded in the least. They all enjoyed the walks in the snowy garden, the nights by the fire, the wassail Mrs Lewis insisted the cook surprise everyone with, and the games Georgiana talked them all into playing.

Darcy smiled as he remembered the look of horror on Elizabeth's face as Mary bravely reached her hand quickly into the dish of Brandy to pull out the prized raisin that flickered with flames, popping it into her mouth without hesitation. Snapdragon was not for the faint of heart. His wife was ever the protective elder sister, and Mary the adventuresome one. It seemed this was a game Mary he found joy in for many years, and even though she had seen her sister's bravery many times, Elizabeth could not keep the look or horror from her features.

The time together had proven to be just what everyone needed—a caring family.

When Darcy came around the corner on his way to find the others, he nearly ran into his sister. He stepped back quickly, but she did not seem to notice him. She was blindfolded and was feeling her way along the corridors. "Georgiana? What are you about?"

She did not answer him. So he tried again. "Georgiana?" He found it odd when she again just continued on her way as if she had not heard him, so he followed after her.

Finally she arrived in the sitting room. She untied the blindfold and jumped, a squeal escaping her lips, when she saw him standing there. "Oh, Fitzwilliam! You gave me such a fright!"

He asked again, "Is something amiss?"

She reached up and pulled wads of cotton from her ears, "I am sorry, I did not hear you. What was that you said?"

"You nearly ran into me, and I just wondered if something was wrong?"

"Oh, no, everything is perfect! How could it not be? I am here in this beautiful home with my three sisters, my brother, and my cousin—as well as three of the most wonderful babes for me to admire. What more could I desire?"

Fitz entered the room, hearing his young cousin's pronouncement. "I have just one question for you. Just when did you decide you now have *three* sisters?"

She smiled, then began her explanation, "Is not my brother's wife my sister?"

"Yes, of course; that I do not deny."

"And is not her sister my sister as well?"

"Hmmm… I can see that also. How you count three is beyond me though."

"Well, as you have already stated, one's sister can certainly be defined by also being a sister—in—law. Your brother has married, so my sister, meaning Mary, is sister to your sister, Lady Milton. Her brother is also married, thus making his wife her sister. As you can plainly see, my sister's sister is sister to the sister of Mrs Bingley, so therefore, she is also my sister!"

He chuckled, "It is truly baffling, however you forgot to count Lady Milton, so that would make four sisters."

She waved her hand in a dismissive fashion, "She never cared for me anyway. We shall just keep her in the distant cousin category. You on the other hand, can now be counted truly as my brother." With a smile at them both she stuffed the cotton back into her ears, tied the blindfold around her eyes, and wondered out of the room once again.

Fitz looked on in confusion, going through the list again until he figured out what she meant. Her sister, meaning Mary, was married to him, so therefore he would be her brother. He chuckled as he thought her skills in this manner would add tremendously to the battles being fought on the continent. When she had left, he turned and asked Darcy, "What was that about?"

He shrugged his shoulders, "I came across her feeling her way through the corridors. I know not why."

Fitz smiled, remembering the conversation he and Mary had with Georgiana a few months before about how Mary lived without being able to hear. When Darcy looked at him quizzically, he replied, "My conjecture is that she is trying to better understand Mary's world."

Darcy thought, she has changed so much in the last few months—she truly was back to her old self, only more outgoing than ever before.

Not wanting to be overcome with emotion, Fitz cleared his throat and shook his head, then patted his cousin on the back, "We have finally completed the monumental task set before us."

"Yes—at last."

"Now she is truly ready to face the *Ton*. So when did you say her coming out will be?"

His face became sour, "Oh, not for at least another four or five years."

Fitz broke out in guffaws. "I feel sorry for Rose even now."

"Speaking of my daughter–would you care to join me as I check on her in the nursery?"

He held out his hand towards the door, "Lead the way. I am certain Bennet could use some time with his father as well."

It was not long afterward when the visitors left for their own homes. Since this property was between Pemberley and Buckley Hall, it was deemed the perfect place for such family gatherings, and in many instances was teeming again with the growing family as the months wore on and the cold of winter set in around them.

It was on one such day in early December that Bingley walked through the familiar halls of Rose Bluff. They were to all dine here this evening, but his wife insisted on coming early to help Mary with something. He was unsure what it was, but really he cared little for the reason as it would give him time to join Fitz in shooting. He found him in his study, and as soon as Bingley mentioned having brought his gun, the former Army colonel jumped up, happy to oblige his friend. There were two things he loved to do more than anything else–ride and shoot. Darcy leaned more towards fishing, and while Fitz did enjoy going with his cousin, it was not his personal choice of activity.

The two rode to Pemberley to invite Darcy along and Fitz passed on his wife's invitation for Elizabeth and Georgiana to join her and Maria at Rose Bluff earlier if they so desired. The ladies were glad to go early, so the carriage was prepared as Darcy saddled his horse and the gentlemen rode off in expectation of a good day.

BOOM!... (boom!) The loud noise rang out through the valleys and ridges, causing it to echo back to them just a few seconds later. Once again Bingley was proving just how proficient he was with this weapon. He had easily shot twice as many birds as Darcy and Fitz combined.

"We had best head back," Darcy said, "or we will clear all my lands. Next time we will have to shoot at your place Bingley."

"Oh no, we must hit Rose Bluff first, as I keep my land quite under control on my own."

"How often do you go out shooting?" Fitz asked as he leapt back onto his horse with practiced ease.

"Much too often, I gather from my steward. He says I will need to give it a few weeks before I go again. I tell you, land management is not for the faint of heart."

Darcy clicked his tongue and the three set out at a slow pace on their way back to Rose Bluff.

"You know us Bingleys though—we are never one to give up too easily."

Fitz smirked, "Oh, your sister is proof of that."

"Yes, she certainly is. I have heard from her again, and I tell you, I just do not understand how we have come from the same parents. Everything I love about being a father is everything she hates about the prospect of being a mother. I could not imagine sending my child away to be nursed for years, then again sending them away to school. No—my children will be tutored at home as I was. I wish to be in my child's life daily, not just when it is convenient."

"So," Fitz asked, "are you and I to become uncles soon?"

"No, no, she is very clear to point out that having a child is not to happen until at least next year. She refuses to have tongues wagging about the possibility of her being with child before she was married—especially with my recent change in marital status and then so quickly to become a father."

Darcy asked, "So I take it your family does not know the truth of the situation?"

"I have told them very little—only that I am happy to have found the love of my life. I am certain they assume we had some sort of assignation last year when I leased Netherfield Park—I know I certainly would assume such if I knew only what they have been told. We see no point in telling them any different. Olivia is mine, whether she carries my blood or not."

Fitz questioned him further, "Are you certain you are comfortable with giving her line everything you possess if you fail to have a male?"

Bingley pulled his horse to a stop and turned to look at the two cousins. His horse danced in agitation, but he held tight to the reins. "It is an honour and a privilege to have the kind of love matches that we all three have made. I care not who my estate passes on to, only that I have as many days as I can with the ladies I love the most."

Fitz nodded, "That is all I needed to hear."

Darcy nodded in understanding, then, with his own horse becoming antsy, he replied, "We need to run these mounts before one of them throws us. Who is with me?"

Fitz grinned, "You know I am always up for a good ride. Bingley?"

"Absolutely. Lead the way."

Darcy clicked his tongue and squeezed his knees together, giving his horse the permission he desired, and soon the three were racing across the fields that would lead them back to Rose Bluff.

They cooled their mounts into a walk when the house came into view, making their way towards the stables. When they came out, Bingley saw a carriage he did not recognize at the front. "Were you expecting visitors?"

"No; why?" Bingley pointed to the carriage and Fitz stopped in his tracks, his face draining of all color immediately. Of course he would recognize that carriage. It bore the crest of the Earl of Danver.

Darcy recognized it too about the time Fitz took off towards the house as quickly as propriety would allow. "It is my uncle's carriage," he said to Bingley, then followed his cousin.

It took Bingley a few seconds to understand what had been related to him, but he quickly caught up with the others and they entered the sitting room together.

Chapter 37

hat Fitz expected to see when he opened the door was a confrontation. He was shocked to see, instead, the ladies sitting together and enjoying tea and sandwiches. His mother was all that was pleasant. His father, however, sat apart from them and wore a scowl on his face.

"There you are," Mary signed to him. "Your parents have come for a visit." She walked over to greet her clearly shocked husband.

Ignoring propriety, he kissed her on the cheek and mouthed silently, "Are you well?"

Mary gave a small smile and signed, "We are perfectly well. We were just enjoying tea. I would invite you to join us, but I fear you are quite underdressed," indicating his disheveled appearance with mud splatters covering his boots and breeches from the three racing their mounts.

With her clear control of the situation, his fears were calmed. He greeted his parents, then excused himself so he could change.

Darcy and Bingley also left to change, their wives having brought their dinner clothing with them since it was known they would be staying the night.

When the three returned to the sitting room, Fitz was still in awe that it was just as when he had left. He took a seat next to his wife on the sofa, then turned to his mother, "I cannot imagine what has brought you here to our doorstep."

Elizabeth saw that they needed a few minutes to speak privately, so she stood, suggesting Georgiana and Maria join her in the garden. Darcy and Bingley followed them as well, leaving Fitz and Mary alone with his parents.

The countess stood facing her youngest son. He had grown into such a good looking young man, and here he stood before her with a wife at his side and a child above stairs. She had missed out on so much of his life. Tears began to form in her eyes. "I have been so wrong. I have not been the mother you needed, and I refuse to allow our family to remain divided like this any longer." She sobbed, reaching her hand out to Fitz, "Oh please forgive me. I am truly sorry for all I have allowed, and all I have said, to the both of you, all these years."

Fitz felt such compassion fill his heart that he too had to fight back tears. He took his mother's arm and helped her sit on the sofa, sitting beside her. He was a little taken aback when she drew him into an embrace, but after a few seconds the physical touch they shared began to heal all the years of wounds between the two. This was what he had needed so many times–his mother's embrace. He never thought he would have her in his life again, and yet here she sat, hugging him. Both were sobbing so hard their bodies shook, but neither one cared. This was just what they needed.

When they were finally calmed and each let go of the other, Fitz looked over to his father. The earl sat there with that same scowl on his face, but there was a look in his eyes that he tried to hide. Fitz saw it though. He turned back to his mother, "Are your trunks upstairs?"

"Oh no, we do not wish to be a burden. We have taken rooms at the Red Lion Inn in Lambton."

Fitz looked to his wife, who gave a small nod of her agreement, then he said to his mother, "No, no, you must stay with us. I will have your trunks brought here."

The earl spoke, "We will be comfortable enough at the inn."

Fitz knew his father would be harder to win over, so he let it go and turned back to his mother. "You are well? The family is well?"

She patted his hand, squeezing his fingers in motherly affection, "Yes, all is well. Now." She swallowed hard, then turned to Mary, "Please accept my apologies for all I have said to you. I should have accepted you into my family with joy, and instead I cut my son off. It is clear you hold deep affection for each other, and above all, that is what I have always wanted for my boys. I cannot say the same for my eldest son–his wife cares not for him, only his title. You are not like that though. I can see in your eyes how much you care for my son. I am sorry I have stayed away so long."

Mary smiled, signing to her, with Fitz interrupting. "I am glad to have you here now. Let us not dwell on the past, for it is in its proper place. What matters most is the future."

The earl sniffed when Fitz voiced what she signed. He clearly saw no reason for such sentimentality.

The countess turned toward her husband of over thirty five years and glared at him with a look he could not ignore. "I just do not see the point in this charade," he replied to her.

She stood, squaring her shoulders, and replied in a firm, solid voice, "I have come to realize just what is missing in my life, and I refuse to let my grandchildren grow up without my seeing them. You forced our son to leave home at an early age, and I said nothing. You have allowed our eldest to gamble away what he could of the estate, and I said nothing. You yourself have had your vices for years, and I have said nothing. I will remain silent no longer. I will stay in Richard's life as long as he and his wife will have me. If you do not like that decision, you may stay at the Red Lion Inn. I will be staying here at Rose Bluff."

She turned, reaching her hand towards Mary, "Come, my dear. We will leave the men to speak in private. I must call for my trunks to be brought."

The two ladies walked from the room and Fitz turned back to face his father. Something was different. He could tell the earl was hiding something. "What has truly brought you here?"

"Your mother insisted we come."

"That explains her being here, but not your own presence in my home."

"I came only out of obligation," he said coldly.

The earl shifted in his seat uncomfortably and Fitz he would learn nothing if he was passive in his assault. "And you care not for anything she has just said? I mean nothing to you still?"

"You are my son—is that not enough?"

"I am your second son; your spare. That is all I have ever been to you," he said with fire in his eyes.

"You know NOTHING of being a father!"

"I know you have not been one in my life! I know Uncle George was more of a father to me than you ever were! I know every day when I hold my son in my arms, I promise to be the best father I can be to him and support him in any way I can."

"You have never had to face the decisions I have had to face."

"And you, sir, have never been be pushed away by your family—the family who should have protected you and loved you. My mother is welcomes to stay as long as she wishes. Unless you are willing to tell me what has truly brought *you* to my doorstep, then it is time you leave."

"It is none of your concern."

"It is my concern. I am your son." Compassion filled his eyes and voice, "Do you not see that I care for you? Is that alone ever to be enough for you?"

The earl stood, striding to the window where he drew back the lace curtains and looked out. He felt his son come up behind him, and he finally said, "I am dying."

It struck Fitz hard. He closed his eyes and sucked in a shallow breath. When he opened them again, his father was looking at him.

"The doctors say I will not make it another year." His hand reached up to his heart. "I have not told your mother—it would crush her. She began to talk of Lady Beaumont and how often she spoke so highly of being a grandmother.

362

Every note your wife sent, and even the drawing she did of you or your son was cherished from the moment it arrived. Your mother continually compared your wife to your brother's, and Viscountess Milton was the daughter—in—law who came up wanting every time. I could see what your mother desired more than anything was to be in your life. Then after receiving a Christmas greeting from your wife, she insisted on coming here." He looked down, not able to look his son in the eye again, "I was certain we would be turned away at the door, our card not even accepted. Yet your wife ushered us in, offering refreshments and being so kind to us. We do not deserve such treatment."

"Your actions do not match the tone of what you say. If you truly feel this way, why are you continuing to push me away?"

"*Do you not understand?*" he said harshly. "I am dying. I will not live past another year, according to the best doctors in London, and the last thing I wish to do to you is step back into your life only to cause you such grief in a few months time." Tears welled in his eyes and began to spill down his cheeks, "I cannot do that to you!"

Fitz now understood. He closed his eyes and took in a deep breath. Opening them again, he focused on his father's eyes, "You are my father. Every day I get to spend with you is worth it to me. As my wife has so graciously taught me, we must look to the past only as its remembrances bring us pleasure. While there is little pleasure to be found there for us, we have these days set before us. Would you forever consign me to the remembrances I hold now? It is my dearest wish to make pleasant memories with you before your days come to an end."

The earl was taken aback. Even after everything he had put his youngest son through, all the years of pushing him away and manipulating for his own gain, Fitz was still able to forgive. He still wished to have him there. The earl knew immediately he could not walk away now. "Your mother is right you know—we have treated you abominably. I am not proud of many decisions I have made, but if it is to be the last one I make in this life, I do wish to make it right between us. I am sorry son. Can you ever forgive me?"

It was hard enough for Fitz to imagine his mother apologizing, but now he was completely in shock as his father's words of contrition as well. He gave a simple nod, "Of course, sir."

They stood silently for a few minutes, then the earl asked, "Do you think Darcy will forgive me as well?"

Fitz looked down at his hands. "Honestly, I know not. He was disturbed to receive that note from you insisting Georgiana marry Milton."

"I wrote that when I was drunk."

"That much was clear."

"I have since stopped drinking. The doctor says it could drive me to my grave even earlier, so I have given it up–along with many other things that have been my constant companions all these years."

"Darcy, I am sure, will at least be willing to speak with you. The harder one to be won over though will be Georgiana."

He was shocked, "She knows?"

"She confided in me recently that she found your letter in the fireplace where Darcy threw it that day."

He walked back over to the chair and sat down heavily, his head held in his hands, "What have I done to this family?"

Fitz did not know what to say, so he waited until his father spoke again.

"I need to speak with her–I must apologize."

"I would suggest you speak with Darcy first."

"Yes, I will do that." His chest began to feel tight and he knew now was not the best time to have another emotional conversation such as this one.

Fitz noticed him wince in pain. "Are you well? Do you need to rest?"

The earl stood slowly, "Yes, it would probably be best. If the offer still stands, I would like to have my trunks brought from the inn as well?"

"Of course you are welcome here. Would you like to go straight to your room, or would you care to meet your grandson first?"

The earl smiled, "It would give me the greatest pleasure to meet my grandson."

Fitz nodded. "Right this way."

"I hear he is quite the healthy boy."

Fitz smiled, "Yes, he is quickly outgrowing Darcy's daughter even though she is several months older."

They turned to walk from the room, the earl saying in jest, "You know what my sister would say about those two if she were here." He put his nose in the air and said in a manner just as Lady Catherine would, *"They are formed for each other from their cradles."*

Both laughed heartily as they went into the hallway. Fitz told the butler to have the trunks brought from the inn and the two ascended the stairs and turned towards the nursery to introduce the earl to his grandson.

Late that night Mary and Fitz lay in bed, cuddled against each other. Mary could tell her husband wanted to talk, so she turned to face him, the light from the candle beside the bed was just enough to see his mouth when he spoke. "What did he say?"

Fitz drew his hand wearily over his eyes. "He did not wish to hurt me further, so he wanted to keep the distance between us."

It was in times like this that she used her voice to talk with him. "Obviously you came to some kind of an agreement, as he is now sleeping just down the hall from us."

"He is dying. The doctors give him a year at best."

"Ahhh, now I understand. He truly does wish to be in our lives, but he cannot fathom burdening you with such a loss?"

"Yes, exactly."

"Does he not see that it does hurt us further by continuing to take these last days from us?"

"That is just what I asked him. He has apologized, but only time will tell if he truly means to be in our lives. Tomorrow he is to talk with Darcy." He sighed, then smiled at her, "You were right. All this time you were right to write to them and continue the connection. I never thought they would come around, but it seems your persistence has paid off. I am shocked at what has occurred and I hope it will last."

Mary smiled, reaching her arms around her husband's neck to draw him closer, "Believe me, the way he was looking at Bennet was very telling. He is quite happy to be a grandfather, and I do not see him shirking that responsibility anytime soon."

"You do not mind them being here?"

"What better way to celebrate the Christmas season than with family and loved ones? Sir William and Lady Lucas will be arriving with their family next week, and Aunt Edith a few days afterward, and we will soon all remove to Pemberley until after Twelfth Night. Elizabeth has planned several neighborhood dinners, there is to be a fox hunt, roasting nuts, wassail, decorating the bannisters, hunting the wood for the best bough of mistletoe," she quirked her eyebrow at him, both remembering well the number of boughs they sought out the previous year as newlyweds, "and parlour games!"

"Yes," he said, tickling her side, "we all know how much you like playing Snapdragon."

She flinched and tried to pull away at his assault to her ribs. When he would not release her, she grabbed the pillow and flung it at him.

Fitz was able to block it easily and the next thing she knew she was flat on her back and her husband was smiling as he looked down at her. "I must say, my favorite part will again be the mistletoe." His smile faded and a fire of passion slowly grew in his eyes. His lips descended upon hers with a soft touch. The exchange was short lived when he pulled back far enough for her to see what he said, "Aside from being the most beautiful lady of my acquaintance," he kissed her lips quickly, then continued on, "you are also the most gracious, understanding, and forgiving person I have ever met. You see the good that no one else sees in every situation. I will be forever grateful you accepted my hand and my heart."

He reached for her hand and drew it to his throat, pressing her fingers just slightly so she could easily feel the vibrations of his voice as he said, "I love you, Mary Fitzwilliam." Once again he leaned down and kissed her soft lips, the two lovers quickly becoming lost in their passionate embrace.

About the
Author

Sarah Johnson is a professional juggler in the circus of life! Married to her own Mr Darcy for sixteen years, they traveled the world thanks to the US Army. Now back in the civilian life and settled in Texas, where she grew up, they focus on homeschooling their six children and participating in church and community activities. She can often be found writing a manuscript between spills, science labs, and pencil wars, or late into the night when the house is finally still enough for her imagination to run wild! When she has a few spare moments, she enjoys just about anything crafty — scrapbooking, painting, sewing, quilting, crocheting — basically anything except knitting, a craft she swears few left—handers truly ever pick up well.

A devotee of all things Jane Austen, she enjoys exploring the story lines Jane never lived long enough to give the world. She is often found discussing with her online friends the intricacies of the novels we do have from our dearest author. It is these discussions that often lead to the plot bunnies that have now become many stories over the last few years, and hopefully further into the future as well.

Connect with
Sarah Johnson

E-Mail:
sarah.johnson.jaff@gmail.com

Twitter:
@SarahJohnsonPL

Facebook:
https://www.facebook.com/SarahJohnsonAuthor
https://www.facebook.com/sarah.johnson.jaff

Blog: 'My Peculiar World'
http://mypeculiarworld.com

Goodreads:
https://www.goodreads.com/author/show/8118710.Sarah_Johnson

Leaving Bennet Behind Series

"Utterly unique and totally charming!"
-Amazon Reviewer Lizzybelle

"Fun book with an interesting premise!"
-Sophie from 'Laughing with Lizzie'

A carriage accident changes the Bennet family for the better. In *Chosen*, the first of the *Leaving Bennet Behind* series, Elizabeth Bennet finds herself drawn to a handsome visitor to the neighborhood, Fitzwilliam Darcy.

Coming Soon!

For more information about books by Sarah Johnson, visit: www.MyPeculiarWorld.com

---

"This heartwarming tale... sure to delight JAFF readers of all ages."
-Amazon Reviewer Jen Red

"...an enjoyable, light read to help pass a rainy afternoon."
-Amazon Reviewer KindleLover

Made in the USA
San Bernardino, CA
30 September 2014